Cool Cat 3

Born To Be Bad

Cool Cat 3

Born To Be Bad

by
Dan Leissner

Midnight Marquee Press, Inc.
Baltimore, MD, USA

Certain characters in this story are inspired by real people; not their real selves but their imaginary alter egos in their songs, those "Neon Angels On The Road To Ruin", on the run in "Dead End Justice". All other characters are entirely fictitious and are imaginary and have no relation to any persons living or dead. This also includes places, names, companies, religious orders or any other names whatsoever.

Cat's Previous Adventures
Cool Cat
Cool Cat 2: Hell on Route 666

Midnight Marquee Press, Inc., Gary J. Svehla and A. Susan Svehla do not assume any responsibility for the accuracy, completeness, topicality or quality of the information in this book. All views expressed or material contained within are the sole responsibility of the author.

ISBN 13: 9781644300855
Library of Congress Catalog Card Number 2019951246
Manufactured in the United States of America

First Printing by Midnight Marquee Press, Inc., October 2019

Dedicated to

Roger Corman, Russ Meyer, Modesty, Honey, Emma, Coffy, Cleopatra, Foxy....

...and to a great band – the Runaways: Cherie Currie, Joan Jett, Lita Ford, Jackie Fox and Sandy West (R.I.P. Sandy)....
...and to my parents, my friends and Cool Cats everywhere

CONTENTS

CHAPTER 1

RED NIGHT

"MMMMMM…MMM…!!!"
She strained against the ropes, her screams muffled by a filthy rag.

Long hot summer. Jagged tenements stood stark against the blood red sky, rows of broken teeth; windowless and desolate. On the abandoned rooftops, the shadows were crushing; like breathing molten tar.

Jeez! I'm boiling…!

A shadow lurked within the shadows. It detached itself and moved swiftly across the flat roof. A living shadow, all in black, costumed for concealment: ski mask, figure hugging cat suit, silent in rubber-soled shoes.

This is too much!

A pale hand tugged off the ski mask. With a shake of the head, long blonde hair tumbled, silvery in the moonlight.
"Whoo….!"
Breathing deeply, she tilted her face to the sky. Beads of perspiration glinted on her smooth brow, sparked like gemstones, ruby red.
She was young, in her early twenties. Her straight, silken hair hung down to the small of her back. Green eyes over high cheekbones, eyes like a cat's, slanted just a little, just enough to be bewitching. Lips that were ripe and pouting, just enough to make her ravishing.
She was tall enough to make her formidable. Her shoulders were strong and her breasts swelled to perfection. Her waist was slender and supple; beneath the second skin of the black cat suit the muscle tone of her midriff was superb. Her splendid hips swung with a lazy insolence, as she crossed the roof with a lithe, athletic swagger.

Time to go to work….

Once upon a time, the park had been a place for simple pleasures.
Mothers cooed to their gurgling offspring as they wheeled them along swept paths, pretty parasols swaying.
Older children ran laughing across green grass dappled with golden sunshine. They raced a bounding spaniel or chased a ball, running rings and playing tag around the tinkling drinking fountains and ornate statuary.
On the shores of the boating lake fathers played Admiral, pointing and issuing commands as their sons launched model sailing boats, surging like white swans on the sparkling water.
Another time, another world.

A long black padded case was slung across her strong back. With a shimmy of her shoulders she shrugged it off. Bending her knees, she ducked down behind the low wall that framed the rooftop.

A zipper rasped softly.

Out you come sweetheart....

It slid out smoothly, eagerly, as if of its own accord, molding itself to her hands.

Mmmm...baby....

In this world, the park was a dark and polluted place, a jungle red in tooth and claw. Its pathways were tangled and overgrown, seething with hidden menace.

The fountains were dry and broken, the statues dismembered, headless and limbless. The discolored grass was scarred by scabby bald patches and spiked with broken glass and discarded needles.

A big beast moved through the jungle, making a slow and stately progress, assured of its supremacy.

It flaunted its status; the leopard-skin trim of its plush upholstery, its extravagant Imperial purple coachwork and massive chrome.

...come to Mama!

She stroked the purposeful contours of the Remington 700 bolt-action rifle. Fine-tuned by the U.S. Marine Corps and fitted with telescopic sights, re-designated as the M40 sniper's rifle and shipped out to the jungles of 'Nam.

With its dulled barrel, customized wooden stocks and the very latest optics, the precision instrument that Cat Warburton cradled tenderly was the upgraded M40A1, locked and loaded and ready to go.

It was a carriage fit for a king. The King of the Jungle; the monarch of all he surveyed.

A man mountain, a colossus. His mighty torso and bulging biceps strained the seams of a cream safari suit. His shaven skull was crowned by a snow-white broad-brimmed fedora with a silver band echoed by the twinkling toe caps of his stack-heeled boots.

The quadraphonic speakers were oozing out mellow tones that wrapped around him, urging him to "...Get It On...". Masked by mirror shades, his eyes were closed; he was mellow, life was good.

Muffled by the sliding smoked glass partition, he heard the CB radio crackle. Opening his eyes, he saw the driver dip his head to pluck the handset from the dash, beside the wide-shouldered silhouette of the bodyguard in the passenger's seat.

Dimmed by deep tinting, the headlights of a long, low-slung escort glowed in the rear window.

"… Ain't no rush, man; we got plenty of time …."

"Wha—?"
In the heat of the night a cold chill washed over her, from her head to her toes.

Hey what…?

And then another, and another. Jaws of ice gripped her, crushing her, bending her till she thought her spine would crack.
"AH—!"
A white flash behind her eyes; cold fear, sudden terror, paralyzing her. Then, suddenly her body was bathed in sweat. She was hot. Then cold. Hot and cold, shivering, panting, now frozen now scalding.

The boastful limo and its escort glided down the derelict side streets, dappled red and purple by the ragged shadows.
Cruising, they slid past the abandoned tenements with their eyeless sockets and the dangling rusting remnants of their fire escapes. They passed the vacant lots heaped with rubble, where fires flickered and furtive phantoms darted, lesser life forms seeking cover as the big beast passed by.
"… this is it, Boss …."
The convoy pulled up to the cracked curb. The doors of the sleek escort slammed open. Dark men, big men in black suits sprang out, stubby sub-machine guns held ready at the hip.
With smooth choreography, they flanked the big beast, looking up and down and all around, gun muzzles traversing, taking in the street and the crumbling walls.
"Okay…."
The big man riding shotgun disembarked and jogged round to the rear.
"… all clear…."
A leg appeared, cream-colored flares billowing around a shiny silver toecap. Then a massive hand, wrapped around a silver skull with ruby eyes that topped an ebony cane.
Despite his imposing bulk, the man mountain flowed out of his carriage with surprising grace. As he emerged his soldiers closed in to ring around him; although big as they were he towered above them.
The giant tilted his head back on the thick neck that merged into the pack of muscle on his broad shoulders. A light glowed in a single window high above.
"Let's go!"

Where did that come from…?

Her palms were slippery on the smooth sculpture of the rifle stock. Angrily, she wiped them down the front of the skin-tight cat suit.

Breathing deeply, she raised her shoulders to peer over the edge of the low wall. She measured the distance to the decaying cliff face of the building opposite and the solitary glowing rectangle.

"MMM…mmmm…ggghh….hhhhh…..!"
The gag muffled her terrified pleadings.
"Shuddit bitch!"
A man's laugh, hard and gloating.
"Plenty 'o time fo' yo t' makes noise later, when th' King gets here!"
"MMMMMM….mmmm….ggghh…hhhhh….!"
He slapped her hard, rocking her head back.
"I said shuddit!"
The walls were flaked and peeling; uneven floorboards. The room was furnished with a rickety table shoved against the wall and the woman's creaking chair, placed beneath a glaring naked bulb.
"….mmmmm….mmnnn….."
Her head was lolling, tangled black hair falling over her glassy eyes. Her taut body was held to the chair by ropes around her waist, on her wrists and ankles.
"Goddamn…!"
The man was lean and mean with narrow eyes and a lipless slit for a mouth. His narrow shoulders were draped by a short shiny blue leather jacket. His belt had a yellow metal buckle in the shape of a star, maroon crushed velvet bell bottoms flapped around polished red toecaps and silver stack heels.
"…uuuuuhhh…mmmmnnn…."
He drew back his arm again, fist clenching.
"Bitch don' hear too good…!"
The door jerked open with a screech of rusty hinges.
"Yo Turkey! Han's off! Yo kin have wha's left o' her when we done!"

Flicking back the lens cap, she made minute adjustments, zeroing the cross hairs on the single rectangle of yellow light.

Sneaking a glance over the edge, she'd seen a giant form take the crumbling stone steps two at a time and disappear into the unlit doorway.

Here we go…!

His deputy paused to issue crisp commands and then turned to follow. The foot soldiers remained by the limousine and its escort. Alert, they watched the dim and dirty street.

Some suspicious instinct made one man look up over his shoulder and she ducked down quickly. Easing up again, she saw movement within the glowing yellow window frame.

"Gotya…."

The woman squirmed wildly in the chair. Above the gag her eyes bulged with terror, glaring out of the shadow cast by the giant looming over her.

His voice was a deep rumble that swelled from his massive chest and filled the room to bursting, making the floor boards vibrate.

"Yo been talkin' to th' Man, bitch…!"

She was rooting in the padded case's side pockets. Dull metal eggs rolled out onto the wrinkled surface of the roof.

One shot and then take out the goon squad….

Tears tumbling down her cheeks, the woman shook her head wildly, the wiry coils of her hair flailing.

"Now yo gonna talk t'me…."

With a shovel-like hand the giant swiped her face towards the table up against the far wall.

His thin lips warped in a twisted leer, his lean henchman displayed the vicious spike of an ice pick in one hand, a pair of heavy pliers in the other.

I'll be gone before the dust settles….

"MMMMM….MMMM…..!!!"

Her body straining against the ropes, the woman screamed through the filthy gag.

"Yo gonna tell me everythin' that Mistah District Attorney knows…"

Filling the glowing window frame, his mighty silhouette was unmistakable. It couldn't be better. She had a perfect head shot.

Say goodnight, Big Boss Man, you won't be selling your poison to school kids any more…!

The cross hairs bisected the massive head.

Fingers brown and elegant, blurring, made gemstones flash and sparkle. Long gold-glitter fingernails clicked rapidly on the keys.

Glowing green characters marched out onto the blank screen, forming ranks and filling it with information:

PERSONNEL FILE
(Classified Level 1)

"Field" name – Cat
Real name – classified
Age – 24
Nationality – American
Base of operations – Bay City Office
Place of residence – classified

• • • • • • • • •

Her finger hovered on the trigger.

• • • • • • • • • •

Special skills – all-collegiate heptathlon champion: can swim, ski, ride,
                        fence and shoot; proficient in several of the martial arts;
                        speaks nine languages
                Weapons – authorized: classified
                        unauthorized: no information available

• • • • • • • • • •

"Wha – ?"
Her vision blurred and wavered. The stark silhouette framed in the cross
hairs shimmered and became watery.

• • • • • • • • • •

                Education: all the best schools – classified
                was inevitably expelled from most of them; dropped out of
                college in her final year in search of excitement and adventure

• • • • • • • • • •

What's going on?

Blinking rapidly, she removed her hand from the rifle stock and rubbed
her eyes. When she tilted her head back to the telescopic sight the image was
sharp again.

• • • • • • • • • •

                Homes – a fashionable penthouse apartment - classified

                tends to live at the beach – classified

        Transport – classified
                Made an impressive debut and considerable impact on the
                        local racing circuits at the age of 19 but was banned after
                        only four races for over-aggressive driving

• • • • • • • • • •

Her finger rested lightly on the cold metal of the trigger. Silently, she
counted to three, drew in a deep breath and then let it out slowly.

• • • • • • • • • •

Status – agent has performed all her assignments with
conspicuous success. Agent is cool and resourceful.
However, her flair for improvisation can spill over into
reckless self-indulgence

• • • • • • • • • •

Wha—!??!!

Her brain sent the command but nothing happened.
"Wha—?"
Her brain screamed the order and she willed it with every ounce of strength in her body – nothing happened. Her finger was frozen on the trigger.

The man mountain made a curt gesture with his hand. His face twisted with cruelty and lust, the thin man wrenched the dirty rag from the woman's mouth.
Writhing in the chair, she threw back her head and screamed, howling for mercy and for rescue.
Towering over her the big man laughed deep and low in his chest. He held out his hand and the thin man slapped the pliers onto his spade-like palm.
Moaning, the woman cowered in the giant's shadow as his bulk blotted out the glare of the overhanging bulb.
"Yo kin make all the noise yo wants, bitch, ain't no one gonna hear yo…!"

Fuck!

Her hand spasmed, trigger finger flexing. The rifle fired; unready, it jarred her shoulder with a wrenching stab of pain.
"AH!"

Abruptly, the woman stopped screaming. She stared, pop-eyed, at the tall black-suited figure of the big man's bodyguard.
A puzzled expression on his face, he stood looking down at his white shirtfront, at a wet red flower blossoming.
"Huh….?"
His knees turned to water. He toppled slowly at first, then came crashing down on his face.
Instinctively, the Big Boss Man drew a chromed .45 and hit the floor beside his fallen soldier, moving with incredible swiftness for a man of his bulk.
The thin man was gone in a flash, out of the door and down a dim unlit corridor. The big man hesitated, then was crawling fast across the floor, making for the doorway.
The woman began screaming again, a seamless needling wail that drew no breath. Her frantic struggles tilted the chair backwards, her legs up in the air.

Pausing, the giant shot her twice, once in the chest and once in the head. And then he too was gone, down the corridor and the back stairs.

I missed!

She heard shouting down below. The bodyguards were storming across the street in her direction, brandishing the sub-machine guns. She could hear them kicking the front door down.

She tried to stand but her legs were made of paper, crumpling beneath her. The rifle seemed to weigh a ton and was dragged from her numb fingers, clattering on the roof top.

I never miss!

She heard muffled shouting, climbing up towards her. And then the icy flood of fear was upon her in a tidal wave, drowning her.

"On th' roof…!"

The voices were getting louder. The door to the roof top crashed open.

Her vision swam; the red sky was revolving above her, the black shadows swirling. There was a roaring in her ears, slashed by a razor-like scream that she vaguely recognized as her own.

The sound of running feet, coming fast at her. Her limbs were paralyzed. Collapsing, she curled into a ball, moaning with terror.

In the black roaring whirlpool of horror, a single thought shone like a diamond.

I'm going to die!

The goon squad stormed the roof, coming at her as a dark mass, feet pounding.

"Take her alive…!"

Her long hair swirling around her face, she lurched unsteadily to her feet.

"…the Boss is gonna wan' t' talk t' her!"

She was dizzy, swaying, scraping the hair away from her eyes. Her vision was blurred, the red night whirling around her.

"UH!"

They came in swinging. A rock-hard fist impacted on her short ribs, low down; the pain was like a knife slashing into her.

"UGH…!"

The fists were scything in on her. She tried to parry and counter; the signals from her brain were scrambled and her limbs wouldn't function.

"…URRGGH…HHH….!"

A pile driver to the midriff. It was a blow her trained muscle tone would have treated with contempt but her reflexes were dulled and she wasn't ready for it. Groaning, she bent double, heaving, trying to breathe.

Someone seized her from behind, jerking her upright, pinning her arms back and wrenching her shoulders painfully.

"AGH!"

"UH—!"

They held her tight between them; one lunged forward and punched her hard in the face, snapping her head round, left-right. The red sky seemed to fill with exploding stars. She could taste blood in her mouth.

Her senses were in splinters; some residual instinct made her twist her body and kick out.

"YOW...!"

She connected, more by luck than judgment. Suddenly she was free. Swaying and stumbling, she lurched towards the edge of the roof.

"Get her—!"

She could hear shouting behind her, distorted by the buzzing in her brain. And then she was over the edge, diving into a rushing roaring blackness.

Suddenly, she wasn't afraid anymore. An absolute certainty came with crystal clarity.

I'm going to die....

A pale ghost, it glided through the veils of shadow, slow and stealthy, lights off, humming softly, its motor barely ticking over.

Leaning towards the wheel, the driver craned upwards, peering through the tinted windshield. She saw movement high above and then a single figure leap into space.

"Oh shit! Cat! No—!"

"AAGHH...!"

Her fall was halted abruptly, snagged violently on the rusting rail of the fire escape. Limply, she rolled off it and onto the metal platform, landing heavily.

"Uuuuhhh....hhhh...."

Groaning, her body one huge draining pain, she forced herself onto her hands and knees. Hauling on the creaking rail, she dragged herself to her feet.

"Uuuhh...hhhh...."

Twisting her neck to look upwards, she saw heads and shoulders silhouetted against the red sky; she saw the guns in their hands. Fear gripped her again, like a fist of ice clenching in the pit of her stomach.

On rubber legs, she began to stumble down the swaying descending zig-zag of the fire escape. It creaked perilously as rivets threatened to come away from the crumbling brickwork.

Up above, her pursuers were clambering over the lip of the roof, jumping down onto the top level of the fire escape.

She could feel the impact of their heavy feet, vibrating through the metal. And then her hand, greasy with sweat, slipped from the rail.

"AAAHHH....!"

She toppled forward and rolled down the next flight of iron steps, her body jarring and jolting.

There was a short burst of gunfire from above. Bullets pinged and whined off the metalwork. Flinching, she put her arms over her head, curling her body into a ball.

"Shit! Cut that out! Ah sed we wants her alive!"

The feet were pounding down the stairs, making the small platform shudder beneath her. Reaching up, she grabbed the rail and pulled herself upright.

She groaned, her body a mass of aches and stabbing pains, the black cat suit ripped and bloody at her knees and elbows.

Every step was a jagged pain that ripped all the way to the top of her head. She made it down the next zig and then the following zag. Coming closer, she heard drumming feet and heavy breathing.

"…Uh!……fuck….!"

She was on the final landing, some twenty feet above the sidewalk. Groaning and grunting, she struggled to release the short iron ladder. Rusted solid, it wouldn't budge.

"Fuck! F-f-fuck you….!"

She jumped. Her feet hit the concrete hard and her knees gave way. She came crashing down.

"….oh……shit…….!"

She rolled over, moaning. Darkness was rushing in from all four corners of the vast red sky.

"Now we gotya, bitch!"

The goon squad came thudding down to the bottom of the fire escape. And stopped short as though they had walked into an invisible wall.

"No way!"

The driver was out of the pale car and was crossing the street.

"Eat lead!"

A young Japanese woman with long glossy black hair and a face like a dangerous kitten, her lithe figure sheathed in a pale jade jumpsuit. Hip high, she brandished a government-issue M16, set to fully automatic.

Bunched together on the narrow landing of the fire escape, they didn't stand a chance. Spitting flame, she stitched them up and down, spent brass tinkling on the asphalt at her feet.

Held upright by the force of the blast, they did a crazy dance, puppets having their strings tugged. When the firing stopped, they subsided in a crumpled heap of bloody rags.

The young woman turned to look up at the single lit window.

You got lucky, Boss Man…you'll get yours another day….

Slinging the M16 across her slim shoulders, she knelt beside the limp figure lying below the fire escape.

"Oh Cat, I was afraid this might happen!"

The blonde's eyes fluttered open momentarily as she mumbled something incoherent through lips crusted with blood. Then her eyes closed and her head lolled sideways.

"...come on, let's take you home...."

CHAPTER 2

COMBAT FATIGUE

"My fellow Americans...."

The President was a square-jawed, stocky individual in his mid- fifties with receding hair that still bore a tint of red. His bright blue eyes were set close together in a square head set on a short, thick neck. He had the look of an old College football player, the kind of guy who, in the privacy of his study, liked to wear a sweatshirt with the faded letters across the chest.

"I speak to you at a time of grave national danger...."

For the TV cameras, he wore his Presidential blue suit. His thick neck bulged above the tight shirt collar and he barely resisted the impulse to tug at the knot of his sober necktie.

Blinking, he leaned forward a little. He struggled with the autocue, they always ran it too fast for him. Beads of sweat defeated the heavy make-up pan-caked on his high forehead.

In the control booth his chief aides, two bland-looking men in identical suits, looked at each other and rolled their eyes, groaning inwardly.

"Jeee-zus!" one muttered. "He's doing it again!"

"Well, you know what they say," his colleague grunted. "Can't think and chew gum at the same time."

She was dreaming.

Where am I?

She was running. Down an alley of shadows that vanished into a void. Something was pursuing her. Something invisible and terrible. Something inevitable.

"She's taken a hell of a beating," the Doctor said. "But she'll mend in time."

Dominated by majestic snow-capped peaks, the woods were deep and dark and secret, veined by silver streams.

The streams flowed into a sparkling lake. A single road, uncharted on any map, led to a large structure hidden deep amongst the trees.

Superficially, it presented itself as an old-fashioned hunting lodge, made of stone and logs, with high sloping roofs, gingerbread house windows and elaborately carved gables.

It was a sanctuary; a place to come and be healed.

Fear choked her. Her body was a block of ice. She blundered through an open doorway. Into a bare room that glared a sickly yellow.

There was a mirror on the wall. She saw her reflection, pale and drawn, staring back at her with blank eyes. She saw her face dissolve like melting wax.

Who am I?

"It's not her body I'm worried about," a mellow voice replied.

The exterior of the lodge presented a false front. Behind the rustic façade, everything was gleaming, streamlined and modern.

There were luxuriously appointed wards with private rooms and state of the art operating theaters; recreation rooms for relaxation and a sauna; a gymnasium and indoor swimming pool.

"No indeed," the Doctor nodded. "When she's ready I would recommend a thorough psych evaluation."

"Where am I...?"

Her eyes fluttered open. Pale blurs solidified slowly and became faces.

"Hey, Cat, welcome back."

The voice was low and rich like golden syrup. Framed by a spectacular afro, a proud beauty, with eyes like Cleopatra that glowed with a fierce fire.

Her beauty was inherited from an ancient, royal race. A culture that built stone cities and cultivated and sang songs and conquered, on an undiscovered dark continent – while Europe still sat and scratched itself in mud huts.

"...Selena....?"

She was magnificent, and ageless. Straight and tall, taller even than Cat. And powerful, in a green robe that draped down to her golden sandals, gold thread trimming its collar and billowing cuffs.

"...wha...?....what's hap—?"

Cat tried to sit up. Pain detonated along the entire length of her body. Her mouth opened but only a tiny sound came out. Weakly, she slumped back onto the pillows, her face drained white, shining with sweat.

Leaning over, Selena took up a small towel and gently mopped her brow.

"Easy, baby, easy...."

She cupped the pale face in her long fingers. Tears rolled out of Cat's wide green eyes.

"I'm s-so scared," she whispered. "S-so scared all the time...."

Swallowing hard to force his Adam's apple past the tight collar, the President squared his shoulders and continued. His voice was oddly high-pitched for someone of such a rugged appearance.

"...the youth of our nation have been corrupted and significant sectors of our society undermined by the tidal wave of illegal drugs that are for sale openly on our streets...."

An aide snorted dismissively.

"Significant my ass", he muttered. "You mean the niggers and spicks."

The sound engineer swiveled in his chair and stared at him, eyebrows raised. The aides withdrew to a more discrete corner.

"…we are engaged in a struggle to save the very soul of this great nation…."

The President had adjusted to the pace of the words scrolling past in front of him.

"…perhaps the greatest challenge we have ever faced…!"

Their heads tilted close together, the aides whispered conspiratorially.

"He can say what he wants…."

"…it won't interfere with the Plan…."

The pages fell from the calendar like falling leaves. Her bruises faded. The months passed in a blur.

At first, she was encouraged gently out of bed and into the pool. She was urged to achieve a few slow lengths, building up to countless fast ones, making the water froth and boil in her wake.

They marched her into the gym, with all its instruments of torture. Cruel to be kind, burly men in grey sweats cracked the whip like slave drivers, till her body burned, a living flame.

These whirlwinds of intense activity were punctuated by intervals of deep introspection. She was subjected to surgical probing by quietly determined men and women who sat in leather armchairs and took notes.

She couldn't help but tell them all they wanted to know, in a quiet voice that barely rose above a whisper, sometimes broken by sobbing.

Despite decay and dereliction, and in the midst of despair, the "Par-tay!" just went on and on, one big bright delirious glitter ball.

A cream-colored Art Deco wedding cake, its gaudy neon hailed **THE JOOK JOINT**. It proclaimed an "All-Nite" carnival and superstardom for everyone on the dance floor – dizzy dreams and fantasies, a life lived to a Disco beat.

The creatures of the night – what music they made…!

By day, few came and went. The club's activities were confined to the back office, where the sunlight never penetrated. Visitors entered and left briskly, men in a hurry, eager not to be seen.

Stripped pine and chrome, the office was ultra-modern, complete with TV monitors that scoped the dance floor. Behind an ebonized executive desk, the Prince of Darkness sat enthroned in padded black leather, his hand caressing the ruby-eyed silver skull that topped his scepter.

One by one, the furtive men came to pay homage. They were a cosmopolitan lot, some white, some black or Hispanic, a few oriental.

They approached the throne nervously; it was set on a slight rise so the Big Man could look down on them imperiously.

Each was handed a shiny black attaché case by one of the hulking bodyguards. An accountant, a slightly-built balding white man with wire-framed spectacles, made entries in a leather-bound ledger.

They exited as if taking leave of royalty, backwards and bowing and scraping. Each received the same words of warning, intoned by a voice so deep it made their bones shudder.

"An' yo makes sure we get every damn penny, muthafucka, else we knows where t' find yo!"

"Oooh baby…!"
The blacktop blurred beneath her wheels.
"…It's good to be home…!"
Cat inhaled deeply; home was all those old familiar car smells.
She was truckin'. She was cruisin', rolling down the highway with the top down, with the sun on her face and the wind in her long blonde hair.
She was dressed for driving in white rubber-soled Hi-Tops and a powder blue brushed denim jumpsuit with the ring pull on the zipper tugged all the way down to her navel.
Sly and the Family Stone were pumpin' out the Funk. The engine was humming.
"Woo!-Woo…oooo…!"
It had the power and poise of a beast of prey. Bright "rally red" with white go-faster stripes on the hood and along its muscular flanks.
Heavyweight chrome and racing wheels, gleaming white upholstery and all the polished wood grain trimmings, more like a luxury yacht than a motor car.
1970 Oldsmobile 442 convertible; the W-30 badge which proclaimed the total package.
"….Woo!...oooooooo…!"
She snuck into the city by the back way. The sun beat like a brass gong on a grim tableau of destruction and dereliction. An industrial wasteland; empty warehouses, vandalized with spray cans, windows shattered. Silent factories decaying slowly or reduced to charred bones, gutted by fire.
Waste paper swirled in the wake of the red Olds as she weaved nimbly down the alleys that ran between the hollow warehouses.
The light at the end of a long dark tunnel exploded with blinding abruptness into a broad plain of glaring concrete with tall weeds spiking its cracks, strewn with rubbish and rubble.
Rolling to a halt, she let the motor idle.
Beyond the bleak expanse of cracked concrete, rose the towering, corrugated frontage of a massive warehouse.
Its high windows were sightless pits, bristling hoists and cranes scabbed and scarred with rust. The bankrupt corporate banners emblazoned on its vast doors were faded and ghostly, their livery blistered and flaking.
Cat shook her head, frowning. She gave it the gun. The big car barreled across the broken concrete, bits of debris crunching under its wheels.
She let it roll on and on. Just when it looked like there was going to be a collision a section of the corrugated wall swung inwards and the red car vanished into the inner darkness. The wall swung shut behind it.

The 442 rolled into a huge steel cage. She switched off the engine. Iron shutters descended with a clang that made her flinch.

The cage was lit by an unflattering chilly light. Cat made a face at herself in the rear-view mirror. She felt the swift descent in the pit of her stomach. It lasted for a full minute.

There was a jolt as the cage stopped. A muffled beeping and the front gates of the cage rose quickly. The pulse was suddenly louder, insistent.

"Okay, okay!"

With a last glance in the mirror, pausing to tease her windblown hair, Cat vaulted lithely out of the driving seat.

Striding out of the elevator, she advanced into a large semi-circular area with stark white walls and a white carpet. Shining corridors, punctuated at regular intervals by polished doorways, radiated like the spokes of a wheel, as far as the eye could see.

All that brightness made her blink, as it always did, she quickly got used to it.

"Ah, Cat. Here you are."

A woman was walking towards her, down one of the corridors. The young oriental woman with a face like a dangerous kitten, neat and trim in a pale blue blouse and darker blue mini-skirt, carrying a thick box file under her arm.

"Oh, hi, Aiko," Cat looked appropriately apologetic. "Sorry I'm late."

The Japanese girl shook her head, smiling.

"It just wouldn't be you, Cat," she said. "If you were on time."

Aiko set off rapidly down a central corridor that ran straight ahead from the elevator, tapering to a far distant vanishing point.

"The Boss is waiting for you."

Cat had to jump to catch up with her. The white corridor was very bright. Young women in pale blue blouses and dark blue mini-skirts were exiting one door and entering another, laden with files and documents.

They gave the new arrival a long, interested look as she passed by, looking her up and down, in her bold costume.

Suddenly, all that brightness was jarring, jangling. And suddenly, that fear jolted her with its cold paralyzing electricity. Cat stopped short, her breath constricted, her hand going to her chest.

"Hey," Aiko turned, reaching out to her. "Are you okay?"

Shoulders heaving, Cat drew in air. She took the lithe girl's hands and squeezed them tight.

"Aiko…", she whispered. "Thank you…!"

At the end of the long corridor, there was a door that wasn't like the others. It was sheathed in padded green leather, with sparking brass studs.

Aiko pressed a brass button. A buzzer sounded and the door opened inwards.

"In you go."

The office was immense, with a plush maroon carpet and a carnival of exotic tapestries on the walls. There were fearsome tribal masks and warrior's shields, hung above leopard skin rugs.

Cat entered to the old familiar greeting.

"There you are," smiled Selena.

The office was dominated by a massive desk, lavishly carved with animal's heads and tribal scenes. On the wall behind it was a panoramic map of the United States and a battery of TV screens. In front, a semi-circle of high-backed conference chairs, upholstered with zebra-skin.

"It's good to have you back."

Selena rose from behind the desk. Cat gazed at her in frank admiration. She was magnificent, and ageless.

"I'm glad to be here," Cat replied.

Suddenly, her eyes were brimming over. She hung her head to hide the tears.

Selena left her desk and walked across the office. The strength of her body was evident in the way that she moved, the long robe flowing.

Framing the beautiful blonde head between her long brown fingers with their golden nails, she looked deep into Cat's jade-green eyes.

"I know, honey...."

Cat sighed.

"I'm so sorry. I'm so sorry I blew it."

Selena stroked her cheek, smiling.

"Don't be. It happens to the best of us...."

Cat's eyes were very moist. Selena returned to her desk and made a motion with a gold-tipped finger. Cat and Aiko settled into the zebra-striped upholstery.

"...And you are the best of us...."

"Right on!" Aiko chimed and Cat smiled at her gratefully.

Selena opened a buff-colored folder that lay on the desk top.

"You're lookin' fine, Cat."

Aiko had the box file on her lap. She lifted the lid and handed a replica of Selena's folder to Cat.

"How are you, really?"

The top page, as usual, was a potted summary; Selena sat back in her chair and gave Cat a chance to peruse it. As she read, her brow clouded. Selena and Aiko exchanged nervous glances. But when Cat looked up from the page she was nodding.

"I can't argue with that."

Selena's relief was plain to see.

"So, you agree with the recommendations?"

Cat shrugged.

"Sure," she replied gloomily. "It's obvious, I've lost it."

Frowning, Aiko stretched over to stroke Cat's arm.

"No way!"

Selena rose from her chair and leant forward across the desk.

"It's my fault, I'm sorry Cat. You're the best I've got and I burned you out."

And then she was smiling again; her warmth charged the room.

"You need a rest, that's all."

"Yep," Aiko grinned. "You deserve a vacation."

It seemed to take all the strength Cat had to bring a pale smile to her face. She stood up slowly and as they came to her side she put her arms around them.

"You know me," she said. "I'm not one for just lazing around in the sun."

"Oh, don't worry, babe," Selena laughed. "We'll find something for you to do!"

"Now, yo jus' chill, sweet cheeks…."

Lean and wiry, he wore a red three-piece suit with billowing flares flapping around his crocodile toecaps, pearl buttons on his vest, a purple silk shirt with a wide psychedelic tie and a broad-brimmed white fedora with a snakeskin band.

"…an' let Papa do his stuff…!"

He set his shiny black leather attaché case down on a small side table. In the soft glow of the bulbs that ringed her dressing table mirror, the dancer was fumbling in a crowded drawer.

"…Ah sed chill, babe, Papa got everythin' yo need…"

She was still beautiful, even before she put her make-up on, but today she looked pale and ravaged. Her blue eyes were lightless, red hair tumbling in disarray, her rumpled silk dressing gown sliding from her bare freckled shoulders.

"…Ah got yo candy, baby…."

She was tugging her sleeve up, struggling to fold it back, the silk slippery in her hasty fingers. He was laying out the kit meticulously on top of the attaché case: the needle, the spoon….

"Ooooo, yes, Papa," she moaned. "I want my candy…!"

He was standing over her, frowning down at the livid tracery of track marks on her arm. He shook his head.

"Jeeez! We's runnin' out o' room!"

Panic flared in her desperate eyes. With hands like claws, she ripped the skirts of the long dressing gown apart, exposing her white thigh.

On the road again. The 442 was a red slash on the blacktop.

Oh man…oh yes…heal me…!

The warm wind was soothing, her hair floating like a golden banner. Marvin's voice oozed like spooned honey from the speakers, as he offered her love and sexual healing.

There was a chromed CB handset just below the polished walnut paneling on the dash, its short curly cord dangling. Its thin, insistent beeping took a while to distract her from the music and her mental image of those soothing hands all over her.

Uncle John…!

"Hi," her voice was brittle and anxious. "Is that you, Uncle John?"

The strength and heartiness in the voice that responded spanned the airwaves, banishing the fuzzy crackle.

"Hey, Princess! How ya doing?"

"Sweet dreams, baby doll...."

He clicked the attaché case shut and closed the door behind him without even a parting glance for the feast of voluptuous flesh exposed by the disturbed dressing gown. He was a man in a hurry; he had business to attend to.

The dancer sagged in her chair. Head lolling, eyes half closed, she was far, far away.

"MMmm...mmmm...."

"...hhhh...hhhmm...mmm...."

"MMM—!"

"—–?"

Her eyes bulged. Her exposed breasts heaved. Red in the face, she strained to breathe. Pink froth bubbled on her twisting lips.

A massive convulsion shuddered through her entire body, from her toes to the top of her head. Then her head fell forward, her chin on her chest. She slid from the armchair onto the floor, the silk gown spreading around her. She flexed, twitched, and then was still.

Suddenly, she was crying again.

Aw shit! That's the third time this morning, why can't I stop it?

Big heavy tears were rolling like stones down her cheeks. Angry with herself, Cat tried to blink them away, and then scrubbed her eyes with the back of her hand.

"I'm not good, Uncle John...."

The response was immediate and positive.

"Well, you just keep on coming, Princess. I'm here for you."

Their passing stirred up scraps of paper, scuffing down the dirty alleyway. A tin can went rolling and clanging.

"Shee-ut, man, cool it...!"

A cave, a refuge, a bunker, made of slabs of rotting cardboard and rusting trash cans, roofed over with boards and tarpaulin.

"Aw, c'mon...c'mon...c'mon....!"

"Fer f-fuck's sake, I'm doin' th' best I can!"

Cursing, fumbling, ragged bursts of obscenity.

"...Oh...ah...that's it...that's the...oooh baby...!"

"...uhhh...ah yeah...yeah...yeah....!"

And then an abrupt and choking silence. A gasp, a strangled exclamation; a violent thrashing that made the rickety structure sway.

A shabby figure emerged, crawling on all fours, long dirty hair hanging down over his face.

"UGH...HHH....IIIIAAAKK...KKK....!"

Vomit sluiced from his gaping mouth. He shuffled forward, subsided and lay face down, wheezing hoarsely. His eyes rolled up whitely, a final convulsion and then all was still.

The empty syringe rolled from his dead yellow-stained fingers. Just one of many that littered this dead zone in the heart of the city.

On the road. The night pulsed with a heavy groove.

Right on...!

Her car speakers were a ringing declaration. Curtis told it like it is.

"Oh, yeah, baby...ain't that the truth!"

When you saw the sign to Free Town, you might be expecting wigwams and campfires, something that looked like Woodstock in the desert.

It was a proper town, a very small town, but a town. Although Cat had been there so many times she never ceased to be amazed.

"Far out!"

It had three parallel main avenues, connected by a grid of side streets, all bathed in the soft radiance of old-fashioned gas lamps. Simple houses, whitewashed wooden cubes, dotted the streets at regular intervals, their windows lit by the same vintage glow.

Old West-style false-fronted stores lined the broader avenues. There were barns and stables and a water tower and a wooden church with a steeple.

There was even a town square with a circular bandstand, a Civil War cannon and a flagpole – only the cannon had a bunch of flowers in its muzzle and the flag bore a large peace symbol and a picture of a dove.

"Crazy..." muttered Cat.

Delighted, she burst out laughing.

Oh, I haven't laughed for a long time....

The mighty V-8 rumbled as she drove slowly down the gas-lit central avenue. The storefronts were dark, an old-fashioned saloon was all lit up and alive with the sound of song and laughter. Down every side street, music was floating from open windows.

Young couples were out strolling, their arms around each other: boy and girl, girl and girl, boy and boy.

I still say they should have called it Free Love....

The red Olds advanced into the town square. On the bandstand, a young man with long hair was plucking the complicated strings of a sitar, before a cross-legged semi-circle of earnest admirers.

Cat could smell the weed from where she was sitting.

She parked the car in front of the small white wooden church. The 442 was already drawing a flock of admirers, drifting across the town square.

"Crazy wheels...."

"Cool...!"

She trotted up the wooden steps to the tall front doors. There was an antique brass bell pull.

She tugged it. Somewhere inside, the bell tinkled.

"Come in, it's not locked."

Cat pushed the doors wide and stepped through.

No matter how many times she'd been there she was still prepared for pews and a pulpit. What she saw was a luxury apartment that went all the way up to the wooden rafters.

The floor was a sumptuous gleaming parquetry of polished woods, the walls lined with stripped pine, hung with iridescent oriental tapestries. At ground level it was one long, enormous space, with richly hued Persian rugs and embroidered cushions tossed around.

Hanging from the beams, brass lamps cast a golden glow. Incense burners stood on slender tripods, wafting their honeyed musk. At the far end, where the altar would have been, the raised area had been converted into a place for dining, seated on cushions around a long, low table.

"Is that you, Princess?"

Cat craned her head back, looking for the source of that old familiar voice.

"Yes, it is, Uncle John."

"Be right with you...."

An iron wrought staircase spiraled up to a platform, supported on flying buttresses, projecting almost halfway into the body of the church, creating a huge loft.

"...make yourself at home."

She waited at the foot of the curling steps. The decorative ironwork vibrated as he descended.

"And how's my favorite niece...?"

John Warburton had the face of a middle-aged cherub, lit by a hearty glow, his blue eyes twinkling behind little round glasses. Long greying hair flowed down to his wide shoulders, complemented by a flourishing walrus moustache.

He was barrel-chested, big but solid, with a mighty girth over which an embroidered caftan hung like a tent, hanging down to the sandals on his feet.

Cat almost threw herself at him, rocking the big man back on his heels. Laughing, he enfolded her in his arms, the billowing sleeves riding up to reveal forearms like hams, emblazoned with faded old Special Forces tattoos.

"Oh, Uncle John...!"

She had promised herself she wouldn't cry; scalding tears were jetting from her eyes, staining her cheeks. Releasing her, John Warburton cupped her face softly in his massive hands with their blunt fingers and scarred knuckles.

"Come on, Princess," he whispered tenderly. "I know what you need...."

With a swift grace surprising for such a big man, he scooped her up in his arms and carried her effortlessly up the spiral stairway.

"...and then you can tell me all about it...."

He took her up the twisting stairs so fast it made her dizzy; and suddenly she was laughing again, snuffling through the tears.

The loft was split in two. To the right were the sleeping quarters and a great big brass bed.

"Here we are...."

To the left was the bathroom, constructed around a large circular sunken bath, rimmed with pink marble, fit for a Roman Emperor.

"Let's wash our cares away...."

Shedding the caftan, John Warburton sat with the steaming water up to his navel, pearls of moisture glinting in the hair on his broad chest and big belly, his mighty arms spread out along the marble rim of the basin.

His impressive biceps were each a pillow for the shining, blue-black head of a beautiful Chinese girl, the one with a round face like a perfect doll, the other more angular and exotic. Their tawny skin was gleaming, firm breasts bobbing on the water.

The girls looked up at Cat and smiled. She smiled back. The exotic girl twisted sideways to reach a small silver-plated flask. She popped the stopper and poured a golden oil into the water. Instantly, the steam became scented.

"Mmmm..." sighed Cat. "That's nice."

Uncle John stroked the girls' long black hair. Smiling, they squirmed closer to him, resting their heads on his shoulders.

Cat didn't wait to be asked. She tugged off the sneakers and her socks and tossed them aside. Down rasped the big ring pull on the zipper and she was undulating out of the blue denim jumpsuit.

Her proud breasts were free and unfettered. She disposed of the skimpy panties briskly, flicking them aside with her big toe.

Stark naked, Cat stood on the edge of the basin.

"Wonderful...!"

The Chinese girls studied her with admiring eyes. Uncle John was beaming.

"You are very beautiful, Princess."

"Thank you, Uncle John."

She waded thigh deep in the water. The warm scented vapors caressed her.

John Warburton marveled at the slow roll of her hips as she advanced across the basin, the supple muscle play of her midriff, the surge of her perfect breasts.

Letting her legs bend, she dipped her body down into the water, up to her chin, her golden hair spread out on the surface. Then she rose, the water cascading down her spectacular contours. She dipped and rose again, her skin gleaming.

"Mmmmmmmmmm....!"

Cat stood with the water lapping at her thighs. She closed her eyes. With a kind of reverence, the doll-faced girl anointed her head with olive-tinted oil. Slowly, luxuriating in the task, she began to wash Cat's long blonde hair.

The exotic girl dipped her hands into a large copper bowl full to the brim with a balm like liquid honey. In a trance, she began to stroke her palms all over Cat's body, smoothing the glistening oil into her skin.

Cat sighed. She smiled, her lips moving, murmuring.

John Warburton watched, enchanted.

Sizzling giggles in the darkness.

"Ssshh…!"

The swish of bedclothes tossed aside. Bare feet padding on the floorboards. Urgent whispers.

"Come on…!"

Vague forms of pale nakedness, flitting fleetingly in the gloom; cloaking themselves.

A window, inching open. A soft creaking, a sharp intake of breath.

"Let's go…!"

Escape.

Sweet smoke mingled with the perfumed vapors.

"So, how are you, Princess?"

The Chinese girls had donned silken robes and departed to the kitchen. Cat and Uncle John sat smiling at each other across the marble basin.

He leaned over to pass her the joint. Cat took from it deeply. She felt the welcome mellowness creep all the way down to her toes.

"I hope you're still enjoying your trust fund."

He wagged his finger at her with mock sternness.

"Now remember, child. I forbid you to spend a single penny of it wisely."

Cat passed the reefer back to him.

"Don't worry, Uncle John. I won't let you down."

She splashed across to his side and cuddled up to him, laying her blonde head on his shoulder.

"I want you to be proud of me."

He touched the tip of her nose lightly with a fingertip.

"I am proud of you, angel."

The tears were never far away. Suddenly, the light went out of her face, which seemed to crumble, as her eyes welled up again.

A terrible sigh was wrenched from her. She shook her head violently, her hair flailing across her face.

"Oh, I haven't done anything to be proud of lately!"

Gently, her Uncle drew the blonde veil back from her large liquid eyes.

"It's not your fault, sweetheart. It can happen to anyone. Believe me, I know…."

His eyes clouded momentarily and in that brief instant Cat had a window on a world of pain. It spanned the bloody jungles of Viet Nam, the glittering ruthless towers of the corporate jungle, all abandoned for the peace and refuge of Free Town.

He squeezed her shoulder and she looked at him with the faintest glimmer of a smile.

"That's better…."

He stroked her bare arm, glistening with a perfumed dew.

"You can stay here with us," he suggested. "For as long as you like."

The night was electric. The air tingled with forbidden excitement.

From the black tunnel of the alleyway, they watched the two-tone patrol car cruise by, making its routine inspection, rolling past the shuttered storefronts and closed saloons.

"Bye bye…Piggies…."

Sizzling giggles.

"Let's go!"

Slim shadows made a dash for it. The side door of the Pharmacy offered little resistance. The locks on the cabinets were child's play.

"Time's up!"

"Go! Go!"

This time the prowler came squealing around the corner, the lights on its roof flashing, in response to the silent alarm.

Too late. Cursing, kicking the tires in frustration.

"Seeya…!"

Hand in hand, they stepped out onto the porch of the old church. In the golden glow of the gas lamps, the night was full of music and laughter.

"You get some sleep, angel," said Uncle John.

A smiling red-haired girl was strolling across the town square towards them, dressed in a simple smock and bell-bottoms.

"Susie here has a room all ready for you in her house."

The door of the "HOMELESS SHELTER" creaked open a crack and someone peered out warily.

"Oh, it's you…."

Sizzling giggles.

"Hi!"

"Here's some more free medicine…."

"For the people!"

Cat gave her Uncle a big hug. He squeezed back and they both laughed.

"Thank you, Uncle John…."

She kissed him lightly on the cheek, tweaked his flourishing moustaches gently, like she did when she was a child.

"I'll stay a few days," she whispered with her face close to his, letting his moustache tickle her, like it did when she was a child.

Her smile had a little warmth in it now.

"But I need to be doing something," she stated. "I'm starting a new career."

CHAPTER 3

ROAD RAGE

The jagged assault of Miles' "Freedom X" was slashing from her speakers as she rolled into the car park.

Heads turned, startled, offended.

Dig it squares!

It matched her mood.

Cat liked her road wide open and free, nothing but her and her music and the vast empty spaces. The four lanes confronting her, the twists and turns like tangled barbed wire, were congested with traffic.

Beneath a pall of smog, seething impatience and frustration, braying horns and angry gestures.

When they saw her, they did a double-take. The red mean machine, top down; a pale blue denim shirt wide open to air her cleavage, held together by a knot that rode up to bare her toned midriff, stonewashed Levi's low on her hips.

"Put your eyes back in, hammerhead!"

She carried her own bags into the lobby.

"Catherine Warburton," Cat told the girl at Reception, ignoring her smile. "You have a room for me."

The motel was modern and clean, in pastel pink and blue. Its tiled balconies looked inwards over a floodlit swimming pool. It boasted a plush restaurant and bar.

The girl went on smiling as she checked the ledger.

"Yes, we do indeed, it's all ready for you."

A tour bus drew up on the neon-lit forecourt and disgorged a small army of salesmen in tired and rumpled suits. On their way back East from a West Coast convention, most of them were still wearing their name tags.

Shoving in through the tall plate glass doors, they headed straight for the bar, ogling Cat from top to toe as they filed past.

"Hey, baby!"

"Guys, we came to the right place!"

Fuck off!

She slammed the door shut. All she wanted right now was a hot bath.

Cat tossed her cases onto the bed. She was undressing as she crossed the room, leaving it all strewn about on the floor.

She looked at herself in a full length mirror. In the bland light, she had no sheen. She had lost her luster.

God, you stink!

Wrinkling her nose, Cat scowled at herself sourly. She couldn't stop them, all the bad thoughts clanging like a cracked bell inside her skull.

She padded across the carpet and lifted the phone from the bedside table. "Hello? Room Service."

"Hi. This is…uh…" she glanced at her key tag. "Room 315. Send me up a Screwdriver. A tall one. Heavy on the vodka."

She poured more than half the scented bath oil into the steaming water, inhaling deeply. She frowned. The bad smell persisted, at least inside her head.

"Shit…!"

She drained the bottle into the steam. Lowering herself by inches, she slid her body into the perfumed water until the surface was tickling her chin.

Closing her eyes, she tried to empty her mind. Whispering, she recited the soothing mantras that had been taught to her, drilled into her. She let herself drift, losing the bad thoughts along with the bad smell.

There was a knock at the door.

"Room Service.…"

The spell was broken. The bad thoughts came crawling back, gnawing at the core of her.

She sat in the bathwater till it became tepid, looking at the tall glass of vodka and orange for a long time. She knew she shouldn't, not on top of the medication.

Fuck it!

She grabbed the glass and tossed it back in one gulp.

Her sleep was full of dreams.

She was running across the rooftops under a churning blood red sky. She could hear heavy footsteps, closing in behind her. Flashlight beams like searchlights in the darkness were lashing wildly from side to side.

The roof's surface was transparent and she could see bloated dead faces, glaring up at her with bulging eyes as she ran by. Their swollen purple lips were moving, their hands reaching up to claw at her ankles.

A shrieking whirlwind flayed her as she tumbled onto a teetering zig-zag of metal steps that descended into fathomless blackness.

And suddenly she was falling, flailing in the roaring void.

Falling…falling……

Cat sat up in bed, wide awake.

She was panting. Cold sweat crawled on her skin. Her nerves were jangling, red raw. She looked at the luminous dial of her watch. It was 1 a.m.

"Shit!"

Stark naked, she crossed the room and peered out through a crack in the curtains. The bar was still open, its neon flashing.

"Hm!"

Cat went to the mirror and ran a quick comb through her hair. She didn't waste time with underwear, slipping on a short pale green silk mini dress that she cinched at the waist with a belt of chain-link silver.

Sliding her feet into a pair of sandals, she grabbed her purse and headed for the door.

The dimly-lit bar was sparsely populated. A lone silhouette at the end of the long counter and shadowy figures in some of the booths, hugging their drinks, pinpointed by the glowing tips of their cigarettes.

Cat chose a bar stool to perch on. She ordered a vodka and orange. The medicine bottle rattled guiltily in her purse but she ignored it.

"Run up a tab...."

A man in an expensive suit took possession of the stool next to her. He looked her over, staring at the unfettered peaks of her breasts, poking through the thin skin of the silk dress.

Cat glanced at him. A slick capitalist; everything about him repulsed her instantly.

Get lost!

Looking at her sideways with his mouth twisted in a knowing grin, he slid a folded bar napkin over towards her. When she ignored him, staring straight ahead, he moved it right in front of her.

"What's that meant to be?" she asked, not looking at him.

He laughed, a cropped unpleasant bark.

"Haw! Don't play games, baby!"

Cat took a long, slow hard look at him, up and down. She lifted the corner of the napkin. A room number was scrawled in pencil. She saw the dollar bills, dealt like a hand of cards.

Cat took a sip of her drink. She dabbed the corner of her mouth with the folded napkin, then screwed it up and flicked it into his lap, sweeping the banknotes onto the floor.

"Shove it, creep, I'm not for sale."

His polished face darkened. He reached out and clamped his hand on her shoulder.

"Don't bullshit me, sweetheart, I know what—!"

The bartender, a chunky balding man in a red vest and bow tie, was moving towards them. Cat moved faster.

"OW...!"

The man in the suit yelped as she seized his hand and bent it back painfully.

"OWWW…WOW….OWWW…!"

Maintaining her grip, Cat flowed off the bar stool, wrenching his arm and making him yell and arch up on tiptoe.

"…OW…BITCH…!"

She dipped and turned and flipped him up and over. He came crashing down flat on his back and lay there winded, flopping about, mouth gaping, like a landed fish.

He was still in mid-air as Cat spun on her heel and was sauntering out of the bar, the brief silk sheening on her glorious contours. Gasps and a gust of astonishment blew after her as she vanished from sight, the doors swinging shut behind her.

The pills and the alcohol made a volatile mix like fire racing in her veins. The lights lining the long corridor to her room were big and bright and dancing.

She felt great.

Sizzling giggles, conspiring whispers.

"Have you heard?"

"Whitlock's replacement will be here this week!"

"She'd better be tough."

"Aw, we'll eat her alive!"

In the pale pink dawn Cat carried her bags out to the motel car park.

Let's go…!

As the red Olds surged onto the empty highway she slotted in the 8-track and turned the volume to maximum – that man Miles again: "Bitches Brew".

They're playing my tune!

She flipped open the wood grain hatch of the glove compartment. A pill bottle rolled out and rattled into her lap.

"Fuck!"

Fumbling, one-handed, she pried the lid off and spilled half the contents into her palm. Mouthing them, she pulled a quart of vodka from the deep recess in the dash.

Releasing the wheel just long enough to twist off the bottle cap, she filled her mouth till her cheeks puffed out and then swallowed hard.

The burn made her blink.

"UGH!"

She took another swig.

The big American stood out from the crowd; six-foot four with wide shoulders straining the seams of his rumpled pale linen suit. A blond government-issue crew cut, eyes masked by mirror shades, mopping the back of his bulging neck with a damp handkerchief.

The customary ranks of petitioners, lined up at the palace gates, parted to let him pass, the eyes in their sad faces downcast. Some tugged the straw sombreros from their heads, lank-haired, ragged and barefoot.

The guards barked something in their coarse colonial Spanish, making wide motions with their arms. The big American ran a practiced eye over them, their sloppy sweat-stained olive drab, oversize helmets and obsolete rifles. They heaved the creaking gate open for him.

A fat flunky came flapping down the cracked and crumbling palace steps, his greasy jowls wobbling, constricted by a tight collar and tie.

"Welcome, Señor, welcome, El Presidente is expecting you…!"

Top down, the wind in her hair; Miles and the miles blurred by.

The 8-track was played out. The only music was the engine. She loved to lose herself in its symphony and savor all the harmonies and counterpoints that delighted her trained ear.

She was spacey, jangling. She was seeing things. She saw dead faces, floating like a pale moon above the onrushing blacktop.

"Shit…!"

Cat slammed on the brakes. The car squealed in protest, its tail swinging sideways as it slithered to a halt.

"Damn it!"

There was a dull ache pulsing behind her eyes. Her skin was crawling like she was covered with ants. She couldn't stop shivering.

"Fuck!"

Scrubbing her face with the palms of her hands, she shook her head from side to side, her long hair lashing. She squeezed her eyes tight shut but the contorted death masks were still there, staring at her.

She stayed like that for a long time, eyes closed, shoulders hunched, her forehead resting on the rim of the steering wheel.

El Presidente's office was a hymn to faded glory. He sat flanked by dusty flags, their tri-colors muted, gold threads dulled.

Above him loomed a massive oil portrait of the National Hero on horseback, the man who had freed them from the bonds of colonialism only to be substituted by the chains of dictatorship.

The paint was so darkened and discolored by age that the proud face was a faint glimmer. All the better, to hide his disappointment.

"Señor ……! 'Eees so good to see you…."

El Presidente was a squat and pot-bellied individual, ill-suited to the contrived sky-blue comic opera uniform he was stuffed into, bedecked with falsified ribbons, encrusted epaulettes and gold braid.

His short neck puddled over his stiff high collar, his eyes small and black in his flabby face, hair combed over slickly in a vain attempt to disguise his advancing baldness.

Normally, he would remain in the raised throne behind his imposing desk when he received visitors, so he could look down on them as they sat before him. This was a special occasion and he came waddling forward, offering his hand.

"Welcome…welcome…!"

The tuneless blare of a car horn shocked her, seemed to stop her heart, freezing her to the marrow.

Something big blasted past her, deliberately, recklessly close. As it blew its harsh slipstream in her face the horn sounded again, a shrill diminishing whine. She saw a head turn, a face, eyes glaring at her vengefully.

It was a familiar face. Twisted with hate, barely distinguishable from the leering lust that had provoked her, the face of the bespoke-suited executive from the motel bar.

Motherfucker!

Ice became fire. Her brain was frying. Blind instinct triggered her. In a smoking wheel-spin she slammed through the gears, put the pedal to the metal and was gone.

She was riding a space rocket. The sky was fizzing and crackling, the tarmac beneath her wheels was sizzling, white hot.

You're mine…!

One second he was cruising, congratulating himself, and then his mirror was full of red. He heard a horn that played a jazzy riff and she was sliding effortlessly alongside, grinning maliciously at him, giving him the finger.

He flexed his foot on the accelerator but she beat him to it. The red beast seemed to sidestep nimbly in front of him and pin him there, too close for comfort.

"Bitch!"

Eventually, she pulled away slightly, making a gap. She extended an arm to wave him on by. He began to edge out nervously.

Her eyes laughed back at him in her rear-view mirror.

Fuck off!

With a touch on the brakes, she kept the 442's rear end in his face. Whichever way he tried to go, she was there in front of him.

It was just a woman! His blood boiled. She'd made a fool of him once; she wasn't going to do it again.

"Fucking bitch!"

He tried to be clever. He slowed, hanging back, then hit the pedal and accelerated, feinting to go outside, then swinging in.

No way man!

He was no match for her instincts. Cat made him think that he'd fooled her. Then she shut the door. His brakes squealed, tires smoking.

The long tail of the glossy sedan swung wildly and the executive's car performed a full revolution, smashing through the barrier. It slid sideways down a steep slope before flipping and rolling over and over to the foot of a deep ravine.

The mangled ruin blew apart. A ball of oily black and orange flame rolled up the steep slope and over the rim of the highway. Spilt gas from the ruptured tank ignited in a curtain of fire all the way across the lanes.

She was as cool as ice.

Everything was big and bright, larger than life, more real than real, like in a dream. She could see the bones in her hands on the wheel, the blood coursing through the veins.

The 442 was a red arrow streaking towards the distant vanishing point. She left the rising smudge of smoke far behind.

He had a wife...?

"A wife he cheated on."

...and kids...?

"Kids he had no time for."

Like your father?

"Yeah, just like my father!"

They're better off without him!

The big American could scarcely keep the curl of contempt from his lips as he took the damp and flabby hand in a crushing grip.

"Pleeeze...pleeeze...sit down...what may I offer you...?"

As his guest wedged his bulk into a deep armchair El Presidente clapped his hands and a venerable orderly in a white jacket hovered at his side.

"Nothing, thank you, Sir."

His tone was hard and businesslike. Gulping, flexing his pudgy fingers to get the blood back into them, El Presidente scuttled back behind his desk and enthroned himself again.

"I'm here about our friends in the South," the big American rasped briskly. "They've been short on product lately. We've had a hard time keeping our people supplied...."

The desert opened like a yellow flower and embraced her.

"Otis Blue" was on the 8-track and she could feel the ache in his voice, a pain so deep she feared it might cut her in half.

"...please wash away all my fears...."

The needle crept past 70 ... 80 ... 90 ... Supercharged, the red Olds sliced through the thick warm air like a sword blade, stirred it and cooled it, soothing her with a cool breeze.

"…A change is gonna come…!"

She saw a familiar shape shimmering in the heat haze, by the side of the highway. As she drew nearer, it took on a recognizable form and solidity and emerged as a modest gas station and diner.

"Hey baby, we've been here before…."

The uppers had made her very hungry.

She nudged the pedal, closing the distance to the sign that declared: LAST GAS FOR FIFTY MILES.

A year seemed like a very long time ago. A lifetime ago; a lifetime of strange fears and excitements, wild adventures – and so many dead faces.

"It hasn't changed at all!"

Long and low, faded yellow with a flat roof and a tin chimney, standing on squat concrete stilts. Tattered red, white and blue bunting hung over its plate glass doorway, framing a board that said: VERNA'S EATS.

The heads that could be seen at the stretched windows wore broad-brimmed hats or baseball caps. When the doors opened and shut, there was a gust of country fiddle and guitar.

"Yee-hah," Cat was smiling.

She let the red Olds roll leisurely onto the large flat area in front of the diner. It looked like something from another planet, beside the battered pick-ups and trailer trucks.

Cat saw Confederate flags and N.R.A. stickers. She twirled a chrome knob and made her urban Soul shout. She laughed when she saw the cowboy hats twitch.

Cat parked the 442 where she was sure she would be able to see it from the window. She tugged the ring pull on the zipper of the tight denim jump suit up from below her navel, to just below her cleavage.

Two good ol' boys in baseball caps and overalls were thudding down the short flight of steps that led to the glass doors of the diner, scrubbing flecks of cheeseburger from their stubble. They stopped and stared in disbelief at the long-legged vision striding towards them.

"Hey, babeee…!"

They looked up into eyes like chips of green ice.

"Er…'xcuse us…."

It was just as she remembered.

A long blue plywood counter and blue plywood booths, the table tops and the counter top in matching yellow Formica. The floor was speckled blue and white linoleum, the ceiling had been white once but wasn't anymore.

Squeaking fans stirred the air tepidly, fanning the aromas of strong coffee and fried onions that wafted from the kitchen, seen through the serving hatch behind the counter. There were Wild West scenes, pin-up postcards that went back to the Fifties of strapping girls posing with trucks, advertisements for brands of beer and cigarettes and faded photographs of ball players and B-Western movie stars.

Ambiance was provided by the sounds of male conversation, cigarette smoke, cooking smells and seamlessly piped country music.

The baseball caps and cowboy hats all turned as Cat strolled in through the door, following her progress as she advanced towards the counter. The hum of conversation dipped, and then swelled again, with sharp intakes of breath, suppressed groans and a wolf whistle or two.

"Jest ignore 'em, sweetheart. They're harmless...."

Verna looked just the same, more careworn, more disillusioned perhaps.

She had been a high school beauty; now she was on the wrong side of forty. A well-built, handsome woman, with a little too much eye shadow and lipstick. Her honey-blonde hair was piled high on her head and had pink highlights, under the glaring strips of neon above the counter.

She looked Cat up and down, in detail, smiling wistfully.

"Hey, beautiful, I know yew don't I?"

Cat smiled back.

"Yes, it's been a while."

Her eyes clouded as she glanced towards the back, the busy kitchen and the wide serving hatch. Remembering; a dark brown-eyed handsome man who had swept her off her feet and made love to her so masterfully, so tenderly.

Verna chuckled, reading her mind.

"Oh yeah, George the cook. Ain't seen him since he left and went looking fer yew. How is the big guy?"

Cat rolled her eyes and laughed. Her laugh sounded strange to her, she hadn't heard it for a long time.

"Oh, he's fine I guess. Not allowed to tell you what he's doing though."

Verna shrugged.

"As long as he's happy. The man deserves some of that, after what he went through in 'Nam."

She grinned, radiating sunshine.

"It's so good t'see yew. What can I getya, honey?"

"Coffee, in a bucket. Ham and eggs."

"Eggs over easy?"

"You remembered. Yes please."

"Gotya."

She barked Cat's order at the serving hatch, out of the corner of her mouth. Cat glanced hopefully in that direction, as though expecting to see that handsome face there, that dashing grin.

The face that appeared was thin and white, with greasy stubble and gaps in its teeth. Cat turned away, shoulders sagging.

"Hey, sweet—!"

Ignoring leery invitations from the truckers and latter-day cowboys, Cat weaved her way amongst the tables, looking for a likely spot.

She saw one, by the window, a table for four occupied only by a stocky, jaded-looking woman with mousy brown hair whose plain-ness and world-weary air had obviously deterred any potential suitors.

"May I join you?"

The plain woman glanced up from the dark depths of her coffee cup which she was stirring slowly and endlessly.

"Sure, why not...?"

Cat judged her to be in her early thirties although she looked older. The woman did a quick double-take, scanning Cat's spectacular attributes. A flicker of envy was swiftly crushed by a great sadness. She sighed, ceased stirring and instead poked at a crumbling slab of cake with her fork, pushing it about on the plate.

Cat felt she had to say something. Forcing a smile, she held out her hand.

"Nice to meet you. I'm Catherine."

The woman hesitated, and then lifted her arm with what seemed an immense effort for a limp handshake. Her hand was damp and cold.

"Fran Whitlock…," her voice was toneless.

For some reason, Cat was compelled to make conversation, although her new companion was clearly unwilling.

"What brings you all the way out here?"

The woman raised her eyes to look at her. Cat saw that they were bloodshot and framed by grey shadows.

"I'm running away," she replied flatly. "From my responsibilities."

Her voice was educated. Cat was intrigued and looked at her, an eyebrow cocked inquiringly.

The woman's shoulders rose and fell in a huge sigh.

"I used to be a Phys. Ed. teacher. At Fairburn Reformatory."

She ran her fingers through a conspicuous grey streak in her brown hair.

"And this is what it did to me!"

Oh Jesus!

The sad woman demolished the slice of cake into a heap of crumbs.

"Now I'm held together by Valium. Whoever my replacement is, I wish her luck. Rather her than me!"

Thanks!

Her companion went back to stirring her cold coffee. When Verna brought the ham and eggs Cat put her head down and ate in silence.

Otis was letting the world know that he "Can't get no satisfaction".

You and me both man….

She agreed with Uncle John, his version was much better than the Stones.

"I can't get no—!"

At 70 mph her left rear tire blew.

OH SHIT!

The tail of the car seemed to go out from under her as the red Olds twisted violently, slewing sideways.

"Fuck…!"

Tires squealing, the car rotated across the highway in a vicious three-sixty. The world became a streaked kaleidoscope of bright sky and sand.

"…aw shit…..!"

Cat's body was jolted forward in her seat. Her forehead impacted on the steering wheel. Everything went black.

"Looks like we got rich pickin's boys!"

Groaning, Cat slumped in her seat, rubbing the back of her neck. A dull pain was throbbing behind her eyes.

"Uuuuhh…hhh…!"

Slowly, her vision swam back into focus. Coated in a film of dust, the 442 had come to rest sideways on the far side of the two-lane blacktop.

"Uuugghh…hhhh…!"

Gingerly, she opened the driver's-side door and heaved herself out. A spasm of dizziness staggered her, her stomach churning. Biting back the impulse to vomit, she shuffled slowly round to the rear of the car.

What the…?

There was a neat hole in the deflated tire. A .44-40 sized hole. Bending stiffly, Cat measured it with a fingertip.

"Now ain't this our lucky day!"

Feet crunched through the gritty crust of the desert.

"A fine bit o' steel and a prime piece of ass to go with it."

Oh shit!

There were four of them. Lean, stringy men in faded overalls, denims and tattered baseball caps, with mean thin faces and a vicious gleam in their eyes. Their leader, taller than the rest, was cradling a long hunting rifle in his arms, fitted with telescopic sights.

As Cat struggled to regain her scrambled senses, one of the men pulled a big pistol and pointed it at her. The leader slung the rifle on his shoulder and reached out behind him. A G.I. surplus walkie-talkie was slapped into his hand.

"Billy Bob, bring the pick-up!"

Cat licked dry lips. Her head was still throbbing. The men fanned out into a line in front of her, staring at her and the car greedily.

"Now ain't yew somethin', sweetcheeks," the leader drawled. "One o' them big city beach bunnies…."

Cat heard an engine gunning. In seconds, it appeared, careening over the top of a ridge, a dusty break-down truck with the crane projecting out the back and the chains and hook dangling.

"Thet fancy wagon o' yours'll fetch enuff t'keep us fer six months 'r more…."

The truck skittered to a halt and the driver got out, a balding fat man in a filthy T-shirt emblazoned with the faded words "White Power". He stopped short and stared open-mouthed at Cat, in the tight jumpsuit with the zipper at half-mast.

"…and yew's jest a right nice bonus…!"

He tossed back the walkie-talkie and stepped forward. His men came with him, forming a half-circle around her as she leant back on the flank of the red 442.

Cat shook her head to try and clear it. A stab of pain speared the back of her neck.

"You bums sure have a strange way of drumming up business."

Her voice sounded far away to her, disconnected. The leader's eyes narrowed into slits with a red spark in them. His arm lashed out and cracked like a whip, the back of his hand slashing across her face.

She saw it coming but her brain sent out the signals sluggishly. She had the metallic taste of blood in her mouth. Someone laughed harshly.

"Strip bitch…!"

He bared his discolored fangs in a lopsided ugly grin.

"Yew can make it hard or yew can make it easy, slut…."

Spittle flecked his thin lips.

"…and I hope yew make it hard, it's much more fun thet way…!"

It was true. She did see a red mist in front of her eyes.

Motherfucker!

Her arm shot out straight with the force of a battering ram. The heel of her hand detonated on the point of his stubbled chin.

"AGH!"

His head jerked back. Something snapped. His eyes rolled like glass balls as his legs crumpled. He descended slowly, going down in stages.

"Yaaaaaahhh…!"

He was rushing at her, arms outstretched, clawing for her. Her brain still struggling, she saw him double, in split focus. She chose one and a spinning side kick sent him cart wheeling away.

Unbalanced, Cat went on spinning. She was rolling in the dirt. As she sat up, legs splayed in front of her, she saw a third man aiming his gun. She was looking straight down the barrel.

"Yew bitch! I'm gonna—!"

Horns played a fanfare, underpinned by the roar of a great beast.

"F — — -!"

It came barnstorming out of nowhere, a big blue and silver Mack truck, with its massively tall cab and long trailer swinging behind. With a swerve of surprising grace, it side swiped the break-down truck and flipped it upside down.

Its wash was a gale that sent the men tumbling. One was scrabbling on his hands and knees in a cloud of yellow dust, reaching for his gun.

Handled by an expert, the big truck came to a precise stop. The high cab door swung open and the driver stepped down, working the slide on a pump action shotgun.

"I wouldn't do that if I was you...."

Oh wow...!

He was built the way Cat liked them, tall with broad shoulders and narrow hips. His skin was the way she liked to take her coffee, dark.

"I suggest you pick up your friend there and start walking."

He gestured with the shotgun. Caked in dust, the men jumped to do as they were told, fear and hate burning in their eyes. He watched them till they melted into the distant heat haze.

"Are you alright?"

Reaching up to lay the shotgun on the elevated driver's seat, he returned and helped her to her feet. She grimaced as small pains jabbed her everywhere, as the dull pain surged behind her eyes.

"I...I think so...."

He let her lean against the red 442 and surveyed the punctured tire.

"I've heard about this racket, first time I've seen it."

Turning back to her, he cupped her face in his hands and looked deep into her eyes.

"A mild concussion, perhaps...."

He was back and forth to the cab of his truck, came back with a canteen and a clean cloth and washed her face gently. She took the canteen from him gratefully and drank deeply.

"Thanks, I owe you one."

He smiled at her. He was standing very close. She liked it.

"You'll be fine in a while," he stated. "You just need some rest."

Without asking, he leant into the red car and took the keys from the ignition. He opened the trunk, hoisted out the spare and the jack and changed the flat tire. He worked quickly and expertly.

She never let anyone touch her car keys. Well, hardly ever. She watched him while he worked.

Hmmm...nice butt....

When he stood up their eyes locked. That significant electricity passed between them.

Yes please!

They made love on the snow-white back seat. She let him make love to her; she put herself in his hands. He did it slowly and skillfully.

In the afterglow she smiled up at him, her long hair like a golden cloud around her face.

"Thanks again."

He sat up, laughing softly.

"This isn't quite what I meant by a rest."

Her eyes were melting, brimming over.

"It was just what the doctor ordered."

She took his calloused hands in hers and looked at them, turning them over. She lifted them and placed them on her cheeks.

"I hate men with smooth hands."

She kissed his hands, her lips brushing the calluses. He laughed again. They made love again, faster this time, with more urgency. He had a schedule to keep and she had places to be.

"Are you sure you'll be okay?"

"I'll be fine."

Alone again, she curled up on the back seat and slept for an hour.

CHAPTER 4

REFORM SCHOOL

A red streak; the snarl of a V-8. A jungle beast. The jungle beat.

The desert blurred by; dotted with small towns—blink and you'd miss them.

The barren expanses between were punctuated by dusty truck stops and diners with faded welcome signs. Highway signs were pitted and sandblasted, pocked with bullet holes, a favorite local past-time.

It was an arid landscape she knew all too well. One that she always seemed to be drawn to, in pursuit of some great evil, man-made or supernatural. Now she was going there to hide from the world.

"A coward," she muttered to herself. "Hiding out in a battlefield."

The dark thoughts and bad memories were like great black bat's wings pursuing her. They blotted out the sun and she shivered in their cold shadow, squirming in the driver's seat.

"Fuck off!"

She twisted a chrome knob, cranking up the Funk. The raw swaggering strut warmed her.

"Oh yeah....!"

She was dressed for the open road again: her powder blue second skin with the ring pull tugged way down. Her white Hi-Tops put the pedal to the metal – the red needle surged across the dial. Her blood was on fire.

"WOOO-OOOO…!!!"

The glowing green characters marched out onto the blank screen:

PERSONNEL FILE
(Classified Level 1)

………..
………..

NOTE ON FILE: Agent currently on the inactive list. Agent on indefinite leave as part of a program of mental and physical rehabilitation following a period of exceptionally arduous duty.

Aiko was curled up in one of the zebra-skin armchairs, her feet drawn up under her. Cat's face smiled up at her from the file cradled on her lap. She sighed.

"I wonder how she's getting on. I really miss her."

Enthroned behind her desk, Selena smiled, her eyes warming.
"We all do. I'm sure she'll be fine."
Aiko sighed again.
"Oh, I hope so. You know Cat, wherever she is, trouble has a way of finding her."
Rocking back in her tall chair, Selena laughed out loud.
"Then Mistah Trouble had better watch out!"

Why not…?

She had time to kill. The sun was banging like a gong and a tall cold one would go down real nice right now.
The turn-off was sign-posted and behind it there was a broad billboard proclaiming: STOP AWHILE IN BARLOW – A REAL FRIENDLY TOWN. A pink-faced jolly bartender beamed at her, his outstretched hand offering a foaming tankard.

You read my mind….

Cat swung the 442 sideways and accelerated smoothly. She could already taste that beer.

A metallic clattering drowned out the jungle symphony, the steady drone of insect life, the shrill piping of exotic birds and the chattering of nimble monkeys.
A column of dust rose high above the densely-packed tree tops, glowing in the harsh sunlight. The whirring clatter of the rotors slowed, their blur thickening.
"Keep the motor running!"
The big American had his combat boots on the ground before the landing skids touched down. He bent his back instinctively, fanned by the idling rotor blades.
"I won't be staying long!"

His wide smile spanned the bar-top.
"An' what kin ah git ya, purty lady…?"
Cat almost burst out laughing.

Hey. It's him!

He was the jolly bartender from the billboard with his round pink face and merry blue eyes. Right down to the snow-white Stetson on his head, his Western string tie and the fancy cowboy shirt.
Cat smiled back at him.
"Oh, the tallest and the coldest beer in the house."
The bartender beamed at her approvingly.

"Yew got it!"

The clearing had been hacked crudely out of the choking jungle, its green fringes frayed and tattered.

Occupying the dusty scar were a cluster of humble wooden shacks. They seemed to shrink away from three long low concrete structures with blacked-out windows and corrugated zinc-iron roofs.

His scalp glowed pinkly through the pale blond crew cut. Scowling, the big American yanked off the mirror-lens Ray-Bans and mopped his face with the tails of the sweat-stained kerchief wrapped around his neck.

Head to toe, he was G.I. olive drab, his big frame clad in mottled combat fatigues. A .45 automatic was holstered at his hip.

Replacing the shades on the bridge of his nose, he stood at the center of the clearing, hands on hips, feet planted wide apart. His thoughts were masked, his face closed, inscrutable.

"Nice place you have here."

The establishment was modeled on the saloons of old, bathed in a mellow glow. A contented clink of cutlery and murmur of conversation emanated from the tables and plush upholstered booths. Tall mirrors were embossed with period advertising slogans; there were reproductions of railroad and Wild West wanted posters.

It was blessed with air conditioning. Cat tilted her head back, letting it flow over her.

"There ya go, purty lady, this'll wash that trail dust away…!"

In the sickly light of yellow bulbs, squat native women sweated in their underwear, with masks over their mouths and noses. Monotonously, robotically, they stood at intervals along a slow conveyor belt, wrapping blocks of a bland white substance in plastic and padding.

At the back, the door of a partitioned office banged open. Two men tried to shove out together, men with lank black hair, in baggy white shirts and pants.

One was tall and thin the other short and fat, their faces shining with perspiration, large dark sweat patches under their arms.

Cursing, they pushed rapidly past the ranks of mechanical dull-eyed women, not even glancing at their semi-nakedness. They burst outside, hands raised to shield their eyes from the sun.

Just what the doctor ordered…!

After the cooling respite of the bar, the glare of the car park was like walking into a wall of white heat.

"Jeez!"

Her shades, with the big round lenses, were hooked into the cleavage of the denim jumpsuit. She grabbed for them and slipped them on.

She'd found a patch of shadow to shelter the red Olds and was striding swiftly towards it.

Must remember to top up the radiator at the next pit stop….

She leant into the snow-white, chrome and walnut cockpit and flicked off the safety switch under the dash.

One day I'm going to forget to do that!

She chuckled. Woe betide any would-be car-jacker who attempted to jump start her ride. The instant he worked the stick shift a tiny needle would prick his palm and knock him out cold.

"Señor ……!"
"We were not expecting you…!"
Their anxious voices trailed away, repulsed by his monolithic blankness. He stood in silence for what seemed an eternity looking down on them. They shuffled their feet and swallowed nervously, their strained faces reflected in the mirror lenses.
"I've come to deliver a message," his voice had an edge of steel.

She heard voices.
"Heeey, man…. C'mon will ya….!"
A shaky and imploring whine. And then a gruff, aggressive retort.
"Don't rush me, bitch! Yo'll git ya stuff…!"

Sounds like trouble….

The men glanced at each other. The fat man took a short step forward.
"Señor …."
"You've failed to meet your quota," the big American stated. "Three months running."

Un-noticed, Cat hunkered down and peered round from behind the tail-lights of the red 442.
"Gotta be sure yo ain't shor'-changed me fust!"
It was a familiar scenario; even in small-town Barlow.
"Awww…man…..!"
Strung out, the mousey girl was painfully thin, her faded hippie regalia hanging off her. Her voice was dry and hoarse and she was sniffing constantly. Her body shivered spasmodically.
"Okay, okay…here 'tis!"
The dealer was a squat man, his bulky frame straining a lime green suit with wide lapels and voluminous flares. A yellow fedora with a snakeskin band was tilted rakishly on his big head and his stack-heeled boots were two-tone

brown and yellow. Several layers of bright gold were draped across his chest, his red silk shirt open to his chunky gold belt buckle.

"T-th-thanks, m-man….!"

Knees quaking, the fat man flapped his hands.

"Señor ….!" He whined gratingly.

The big American's thumb unlatched the flap of his holster. The blue-black .45 was in his hand. He fired twice – bang-bang, one in the heart and one in the head.

Jerkily, the girl turned and stumbled away across the sunbaked car park. She was swallowed up by the deep shadow of a narrow alleyway, a short distance away.

Cat's blood boiled.

Motherfucker…!

She rose from behind the red car.

"Motherfucker!"

Startled, the pusher spun in her direction, his hand darting inside his jacket. A hint of blue steel glinted.

"Wha th' fuck?"

Cat was walking towards him swiftly. The dealer relaxed, letting his hand drop. His wide eyes devoured her.

"Heeey, mama…!"

Her eyes were narrow slits of fire.

"You murdering bastard!"

The dealer frowned.

"Hey now blondie, I don' let no bitch talk t' me that way!"

His hand slid into a side pocket and slipped out a pearl-handled cut-throat razor. The broad blade flashed in the sunlight.

"Yo watch yo lip or else I gonna slice up that cute face o' yores!"

Cat just kept on coming, closing the distance between them. Suddenly, she was as cold as ice, an old familiar feeling that she hadn't felt for some time.

"Give it your best shot, asshole…!"

Hissing viciously, the pusher lunged at her, the wicked razor like a flickering lightning bolt.

"YAAAHH….!!!"

Instinct took over, mind and body, everything in place.

I'm back…!

"HAH!"

Cat feinted and flowed. Swaying sideways, she blocked his arm and then locked it. There was a muffled snapping of bone.

The dealer screamed like a wounded animal. The open razor clattered on the ground. Cat kicked it away.

"Awwww, bitch! Yo broke mah fuckin' arm!"

He staggered backwards, folded over an arm bent the wrong way. Cat stepped in and towered over him. The edge of her hand scythed down on the back of his neck.

"UH!"

It was the last sound he would ever make. He crumpled and lay curled up on his side, his bulging eyes sightless, a thin strand of blood dangling from the corner of his mouth.

"UH!"

The fat man flung his arms out wide; his head rocked back, bursting in a pale pink halo. A stain of dark blood spread on his white shirt front. He fell flat on his back and lay with his arms outspread.

Cat scarcely glanced at the dead man at her feet. He was still twitching as she turned and jogged towards the mouth of the alleyway.

Oh no…!

The girl lay face down, her arms straight by her sides.

"No!"

It had happened quickly. The needle was still in her arm, the short length of thin tubing still wrapped round. She had obviously fallen instantly; her nose was smashed and her face rested in a pool of blood. There was a film of grey foam on her lips.

"Oh no, no, no…!"

Tears scalded Cat's cheeks. She knelt and raised the limp body in her arms, rocking it gently.

The thin man's jaw dropped. His eyes bugged out. He fell on his knees, hands clasped in supplication.

The big American holstered the .45.

"You're in charge," he told the shaking thin man. "We expect an improved performance."

The helicopter was lifting off as his boots left the ground.

"Oh, baby…."

Cat set the girl softly back on the ground. She plucked the empty syringe from the pale stick of her arm and then stood up slowly, wiping away the tears.

She took a deep breath and was ice cold again. Returning to her car, she unclipped the CB handset; it crackled into life.

"Hey, Cat," responded Aiko. "We weren't expecting to hear from you so soon."

She sounded like she was a million miles away. On another planet. Cat sighed, then steeled herself again.

"I'm going to send something to you," she balanced the syringe carefully on her palm, eyeing the traces within it. "I'd like it analyzed. Something bad is going down."

Distance distorted Aiko's chuckle.

"You're meant to be off duty, Cat…."

There was a pause.

"But good to have you back."

Cat switched frequencies and summoned the emergency services. She looked across the sun-drenched car park, glittering with chrome and hot metal, at the dead man in the crumpled green suit and beyond him the dark mouth of the alley.

She didn't give a damn about him; the girl deserved to be found and returned to her people, if only for a decent burial.

Yeah, I'm back…!

She climbed in and drove away.

"Hope you had a good flight, please fly with us again…."

Her bright smile fixed firmly in place, the stewardess recited her parting mantra as the airline passengers disembarked, blinking in the sunlight.

The big American looked every inch the returning tourist as he descended the long flight of steps and strode across the airport tarmac towards the gleaming glass frontage of the Arrivals terminal.

His eyes were masked by the impenetrable shades, his face was tanned. A Pan Am shoulder bag was slung across his broad shoulders, his barrel chest straining the blue and white striped shirt that hung down almost to the knees of his casual beige Chino's. The combat boots had been replaced by suede loafers.

Inside the terminal, no one contested him for space at the luggage carousel. His looming bulk, bull neck and the monolithic blankness of those mirror lenses cleared a space around him. When his heavy suitcases came tumbling out he hoisted them off the turning wheel effortlessly, one in each hand.

The automatic doors swished open and he exited the terminal. The hubbub of comings and goings seemed to part before him as he made for the cab rank and no one protested when he ignored the people waiting and took the first in line.

"The Skyline Motel. And make it snappy…!"

Holy shit…!

The sign said FAIRBURN REFORMATORY in a forbidding typescript. Below it was posted a warning NOTICE TO VISITORS listing banned items and "contraband" and a longer list of RULES AND REGULATIONS.

"Jeez! What a downer!"

Cat thought about her stash, in the secret place below the dashboard.

This is one heavy scene…!

It was a grim parody of a school.

Surrounded by the shimmering heat of the desert, there was nowhere to run to. That is, if you could get past the tall fences topped with razor wire. And the lights mounted on high posts that would turn night into day.

Cat saw the intercom on one of the main gateposts. Vaulting out of the driver's seat, she strode towards it. She pressed a small red button.

A moment's pause; then a distant crackle.

"Yes?"

"Uh …."

"Speak up please!"

The voice had the ring of authority.

Cat leant forward till her lips brushed the small speaker.

"Cat, er, Catherine Warburton. I'm the new Phys. Ed. teacher."

A faint whirring above her head was the glass-eyed close-circuit camera atop a gatepost, swiveling and dipping to examine her. Cat twisted to smile up at it.

"Hold on!"

The tall gates swung open smoothly and silently.

Yet another motel room….

The big American lived a life on the move – motels/hotels; safe houses in the seedy backstreets of some foreign shit hole; the Code Room of a U.S. Embassy in a faraway trouble spot; a tent in the jungle.

He sat sprawled in a deep armchair and took a swig from the quart bottle still in its brown paper wrapping, not really watching the old movie playing on the grainy TV screen in the corner of the bland room.

A blue-black .45 automatic was in easy reach on a small table next to his chair, its checkered grip worn smooth. He was used to waiting; he had the patience of the trained sniper.

The main building was a brutish brick fortress designed not to keep people out but to keep them in. Nearby, concrete barrack blocks, with heavily barred windows that would only open to let in a sliver of air.

"Hey there," said Cat.

That dangerous age, the girls were dressed uniformly, in white T-shirts and pale grey track suit bottoms.

They were both very blonde, with hard bright eyes and hair chopped off severely at the napes of their necks. At twenty-four, Cat suddenly felt very old. She smiled, warming, seeing herself as she was, a very long time ago.

Their sharp eyes devoured her, as she lounged in the driver's seat, in her pale blue brushed denim jumpsuit with the ring pull on the zipper tugged all the way down to her navel.

"Cool threads…." observed the slightly taller one.

"I wish I had a body like that," her companion stated boldly.

Her spectacular cleavage made them gulp, as she swung up lithely out of the driver's seat. Cat grinned at them.

"I'm sure you will have, you still have some growing to do."

They both sulked slightly at that, being reminded that they still had one foot in childhood.

"You're both mighty fine as you are."

They appreciated that, pinking lightly and smiling back at her.

Cat extended her hand.

"Hi, I'm Catherine Warburton, your new Phys. Ed. Teacher."

Cat strode briskly round to the rear of the red Olds and heaved open the trunk. The girls jumped to help her lift out her suitcases. They wouldn't let her carry them.

A broad flight of concrete steps rose up before them. The girls were surging ahead, bumping the heavy cases upwards.

Cat winced inwardly but let them carry on.

"Follow us...."

"We'll take you to Warden Hansen's office."

There was a knock on the door.

The big American knew better than to peer through the peep-hole and invite a bullet in the eye. Scooping up the .45, he propelled himself out of the armchair and was beside the double-lock and chain, his back to the wall.

"Yeah...?"

The knock was repeated, coded this time: twice, three times, then twice again.

"Okay...."

He unsnapped the locks and slid the chain from its slot.

"Come in."

The dark bodyguard came in first, so tall his shaven skull nearly brushed the low ceiling. Dressed in black, his right hand was inside his jacket, ready to draw the gun holstered there. With his left he twitched his shades down the bridge of his nose, his eyes darting around the room.

He scanned the big American from top to toe. The blond man looked right through him.

"Mah man...!"

He filled the doorway and entered with a single giant stride. He lit up the room, his mighty bulk bedecked in a sky-blue suit with leopard skin lapels, gold nuggets flashing on his fingers, ropes of gold draped across his chest.

"Have a seat...."

Mr Big took off his broad-brimmed white fedora and skimmed it onto a sofa. He sat down beside it, his huge hands clasped across the silver skull that topped his ebony cane. The towering bodyguard stationed himself close by.

The blond American drained his quart bottle into two glasses. He handed one to the giant on the sofa and then took the other with him to the armchair. He settled himself and the two big men raised their glasses in a silent toast to each other.

"We're pleased," the big American began.

Mr Big flashed his teeth. A diamond set there twinkled.

"But it could be better."

The wide smile vanished.

"Shee-ut, man, we shiftin' th' stuff as fast as yo cin pro-vide it!"

He frowned darkly.

"Hell, we bin givin' yo muthafuckahs th' best damn org-nizashun on th' fuckin' planet…!"

His eyes flashed thunder and lightning.

"Yo'all needs t'git yo' act t'getha! Goddamn Yo-United States Gov'ment, muthafuckin' C-I-A…!"

The big American tensed, leaning forward out of the armchair. Behind the sofa, the bodyguard's spine stiffened. His hand edged deeper inside his jacket. The blond American impaled him with eyes like chips of blue ice; the hand froze.

"You should watch what you say," the big American said quietly. "We're paying for your discretion as well as your…services."

For the first time in his life, Mr Big felt a tiny worm of fear wriggle deep inside him. It surprised him and it showed in his face, just for a second.

The big American saw it and relaxed. He sat back, satisfied. He shrugged diplomatically.

"Yeah okay," he admitted. "We've had some problems with the supply – it's been dealt with."

Mr Big appreciated the conciliatory gesture. The diamond twinkled in his smile again.

"Yo! Ah 'cin dig it!"

"We need to step up the operation," the blond American continued. "We're perfecting the formula and when we're done we'll want to saturate the campuses and the ghettos with the stuff."

Mr Big fancied himself as a student of history. He saw himself as a leader of men and took his inspiration from the great leaders down the centuries, from Genghis Kahn to Adolf Hitler.

He sat up straight, inflating his broad chest to epic proportions.

"Yo give us th' tools," he declared, paraphrasing Winston Churchill. "An' we'll do th' muthafuckin' job!"

CHAPTER 5

FALSE IDENTITY

The girls led Cat down bleak corridors lit by a cold forbidding light. They advanced before her swiftly and silently as though wanting to get this over with quickly.

Cat saw placards on the wall: NO RUNNING OR TALKING.

"Wow," she commented. "You sure have a lot of rules in this place!"

The girls merely glanced back at her and grimaced. Cat pined for the shining, inviting avenues that led to Selena's door. A door behind which new excitements were always waiting for her. This bland passageway looked a lot less promising.

They turned a corner and then another one and one after that. Past doors that were ironbound, with small hatches and shutters tight shut. Muffled, Cat heard what sounded like sobbing, cracked laughter; and a scream.

They arrived at a cramped antechamber with an old sofa shoved against the wall, the stuffing protruding from a rent in its scuffed leather.

It was occupied by a thin pale girl with stringy hair clad in the regulation white T-shirt and grey track suit bottoms. She sat hunched over staring down at her feet, her fingers twisting nervously in her lap.

Startled, she looked up as they turned the corner.

Cat smiled at her.

"Hey, the Principal's Office, huh? I've been there...."

Tears welled in the girl's eyes and then her head drooped again.

There was an oak slab of a door and a dulled brass plate that said: MARGARET HANSEN – WARDEN. Cat's escort knocked in stereo.

"Come in!"

The girls pushed the door open, spun on their heels and were on their way, rolling their eyes at Cat sympathetically as they brushed past her.

"Ah, Miss Warburton, I'm glad you found us...."

Margaret Hansen was on the wrong side of fifty. Athletic in her prime, she was matronly now, thicker in the waist, heavier on the hips. Her face was plain but there was strength in it, her slate grey eyes penetrating.

Streaked with grey, her dull brown hair was piled high on her head. Her stocky frame was confined by sober brown tweed, a short jacket and tight skirt down to her knees. Her only adornment was a simple strand of pearls.

"I've been waiting for you."

It was more like a bureaucrat's office than an academic's study. The floor was bare unpolished wood with only a faded throw rug tossed down in front of a large grey metal desk. On its scratched surface were three telephones, the microphone for a public-address system, an ugly angle-poise lamp and overflowing "In" and "Out" trays.

On the wall behind the desk was a large and detailed map of the State. There was an architect's plan of the Reformatory and charts and calendars detailing various rosters. The industrial metal framework of tall shelving was full to bursting with box files and stacks of cardboard folders.

Jeez!

Cat's heart sank. It had none of the tingle, the buzz, when she entered Selena's command center with its exciting blend of gleaming high-tech and rare exotica.
"In future, punctuality at all times would be appreciated."
Warden Hansen's smile was a mere formality, her handshake brusque and mechanical.
"Uh…oh…yes, sorry…I was held up on the road…."
Cat sized her new boss up and didn't like what she saw.

A cold fish….

Margaret Hansen looked Cat up and down, taking in every detail. Cat felt like she was being x-rayed.
"I trust, Miss Warburton," the Warden's lips pursed slightly. "That you will find more suitable attire when you take class."

AW SHIT!

Cat gulped and tugged the jump suit's ring pull up towards her chin.
"Uh…yes, of course…er…I just wear this for comfort when I'm driving…."
Warden Hansen moved towards a panoramic window.
"Indeed…?"
Bending slightly, her gaze lasered through the thick glass.
"And I would be grateful if you would move that…."
Her sneer was audible.
"…vehicle…and park it around the back in the spaces provided."
Cat gulped again.
"Uh, yes Ma'am, er, Warden," she responded automatically.
The Warden gave the impression of floating an inch above the floorboards as she returned to her desk. Her blunt finger, with cropped unpainted nail, depressed a small button on the corner of her desk.
A responding crackle came from a small white plastic intercom, tucked behind the telephones.
"Yes, Miss Hansen…?"
"Miss Brewster, Miss Warburton has arrived. Please come and show her to her quarters."
Warden Hansen ushered Cat to the office door.
"When you've unpacked, Miss Warburton, come back and we can discuss your duties."
"Yes…er, Warden…."

"Gentlemen…."

The War Room was a stark iron box with cold steel walls and a low ceiling hung with strips of neon that gave everything an eerie greenish cast. A long metal table shaped like a stretched oval filled the room, ringed by chairs fashioned from steel tubing and padded black leather.

Along the wall, running the full length of the table, there was a map of the World. It hung in semi-darkness, indistinct.

"Gentlemen...."

Miss Brewster was a thin-faced greying spinster in a drab two-piece, peering at the world through steel-framed spectacles with lenses like bottle glass.

"I am Warden Hansen's Administrative Assistant....," she was saying, in a tone that denoted great importance.

She proceeded at a fast pace, clutching a thick wad of cardboard folders to her chest; Cat imagined that she never went anywhere without them.

"If you have any questions or problems please come straight to me...."

Cat adjusted her stride and fell into step with her. Miss Brewster conducted her down a maze of chilly balefully lit corridors.

Occasionally, they encountered the inmates, singly or in pairs, in their T-shirts and track suits, dawdling there. The girls would cease their chatter abruptly, stop and step aside, averting their eyes.

"What are you doing here?" Miss Brewster would snap at them. "I'm sure that you have somewhere to be. Move on!"

"Yes, Miss Brewster!"

They all looked at Cat, up and down, with those young x-ray eyes.

"Yes, Miss Brewster!"

Heads down, they scurried off. Cat heard the words "old witch!" being whispered.

She was led up a narrow back staircase, to a door at the top.

"Here we are!"

The big blond American was the only man standing.

Gone were the crumpled linen suit and the sweat-stained jungle fatigues. He was resplendent in the dress uniform of a Special Forces Colonel, from the rakish slant of the green beret on his head to the mirror polish of his shoes.

His insignia glinted in the half light, reflected as hard dagger points in his eyes. His broad chest was decorated with a rainbow of ribbons.

"If you are ready gentlemen...."

A low masculine murmur faded.

The Colonel stood at the head of the table. Two pale colorless men in identical grey suits sat opposite him. For once, they had removed their impenetrable sunglasses to reveal their all-seeing unblinking eyes.

At intervals around the table, men who sat up straight, the way they'd learned as cadets at West Point and Annapolis. Middle-aged men with hard faces and keen eyes.

An Admiral, with steel grey hair and a hawk-like expression, cleared his throat harshly.

"Yes, we're ready for you Colonel, you may proceed."

Be it ever so humble....

Lit by sloping attic windows, her quarters were basic but adequately furnished and clean. There was a small galley with a cooker and fridge and the bathroom had a shower.

"Thank you," Cat said to Miss Brewster. "This is fine."

"Good," Miss Brewster sniffed thinly and was gone, her parting words left hanging behind her. "Please report again to Warden Hansen when you are ready."

Cat went into the small bedroom. Her cases were on the floor beside the narrow bed. She caught sight of herself in a full-length mirror, in the pale blue denim second skin. Her shoulders rose and fell in a heavy sigh.

"That won't do, babe. Time to be someone else...."

Suddenly, the huge map of the World leapt out of the shadows, as angled floodlights illuminated it. Deep in a vast sparsely populated wilderness at the core of Central America red pin lights were winking.

"The plan, gentlemen, remains essentially the same," the Colonel commenced his briefing. "There are a few modifications which you will find in the supplementary files provided for you. Please take a few minutes to acquaint yourselves with them...."

On the gleaming table top, each man had a grey cardboard folder with his name on it. Quickly, they flicked back the covers and began to read.

The Colonel was quivering with excitement. His eyes were gleaming in the cold light as he looked around the table.

One of the grey-suited men tossed down his folder and jabbed a finger at the map.

"Those lights represent the processing plants where the...product...is refined?"

The Colonel nodded. The dagger on his cap badge flashed.

"That's right, Sir."

The grey man's thin lips pursed doubtfully.

"Can we rely on these people...?"

His twin finished the sentence for him, rattling the pages.

"It says here that they haven't been meeting their quotas."

"That's much better," said Warden Hansen.

Cat looked the part. Her golden mane was under control. Her blouse was a neutral beige and her brown skirt came down to her knees. She wore stockings and sensible shoes.

"Thank you, Warden."

"Please sit down," Warden Hansen indicated a leather-bound armchair.

"Thank you."

The Warden lifted some papers from a box file and shuffled through them. She extracted a document.

"Your C.V. is certainly impressive, Miss Warburton. You come well qualified and thoroughly recommended."

Cat smiled inwardly. Selena had people that could forge any identity and make anything a matter of public record.

"Your references are impeccable."

Warden Hansen replaced the papers and closed the box file, snapping it shut.

"You will begin with Gym class first thing tomorrow morning. You will be taking on our chief trouble makers, our hardcore element."

Jeez!

"In at the deep end," Cat ventured lightly.

"Indeed," the Warden blanked her. "You will find your weekly timetable posted on the board in your rooms. You will be notified of any changes or extra duties."

She fixed Cat with a steely stare.

"I hope you are up to it, Miss Warburton. Your predecessor was something of a disappointment."

Cat remembered the worn out, deflated figure from the diner.

Yeah, I could see the scars!

"Yes, Warden. I'll do my best."

The Warden pursed her lips.

"Then let us hope that it's good enough."

The Colonel squared his wide shoulders.

"They have had difficulties with the local rebels," he admitted. "We're taking measures to give the government the support it needs."

The Admiral closed his file and dropped it on the table top.

"I hope so, Colonel. But you must remind President Romero that the degree of support we give him depends upon his maintaining a good supply of the...."

"Product," a grey man finished for him.

The Warden rose from behind her desk and went over to the window.

"What do you know about this establishment, Miss Warburton?"

Cat found herself sitting at attention.

"Well, I know of course that it has a high reputation...."

"The very highest, Miss Warburton."

"Yes, yes of course...."

Her brain was scrambled.

"Uh...and...er...that it specializes in...in...."

Warden Hansen swiveled, stepped back into the room and loomed over her.

"In difficult girls, Miss Warburton."

"Uh…yes…."

"Difficult girls from the most dysfunctional backgrounds."

She was back behind the desk again but still gave the impression of looking down on Cat from a great height.

"They can be the worst, Miss Warburton, don't you think? The worse the family the more difficult the child?"

Cat swallowed hard.

Yeah and I'm one of them!

"We know how to manage them."

She leaned across the desk, transfixing Cat with a hard stare.

"Do you think you can cope, Miss Warburton?"

Cat swallowed hard.

"I…I think so, Warden Hansen…."

The Warden frowned.

"You'll have to do better than think so, Miss Warburton."

And then she was up and showing Cat out of her office.

"We'll see how you get on when you take your first Gym class tomorrow!"

The door shut behind her like the clap of doom.

The door chimes sounded a disco beat.

"Come in!" said Selena.

Selena's penthouse pad was a funky festival of oriental carpets, rich tapestries and carved tribal masks, its bamboo furniture upholstered in tiger skin prints.

"Hi, Chief!"

Aiko stepped in briskly, sleek and supple in a satin jade one-piece with flaring bell-bottoms. There was a cardboard folder tucked under her arm.

The lava lamps seemed to pulse in time with the smooth Funk oozing from the hi-fi speakers. Selena reduced the volume.

"Sorry to intrude on your down time, Boss, but you said you wanted to see this."

Selena held out a hand with the long glittering fingernails.

"Show me…."

Oh man!

Conformity – it was a word that was absent from Cat's vocabulary.

What a downer!

A total stranger stared back at her sullenly, framed in the full-length mirror.

Who the hell are you…?

This stranger had hair that was combed back severely. She wore an unflattering long-sleeved beige blouse, done up chastely to the top button. Worse still was a navy-blue skirt, down below the knee. And worst of all, flat brown shoes. Sensible shoes; sensible, another word missing from Cat's dictionary.

She pouted and the stranger frowned back at her.

"I hate you!"

"Heey, man, we've been waiting for you…!"

The contrast could not have been starker.

"You got the stuff?"

Long hair, beads and bangles, badges with brash anti-establishment slogans.

"Yes, we have it."

Two well-built pale men in black suits with regulation crew cuts, their eyes masked by impenetrable shades, carrying bulky attaché cases.

They laid the cases on the stained top of a small coffee table. Their customers jostled round eagerly.

"Far out, man!"

"You guys are the squarest but you've always got the best stuff!"

One of the big men smiled thinly.

"That's right. The best stuff."

Selena closed the file.

"So, Cat was right.…"

Aiko took it back from her.

"Seems so," she replied. "There's some bad dope going around."

Ain't this the pits!

She'd seen the dining hall before, in all those old prison movies.

A sea of uniform grey, the inmates sat at long metal-topped tables. The aisles between the tables were patrolled by watchful, grim-faced beefy women in tight blue tunics and long skirts, black stockings and flat shoes.

What am I doing here?

Shoulder to shoulder, the girls ate in silence, heads down, focused on their plates. The only sound was the dull clink of cutlery.

As Cat entered and advanced down a broad center aisle a slow tide of pale upturned faces marked her progress. She tried to smile at the few who dared to make fleeting eye contact. The chunky wardresses glared and they looked down again quickly.

The top table was raised above all the others, overlooking the crowded hall. It was reserved for the senior staff.

At first sight they were bland and indistinguishable, all conforming to the dull dress code of blue and beige and brown.

There was an empty throne at the middle of the top table and as far as possible from it, way down the pecking order, an empty chair.

That'll be for me I guess – the new girl

"You must be our new Phys. Ed. coach…."
"You're just in time…"
"Warden Hansen likes us all to be here before her…."
There were no further introductions. They were all blank, unsmiling. Cat nodded dumbly, one hand fiddling nervously with her constricting top button.
"UP!" one of the patrolling wardresses barked. Cat jumped, gulping.
At the distant end of the dining hall, broad doors seemed to swing open slowly of their own accord. There was a cacophonous scraping of chairs as the girls at the long tables all jumped to their feet.
At the top table, everyone was standing. Caught by surprise, Cat was a split-second behind them. In the aisles, the intimidating women all stood rigid at attention. The girls did their best, arms at their sides, face front.
"ATTEN-HUT!"
Warden Hansen came in like a galleon in full sail, armored in her brown tweeds. No one dared look at her as she strode down the center lane. All remained standing and at attention until she arrived at the top table and was enthroned.
"Be seated!"
The clatter of knives and forks resumed.
The top table had a waitress service provided by some of the more senior girls.
"Thanks."
Cat tried to smile at the girl who filled her plate. The girl looked surprised and then alarmed and turned away quickly.
"Are you settled in, Miss Warburton?"
Warden Hansen noticed her eventually. Cat almost stood up to reply.
"Oh, uh, yes, I have, thank you…."
The Warden's mouth warped in a brief glimmer that passed for a smile.
"Excellent."
A chunky bracelet clanked as she gestured round the top table.
"These are your new colleagues, Miss Warburton…."
She introduced them all by name and function, some academic and some administrative. Their grey faces appraised her coolly. Some nodded, none smiled.
"I recommend an early night, Miss Warburton. First thing in the morning you will be taking a class with some of our more challenging girls…."
Their dull eyes were dissecting her, stripping her to the bone.
"You will be expected to provide a means of diverting their more dubious and destructive energies…."
Cat swallowed hard, nodding dumbly.

Yeah, that's what they tried with me!

The house was rocking. Literally, rocking, shaken on its foundations.
"That's it – I've had enough…!"
The crashing and pounding of a psychedelic lightning storm blasted out of the wide-open windows and reverberated down the polite suburban side streets. It made neighboring walls quiver and glass panes vibrate.
Curtains twitched and were wrenched aside, revealing angry faces.
"I'm calling the Police!"

The two-tone prowler with the gold stars on the doors was there in five minutes. Two big patrolmen parked and climbed out wearily.
It had been a long and arduous Saturday night and neither was in the mood to take the usual shit from some hopped-up radical long-hair.
"Aw fuck, why us…?"
Then finely tuned instincts kicked in. Something was wrong.
"Huh?"
The sonic assault of that damn hippie crap was the usual thing. But something was missing from that wall of sound.
There were no loud voices, no laughter; and no one already there out front to bad mouth them before they even got a foot in the door.
The cop's fingertips tickled the worn grips of his holstered revolver.
And then he saw it.
Wha – !"
A body, spread-eagled on the grass of the front lawn.
"What the f – –?"
He knew death when he saw it. The patrolman drew his pistol.
Two more sat slumped side by side on a porch swing, a young man and woman – at least he thought it was a man and a woman, it was always hard to tell with all that hair.
He stepped over a fourth, as he entered warily through the half open door into a maze of multi-colored rainbows pulsing in time to the throb of the music.
There were bodies in the passageways and on the stairs. The living room was full of bodies, all over the floor and the furniture that had been shoved back to clear space for dancing.
Some were still alive, moaning and vomiting. Others were just standing there, backed up against the wall, staring blankly.
In the middle of the room a girl was kneeling, her hands clamped to her head, wild-eyed, her mouth gaping in a soundless scream.
"Charlie, call for back-up, we gotta situation here!"
Across the street, a darker shadow separated from a pool of shadow and rolled away slowly and quietly. A black car with tinted windows, crewed by pale men in black suits.

When Cat returned to her modest lodgings she was annoyed to see that the board on the wall above her desk had been re-arranged to make space for a weekly timetable headed "MISS WARBURTON – PHYS. ED.".

It meant that they had pass keys and could come and go as they pleased.

Bummer…!

Then she shrugged. Best to toe the line. Her fierce independence would have to be put on hold, she told herself, for as long as she was here.

Her eyes saddened, her shoulders sagged, as she stared back at herself in the bathroom mirror. She finished brushing her teeth and rinsed and spat into the basin. She spat loudly, a comment on her predicament: worn out; hiding out.

"Shit…!"

Normally, she slept naked, this environment called for the baggy blue flannel pajamas, the pants flapping around her ankles as she walked back into the cramped living room.

She studied the timetable; her first Gym class was bright and early in the morning.

The sight of the timetable prompted a twinge of alarm. Maybe they'd searched her bags.

"Uh-oh!"

Her luggage was under the bed. She ignored the small travel case that held her feminine necessaries. And the smaller of two battered suitcases.

The larger suitcase was empty, its contents hanging in the wardrobe.

"Okay…."

The deep case had a false bottom, an optical illusion. Its hidden clips clicked open.

Cat made a swift inventory of its contents: a .380 Colt Commander automatic with a well-worn dulled finish; four spare magazines all loaded and two cartons of cartridges; a mean government-issue M3 fighting knife, its blackened blade sheathed in scuffed leather with military markings; a modest selection of color-coded stun, gas and shrapnel grenades….

It was all there. Cat knelt by the open case, considering it for a long time. Then she sighed again and shut it, shoving it back under the bed.

I guess I won't be needing you for a while….

A grey man rose from his seat; taking his cue, the Colonel sat down. His pale hand twitching the knot of his sober tie, the grey man addressed the meeting in dry and penetrating tones.

"May I remind you all, gentlemen, that we require a constant supply of the product to feed and indeed encourage the need for it in the ghettos and on the campuses…."

All around the table, the military men were nodding.

"…wherever the flames of dissent and sedition burn. There will be no revolution here!"

Cat lay there for a long time staring up into the darkness.

Oh man…!

She thought about her new charges.

Sweet sixteen....

Cat remembered it well, the scrapes and escapades, the routine of expulsions from a succession of exclusive private schools.

She only felt at home in the rough and tumble of the sports field, breezing into college on a sports scholarship where she excelled in track and field, with trophies and medals to prove it.

The only people she could get on with at college were the simple-minded, single-minded jocks. At least they only wanted her for her body and weren't trying to mess with her head like all the freaks and self-proclaimed radicals.

Or complete bull-shitters, like the "turned on" college professors, who pretended to admire her mind but only wanted to fuck her.

So, she played the professors for the grades she needed without having to work for them. And she shared the hippies' dope, not their wide-eyed ideals, just so she could escape her mind and the pain she carried with her of an uncaring home.

She lasted until mid-way through her sophomore year, before bailing out. Her mother was ever the busy socialite, too busy to notice. Her father blew his top because it made him look bad. She just let it all wash over her; and anyway, he soon washed his hands of her and went back to rubbing shoulders with Presidents.

Uncle John congratulated her, and promptly took the lock off her five-million-dollar trust fund. That was just before he did his own disappearing act, without so much as leaving a farewell note on his executive desk, deserting it for the alternative lifestyle of Free Town.

Cat, meanwhile, embarked on a journey of twists and turns, of exploration and self-discovery, which found her working undercover for Selena's crime-busting, super-spying mysterious "Agency".

Right now, however, she seemed to have hit a dead end....

"Very bad dope."
"And it's no accident."
"No, it's been deliberately contaminated."
"And if that report is right..."
"...by some very sophisticated shit...."
"...that should be on the secret list."
Selena span on her heel and was making for the bedroom, tugging at the cord of a burgundy silk dressing gown.
"Okay, let's get back to headquarters. We need to do something about it."
The silk pooled around her bare feet.
"Get the word to Cat. She'll want to know."
Aiko nodded.
"Do I tell her she's re-activated?"

Selena paused and stood there in the doorway to her decadently appointed bed-chamber, spectacularly naked.

Aiko could only stand and stare in frank admiration. Selena shook her head slowly, her regal brow furrowing.

"Dunno...."

And then her eyes flashed decisively.

"No! If Cat is ready then let her find out for herself!"

CHAPTER 6

THE HARD CORPS

The knock on the door jarred with the cool cadences of Cat's Jazz-Funk.

"Er…wha…?"

She was jerked out of her reveries, her morning meditation. Cat couldn't start the day without her music. A portable record deck with its twin hi-fi speakers was one part of her true self that she couldn't do without.

"…come in…."

At night, to soothe herself to sleep, it might be Marvin's healing honey. In the morning, when she needed to stiffen the sinews and summon up the blood, it had to be Miles, her call to battle.

The knocking persisted. Cat sat cross-legged on a small rug face-on to the pulsing speakers. Her closed eyes snapped open. She came upright effortlessly, her long legs unfolding.

"Come in!"

The door to her small apartment creaked open.

"Hey."

A Bad-Ass, a leader – Cat saw that straight away.

Her hair was a jet-black mop ragged at the fringes. It fell across her pale forehead over eyes that burned like dark coals.

There was a street-tough pugnacity in her intriguing prettiness, a challenge in her expression. She had a slim-hipped boyishness in her swagger; a physical presence, and something ambiguous in her potent sexuality.

"I'm Janey."

Her voice had the rough energy of the streets. Cat had rarely been struck so forcefully, so immediately, by the strength of someone's personality.

She looked much wiser than her sixteen years; street-wise. She wore her lightweight gym kit: a short sleeved pale blue cotton T-shirt and deeper blue shorts, with white socks and sneakers.

Cat admired her trim figure. And suddenly felt very old again, at twenty-four.

She extended her hand.

"Pleased to meet you. I'm Catherine. You can call me Cat."

The girl was surprised but clearly appreciated the mature gesture of respect. She took Cat's hand and shook it firmly.

"I think I'd better call you Miss Warburton, at least in public."

They grinned at each other. Janey's eyes rolled all over Cat's magnificent contours, her obvious athleticism emphasized by a blue track suit.

"I thought I'd come and make sure you weren't late for your first class and knew where to go."

Cat laughed. She was pleased and relieved; she already had an ally.

"Thanks! I wouldn't want to get off to a bad start with Miss Hansen!"

Janey shrugged, an amber spark in her eyes.

"Aw, she's no trouble."

She nodded towards the record player.

"But I'd keep that turned down if I was you."

Head tilted slightly, Janey listened, her eyes suddenly intense.

"Cool sounds."

Cat looked hopeful.

"You into Miles?"

"I can dig it...."

The girl's body was moving slightly, in perfect synch with the challenging rhythms, as if identifying with them. Her eyes locked on with their dark fire and sent a shiver of electricity down the length of Cat's body.

"....it's like a jagged edge...."

Cat smiled.

Oh I love that!

The gymnasium tingled with expectant echoes.

"Hey, hey!" Janey sang out. "The gang's all here!"

In their identical gym kit, they stood against the far wall, projecting a pose of cool nonchalance. Janey introduced them one by one.

"Cheryl...."

Beautifully wasted; bewitching; so pale; framed by a bold platinum crop that came down at the back to caress her slim shoulders. Sultry deep blue eyes and pouting lips, the face of an evil angel. Slender, leggy, coltish, her poise provocative; a wanton Wild Child.

"Lina...."

The Bombshell with a very short fuse. A predator with lusting eyes and devouring lips; long satin-blonde hair flowing down to the small of her back. Her strapping body was all curves: top heavy breasts, voluptuous hips and thunder thighs; outrageous at 16. Everything about her screamed **DANGER!**

"Josie...."

The privileged Princess on the road to ruin. A deep intelligent beauty; an elegant brunette, tall and self-possessed with cover model looks and charisma, long legs and a perfect body. An aloof arrogance on the outside, hellfire burning within.

"And last but not least – Sammy...."

An outgoing unabashed Tomboy with strong shoulders and impressive biceps. Not conventionally pretty, an attractive earthiness amplified by her shaggy sandy mane. And something fetching too, she had lovely blue-grey eyes. A sunny brutality; she smiled a lot but something suggested that she could snap your spine in an instant.

They stayed where they were, in a line, leaning on the wall. Appraising Cat clinically, they scanned her up and down. Cat sensed the unspoken challenge thrown out to her; the provocation.

"It's okay, guys," Janey told them. "She's cool."

The blonde hell-kitten's pout curled contemptuously.

"Oh yeah?" Cheryl drawled. "How cool…?"

Coordinated, united by a single thought, they detached themselves from the wall and spread out around Cat, circling her.

They had shark's eyes: cold, blank and unrevealing. Cat shot a glance at Janey. The girl shrugged, her eyes glowing. She stood aside.

"You want respect, you gotta earn it."

Oh I like them!

For a moment, their tough mask slipped and they looked surprised when Cat just stood and smiled at them.

"Okay, ladies, try me!"

They came at her from all sides, all at once.

"HAH…."

"…YAH!"

And all at once they were sat down hard on their backsides.

"Aw…!"

"Owww…!"

"Yow!"

"Fuck!"

Janey laughed out loud.

"Told ya!"

Cheryl got slowly to her feet, rubbing her ass ruefully. Wincing, Josie was reaching down to haul Lina upright. Sammy stayed where she was, sitting on the polished wood floor, grinning broadly.

"Wow!"

The atmosphere was decidedly warmer.

"Happy now?" Cat asked.

They held their hands up in mock surrender.

"Holy shit!" Cheryl exclaimed, rubbing herself again.

I really like them!

Cat offered her hand and Sammy laughed and grabbed it. Cat hoisted her effortlessly to her feet.

"Wow!"

Janey stepped up to Cat's side. Her easy grin beamed recognition and solidarity.

"How did you do that?"

Cat grinned right back at her.

"I can teach you!"

The room was a cold steel box, secret and sealed and deep underground.

"Well, gentlemen," the Colonel declared. "I think we can state with confidence that our distribution system works!"

"Holy shit!" panted Sammy. "That was the best damn Gym class we ever had!"

Rubber mats had been dragged out to the middle of the floor and assembled as a triple-layered padded carpet.

Nimbly hip-thrown, Lina lay splayed out on her back, her chest heaving.

"Yeah…right…!" she gasped.

Smiling triumphantly, Josie stood over her.

"I could do this all day!" she declared.

Lina glared up at her, lurching awkwardly to her feet. Josie's laugh was snapped short as she was flipped up and over, landing with a slap on the rubber mat.

Grinning, Cat clapped her hands.

"There you go! You've got it!"

Exhausted, Janey and Cheryl were leaning on each other, arms draped casually around each other's shoulders. Cat could sense the spark between them, their electricity.

"Jeez!" Janey exhaled. "I need a cigarette!"

Bright lights transformed the thick lenses worn by the scientists into stark blanks. In white lab coats, they sat around the stretched oval of the metal conference table, their clipboards close to hand.

His high domed forehead gleamed as their chief craned forward in his tubular-framed chair, straining to read the small name tag on the Colonel's broad chest, opposite his formidable array of medal ribbons.

"Uh, Colonel…I must say that we are somewhat concerned by the…um… level of fatalities…if the news reports are to be believed…."

Steam fogged the white tiled changing room. Condensation glistened on the walls and made the floor slick.

The facilities were basic and communal. They lathered up together, side by side, standing below the row of chromed shower heads.

They weren't shy in front of her, laughing and enjoying the caresses of the warm water, turning this way and that, posing for her, challenging her.

Cat joined in the laughter.

"You guys are something else!"

She retaliated with a show of her own, soaping herself slowly and generously. Tilting her face up, she put her hands behind her head, undulating, letting the water flow over her, the slick lather cascading down her body.

"Oh man!" Cheryl pouted jealously.

Closing in on Janey, she jerked a thumb at Lina and Josie, showering behind her.

"Some of us have got more than we need," she complained.

"Wow!" Janey exclaimed, staring at Cat. "I wish I had a body like that!"

"Right on!" Sammy chuckled, stepping out of the shower with the water dripping from her muscular frame, reaching for a towel.

Cat laughed again, standing full square to them, hands on hips.

"Ladies," she declared. "What some of you may lack in inches you more than make up for in Attitude!"

The chief scientist's voice trailed away as the Colonel seemed to swell in stature, casting his shadow across the long table.

"What better way, to estimate our progress accurately, Professor?" he demanded, in a tone that brooked no argument.

The scientist slumped back in his chair. The Colonel raked his steely gaze around the table, pausing momentarily at each pale anonymous face.

"You eggheads like your numbers and statistics. What's better than a body count?"

No one dared to challenge him. One by one, their faces dropped, as they fiddled with the pens in their top pockets or ruffled the dog-eared pages on the clipboards.

"Alright then...."

The Colonel turned the pages of a thick document laid out on the table in front of him. Much of it was layered with mathematical symbols. Frowning, he returned to the top page which was in a different color and headed "SUMMARY".

"Now I don't get any of this scientific mumbo-jumbo," he rasped. "But can I take it that the formula is now ready to go into mass production?"

The chief scientist glanced at his colleagues and was rewarded by nodding all around the table. He cleared his throat nervously.

"Uh...ah...yes, Colonel, it is. We have verified the sample and you may go back to your laboratories in...in...."

The Colonel's eyes flashed.

"That's on a need-to-know basis Professor and you don't need to know!"

The chief scientist shrank in his chair.

"Yes...yes, indeed," he gulped. "I'm sure that they will now find the Doctor's formula simple to follow and reproduce...."

The Colonel scowled, his brow like thunder.

"You don't mention that name again," he growled. "You forget all about the Doctor!"

The nights were the worst.

Wake up...!

That's when the bad dreams came.

Wake up, damn you...!

The absurd anxiety dreams. She might be traveling somewhere – she had somewhere to be – and never getting there; the road went on and on and the panic escalated.

Please wake up...!

Or the repetitive nightmares – being chased up a long pitch-black alley by an unseen horror close behind her, a flapping of great wings, the gust of an icy breath on her naked shoulders.

And the faces, pale and ghostly, floating in the darkness, mouths warping as they called out to her, accusing her, the dead faces of those she couldn't save.

PLEASE…!!!

The invisible demon was upon her; she felt the slashing rasp of its talons ripping her flesh.

"AH—!"

Cat's scream choked off as she was jolted awake. She sat bolt upright, the thin blanket slithering off the bed and onto the floor. She had abandoned the unfamiliar nightclothes and was sleeping naked; the sweat was like ice, scalding her skin.

She got her bearings, identified the shadowy shapes of the furniture in her cramped bedroom, and warming relief washed over her.

Reaching out, she took her watch from a small bedside table and checked the luminous dial. It was two a.m. and the muffled glow of the moonlight radiated dimly through her curtains.

"Aw, shit!"

Some sixth sense pricked her. She had learned long ago to trust it; but why here and now?

"Hmph…!"

Cat swung her long bare legs out of bed. Bending, she scooped up the blanket and draped it around her shoulders. Cautious, although she wasn't sure what she had to be cautious about, she made a crack in the curtains and peered out.

At first, she didn't see anything unexpected. Geometric expanses bathed in moonlight, made up of yards and quadrangles, bordered by gates and wire fences. The ordered rows of barracks blocks, with deep pools of shadow trapped between them.

And then she thought she saw something. Quickly, she rubbed the sleep from her eyes. Maybe she'd imagined it.

There it was again. Something – someone – moving. Someone who didn't want to be seen.

"Hey…?"

Cat didn't bother with underwear. She climbed into the denim jumpsuit and was zipped up in an instant. She laced her sneakers onto bare feet.

Let's go!

Although her rooms were on the top floor, there was a convenient drain pipe within easy reach. It was child's play.

On the ground, she moved swiftly, silently, in a crouch, on the balls of her feet. A splash of shadow swallowed her.

Concealed, she hunkered down and waited.

I see you now!

They'd obviously done this before. They knew where the blind spots were, the shadowy angles and corners that the floodlights didn't reach. They flitted from one to the other, tacking their way from the slumbering barracks to the tall wire mesh barrier of the main perimeter fence.

Impressed, Cat mirrored their movements. She waited a few seconds and then followed in their silent footsteps, till she was within fifty feet of the wire, swallowed by a pool of shadow.

Now what are you up to…?

The girls were wearing their street clothes: short leather or denim jackets decorated with studs and patches over cut-off T-shirts and tight faded jeans, their swift feet encased in scuffed Hi-Tops.

Oh that's neat!

There was a square hatchway cut out of the woven wire of the fence. It could be folded out and then back again so it was invisible.

That's so clever!

Janey did the honors, bending back the square cut-out. Cheryl went through first, swift and supple, the others close behind her. Cat smiled as she watched Lina's voluptuousness make heavy weather of it; likewise, Sammy's broad shoulders.

Janey shot a sharp glance back towards the quiet barracks huts and the main school buildings. Her gaze was so penetrating that for a moment Cat thought she had been discovered. And then Janey was gone, closing the secret door carefully behind her.

Cat gave them a few seconds and then exited her hiding place. At the fence, she followed their example. It was a tight squeeze for her athletic frame.

Beyond the fence, the glare of the high floodlights faded until it was sucked up by the surrounding blackness. Cat could make out the dim grey ghost of the desert highway and the girls waiting there.

Ah, I get it.…

She got down flat and crawled as close as she dared, making use of hidden folds in the ground.

"Here goes," she heard Janey say.

Closing the distance, the twin orbs of glowing headlights.

"Okay Jugs, do your stuff!"

In the shadows, Cat was smiling again. Lina clearly had a lot of practice, stepping out onto the blacktop and striking a pose, thumbing the driver down. It was obvious why she was chosen; her bountiful contours could be seen a mile away.

Predictably, the driver couldn't resist. He scraped and slid his dusty pick-up to a halt, flashing a lop-sided grin that lit up the dim interior of the cab.

"Heey, baby…where ya headin'?"

He leaned across and swung the passenger side door open, creaking on rusty hinges. Hip-swaying, Lina swaggered across and undulated in beside him.

"Hey…!"

Before he knew it, Janey and Cheryl had sprung out of the surrounding gloom and were piling into the cab and squeezing in. The pick-up bumped and swayed as Josie and Sammy ran up and vaulted into the back.

"We're going as far as Barlow," Janey commanded.

The driver merely swallowed hard and nodded. The pick-up jerked into forward motion, the gears squealing in protest as he fumbled with them, his eyes attached to Lina's swelling frontage.

"And keep your eyes on the road!"

Cat stood up and walked towards the blurred edge of the highway. Chuckling, she watched the tail-lights diminish to bright pin pricks in the distance.

What are you up to…?

She turned and looked back hopefully into the vast darkness of the desert. She didn't have long to wait before she saw the bright dots of an approaching vehicle.

Cat stepped out and threw the shape that served Lina and countless nubile hitchhikers so well. She tugged the ring pull of the zipper down towards her navel.

"Hi there! Can you take me to Barlow…?"

The air field didn't appear on any maps.

"We're fueled and ready to go, Colonel."

It was a rudimentary affair, befitting its clandestine status, just a single runway that blended into the surrounding desert and a squat control tower similarly camouflaged.

"Then start her up!"

The Colonel was dressed for rough country, in olive drab fatigues and combat boots, a.45 automatic in a webbed holster on his hip. The floppy-brimmed hat on his head was tiger-striped, souvenir of a tour in 'Nam.

He had two pieces of luggage. One was a bulky kit bag covered with faded stencils, slung over his shoulder. The other he hefted in his right hand by its sturdy handle, a strange cube, its slab sides fashioned from dull metal, heavy protection bolted to its corners.

"Yessir!"

The executive jet was a streamlined twin-engine dart. It had no markings and was painted grey designed to make it blend into the sky. The Colonel mounted the short ramp swiftly and vanished inside.

The short stairway retracted behind him. The engines whined.

"Let's go!"

The pusher man snapped his fingers impatiently.

"C'mon man, get wit' it…!"

He was parked within the curtain of shadow that slanted down broadly at the shabby cluttered rear of the "All-Nite Bar and Grill".

A musty light glowed in the dirty windows of the kitchens from which came a muffled clatter of pots and pans and raised voices. Rusting drainpipes gurgled into clogged drains. Tall industrial waste bins overflowed, their lids askew, releasing stale odors.

"C'mon, make wi' th' green!"

He had cause to conceal his gaudy ride. A hulking white Eldorado, pimped up with a ton of extra chrome, it stood out starkly amongst the workaday jeeps and pick-ups, the occasional drab sedan of a transient salesman.

"Now that's what I'm talkin' about…."

His narrow eyes glittered in a face that was lean and mean like a switchblade razor, adorned by a pencil thin moustache and pointed goatee. He wore the uniform, a sharp suit in maroon crushed velvet, a yellow silk shirt and sky-blue tie, his feet sheathed in stack-heeled crocodile.

"Oh yeah….!"

His customers were a matched pair of heavy duty bikers. Leather-clad hunks of solid muscle, their sullen battered faces were masked by blank black shades they wore even at night. They might have been twins except that one sported a steel helmet with the Nazi swastika prominent, the other a scarlet bandanna.

UGH!

Cat wrinkled her nose. She was close enough to catch their body odor, carried on the nervously twitching night breeze. Invisible, she had concealed herself in the pool of shadow beneath a parked pick-up truck.

Her eyebrows rose, surprised, when she saw the size of the rolled wad of banknotes that the helmeted biker handed over. As she watched, the pusher flipped off the rubber bands and counted it quickly.

"It's all there, brother, yew can trust us."

Satisfied, the pusher slipped the brick of cash into a side pocket.

"I ain't yo' brutha and I don' trust nobody!"

The pusher slid his right hand inside his jacket, fingers tickling the pearl handle of his nickel-plated pistol. He kept it there and one eye on the bikers, as he reached round behind him with his free hand through the rolled down window of the white Cadillac.

"Here's yo goods…"

Hey, this is big time!

Cat saw the brass catches glint on the fat attaché case that the pusher hoisted off the pink fake fur upholstery of the passenger seat. He tossed it over and the leather clad hulk with the bandanna caught it in both hands.
"Thanks man!"
The pusher scowled, jabbing at them with his finger.
"Now yo be sure and spread that aroun' in all the right places. Yo's had yo orders!"
Nodding dumbly, the bikers exited backwards, before spinning and sprinting away across the unlit car park. Cat lost sight of them and then heard the distinctive sound of their Harley's igniting and rumbling away into the distance.

Oh yeah, there's some higher power at work here.…

The pusher leant back on the flank of his fancy ride, flipping a long cheroot between his thin lips. Illuminated briefly by the flame of his gold lighter, the hollows of his face made him look almost satanic.
Concealed but also confined by her narrow hiding place, Cat seethed with impotent rage. She wanted to take him down right there and then.

Oh – Mistah Evil!

"Hey Mister…?"
Startled, Cat heard a voice she recognized.
"You looking for a good time?"

Oh boy!

The pusher spun around, his hand sliding inside his jacket again.
"How about it?"
Thumbs hooked in the belt loops of their tight jeans, Lina and Josie were strolling coolly towards him; Josie all long legs and smooth swagger, Lina leading with her spectacular curves.
The pusher's gun hand dropped free and hung limply. His jaw sagged as he stood and stared. The girls advanced till they were almost close enough to touch, in his face, smiling brazenly.
"Well, how about it…?"
Lina shimmied voluptuously; Josie posed with her hip cocked provocatively.
"You want it, we got it!"
In her hiding place, Cat stifled the impulse to laugh out loud. She could sense what was coming.

You guys are good!

The pusher gulped audibly. They could smell the surge of lust radiating from him, sweat overpowering his aftershave.

"If you can afford it!"

Cat could smell it too.

Go on! Go for it motherfucker!

Muttering something obscene under his breath, the pusher ripped the wad of banknotes from his hip pocket.

Yeah, you dig it, creep! Forbidden fruit is always the sweetest….

Dollar bills crackled. Some fluttered from his fingertips and floated to the ground. Josie laughed huskily and made her body sway. Lina hooded her eyes and put her hands up and behind her head, gyrating.

The pusher bent awkwardly and scrabbled to scrape up the banknotes. Lina took a swift step forward and flicked up her foot, catching him square in the face.

"UH!"

He jerked upright, blood dripping from his mashed nostrils, his eyes wide with surprise. Coordinated, Lina stepped aside and Josie took her place. Her fist snaked out and impacted solidly on the pusher's cruel mouth.

"UGH!"

Arms flailing, he stumbled backwards.

"Where ya goin' dickhead?"

The hard voice belonged to Janey, emerging from the shadows behind him. Rubber-legged, the pusher twisted clumsily, fumbling to get at the gun in its shoulder holster.

"Oh no you don't!"

Cheryl was clamped to his side, jerking his arm up behind him painfully. As the pusher yelped and struggled, Janey jumped in and seized his other arm. He twisted and kicked, hissing viciously, the girls hung on, pinning him between them.

"Sammy…!"

Without breaking stride, she marched right up to him and released a perfect uppercut with all her strapping frame behind it, detonating on the pusher's chin.

Ouch!

The pusher's body arched, his head snapping back. For a split second he stayed frozen like that, up on his toes. Then his eyes rolled glassily, his head lolled forward and he shuddered and went limp.

Janey nodded at Cheryl and they let him go and fall heavily on the tarmac. He lay sprawled within the faded gridlines of an empty parking space, the dollar bills spread around him.

Yeah, you guys are really good!

Sammy was blowing on her knuckles. Grinning nastily, Janey slapped her on the shoulder.
"Nice goin' Biceps!"
Sammy grinned back at her. Straddling him, Lina sneered down at their fallen victim.
"Jerk!"
Cheryl scooped up the banknotes and handed them to Josie. Smiling darkly, Josie counted them.
"Well?"
"There has to be a thousand dollars here!"

Whooping and backslapping, the gang was leaving the gloomy car park, heading for the lights of Main Street.

Now what…?

Cat waited, watching their swift silhouettes recede and melt into the street lights. She crawled out from under the parked pick-up and moved swiftly to follow them, with barely a parting glance for the unconscious pusher.

Poor sap! You didn't stand a chance!

Cat maintained a discreet distance, keeping the girls in sight, as they made their way along the darkened store fronts.
The gang stopped suddenly, in front of a squat red brick building that looked like it had once been a store house. A painted sign proclaimed: SAINT JUDE'S HOMELESS SHELTER.

Huh?

As Cat watched, the girls held a brief huddle. Janey was doing all the talking and there was nodding all around.
Josie checked on the thick wad of cash in the breast pocket of her short denim jacket. And then the others stood back and waited as she disappeared inside.

Well, well, well.…

Minutes later, Josie reappeared, all smiles. They clapped their hands; Sammy was laughing, her brawny arm flung around Janey's shoulders.
"Let's go!"
They turned to leave and then stopped in their tracks, surprised.
"Hey there.…"
Cat was standing across the street, grinning at them.

"I like your style!"

Suddenly, they all looked very young and awkward. It made Cat melt inside; she saw her younger self in all of them.

She crossed the street and joined them. They stood there, looking down at their feet, glancing at each other, waiting for someone to say something, like little kids caught with their hands in the cookie jar.

"Um," Janey managed. "How much of it did you see?"

Cat chuckled in a warming way that made them feel much better.

"Oh, I saw it all."

Then she laughed out loud.

"And I dug every minute of it!"

Cat glanced at her watch.

"Don't you think it's time to find a ride back?"

Janey grinned at Lina.

"That's your department, Jugs, you got skills!"

Oh yeah, you all have skills that I can use!

Their laughter floated behind them as they headed out of town, making for the highway.

"Untermenschliche sau!"

Cowering fearfully and babbling entreaties in her native tongue, the old woman backed away through the open doorway, her tattered broom dragging on the floorboards.

"Geh mir aus den augen!"

Scowling, the Doctor bent stiffly and began retrieving the broken pieces of porcelain from the faded rug laid out in front of his desk.

Only the ornate handle and the embossed pewter lid gave clues as to its former identity.

"Scheisse…!"

He took out a large handkerchief from the hip pocket of his crumpled linen jacket, unfurled it and spread it out on the desk top.

"Verdammt!"

Grunting stiffly, he stooped to collect all the pieces from the floor. His back spasmed and he grimaced, cursing and clutching at himself.

A tall shadow fell across the room.

"Had an accident?"

The Colonel's broad silhouette blocked out the bleary wet light that oozed in from the surrounding jungle and the blank skies above.

"Need a hand?"

Shaking his head, the Doctor straightened up gingerly. His rumpled white linen suit hung loosely on his slight, stoop-shouldered frame. His grey hair was thinning on top, the scalp glistening through the sparse scraped back strands.

Cupping the broken shards carefully in both hands, he laid them reverently on the handkerchief and then folded it over, making a neat bundle which he stowed away carefully in a desk drawer.

"Clumsy bitch!" he spoke in thickly accented English. "It was a gift from the Fuhrer himself!"

He gestured towards a tilting picture frame on the wall behind the desk. It displayed a younger and sleeker version of himself, with gleaming black hair and a pencil moustache, shaking the Dictator's hand. Both were smiling for the camera.

The Colonel was impressed; that man had certain qualities that he admired.

"Sorry about that."

Slumping into the chair behind the desk, the Doctor reached for a fat brown bottle and filled a dusty glass which he then drained noisily. He offered the bottle to the Colonel, who shook his head impatiently.

"You've had a chance to review the formula, Doctor. What do you think?"

Pouring himself another, the Doctor shrugged his narrow shoulders.

"Ja, ja, es solte einfach genug sein…"

He tossed back the contents of the glass.

"Yes, yes, it should be simple enough, my people will refine the, the…das produkt…?"

"The product."

"Yes – the product – in the quantities you require…."

The Colonel never smiled. But his eyes warmed slightly.

"It's a pleasure doing business with you, Doctor."

CHAPTER 7

BASIC TRAINING

"So, Miss Warburton, how long have you been with us now?"
Cat sat at attention in the chair placed opposite Warden Hansen's desk.
"Almost three months, Miss Hansen."
In her capacity as Phys. Ed. Instructor, she was permitted to go about in her official blue tracksuit. It was much more her style than the starched blouses, unflattering skirts and clunky shoes prescribed by regulations.
"Uh…yes…three months…."
She still felt uncomfortable in the Warden's presence, like a naughty schoolchild summoned to see the Principal.
Margaret Hansen leant forward, elbows on the desktop, chin resting on her steepled fingertips. Her face was slab-like, expressionless, giving nothing away. Her slate grey eyes were mobile, scanning Cat from top to toe.

Oh my God – she's undressing me with her eyes!

"Well, you certainly appear to be up to the job, Miss Warburton…."
Cat maintained her neutral expression and compliant posture. Inside, a sudden stab of revulsion made her queasy.
It wasn't something she was proud of, she'd always found it hard to connect with anyone that she found physically repellant, male or female, especially when that person was so obviously attempting to connect with her.
"…you've made quite an impression…."

On you, you mean….

Cat's skin crawled, tracking the slow searching progress of the Warden's hungry eyes. Suddenly, she felt naked and exposed.

I'm going to puke!

Everything about Margaret Hansen repulsed her. The thick body encased in unglamorous brown tweed; the way she constrained her hair, piled on top of her head. The permanently unpleasant set of her features; the heavy bags under her eyes and the downward curve of her mouth.
Cat thought about Selena; exotic and magnificent. And Aiko, such fun and so uninhibited.

Oh I miss you!

She wanted to wrench her body up out of her chair and make a run for the door. And then it struck her, like a lightning bolt.

I've got something over you!

Cat looked straight back into the Warden's steely eyes. And smiled.

The Warden blinked. She dropped her hands and sat back stiffly. Swallowing hard, she fiddled nervously with the strand of pearls around her thick neck.

"Er…ah…yes…." She forced out the words. "I have noted that some of our more difficult charges seem to have benefited greatly from your presence."

Cat just sat and smiled right at her. Margaret Hansen was blushing, perhaps for the first time in her life.

"Yes", she gulped. "They've fallen under your spell, one might say…."

Gotya!

"…under your spell…."

Cat was enjoying herself now. She toyed with the brass ring pull of her tracksuit top, easing it down an inch or two.

"Thank you, Miss Hansen, I'm glad you think so."

Another inch, idly, then up, then down again. The Warden's colorless lips parted, her eyes widening.

"And I do have some ideas for an extended program above and beyond what can be achieved in the gymnasium," Cat enthused. "You know, hikes, road runs, that kind of thing."

Margaret Hansen frowned.

"I don't think so, Miss Warburton. We rarely allow the girls to pursue activities outside of the compound."

Cat wanted to laugh out loud.

Oh Warden, if only you knew!

She flipped the ring pull with her finger. Its glitter was reflected in the Warden's devouring eyes. Cat made her body undulate subtly in her chair. Her smile was dazzling.

"Yes, Miss Hansen, but I do hope I'll be able to persuade you…."

"Are you thinking what I'm thinking?"

The crop duster was an historical relic, a faded blue and yellow biplane, held together by string and faith.

"I don't know, Colonel…."

Coughing and spluttering, it trailed a smudge of oily vapors across the bright sky. Executing a laborious turn above an expanse of shimmering gold it was banking to come back round again.

"What are you thinking?"

There was a bulky metal hopper slung beneath the biplane's patched fuselage. A flap fell open and it disgorged its contents. A pale cloud that glowed in the sun. Ejected in a long ribbon it expanded till it spanned a broad section of the crop field below before starting its slow descent all the way down to the ground.

Their anonymous sedan was parked at a discreet distance. The two men stood by the barbed wire fence that enclosed the field, watching the crop duster do its work.

Mopping the back of his bull neck with an olive drab kerchief, the Colonel flashed his teeth at his companion, a faceless man in a rumpled grey suit, its sharp creases erased by the humidity.

"It might just work", he stated. "I think we might revise the Plan."

"Make yourself comfortable, Catherine…."

The décor of the Warden's apartments reflected her austere personality. Drab walls sparsely decorated with old prints of municipal buildings, beige upholstery, bland lighting.

"I may call you Catherine?"

Cat was dressed to seduce in a low-cut paisley mini dress cinched in at the waist by a silver link belt, her calves sheathed in kinky boots.

"Yes, yes, of course, Miss Hansen."

"Call me Margaret, please; we're informal this evening."

Crockery clanked and cutlery rattled as the Warden cleared away clumsily, unable to tear her greedy eyes away from the bounty at her table. A fork fell onto the grey carpet and Cat lunged from her chair.

"Here, let me get that…Margaret…."

As she stooped to retrieve it, she gave Margaret Hansen an eyeful of her plunging cleavage. The Warden stared, magnetized, then reached out and jerked the fork from her grasp.

"I—I'll p-put some music on, shall I?"

Her voice was strained. Cat smiled and nodded.

"Yes, that would be nice."

Cat settled back into an armchair and crossed her legs slowly and extravagantly, flaunting her superb thighs. The Warden gulped, backed up and rebounded off the table, then turned stiffly towards the phonograph perched on a shelf.

The sounds were light classical. Cat hated light classical.

Boring!

"That's lovely," she cooed.

"I'm glad you like it."

The Warden approached Cat's chair with a full wine glass in each hand. She had made the effort to mellow for the occasion. Wearing her hair down in heavy coils, her thick body was draped by a long deep blue cocktail dress, her ankles bulging in high heels.

"Here you are…."

Awkward in such unaccustomed attire, she bent her knees to hand Cat's glass to her. The long dress didn't suit her stocky figure; and trying to wear her hair young only made her look older.

Cat wanted to feel sorry for her but couldn't. She represented everything she hated.

"Thank you."

The wine was cheap and tasted it, Cat made a show of savoring it. She looked up into the Warden's eyes and smiled.

"Lovely."

Margaret Hansen stood rooted over her for what seemed an eternity, gazing back at her fervently, a fever glowing in her eyes.

She took a sloppy gulp of wine, wrenched herself about and marched across the room to a beige leather sofa. She threw herself down, wedged at one end of it.

There was a strained silence. The Warden's eyes jerked back and forth, from the carpet to the spectacular form decorating the armchair. Cat prolonged the agony, playing her like a harp string.

Oh yeah, you're mine!

She took another slow sip of wine and let the tip of her tongue tease her smiling lips.

"Mmmm…yes…lovely…."

Cat rose sinuously up and out of the deep armchair. Smoothing the fine fabric of the mini dress down her flaring hips, she sashayed lithely across the room, chuckling softly, provocatively, deep in her throat.

"Oooh, it's going to my head…."

Cat plopped down at the opposite end of the sofa as the Warden sat wide-eyed and mesmerized. She drained the glass.

"Lovely!" she repeated.

Margaret Hansen gulped audibly.

"You're lovely!" she said hoarsely.

Laughing, Cat slid along the sofa until her thigh and her flank were pressed against the Warden's body. An ample breast brushed against Miss Hansen's upper arm, an excited nipple all too obvious beneath the thin stuff of the skimpy dress.

"Oh God!" Margaret Hansen groaned. "Oh my God!"

"She's a babe…!"

Their faces floated pale and ghostly as the dawn seeped through the wire mesh sealing the windows of the barracks block.

"She's so cool…."

They sat cross-legged in a tight circle at the foot of their steel hard-sprung beds, wrapped in their thin grey blankets.

"Aw, I wish I had a body like that…!"

Ugh…!

Cat grimaced, wrinkling her nose.

Yuk!

Her long legs were tangled in the damp disrupted bed clothes. Twisting her body, she rolled onto her side, turning her back on the large lump in the bed beside her.

The things I do for my country!

The shapeless mass was hogging most of the bed. It stirred and mumbled, its sluggish movements exhaling a gust of stale sweat and body odor that made Cat's stomach churn.

That was disgusting!

It wasn't just the woman's ugliness and fumbling, desperate clumsiness. Or that trying to visualize Selena and Aiko – their beautiful fragrant bodies and skilled hands and inventive tongues – had failed to blot out her grunting like a pig.

No, the worst of it was striving to simulate passion to the tune of those bland light classics. Cat's idea of music to make love by was the inspirational sweet Soul of Otis or Marvin.

A clammy hand squeezed her thigh.

"Good morning," said Warden Hansen.

"'Cat', that really suits her."

"She's a real Cool Cat."

"I think she likes us."

"I think she's got plans for us...."

Pillow talk.

"Oh, don't go...."

Cat sat bolt upright in bed and swung her legs over the side.

"...we have lots of time."

The damp hand was caressing her naked hip.

Oh God...!

"I'm sorry," she said through a forced smile. "I have a class first thing."

Cruelly, Cat arched her back, raised her arms and stretched, yawning. Then she looked straight at the Warden and laughed, with a low throaty chuckle that made little plays down the length of her splendid body.

The Warden's jaw dropped; her eyes looked like they were going to fall out of her head. Her cheeks glowed hotly.

"Don't worry," Cat said huskily, hip-swaying towards the armchair where she'd piled her discarded clothes. "There will be another time."

The Warden gulped, nodding dumbly. Transfixed, she watched as Cat shimmied lithely into the silk mini-dress.

"Oh yes," Cat said, cinching up the chain-link belt. "Now about taking the girls out for that road run…?"

"Don't go walking alone on the beach at night…!"
The guide book made it perfectly clear – the bars along the beach front were safe enough as long as you went as a group – "But don't go walking alone on the beach at night!"
She was young and she was drunk. She'd had a row with her boyfriend and he was drunk and angry and let her storm off into the night.
And now she was lost, feeling the chill, stumbling through the gloom as her sandals sank into the pale sand. She saw only the dim glimmer of the surf on one side and the occasional winking light through the black canopy of trees on the other.
"Oooohhh….!"
She felt sick; her belly churned and she stopped and bent over abruptly, the fringe of her short blonde bob falling over her eyes, wanting to vomit.
"Uuuugghh…!"
She gagged but nothing came. And when she straightened up there were dark shapes around her.
"AH!"
Her arms were seized and twisted up painfully behind her. A calloused hand was clamped over her mouth.

"C'mon, ladies, pick up the pace…!"
Sweat glued the white T-shirts to their bodies. In blue running shorts their bare legs gleamed.
The sun beat down on their shoulders. All had canvas haversacks strapped to their backs.
"Awww….heck….!"
Lina simply wasn't built for jogging.
"If I go any faster I'll give myself two black eyes!"
Grinning, Sammy surged muscularly past her.
"Told ya to wear a bra…."
Their footfalls crunched into the gritty surface of the desert, on its blurred and dusty border with the two-lane blacktop.
Loping with a long-legged elegance, making light of her bulky backpack, Cat was way out front, in a sleeveless singlet made of a silvery synthetic mesh and shiny blue micro-shorts with a white go-faster stripe.
"Jeez!" Josie panted. "I bet her sweat smells like roses!"
"Yeah!" Janey was gasping, her legs turning to rubber. "I bet she pisses perfume and shits marble too!"
Still grinning, Sammy drew up to Cat's shoulder and tried to match her stride for stride.
"Aw, no way!" she laughed. "Your legs are twice as long as mine!"
Cat flashed her a sideways smile.
"You're doing great."

Fluidly, Cat turned and was jogging backwards, looking back at her charges, strung out behind her.

"C'mon, you can do it, close up there!"

Bringing up the rear, Cheryl bent over with her hands on her knees, her shoulders heaving. With a loud groan, she let her coltish legs fold under her, sitting down on the hard ground.

"Oh fuck! I need a cigarette!"

The Doctor shrugged wearily.

"Nein, herr Oberst," he sighed. "We cannot adopt the formula to target homosexuals...."

He drifted far away, his eyes misted by nostalgia.

"Ach, but we knew how to deal with those degenerates in the old days!"

The Doctor tugged off wire-rimmed spectacles and scrubbed them with a dingy handkerchief. When he replaced them on the thin bridge of his nose the thick lenses magnified his pale eyes and the fanaticism in them.

"Perhaps a practical demonstration will make it clearer for you, herr Oberst...."

Sweating in his drab fatigues, the big Colonel scowled. He saw himself as a simple soldier and disliked being blinded by science.

"If you please...."

Eagerly, the Doctor ushered the giant American towards a far corner of his cluttered laboratory. It was dominated by a hexagonal structure of dull riveted iron with thick plate glass windows framed by rubber seals.

"As you can see, the design is not unlike the execution chamber in your American prisons."

Through the thick glass, the Colonel could see a tall chair, a construction of steel and leather strapping.

"Jesus!"

The chair was occupied, by a girl with short blonde hair.

"Hell, Doc!" the Colonel barked. "She's a white woman!"

The Doctor smiled.

"That is necessary for the purposes of the experiment."

The girl's sturdy body was squirming in the chair, straining against the straps. Her mouth gaped, her screams were muffled by the sealed glass.

"Don't worry, herr Oberst, she is not one of your fellow citizens, a native of Sweden or so I believe...."

The Doctor was stooped over a sloping panel of knobs paired with glinting dials.

"And now, if you will observe...."

His hands fluttered over the panel. Inside the iron chamber, a glistening mist was descending. The girl's writhing became frantic, her face contorted with terror.

"Jesus...!"

The mist came down and enveloped her, thickening until it obscured her completely.

"Ach so....!"

"So," Cat chuckled. "Do you all hate me now?"

They were slumped in a semi-circle, their backpacks tossed down in front of them, ripping at the straps and tugging out plastic water bottles. For a full minute there was nothing but the sound of liquid gulping and long sighs of relief.

"You didn't tell us," Janey growled. "That you're a fucking sadist!"

Cat stood smiling down at them. The perspiration shining on her bare arms and legs made her golden, radiant, the bright blue sky singing above her. In her shadow, they all felt inferior.

"Awww…shit…..!"

Lina stretched out on her back, her chest rising and falling. Groaning, Cheryl collapsed beside her.

"We're from L.A. for Chrissakes!" she moaned.

"Nobody walks in L.A.," Josie finished for her. "And you've got us running!"

Cat flicked back her long blonde hair, laughing.

"You'll amaze yourselves, ladies, you have great potential."

Raising her arms, Cat arched her body, stretching. For an instant, they all stopped breathing, awestruck by her spectacular beauty.

"Uh…."

"Er…..?"

"Potential…?"

"That's right," Cat stated. "I've seen you in action; you have the makings of a truly badass commando squad!"

The Doctor flicked a switch. Fans whirred within vents that opened in the roof of the iron chamber.

"Ach!" the Doctor exclaimed. "Do you see, mein freund?"

The blonde girl was still squirming in the chair, her eyes wide and mouth gaping.

Frowning, the Colonel shrugged.

"Yeah? So what? She's still alive!"

His eyes manic behind the thick coke-bottle lenses, the Doctor was rubbing his hands with glee.

"Precisely, herr Oberst! Precisely…!"

"You gotta be kidding!"

Carpeted treacherously by grit and small stones, the towering slope loomed at a perilous angle, its summit blurred by the glare of the sky.

"No way…!"

A man-made aberration in the flat desert landscape, a giant slag pile left over from a major pipe-laying project, parallel to the dusty highway.

"No fucking way!"

Squinting and shading their eyes against the battering sun, they stood at the foot of the artificial mountain, jaws dropping in disbelief.

"Aw, Jeez…!"

Ignoring the chorus of protest, Cat was already halfway there, her long legs moving with a strong determined rhythm, devouring the distance with intimidating ease. A small avalanche cascaded behind her in sandy streams and plumes of pale dust that glowed in the sunlight, pooling at their feet as they looked on dismayed.

"Okay, your turn!"

She looked very small and very far away, silhouetted against the blinding sky.

Lina puffed out her cheeks, shaking her head; Josie took a step backwards. Leaning on each other, Janey and Cheryl exchanged nervous glances; Janey dipped her head to rest on Cheryl's shoulder.

You're on!"

Sammy squared her strong shoulders, coiled her body like a sprinter in the blocks and was surging upwards. She took the teetering slope in one concerted effort, legs pumping, grunting, putting her hands down and scrabbling on all fours.

Down below, Janey glowered, Cheryl pouted. Lina threw her hands up in exasperation. It was Josie who surprised them by laughing out loud as she stepped forward.

"Go Sammy…!" she yelled.

Sammy scrambled up and fell at Cat's feet, a mantle of fine dust draped around her.

"Holy shit—!"

She was laughing, panting and laughing, sweat dripping from her face. Cat reached down and hauled her to her feet.

"Wooo…!"

Sammy swayed; and Josie was right behind her, tall and upright, her eyes blazing, possessed.

"Wow!"

As Cat strode forward to greet her, the light flickered in Josie's eyes. She staggered and looked around her in confusion.

"Wha…what d-did I just do…?"

Way down below, Janey's frown was volcanic.

"Aw shit, if Her Majesty can do it then we got to!"

"Fuck yeah!"

It looked like a sheer cliff face to them. Taking a deep breath, Janey and Cheryl linked arms and began to plod up the steep slope.

"C'mon…!"

Halfway there, they had to pause for breath, bent over double and sucking in great rasping lungsful of air.

"You can do it!"

Cat was clapping her hands, urging them on. She flung out her arms to embrace them as they lurched to the top and crashed into her.

"Awwww……!"

"…..Jeeeezzz….!"

They reeled, gasping, glaring at Cat accusingly.

"Alright!" Cat declared. "Badass!"

They turned and looked all the way down, at Lina, still standing there, still shaking her head.

"Let's go, Jugs!" Sammy shouted. "Haul those melons up here!"

"I still don't get it."
The body strapped into the steel chair was dark and wiry. Tossing her mane of black curls, she jerked violently against the straps, grinding her teeth, terror glaring from her eyes.
"She is not an American negerin", the Doctor stated. "However, der prinzip – the principle – is the same."
Once again, his thin and bloodless hands played over the control panel with the dexterity of a true maestro at the keyboard.
The lithe brown body arched against the straps as the silver cloud descended.

"Yay!"
"Wooo…Lina…!"
Lina made the climb almost entirely on her hands and knees, cursing and complaining all the way.
"Oh fuck oh fuck oh fuck oh fuck….!" She was chanting as she collapsed and rolled over at the top.
"No fair!" she blared. "I've got all this extra weight to carry!"
The summit of the artificial hill was squared off as a flat plateau shimmering in the noonday sun. Cat was strolling across it; she slipped the long backpack off her shoulders and dropped it at her feet.
She glanced back at them as though expecting them to follow. The girls stayed where they were, sitting in the dust with weary legs splayed out, their frowning faces signifying collective discontent.

That's it; I need you to hate me a little….

Cat's smile radiated across the flat plain and rubbed salt into their wounds. With the rubber soles of her running shoes she was testing the composition of the dirt surface, satisfying herself that it was solid.
Groaning, Janey heaved herself onto her feet.
"What the hell is she doing?"
"Fuck knows."
"Thinking up some new torture for us."
Still smiling, Cat bent and was delving into the side pockets of her backpack. She came up with a heavy hunting knife. Sliding it out of its sheath, she moved her hand, making the broad blade flash in the sunlight.
"Jeez!"
"You ain't joking!"
Cat flowed into fluid motion, a deadly ballet, making flourishing passes with the knife, making it jump from hand to hand, the bright blade a streak of light.
Oh…!"
Now they were all standing and watching, open-mouthed.

"…wow…!

Almost without realizing it, they were walking towards her, as though she was some irresistible magnetic force, drawing them to her.

Cat stopped and swiveled to face them, her face an inscrutable mask, her breasts rising and falling in a controlled rhythm beneath the thin mesh of the singlet.

There was something in her expression that they hadn't seen before. There was nothing in her eyes; the hard blankness of a shark's eyes, the eyes of a killer. It stopped them in their tracks and they just stood there, chilled in the blaze of noon.

With a flick of the wrist, Cat released the dagger. Flashing, it rotated in the air in a downward spiral before impaling the dirt between Janey's feet, making her jump backwards. It stuck there quivering.

Always start with the leader….

"Pick it up…."

The voice that came from the cold mask froze her bones. She couldn't move.

"Pick it up!"

Hypnotized, Janey bent and plucked the blade from the earth. As she straightened slowly the others fanned out away from her.

"Come on then…."

Dull-eyed, Janey was looking at the knife in her hand. The sweat that glued the T-shirt to her body was suddenly cold and clammy.

"You know you want to…after what I've just put you through…."

The steely voice was low and insidious, getting under her skin.

"I betya carried a switchblade all the time…."

And now the sweat on Janey's skin was getting hot, starting to steam.

"C'mon, tough girl, show me whatya got!"

Here it comes!

"F-F-FUCK YOOOOOOO…!"

Her face contorted and ugly, Janey was propelled by pent-up teenage resentment, a rage at all the world. She was an unguided missile, a shot fired from a loose cannon.

"FUCK YOU! FUCK YOU! FUCK…!"

Frenzied, she slashed and stabbed. Yelling, the others scattered, throwing up their arms to ward off the expected chunks of flesh and fountains of blood.

"HAH…!"

There was no flesh. There was no blood. Cat, with a subtle shimmy, seemed to melt and become air. She was there but not there, as the blade passed right through the insubstantial supernatural ghost of her.

"YAH!"

The knife, jarred loose from Janey's numbed fingers, was looping up into the bright sky.

"AAAAAAHH…!"

The earth was where the sky should be and the sky was below her as Janey somersaulted, limbs flailing.

"….GGGHH!"

And then the ground fell on top of her with a crash that jolted the breath from her body. Her insides churned, earth and sky rolled over and over.

"Uuuuuhhh….!"

Fluttering like a silver leaf, the knife dropped out of the sky and Cat caught it deftly. Straddling Janey with her thighs astride, she flipped it from hand to hand, left-right, left-right.

"….oooowww…!"

Janey sat up gingerly, rubbing her head.

"J-Jeez-us!"

Cat was all golden warmth and smiles, as she knelt and put an arm around Janey's hunched shoulders.

"You okay?"

Janey grimaced, wincing.

"I'll live. What the hell did you do to me?"

Laughing, the others clustered round. Grinning broadly, Sammy heaved Janey to her feet.

"You gotta show us how to do that!"

The fans did their work, sucking up the sinister vapor.

"Goddamn!"

The Doctor was beaming. He took off his glasses again and polished them vigorously.

"You see, herr Oberst…?"

The body slumped in the chair stared with eyes bulging and sightless.

"….do you see?"

Her wrists tied behind her back, ankles lashed together, the blonde girl writhed on the floorboards as the Doctor bent over her, a dirty gag reducing her screams to muffled squeals.

"Ah, meine leibe, still so full of life…."

The Colonel stood looking back and forth from the dead dark body to the live pale one.

"Goddamn!"

The Doctor was stroking the blonde head, savoring all the palpitations of her flesh as she lay there trembling.

So, herr Oberst, I believe that I have found the solution to your problem…."

CHAPTER 8

HIT SQUAD

Their exertions left them with a healthy glow, shining on their faces.
"Who are you?"
Josie was helping Cat manhandle the wooden vaulting horse into a corner.
"Who are you really?"
The others gathered around in a tight semi-circle.

I knew you were too clever!

"What do you mean?"
The tall teenager's eyes were intense and penetrating.
"You're a great teacher," Josie said. "But that's not who you are."
The boldness of youth; it pinned Cat to the wall.
"What are you?"

Okay, I think you're ready for it....

"I'm no cop, if that's what you mean," she replied. "I'm not spying on you."
Josie nodded.
"Cop no. Spy. Yes, that's what you are."
Cat shrugged and flashed a grin, trying to make light of it.
"I prefer secret agent."
Those beautiful deep eyes were smoldering. The others were watching closely.
"Have you ever killed anyone?" Josie asked.
Cat's eyebrows arched in surprise.
"I have," Josie stated calmly.
Cat took a sharp step backwards, bumping up against the wall bars.

What!

Alarmed, all eyes jerked in Josie's direction. Janey grabbed her arm.
"Hey...!"
Josie shrugged her off. Their eyes met. Janey nodded.
"Okay, go on, tell her."
Josie dipped her head, her long brown hair falling across her face. Cat moved closer to her.
"Tell me what?" she asked softly.
When Josie looked up her eyes were glowing intensely.
"My folks were rich...."

Poor little rich girl – just like me!

Josie sucked in a huge sigh and then heaved it out.
"It was all about them, they didn't care about me...."

Welcome to my life!

"My Uncle did. He cared about me a lot!"
It came out in a rush, without a pause for breath.
"They'd send me to stay with him when they wanted me out of the way. Which was nearly all the time. And he'd come and visit me, in my bedroom...."

Oh God...!

"It started when I was ten. He made me do...."
Cat reached out and touched her shoulder tenderly.
"I get the picture."
Josie didn't shrug her off and Cat left her hand there, looking deep into those dark wells of pain.
"One night, when he came to the top of the stairs...."
Her lovely mouth was twisted, ugly now.
"I was waiting for him. I pushed him and he rolled all the way down. He was still moving when he reached the bottom. I grabbed a kind of heavy statue thing and hit him."
She spoke in a hollow monotone.
"I went on and on hitting him till he stopped moaning. I could see his brains on the carpet."
Janey's breath hissed out through clenched teeth. Sammy muttered something vicious. Lina reached out and then let her arm fall. Cheryl's eyes were wide and agonized.
"I didn't feel a thing."
Josie was searching Cat's eyes, demanding a reaction.
"The cops believed me when I cried a lot and told them it was burglars," she sneered scornfully. "And my parents didn't want any scandal!"
Her dark eyes gleamed maliciously.
"I gave them scandal alright!" she declared. "I went B-A-D!"

Yes, I know – me too – just to spite them!

"They tell people I'm at school in Switzerland!"
Cat tilted her head, gazing back at her benignly.
"Good," she stated. "Well done."
"Yeah?" Janey blurted.
The others looked at each other and released their trapped breath in a concerted gust of relief.
"Absolutely. If you ask me, you made it too easy for the bastard!"

The fire in Josie's eyes began to mellow as everyone relaxed. And now Cat could see it in their faces. They all had stories to tell.

"Okay, come on, spill!"

Flash-back....

Cat loved the smell of gun oil in the morning.

"Hello, baby...."

In its narrow case made of high-impact composite, it slotted neatly into the false bottom of her battered suitcase. The latches opened with a crisp snap that excited her.

You beauty...!

Smiling, she extracted the familiar components from the customized recesses cut into the foam lining.

Deftly, she assembled it: the sculpted black plastic butt stock, the machined lightweight blow-back semi-automatic action, the screw-in aluminum barrel with its rifled steel liner.

She slapped in the magazine.

Cool!

Sammy went first. She told it straight out, like it was no big deal.

"I went to a really rough school...."

She laughed.

"When I bothered to show!"

Her tomboyish grin was indefatigable.

"I was the ugly duckling. There was a gang of foxy girls that were really brutal to me."

She was relishing the memory.

"I snapped and slapped the leader. I made her bleed."

Savoring the image.

"So, one time, when I was playing hooky as usual, she got some of the older boys that hung around her all the time to drag me onto some waste ground. She told them to tear my clothes off and rape me. She wanted to watch."

The grin evaporated. Sammy's face turned to stone.

"When they said I was too ugly she said put a paper bag over my head."

The girls were growling deep in their chests. Sammy laughed; a harsh bark that echoed off the walls of the gymnasium.

"I fought them off. Beat the crap out of them, all five of them! That's when I found out how strong I was."

"And the bitch?" Cat enquired, although she knew what was coming.

Sammy tossed her shaggy mane and laughed again.

"Aw, she was shitting in her pants. She ran for it. I found her later. I just put my hands around her skinny neck and squeezed and squeezed....!"

She was looking at her hands, which were demonstrating how she did it.

"No one believed that a girl could snap anyone's spine like that!"

Weighing in at a mere 2.5 pounds, the .22 caliber ArmaLite AR-7 had been developed from a U.S. Air Force aircrew survival weapon.

Okay, let's see if I've lost my touch….

The top of the frame was grooved to take a telescopic sight. She slid it on and tightened the small screws.

"Next…."

The tapered muzzle of the dark blue barrel had been modified for the smooth cylinder of a silencer; she fixed it there with a swift twist.

"Okay…."

Laying the short rifle on the bed, Cat crossed to the window and heaved it wide open. Retrieving the weapon, she stayed well back in the room. She hooked back the bolt and raised the gun to her shoulder.

Perched on a sagging telephone wire, a small bird was greeting the dawn with its shrill song. Cat smiled.

"Don't worry, honey, you're safe from me."

Beyond the yards, and then beyond the still sleeping barrack blocks and the high wire perimeter fence, there was a green metal signpost on the highway, pointing the way to "BARLOW".

You'll do….

Cat peered through the sight, focused on the etched cross-hairs. Exhaling slowly, she held her breath and squeezed the trigger lightly. The silencer reduced the report to a faint cough; the recoil was the merest vibration.

"Hmm!"

Magnified, she saw a black dot appear on the fringe of the "O" in "BARLOW". Frowning, she made minute adjustments, twiddling calibrated screw heads.

She caressed the trigger again. This time the black spot was dead center within the frame of the "O".

Yep, I've still got it!

Lina smirked sourly.

"I've had these goddamn basketballs on my chest since I was twelve…."

Yeah, I grew up fast too – a blessing and a curse!

"My folks couldn't afford to give me an allowance so I'd make the local boys pay to look at them."

Janey shook her head, rolling her eyes. Lina chuckled, made her jutting frontage shimmy. Janey glared at her.

"It was always you-can-look-but-don't-touch, I made that clear!"

Lina sobered, frowning.

"There was an older guy, a local gang-banger, a real low-life. I shouldn't have done it but he could pay more."

Unconsciously, she put her hands on her breasts. Cat saw a flame ignite in Janey's eyes and Cheryl pout enviously.

"Anyhow, he'd touch alright. Sometimes, he'd hang on and wouldn't let go. He wanted to touch them with his mouth and his breath stank and his teeth were yellow!"

She paused, pursing her lips.

"I did warn him...."

Silly girl....

"So next time I brought a big kitchen knife with me from home. When he did it again I showed it to him. He just laughed at me and crushed me. He hurt me bad."

Oh boy...!

"Next thing I knew, the knife was sticking in his gut. He looked so surprised...."

She grinned nastily.

"Everyone said he must have done one bad dope deal too many, the cops didn't ask any questions."

Population sixty-seven, the village was barely that. Its crude shacks were crammed this way and that into a rough clearing hacked out of the steaming jungle.

Barefoot and threadbare, its inhabitants scratched and scraped for a meagre survival while they waited for their inevitable displacement by the ruthless advance of the corrupt logging companies. They were dispensable.

"Move in...!"

These soldiers were a new phenomenon. The olive drab was all-too familiar; and the guns and the grim pitiless expressions. The white faces were not, the foreign twang in their voices and the strange language.

"Okay, round 'em up!"

Janey opened her mouth but Cheryl stepped in front of her.

"My turn."

This ought to be good!

"My mom was a junkie and a whore," she declared defiantly. "I never knew my dad, he could have been anybody."

She stared hard at Cat, challenging her, ready to repel any hint of disapproval.

"Go on...."

Cheryl's pale brow furrowed, unused to such calm acceptance.

"Mom was desperate. She needed her stuff."

Oh, the old story!

"Her pimp was also her supplier. But he was holding out because she was in bad shape and wasn't bringing in the green like she used to."

It wasn't pain that inflamed her eyes, it was hate.

"So she got the idea of giving me to him. I was thirteen. He told me I was a piece of prime merchandise."

A cold shiver shuddered through her slim frame. It was infectious, they all felt it.

"My mom told me to make her proud!"

Tears pricked Cat's eyes and she blinked them away. This girl wasn't looking for pity.

"The first time, he doped me up till I hardly knew what was happening...."

Her pale face contorted. The others were looking down at the ground.

"I did the next time alright and the time after that... I didn't know anything could hurt that much...!"

Janey swore viciously and wrapped her arms around the slender blonde who, for a moment, looked like she might break in half. Infused with strength, Cheryl swallowed hard and carried on.

"He had me too, whenever he wanted. When he was sleeping, I snuck his piece from his coat pocket and blew his head all over the pillow. I kept firing till the gun was empty."

She patted Janey's arm and her friend released her.

"The Fuzz had Mom in the frame for it. She overdosed three weeks later."

Used to being pushed around by men in uniform, the villagers congregated docilely in an irregular patch of dirt that passed for the town square.

"Okay, stay there!"

They were ringed by the strangely tall and pale foreigners, under the muzzles of their guns. The dark-skinned men, women and their naked children clustered and stared at each other dumbly, puzzled and apprehensive.

"Here it comes!"

A growing whine and whirring clatter, approaching rapidly, down low, skimming the tree tops. The villagers were cowering, clutching their frightened children to them. The tall men ducked instinctively, hanging onto their shapeless forage caps.

Mottled drab, the insect-like chopper hovered close above them, stirring columns of yellow dust and making the surrounding green canopy sway and swish vigorously.

The noise was deafening. And penetrating it, a thinner sound slicing through the roar of the rotors. A seething hiss, jetting from two long grey cylinders mounted on the chopper's long landing skids.

"Steady men!"

The gas was invisible, evidenced only by a slight distortion of the air around the nozzles.

"Hey, Sarge, it's workin'!"

Janey shrugged.
"No big deal...."

I'll bet!

"Mom worked as a waitress, when she wasn't drunk. Dad didn't have a steady job, did things he didn't want to talk about."
She seemed almost nostalgic.
"They were always fighting; my dad hit her a lot, when he was around. They wished I didn't exist, which was fine by me."

Oh yes, you all grew up too fast!

"I lived in the streets," she was proud of it. "I hustled, ducking and diving...."

Surviving, hardly what you'd call living....

"Some fat cop tried to put the arm on me. Caught me peddling weed. He shoved me into his prowler, drove me to an empty lot and told me that if I went down on him in the back seat he wouldn't run me in."
She shook her unruly black crop and laughed coarsely.
"I twisted his balls till he squealed like a little girl and said that I'd rat on him for having sex with a minor."
That got a chorus of laughter.
"The motherfucker had connections," Grinning, Janey milked her applause. "He hired a pair of bad asses to waste me and dump me somewhere and make it look like just another street killing."
"And they lived to regret it?" Cat was impressed.
"No they didn't," Janey's grin was pure evil. "I was packing heat, a Saturday Night Special I stole from my dad. I let them take me to the alley and then got the drop on them."
"Neat!" exclaimed Sammy.
"That wasn't all of it," said Janey, showing her fangs. "I went and found that fat pig in one of his regular night spots being serviced in his black-and-white by another underage street kid...."

Oh wow...!

"She was begging him not to and he was just laughing. I popped one in his thick skull. She had her head in his lap, never even saw me."
Janey turned that bold grin on Cat who smiled right back at her.

"Oh, I admire your sense of justice!"

And the way you get away with murder....

Which begged the question: what were they in for?
Blithely, they recited the alphabet, the A to Z of juvenile delinquency.
"Aw!" sneered Janey. "We can do this standing on our heads!"

But that's not really it, is it? You're all here because you're unwanted, disrespected and rejected....

The desert was where the bodies were buried. The disloyal gangsters; the gamblers who didn't pay their debts; the hookers who disappointed their pimps; the teenage strays who were used, abused and discarded; plenty more where they came from.
"It's no use, Dear...."
The deluxe mobile home was a gleaming juggernaut of chrome and wood paneling. Year in, year out it had served the Baxter clan well, vacationing coast to coast.
"I'll have to go and get some help."
And now, in the middle of nowhere, something went "bang!" and then wheezed and they ground to a shuddering halt on the crusty fringe of the blacktop.
"Aw, heck...!"
The Baxters disembarked and gathered on the shady side of their towering vehicle. Head of the clan, Mister Baxter was balding and fleshy with a pink face and small eyes, in a loud floral shirt and striped Bermuda shorts.
He shaded his eyes, looking out across the broiling expanses, then raised the binoculars he took with him everywhere.
"Hey, looks like we're in luck."
His wife cut an ample figure not flattered by a tight floral T-shirt and stretch pants that emphasized every bulge of surplus flesh. She lifted enormous panoramic sunglasses from the bridge of her blotchy nose and strained to squint through the sizzling heat haze.
"What is it....?"
Dark shapes floated in the distance, a jumble of mysterious architecture, wavering and melting.
Two plain, bland overweight children came and stood by their father, a boy and a girl, maybe six and ten.
"What is it, Daddy?"

"Come on! Faster! Faster...!"
They were getting fitter, Cat could see it.
"That's it! Good! Come on! Hup! Hup...!"
The gym reverberated with their physical effort. Step by step, Cat had ramped up their regime.
She had them sprinting lengths, wall to wall, punctuated by vigorous star jumps on the spot, leaping spread eagled into the air, then dropping to the floor for squat thrusts and push-ups.

"Okay…and rest….!"

They no longer collapsed and lay sprawled on the mats, panting and complaining loudly. Automatically, they formed a line and faced her expectantly, breathing evenly, glowing.

Yeah, you're getting it….

Cat was satisfied. She had succeeded in tapping into their rebellious spirit and was channeling it into a new kind of pride and purpose and unity.

She relished the challenge in their eyes. They knew that she wanted them for something special and they wanted to know what it was.

She scanned their young – so young – faces.

Cheryl, so wanton, so wild, so dangerous.

Janey, her fierce fire smoldering, ready to ignite recklessly, no holds barred, no inhibitions.

Lina, that outrageous body such a deadly weapon and so ready to use it.

Josie, drop-dead gorgeous; her cool exterior concealing cruel passions.

Sammy, that easy-going affability disguising a cold capacity for extreme violence.

Five unique individuals, thought Cat, striking sparks off each other. Those tensions were what made them such a strong group. And what they had in common was utter fearlessness and a thirst for excitement – and they could kill.

What they wanted more than anything, in their bruised and battered lives, was respect, and self-respect. And she could provide it.

Yes, you'll do!

Cat mopped her face and draped the towel over her shoulder. She grinned at them brightly.

"Well done, ladies, now hit the showers!"

Mister Baxter had flown a desk in the Air Force, when he still had hair. That layout looked familiar to him.

"I think it's an airfield!"

His wife frowned and masked her eyes with the shades again.

"What's it doing all the way out here?"

Mister Baxter shrugged, tugging out a large handkerchief and wiping his greasy face.

"Dunno. But it's a stroke of luck, that's what it is."

Then his children pointed and sung out in chorus.

"Someone's coming!"

Margaret Hansen stifled the groan of agony and ecstasy until it almost choked her. She didn't want to wake her.

Her dumpy figure swathed in an ankle-length towel robe, the Warden hovered over the bed, mesmerized.

Cat lay naked in the mellow first light, splayed across the storm-tossed sheets, her golden mane spread over the pillows.

"Oh, dear God…!"

Cat stirred slightly in response to the Warden's choked whisper and the movement played delicious tricks along the length of her body. Alarmed, Miss Hansen raised her hand to her lips, strangling the cry of lust that was so desperate to escape.

She stood at the foot of the bed, her wide eyes burning, devouring every breathing contour of the spectacular nakedness displayed before her.

"Oooohh…mmmmmnn…."

Some sixth sense drifted Cat back gently to consciousness. Her long lashes lifted and the green eyes seemed to glow in the half light.

It all came back, in a repulsive rush.

Oh fuck!

"Hi there," she cooed invitingly.

The Warden was trembling visibly, clutching the robe to herself with twisting claws. Smiling, Cat extended a long smooth bare arm.

"Why don't you come back to bed…?"

Miss Hansen gulped audibly and took one jerky step forwards and then two stumbling steps back.

"I—I c-can't," she stammered. "I have m-meetings…things to d-d-do…!"

Yay!

"Awww….!"

Cat was the picture of disappointment.

"Uh…another t-time…?" the Warden was begging.

Cat sat up suddenly with a shimmy of her shoulders, thrusting with her glorious breasts. The Warden's eyes almost popped out of their sockets.

"Sure thing," Cat smiled voluptuously. "Before you go, I have a favor to ask of you…."

Miss Hansen nodded so violently Cat feared her head might fall off.

"Anything!" she croaked. "Whatever you want!"

Flickering phantoms in the heat haze, the figures advanced towards them.

"Hey!" Mister Baxter called out and waved. "Hey there!"

As they approached, the shapes took on form and solidity. Flanking him, the children danced with excitement.

"Daddy!"

"They're soldiers!"

Mrs Baxter took a step back, her hand rising nervously to her throat.

"Frank, those men have guns!"

Her husband waved her off complacently.

"Well, of course they do, Dear…."

Relieved and wreathed in smiles, he was stepping out to greet them.

"Hi guys! You're the answer to our prayers! Can you — ?"

The man on point jerked an M16 to his shoulder and fired.

"Oh my God!"

Baxter's wife shrieked as she saw his head snap back, his skull erupting pink and pulpy.

"Oh my God oh my God oh my — !"

His legs were crumpling and he was still sagging slowly to the ground as the whole squad opened fire.

The desert was where all the bodies were buried – the innocent and the guilty and those who were simply in the wrong place at the wrong time.

"…. **FASTER PUSSYCAT … KILL! KILL!** …."

The print was old and worn, speckled, scarred and streaked, the soundtrack crackly.

"…. **Superwomen Belted, Buckled and Booted!** …."

…. Careening wildly down the desert highway in sports cars supercharged by the sheer force of their personality, hair flying free in the wind, screaming ecstatically ….

"Oh wow…!"

"That's what I wanna do!"

…. Trying to impress his dumb girlfriend, the handsome hunk thought he could out-race the three strapping go-go dancers. Laughing, they blew him off the crude dirt track ….

Oh that takes me back!

They read her mind.

"Bet you could do that!"

Cat laughed.

"Yeah, that's what got me disqualified!"

…. His pride hurt, the hunk tried to get tough. He tried to play it rough ….

"Bad idea man!"

…. She snapped his spine ….

"Oooh!"

"Nice!"

…. Snarling, wheels grinding, she crushed the lecherous muscleman to pulp with her black Porsche, mashed him into the wall ….

"Go girl!"
"Hmph!" Cat sniffed. "Should drive American!"
They were packed into the red Olds 442; Janey and Cheryl wedged shoulder to shoulder in front with Cat while Lina, Sammy and Josie filled the back seat.
Parked at the sparsely attended drive-in, they watched the screen that towered above them as the closing credits rolled by.
"Far out!"
Janey clapped her hands.
"That was so cool," Cheryl sighed.
"Awesome!" Sammy declared.
Lina rolled her eyes.
"Holy cow! Those babes made me feel flat-chested!"
Josie leant forward and tapped Cat on the shoulder.
"I think we get the message."
    Cat laughed again.
"I knew you would."

One by one, and then in bunches, the shabby villagers were collapsing, their eyes rolling up in their sockets, their mouths opening slackly, some vomiting. They lay in a heap, twitching, the children draped across their mothers' bodies.
The tall white men remained standing and intact.
A short rope ladder unfurled and came down from the hovering helicopter. The ring of armed men snapped to attention; their Sergeant saluted.
"At ease…!"
The Colonel was in his element, in the jungle, and in command. Arms folded across his chest, he surveyed the pile of contorted brown corpses and the ring of white men standing tall around them.
"Well," he observed. "I think that proves it."

"Uh oh!" said Sammy.
They heard rusty hinges creak and metal slam.
"Hey lay-dees, wanna par-tee…?"
They spilled out of the cab and off the back of a battered blue pick-up, half a dozen of them.

Oh great!

They were faceless stereotypes, local good ol' boys. Some were gripping beer cans. Glassy-eyed, everything about them was slightly askew, their baseball caps and cowboy hats.

Young, dumb and full of … shit …!

Cat just sat back and let it happen. She saw the expression on the girls' faces.

…. FASTER PUSSYCAT … KILL! KILL! ….

"Fuck off, numb nuts!"

Janey and Sammy had stepped quickly out of the car, blocking their path. But they were looking right past them, zoning in on Lina's exceptional cleavage.

"Oooh, baby, gimme some 'a thet!"

As he fumbled for her, Lina slapped his hand away and then backhanded him hard across the chops. He cursed and lurched backwards, wiping blood from the corner of his mouth.

"No you don't!"

As he lunged forward again, Janey stepped in quickly and brought her knee up sharply into his groin. He doubled up, spewing, and she rabbit punched him hard on the back of the neck. He went straight down and didn't move.

"Bitch!"

He came in, fists swinging. And then his mouth gaped and his eyes popped as the ground seemed to fall away from under him.

"NNGHH…!"

Grunting, Sammy hoisted him onto her shoulders and flexed her strong arms to raise him high above her head.

Yelling, he kicked and flailed uselessly as she walked him over to the pick-up and tossed him into the back.

"Uuuuhhh…hhhh….!!!"

When he groaned and sat up groggily, Sammy pole-axed him with a short-left hook.

"Pussy!"

Two down and four to go….

With a shrill war cry, Cheryl launched herself out of the red car and came down on her victim like a bird of prey. He crashed down flat on his back with the blonde fury straddling him.

"Motherfucker!"

He shrieked as she hooked her thumbs into his eye sockets. Wailing, he crawled away; she kicked him in the head, once, twice, till he lay still.

Three….

He made the mistake of grabbing Sammy from behind, wrapping his arms around her sturdy frame. Frowning, she arched and slammed her head backwards, pulping his nose and blinding him with blood.

She took her strength from the ground, putting it all into a mighty uppercut that lifted him off his feet and deposited him in the back of the pick-up, lying next to his buddy.

Two….

"Look out Janey!"

He had a knife and was slashing clumsily with it. Janey dived and rolled away.

As he lurched and tried to regain his balance, Josie materialized beside him. Deftly, she seized him by the wrist and elbow and wrenched his forearm downwards.

The crack echoed across the concrete car bays. He screamed, the blade falling from his numbed fingers.

"Lina…!"

Josie drove the flat of her hand into the center of his chest, hurling him back against the side of the red Olds.

Stood up in the back seat, Lina was waiting. She wrapped her arm around his throat and squeezed until he went limp. Her lips curling contemptuously, she let him slide to the ground.

One!

He panicked and pulled a gun. A worn-out Saturday Night Special with the stub of a sawn-off barrel.

"Git away!" he squawked as he stumbled backwards towards the pick-up. "I'll use it! I will! I'll use it!

Cat flowed lithely out of the driving seat.

"My turn!"

She strolled languidly towards him, making every curve work for her. Frozen, he stared at her, the tip of his tongue darting nervously.

"Now, why don't you be a good boy and put that down…?"

She made her voice husky, hypnotizing.

"Go on, be nice…."

Dumbly, he gulped, swallowing hard. As his eyes glazed over, his hand opened slowly and the pistol clattered on the ground between his feet.

"That's a good boy…."

Cat launched her right foot into an explosive high kick that impacted on his chin. For a moment, he stood stock still and then his eyes rolled up into their sockets and his legs folded, sinking him to the ground.

"Oh wow….!"

"That was amazing!"

"You've got skills!"

"Shit! You've got magic powers!"

Cat grabbed Janey and hugged her.

"And you guys learn real quick. Now let's get out of here!"

CHAPTER 9

WILD THING

I need to get laid!

Pillow talk.

I need to erase these pictures from my brain!

Lying there in the steam bath of the Warden's sweat, Cat fought back the impulse to retch.

She lay with her back to her. Stiffening her spine, Cat rolled over to gaze into the sagging face. She made her mouth smile.

"Good morning...."

Margaret Hansen blinked and stirred sluggishly, reaching out automatically to grasp Cat's breast. It took a supreme mental effort to stop her from ripping the clumsy fat fingers from their sockets. Instead, she patted the groping hand softly.

"Gently, gently...."

The Warden mumbled something desperate. Cat twisted to lie on her back and the hand fell away. They lay side by side for a while as the dawn glow expanded across the ceiling.

"I'd like to take a long weekend off," said Cat. "I'll leave at lunchtime and be back on Wednesday."

The Warden's hand was on her bare belly, creeping downwards past her navel. She was nodding eagerly.

Jeez! If I told you to shave your head and paint it green you'd do it!

"Yes, yes, of course," Miss Hansen replied hoarsely. "Whatever you want!"

They weren't happy about it.

"It's only four days, I'll be back before you know it."

Lined up on the gym mats, they radiated disapproval.

"Aw, c'mon you guys!", Cat held up her hands.

Janey's frown flashed thunder and lightning.

"We like having you around."

Oh, I love them!

She flung out her arms as if to embrace them all.

"Thank you, that means a lot!"

They mellowed somewhat but still looked disappointed.

"Bummer," Cheryl's pout deepened. "We were hoping you'd be taking us out again."

"It's the weekend!" Sammy laughed. "Time to par-tay!"

Cat smiled, snaking her arms around their shoulders.

"I tell you what," she suggested. "You guys up for a dare?"

Sixteen-year-old women of the world, Lina and Josie stood aloof. This sounded like some childish game.

Other eyes lit up.

"A dare?"

"Oh yeah!"

Cat grinned at them, her eyes challenging.

"Okay, you know the drill. Break out, do some good. Impress me!"

I'm back!

The moon was out and the night-life was roaring.

Oh yeah! It's Friday night! Let's party…!

It was there to welcome her, the pulsating rainbows of neon that proclaimed: **THE JOOK JOINT**.

The car park was crammed bumper to bumper with prestigious limo's, brash American Muscle, chic European sophisticates and outrageous pimp-mobiles.

"Right on…!"

Straining the seams of their purple tuxedos, the huge doormen took one look as she hip-swayed and swaggered towards them and flung the doors wide open.

"Heeey, Mama…!"

"Have a good night…!"

Oh, I intend to!

Cat was a feast for the eyes. Her breasts were thinly veiled by a futuristic halter top, a translucent weave of light. A twist of sparkling links secured iridescent harem pants, her feet shod in golden slippers.

An emerald that matched her cat's eyes was a green star twinkling in her navel. Her face and the bold bare flesh of her toned midriff and flaring hips were powdered by a silvery glister.

Oooooo… So much choice!

Her senses were overloaded by a boogie wonderland of sound and light. A riot of whirling spotlights, pulsing strobes and colored gels and glitter balls.

Let's get it on…!

Sparks and lightning bolts and showers of stars, effervescent rainbows washed over the heaving mass on the dance floor.

And the Beat. Always the Beat. Seamless, relentless, intoxicating, the best drug of all. One great almighty high.

Smiling, Cat inhaled deeply. It gave her a rush, the heady cocktail of body heat and Sex, Sex, Sex.

Already men were scoping her, as they prowled the fringes of the crowded dance floor, a giant chessboard of luminous, multi-colored squares, lit from below. Macho men with silk shirts unbuttoned to the waist, heavy gold medallions clanging on their hairy chests.

Sorry, not my type….

Cat sashayed right by them and the medallion men backed off, intimidated. And then she saw what she was looking for.

Ooooh yeah!

She recognized them from the sports pages. Crew cuts, thick necks, broad-shouldered, beef on the hoof. Two notorious linebackers and an All Star running back.

Come to Mama!

The massive young men had dance partners, three foxy women with conquest in their flinty eyes. The men were dancing automatically with no passion in it, going through the motions for the reward of the easy lay to come.

No contest….

Cat strode onto the pulsating floor. Her dance was subtle at first, her feet hardly moving, hips twitching to the beat. Slowly, she became more expansive, until her whole body was working in voluptuous undulations and gyrations.

She looked like she was sculpted by starlight, the bare expanses of her skin glistening, the pearly silk and the silver gleaming. She was supernatural.

Slowly, she moved towards her target. She created a space around her, illuminated by her aura. The hulking athletes couldn't tear their eyes away and the women were stabbing angry looks at her.

Making her fabulous body move in ways that became more and more suggestive, Cat made a show of looking the three young men over, her hooded eyes and parted lips provocative and inviting.

You're just what I need, boys….

Still dancing robotically, the young hunks could scarcely tear their eyes from her. She was a mythical beast, primitive and strong, a force of nature.

    simple-minded meatheads who'll just love me for my body!

Furious, the dance partners felt like they were invisible. One gave Cat the finger, spun on her heel and stormed off the dance floor. The other two just stopped dancing and stood staring coldly at her.

Smiling like the cat that got the cream, Cat gave her defeated rivals an emphatic look of triumph and strutted off the dance floor, her hips rotating extravagantly.

Gotya!

She weaved her way through the heaving throng to the long chromium bar way at the back, lit up like a fireworks display. She was glowing, golden; the bartender saw her at once and came running.

"Bourbon, double, on the rocks...."

A heavy hand touched her arm with unaccustomed shyness.

"Uh, why don't you let us...er...Miss...?"

Cat lit up her biggest smile and turned to face them. Their looming bulk made them look even more like bashful schoolboys.

Cat was graciousness itself.

"Oh, thank you, that's very nice of you."

They ordered what she was having, sipped, and then stood shoulder to shoulder, looking down into their glasses.

"Uh...uh...."

"Yes?"

Cat smiled again and tried to look less intimidating.

The enormous linebacker swallowed hard, rubbed his chin and then blurted it out.

"Well...it's like this, Miss...we...er...we...."

The running back picked up the ball and carried it for him.

"We all agree, Miss," he said in a rush. "That we'll never be able to live with ourselves...."

"Or die happy...."

"If we don't all make love to you, Miss – right now – tonight!"

Suddenly, all three looked like they wanted the floor to open at their feet and swallow them. Cat let them suffer for what seemed an eternity. Then she tossed her golden mane and laughed.

"Why, you dear sweet old-fashioned boys – so you shall, so you shall!"

Sizzling giggles. Through the fence, running into the night.

"C'mon...!"

Beneath a full moon, the desert shone like silver. It was a moon for werewolves and vampires – and for dead end kids in the danger zone – it showed them the way.

"Let's go!"

They all felt it. Thanks to Cat. Like they could run forever, like nothing could stop them.

They followed a route that they had run with her, but now they were on their own. It took them to the craggy high ground from where they could get the lay of the land.

"Okay...."

"So...?"

Isolated clusters of light twinkled in the distance. Occasional headlight beams marked the path of the dark desert highway.

"Well?" demanded Lina.

Knitting her brow, Janey scratched her black thatch.

"Okay," she decided. "We got Barlow and then there's Fairfax...."

Cheryl looked unimpressed. Josie just shrugged.

Janey flared up.

"Well fine! If you can think of anything better why don't you—!"

"Hey...?" said Sammy.

She was a little way off, leaning perilously over the edge of their precariously crumbling perch.

"What's that?"

Sammy was pointing downwards to the floor of the moonlit desert. The others gathered around her. Janey was muttering and darting black looks at Josie who ignored her coolly.

"That doesn't look right."

A shallow, barely perceptible elevation picked out by the moonlight, a slight hump in the ground. Its strange symmetry stood out, in the irregular rough-hewn landscape.

"Yeah," agreed Lina. "It's square."

"Rectangular," Josie corrected her.

"Oh, I'm sorry," Lina retorted. "Some of us haven't had the benefit of a private education!"

They made faces at each other.

"Okay, okay," laughed Janey. "Let's go down and check it out."

The slightly raised rectangle was large enough to accommodate them all with plenty of room to spare. They stood just inside its border, looking down and around.

"It looks like a fresh grave," observed Sammy.

"What do you know about fresh graves?" asked Cheryl.

Sammy tried to look mysterious. Cheryl rolled her eyes.

"Big grave," said Lina.

"Maybe there's more than one body buried in it," Josie suggested.

"Cool!" said Janey. "Start digging!"

They all stood and stared at her, except Sammy, who guffawed and fell on her knees, pawing at the dirt, using her strong hands like shovels.

"Well, come on...!"

Half an hour later, they were spread out around the frame of the odd geometry, shaking their heads in confusion.

"What the fuck...?"

They'd scraped away a substantial patch of dirt. Bewildered, what they were looking at now was a dulled surface of steel.

"Okay...."

The others looked dubious; Janey stepped out boldly and advanced to the center. Squatting, she carved away energetically with her bare hands.

"Huh!"

Rising, she stomped down hard with her foot, then hunkered down again and banged with her fist.

"Hey, I think it's hollow!"

Tentatively, like walking on thin ice, they ventured forth to join her. And then they were all stamping and banging.

"Wait! Wait! Stop...!"

Sammy was pointing again.

"What's that over there?"

Shoulder to shoulder, they stooped to scrape away a skin of dust and grit.

"It's some kind of hatch!"

Janey produced a vicious switchblade and was probing skillfully. The hatch was narrow and made of thick Perspex with an aluminum frame. The catch succumbed to her expertise easily.

"Yeah!" Janey triumphed.

On her hands and knees, she lowered her head and peered into the darkness within. Cursing, she recoiled violently.

"Aw shit! What's that smell?"

They all took a step backwards, covering their mouths and noses.

"That's death," said Sammy.

Janey and Sammy stayed where they were, the others backed away further. Sammy shook her shaggy mane.

"Too tight for me."

To make her point, she flexed her biceps, grinning.

"Jeez!" exclaimed Lina. "What've we got here?"

"Well," said Josie. "Cat said she wanted us to impress her."

Janey turned to look them over. She lit on Cheryl.

"Okay, Slim, get yer little ass over here!"

Cheryl's mouth opened and closed. Before she could say anything Sammy had reached into the pocket of her short jacket and was slapping a neat flashlight into her hand.

"Go for it!"

Gulping, Cheryl stepped forward and then jumped back, gagging.

"No fucking way!"

Janey was wearing a biker's flamboyant red kerchief around her neck, to set off her studded black leathers. She untied the loose knot and secured the cloth over Cheryl's nose and mouth.

"Now go!"

Reluctantly, Cheryl approached the open hatch. The smell was barely muted by the kerchief but this was all about the respect of her peers and she wasn't going to risk that.

"Okay, okay! Lower me down!"

She held out her arms. Janey and Sammy seized a wrist each and let her dangle into the dark opening.

"Go easy!"

They lowered her slowly until the top of her blonde head dissolved in the gloom. Her muffled voice floated up to them.

"Okay, you can let go now!"

They saw the open hatchway glow a musty yellow as Cheryl switched on the flashlight.

"I can…It's…."

There was a brief pause as they heard her moving around beneath them.

"It's a motor home…! It's a whole fucking motor home…!"

And then there was an awful shriek from down below that seemed to slice through the steel beneath their feet and turn their bodies to ice.

"OH MY GOD OH MY GOD OH MY GOD…!!!!"

They saw her hands, flapping desperately, reaching up to them from below.

"Get me out of here!"

Sammy reached in and hauled the slender blonde out effortlessly. As she landed on the steel surface, Cheryl staggered, gasping. Janey steadied her, wrapping an arm around her shoulders.

"Oh fuck! Oh fuck…!"

The others maintained their distance, on the edge of the rectangle. Janey shook Cheryl by the shoulders, smoothing her fair hair back from her face.

"What was it?" she demanded. "What the fuck did you see?"

Cheryl struggled to breathe.

"Dead people!" she croaked. "I saw dead people!"

Intrigued, Sammy went to the rim of the hatch.

"Yeah…?"

"A whole fucking family!" Cheryl panted. "Kids too!"

Sammy removced the flashlight from Cheryl's numb fingers. Returning to the hatch, she lay down and leant in as far as she could.

"Yep," she pronounced. "They're dead alright."

Her face darkening, Janey reached down and pulled Sammy out of the way. Sammy passed her the torch.

"Take a look."

When Janey stood up, her eyes were blazing.

"Who could kill little kids like that?"

Peer group pressure obliged Lina and Josie to lean down and look. Lina just said "Fuck!" and then walked away, her hand over her mouth. Josie's face turned to stone as she blanked it, as a childhood of abuse had taught her.

Cheryl was sitting on the ground, shaking. Janey embraced her, their faces very close.

"Mmmm…nnnn!"

Cat awoke in the middle of the afternoon. She was splayed stark naked across a vast circular water bed that dominated the high-tech penthouse suite abandoned long ago by her Uncle John for Free Town.

"Ooohhhh….!"

She sat up gingerly and looked around her. At all the mod cons and clever gadgets that reminded her why she rarely came here and why she preferred the soulful simplicity of a beach house.

Huh?

A naked man mountain of muscle lay sprawled face down across the curved horizon of the bed, below her bare feet. The sound of deep snoring was muffled by the rumpled black satin bedsheets.

It all came flooding back in flashing images like a strobing jump-cut garish porno flick.

Oh my God!

Did I really do that!!?!

That's not physically possible!!!

The expanses of the circular bed rippled as something stirred beside her. "Nnnngghh…hhhhh….!"

His broad bare torso was sculpted marble; a Greek god. She marveled at its sheer perfection as he breathed deeply, mumbling in his sleep.

Ooooooo…did I?

His powerful thigh rested across her knee. Gently, Cat extricated herself and swung her long legs over the curved rim of the water bed.

When she stood up she discovered the third one. As naked as his team-mates, he was lying curled up on his side cushioned by the deep pile of a white fur rug. He looked so cute, to Cat, smiling down at him.

Oh yeah – I did!

Her daring costume lay strewn in a trail on the floor that stretched all the way from the distant door to the water bed. Her ivory satin G-string dangled from a chromed sci-fi chandelier. The young jocks' disco wardrobe, ripped off in haste, was tossed here there and everywhere.

Cat felt replete, satiated, mellow inside and out, as she padded across a room that vibrated with snoring and shut the bathroom door behind her.

The sounds of her singing in the shower didn't wake them. When she emerged she was radiant, wrapped in a long robe, crossing swiftly to her dressing room.

Oh shit! Look at the time!

Totally drained, the big men slept on. Cat reappeared, frowning at her watch, casting around for her car keys.

She was transformed, dressed for work, in stone washed denim snug on her hips, a darker blue embroidered denim shirt loosely buttoned and tied up to expose a flash of midriff.

Juggling the keys on her palm, she stood in the middle of the room, surveying the slumbering, utterly spent bodies of her victims.

Thanks guys, I hope you're dreaming about me....

Gradually, the numbness faded. It receded from them one by one – starting with Sammy – leaving only Cheryl sat on the ground, staring blankly.

"What are we going to do?" asked Lina.

"Tell the cops?" suggested Josie.

"No fucking way!" Janey rounded on her.

Loftily, Josie raised her hands, turned her back and stalked away. Her face contorting, Janey made to go after her. Sammy stepped between them.

"Aw, c'mon guys! We gotta stick together!"

Janey and Josie stood and looked at each other. The tension seeped out of them.

"Sorry...." they both said together.

"Well," repeated Lina. "What are we going to do?"

Janey opened her mouth and then saw that Cheryl had stood up and was pointing dumbly.

"Hey, what the...?"

The moonlight made it easier to pick up the fragmented traces of broad caterpillar tracks. Someone had obviously tried to erase them.

"There's been a digger out here!"

"Well yeah, how else could they have done this?"

"They – who?"

Janey shrugged. Sammy surged past her.

"Come on...!"

She was marching out onto the broken trail that stretched to the silvery horizon and the great glowing moon hanging above it.

"Come on!"

"Oh Cat! It's so good to see you!"

Aiko pounced and squeezed the breath out of her.

"Whoa! Whoa!" Cat wheezed. "I'm feeling fragile!"

Aiko stood back and looked her up and down.

"Yeah right," she raised an eyebrow. "And glowing too."

Her exotic eyes were penetrating.

"How many of them were there?"

Cat made a show of looking bashful.

"Come on! How many?"

"Oh, just three," Cat replied casually.

Aiko shook her head, feigning disappointment.

"Not up to your usual standard, Cat; what's the record…?"

The studded leather door swung open and Selena entered her exotically appointed office.

"Hey, sweet thang, how are you?"

She was, as always, regal, powerful, in her flowing tribal regalia, accented with chiming gold.

Their embrace was long and lingering, as Cat clung on, taking so much strength from her.

"I'm okay, Boss."

Selena looked deep into her eyes, cupping the golden head gently in her hands.

"Good. Then let's talk."

The ground folded upwards to form a shallow ridge. They lay side by side on the up-slope, peering over the edge.

"What the f—!"

"What's that doing there?"

As they watched, the seemingly deserted airstrip sprung into life. A single runway revealed itself in parallel strands of glowing beads of light. Light blazed through the crack as a hangar door split open and slid apart to reveal a bright cave bustling with activity.

A distant hum grew in volume and intensity, coming up behind them. Then they could see the winking red and green navigation lights. In seconds it was low and close enough to make out the silhouettes of the crew in the lit cockpit.

"Holy shit!"

They were on their backs, propped up on their elbows. As the twin-engine Cessna swooped down low right over them, they rolled over and pressed their bodies into the ground, clamping their palms over their ears.

"Fuck…!"

When they looked up again, the small plane was taxiing towards the hangar. Figures emerged from the light within and surrounded it.

In the pool of yellow light that flooded from the gaping hangar, boxes were being tossed down and transferred along a chain of hands that snaked back inside.

"Wow!" said Sammy. "Wait till Cat hears about this!"

"Let's get out of here," said Lina nervously.

"Good idea!" agreed Josie.

Cheryl was already sliding herself backwards gingerly, down below the lip of the shallow rise.

Janey ignored them, her keen eyes flashing.

"It's gotta be dope!" she stated. "It's—!"

Cheryl yelped.

They seemed to rise out of the earth, walking swiftly towards them in a tight crescent formation, their M16s aimed from the hip.

"Put your hands in the air!"

They didn't get the fearful and docile response they expected, from what looked like just a bunch of nosy kids.

Their instincts fine-tuned by young lives spent dodging Police sirens, the gang gave themselves the best chance by scattering. They weaved and zig-zagged, their evasions dictated by the sparse concealment offered by folds and hollows in the ground.

"Halt!"

"Stop or we fire!"

They'd heard that before, so many times, and just kept right on going. This time, the firepower was substantial; and fully automatic.

"Aw, shit!" Janey bawled, as lead spat past her ears and raised dust near her blurring feet.

"Fuck!" Lina yelled, as a bullet flicked her long flailing tresses.

Sammy wasn't running with them. The armed men had formed a firing line and she charged and took them sideways on like a pro tackle, tumbling them into each other like bowling pins.

"Run!" she screamed. "Get outta here…!"

One was scrabbling on his hands and knees, groping for his rifle. Sammy kicked him in the head with all the might of her sturdy thigh. He rolled over on his back and lay still.

"UH!"

She felled the next one as he lurched upright with a brutal forearm smash across his throat. The third was still on his knees when she kicked him in the teeth.

And then they were all on her. It took five of them to drag her to the ground. She bellowed curses, heaving and thrashing and lashing out with her feet and her fists.

She broke one man's nose and blood spurted; she knocked out some teeth. "MOTHERFUCKERS…!!!!"

Finally, they pinned her by her arms and legs, grunting and cursing. A short baton detonated on the back of her skull. The starry sky came crashing down on her; the huge moon shrank to a pin prick and winked out.

"That's a bad scene," said Cat.

"And getting worse," Selena replied.

Aiko was reciting from the open folder on her lap.

"There's been a dramatic increase in deaths by drug overdose," she confirmed. "And not just in ones and twos."

"Lately in whole batches," added Selena from behind her massive carved desk.

Cat shook her head, her face clouding.

"Yes, I saw the headlines…horrible!"

"There's some very bad stuff out there," said Aiko.

"Well, that's nothing new," Cat replied. "Dealers can cut the stuff wrongly."

Selena shook her spectacular Afro.

"Not on this scale. And there's something planned about this, something deliberate."

Aiko extracted a sheet of paper covered in chemical symbols and technical jargon.

"We've analyzed some blood samples," she scanned the sheet. "And the results are disturbing."

"In what way?" Cat asked keenly, galvanized by the prospect of new excitements.

Selena smiled, noting Cat's eagerness. She held out her hand and Aiko stood and passed the sheet of paper to her.

"The results," Selena explained. "Show an entirely new blend...."

"Yes...?" Cat craned forward in the deep zebra-skinned armchair. Selena smiled again.

"Rare ingredients found only in Central America and a formula that we traced back to secret Nazi experiments in World War Two."

"Holy cow!"

Selena put the paper down and leaned across the desk towards her.

"We need someone to go down there."

She registered the flame that sparked in Cat's green eyes.

"How are you feeling, honey?" Selena asked gently. "Are you ready to go back to work?"

"Well?" barked Warden Hansen.

They stood at attention lined up in front of her desk. All maintained the same stony blankness, staring at a point above and beyond her.

"What do you have to say for yourselves?"

Janey shrugged.

"Dunno, Miss Hansen...."

"When we woke up this morning she was gone," Cheryl finished for her.

"Gone," affirmed Lina.

"Real gone," smirked Josie.

Reddening, the Warden slammed her fist down on the desk.

"Do you think this is funny?"

Cat knocked and entered, restored to her regulation track suit with the coach's whistle around her neck.

"Sorry I'm late, I only just got...."

Anger made Margaret Hansen even uglier, her eyes bulged and she looked like she was about to turn purple. Cat recoiled, taking a step backwards.

"It seems that we have lost one of your class, Miss Warburton!" the Warden snapped. "She escaped last night!"

The girls all glanced sheepishly at Cat and then looked down at the floor.

"And these say they know nothing!"

Oh God! Sammy...!

Cat made a display of glaring at them and they all flinched. Sucking in a deep sigh, she approached the desk.

"If I may have a word with you in private, Miss Hansen…?"

They were waiting in the gym.

"Okay, I convinced her…."

Cat entered briskly and they swarmed around her urgently.

"I told her that Sammy had let slip that she knew someone who could meet her with a car outside Barlow and then head for the East Coast. That ought to have the Fuzz looking in the wrong direction."

Janey looked doubtful.

"And she believed you?"

Cat smiled mirthlessly.

"She'd believe anything I tell her."

"Oh yeah…?"

They wanted to know more about that. Cat's eyes sparked impatiently.

"Never mind – now tell me all about it!"

"UGHH!!!"

He hit her again.

"OOOOGGHHH…!!!"

Sammy coughed and spat blood. When she raised her head and flicked back her hair she was grinning, her teeth stained red.

"That the best you got…?"

She was strapped with her hands behind her into a metal-frame chair, in an old shed with flaking corrugated walls.

"You hit like a little girl!"

She'd lost her bomber jacket and was in her T-shirt and faded jeans. Bright lights blazed into her face, almost blinding her, she could just make out figures hovering behind them.

"UH!"

"AGHH!!"

"UURRGGHH…!!!"

Sammy sagged in the chair, panting, blood dripping from her chin.

"Well?" said the voice from behind the bright lights. "How much do you know?"

She lifted her head slowly, her eyes sizzling with anger.

"I told ya," she shouted hoarsely. "We were on a break-out from Juvie, we were on a dare that's all!"

She heard low voices behind the lights. Discussion; and then a clipped command.

"URGHH!"

"AAAGGHH!!!"

Oh God!

Gagging, Cat hoisted herself up and out of the Perspex hatch. She stood on the dusty steel rectangle, sucking in great draughts of cool clean night air.

Those poor kids!

It was just as they had described it to her; as she stood and looked out over the faint traces of the caterpillar tracks that stretched out towards the silvery horizon.

She was dressed for war, her body sheathed in the skin-tight black catsuit. Her fair hair shone like a beacon in the moonlight and so she concealed it with the black ski mask.

The short AR-7 rifle was slung across her shoulders, with the scope and silencer attached.

Hey…?

And then suddenly the gun was in her hands and she was crouching, spinning, aiming from the hip.

"HEY!"

Alarmed, Janey raised her hands high in the air. Close behind, the others imitated her hastily, wide-eyed.

They'd never seen her like this before, dressed to kill.

"Oh wow!" breathed Janey. "Look at you…!"

"You really are a secret agent!" Cheryl exclaimed.

Cat clicked on the safety catch and let her breath hiss out through clenched teeth.

"What are you doing here?"

Janey grinned at her boldly.

"You didn't think you'd do this without us, did you?"

"Sammy saved our asses," said Lina.

"We have to do this," Josie insisted.

Through the slash in the black ski mask, Cat was smiling proudly.

"Okay, okay, let's go," she surrendered. "I only hope we're in time!"

"Come on, bitch, spill!"

Beads of sweat flew in a glittering spray as Sammy shook her head violently, her damp tresses flailing.

"Tell us what you know!"

"Oh boys…?"

The patrol stood and gaped, their gun barrels drooping.

A jaw-dropping spectacle, Lina and Josie displayed themselves, exposed on a hump in the ground.

"My, what big guns!"

They flaunted it.…

"Want some fun?"

Janey and Cheryl lay side by side in concealment, hugging the dirt.

"Huh!" Janey muttered. "That's all it takes in this world – big tits!"

Mechanically, one began to lift his rifle. The man beside him slapped it down.

"Are you crazy?"

Cat had worked her way silently behind them.

"Aw, c'mon you guys…!"

"Don't you want a good time…?"

Cat juggled the gas grenade like a metal egg on her palm.

One…two…three….

It landed just behind their bootheels. A dull crack and a hiss and the patrol was enveloped in a dense yellow cloud that wrapped itself around them like a blanket.

"AAA-AAaaarrrgghh-hhh…!"

One man managed to tear himself free from the gaseous coils. He staggered forward, his brain scrambled. Josie and Lina swaggered across to meet him.

"Oh my God…!" he drooled.

He reached out like a kid in a candy store.

Josie picked up his M16 and handed it to Lina.

"Yours…."

Lina swung it like a baseball bat. He fell flat on his back, blood pooling beneath his head, black in the moonlight.

"Home run!" declared Lina.

"Naw," said Janey, emerging from cover. "More like a double."

Lina scowled; and then saw Cheryl gazing at her raptly.

"Want some…?"

Smiling smugly, Lina advanced on her.

"Want me to lend you some of this?"

Josie was laughing.

"I've got enough for both of you!"

Janey and Cheryl clenched their fists.

"Okay, ladies, that'll do…."

Cat was circling back to them, tugging off the ski mask, her face bright and smiling in the moonlight.

"And you two put your clothes back on."

She applauded them.

"Nice job!"

They grinned at her vengefully. The precocious attributes which had made them a victim were now a weapon and they relished it.

Cat saw Janey and Cheryl looking left out and downcast.

"Hey, don't worry, guys, you've got skills of your own."

They waited till the clinging yellow cloud had dissipated.

"They'll live," said Cat. "But they'll be tripping for days."
"Far out!" laughed Cheryl.
Janey frowned.
"Let's go get Sammy!"

"AAAAAAIIIII-IIIIGGHH…HHHHH!!!"
Sammy screamed as much in anger as in pain, glaring at them through the veil of matted hair glued to her face.
"F-F-Fuck…you….!"
Her head lolled, her chin coming to rest on her heaving chest.
The lights dimmed. A door slammed.

"She must be in there somewhere…."
In the moonlight, they could see it all clearly; the single stretch of runway, the big hangar and a cluster of smaller structures close by it.

Unless she's already buried out there…!

Cat kept her fears to herself. Charged by the eternal optimism of youth, they were itching to get at it. Suddenly, she felt very old again, at twenty-four.
"Let's go…."
Crouching low, they spread out and crept forward towards the dark airstrip, weaving through tufts of long grass and crusty humps of sand and rock.
As they neared the sheds huddled against the high wall of the hangar, a sentry walked around the corner and slap bang into them.
"Wha —!"
That was all he had time to say. Cat was on him, a blur of motion, swift and precise. A blackened blade gleamed dully. A gasp, a brief gurgle, and then she was easing him down to the ground.
"Hey!"
As she crouched over her prey, a second man loomed above her, lifting his rifle to club down with the butt.
Before Cat could react, the gang was all over him.
Cheryl clamped herself around his legs; Lina and Josie pinned his arms; Janey choked him with a vice-like headlock. They dragged him down and covered him and when they stopped and stood up he lay motionless, his head at an awkward angle.

Oh yeah – you'll do alright!

They looked at her expectantly, a class hoping for praise from its teacher. Cat rolled her eyes and grinned, giving them a big thumbs-up.
"Hey…."
They were startled by a low voice coming from the shadows and a slow soft hand clap.

"Good job, you guys!"

They jumped and turned around. Sammy was walking slowly and carefully towards them. She was battered and bruised and grinning at them broadly with her bloodstained teeth.

"So what took you so long?"

They stood amazed and speechless. Sammy saw the deadly AR-7 slung across Cat's shoulders.

"Can I borrow that?"

"Uh, sure."

Cat handed it over.

"Thanks. Back in a minute...."

Sammy strode stiffly to the tall doors of the hangar. She cocked her head, listening, and then her battered face lit up with a smile that was pure evil.

With a grunt, she hurled the heavy slide door wide open.

"Hey, dickwads!"

There was a shout of alarm. Cut short when the gun went "pop!-pop!-pop!"

Sammy stood for a moment staring into the bright glow inside the hangar. Then she turned on her heel and was walking back to rejoin the others.

"Thanks."

She tossed the gun to Cat who caught it one-handed.

I like your style!

"My pleasure."

"Aw...I think I lost a tooth...!"

Sammy fingered her black and blue jaw gingerly.

Putting a safe distance between them and the airstrip, they besieged her with questions.

"So what happened?"

"How did you get away?"

With relish, Sammy hawked and spat a gob of blood, making Cheryl jump backwards.

"Hey!"

Sammy flashed her stained teeth.

"They were a bunch of pussies!"

"Yeah?"

"C'mon!"

"Tell!"

Smiling, Cat squeezed an arm around Sammy's broad shoulders.

"I'm proud of you!"

Suddenly, Sammy's eyes were brimming over.

"Nobody," she whispered. "Nobody's ever said that to me before."

The moment passed and Sammy was grinning boldly again.

"Aw it was easy," she declared. "Two of them assholes decided to untie me so they could have a little fun...."

She let rip that hearty guffaw.

"Big mistake!"

Her laughter was infectious and Cat let them all savor the moment and share in the victory.

And then they were all looking at her again, for affirmation and approval.

"I'm so proud of you all!"

They looked suddenly shy and tongue-tied.

"Well," said Janey. "We have a good teacher!"

Oh, I adore them!

"Back to Juvie?" asked Cheryl.

Cat shook her head.

"No," she said mysteriously. "We have other places to be."

This time they didn't ask any questions, trusting her. Cat marched them across the moonlit desert for about a mile. They chattered all the way, extracting every gory detail out of Sammy.

"Awww, shit…!"

"Ooooh! That must have hurt!"

Not as much, my darlings, as the pain inside!

Cat stopped.

"We're here."

"Uh, where?"

It looked for all the world like a long, ragged hump in the ground, mottled and bristling with tufts of grass.

"What's she doing?"

"Search me…."

Cat reached out with both hands and tugged. The entire surface rippled, shifted and then slid away.

"Holy shit!"

The red Olds 442 stood gleaming in the moonlight.

"How the—?"

Cat hauled off the remaining folds of the camouflage netting and tossed it aside.

"Let's go, team!" she clapped her hands. "Climb in!"

CHAPTER 10

ACTION STATIONS!

"Warden!"

"We've got trouble!"

"They're all gone!"

"And Miss Warburton!"

"Her car's gone!"

The phone rang on Margaret Hansen's desk before she could quell the invasion of her office.

"Uh…yes….?"

The female voice was clipped and businesslike, made sinister by its electronic disguise.

"Warden Hansen? This is…."

It was the name of a very secret agency.

"Oh! I—!"

"Please don't interrupt…!"

The voice verified itself with a coded number provided to all public officials, major and minor, to establish its absolute authority over them.

"The five young women and their teacher – you will not contact the Police – you will destroy your records and you will forget that they ever existed!"

The Colonel looked like he'd just returned from his vacation, in a short-sleeved Polo shirt, strained by his broad chest and biceps, and casual slacks. The regulation crew-cut gave him away, even more so the .45 automatic wedged in his waistband.

"What the fuck happened here?"

He stood looking down at the bodies laid side by side on the concrete floor of the hangar. It was a gruesome display: one with his throat cut from ear to ear; one with his neck snapped; three with a neat .22 caliber hole in the middle of his forehead.

Standing beside him was the only man who could make the Colonel look average; Mr Big, the Colossus, King of the Jungle, resplendent in a cream-colored suit with diamond buttons on his vest and leopard-skin lapels.

He used his skull-topped cane as a pointer, indicating a lens mounted in the steel rafters.

"Mebbe that's tell us…."

It's done!" said Aiko.

"Everything?" asked Selena.

"Yep," Aiko replied. "Those kids can start again with the slate wiped clean."

"And a new family," said Selena.

A small speaker bleeped on her desk.

"Hey, it's me!" the CB handset made Cat's voice thin and crackly. "We're on our way!"

Selena smiled warmly at the sound of her voice.

"We're waiting here for you, honey, have a safe trip."

Aiko craned closer to the small speaker. They could hear music in the background.

"Those aren't your usual sounds, Cat?"

"Tell me about it!"

Aiko chuckled as Cat signed off.

"Well, she used to say she always wanted a crazy little sister; now she's got five of them."

"Cat Warburton – role model; now that's a scary thought!"

The Colonel watched the grainy images flicker on the TV monitor.

"Jesus!"

Mr Big shook his massive shaven head.

"Taken down by a bunch 'o wimmin," he rumbled. "Looks like lil' girls!"

There was a military spec radio mounted on a metal table. The Colonel grabbed the handset.

Mr Big heaved a massive sigh that stirred vibrations in the metal furnishings.

"Girls wi' guns, dunno what th' world's comin' to!"

The Colonel's report was typically clipped and precise. The response on the line was immediate.

"Find them, Colonel – you know what to do!"

On the open highway, Cat drove with the top down, the music blaring and the wind in their hair.

She had made the supreme sacrifice. Resisting any impulse to try and convert them to her Funk and smooth Soul, she made a rare concession by catering to their taste – The Stooges, MC5, Deep Purple....

The things I do for my country!

Unable to by-pass every pocket of civilization, Cat did her best to persuade them to modify their behavior so as not to draw attention to themselves.

A car loaded with such an abundance of charms was hardly inconspicuous. Cat gave the gang strict orders not to provoke the wolf whistlers by giving them the finger, mooning them, or lifting their T-shirts.

It was hard work but they managed it, although once or twice they had to virtually sit on Lina, whose generous curves made her a focus of attention.

They stopped for supplies at lonely gas stations and small-town stores. The carpets and gleaming white upholstery of the red 442 were polluted by junk food wrappers and empty soda cans; they wanted beer – Cat forbade it.

When they yelled at her to go faster, to do the ton, Cat only laughed and nodded towards the Highway Patrol prowlers lurking behind giant billboards.

They wanted some target practice, to lob the empty cans at the road signs as they flashed by. Sammy asked to borrow Cat's gun again.

"Just chill out and listen to your music...!"

As darkness descended, it all began to catch up with them.

Hooray!

Wedged in the corner of the back seat, Sammy was snoring, her head tilted back, mouth open. Lina couldn't stop yawning and Josie's eyelids were drooping.

In the front, next to Cat, Janey and Cheryl were leaning on each other, their faces close together, eyes closed.

You're so sweet...!

She dared to turn the music down. Janey's eyes popped open.
"Hey!"

They could have roared past those watchful prowlers doing a hundred and ten, buck naked, throwing beer cans and firing guns and nothing would have happened.

The Highway Patrol would have stayed right where it was, tucked behind the tall billboards.

Seething with frustration, the driver wrenched his radio handset from the dash.

"It must be them, Sir. A blonde woman and five kids, heading South in a red Oldsmobile."

The Colonel's voice came back promptly.

"Alright, pass it down the line. Tell them to let me know when they stop for the night!"

The driver cupped his hand over the mike and cursed. The man riding shotgun banged his fist on the dashboard.

"We could have taken them, Sir. We — !"

"They would have eaten you alive, asshole! Now do what you're told!"

Cat took them to another world. A rolling vista of sinister whispering grey corn fields, under a starless sky. The black angular silhouette of a gaunt farm house, stark against a vast blood red moon.

There were signs in big bold letters: **TRESPASSERS WILL BE SHOT!**
"We're here...."

She stirred and unloaded them and ushered them towards the warped porch steps and a flaking door with cracked glass panels made opaque by the passage of time.

"We'll be here for the night."

Her charges hung back skeptically.

"I've seen this movie," said Cheryl nervously.

"Yeah, me too!" Janey echoed.

Cat's eyes glittered in the deep pool of shadow below the porch's sagging wooden awning. They heard a bunch of keys rattle like something from a medieval dungeon. Hinges creaked loudly, making them jump.

"You'll be fine," said Cat. "This is one of our safe houses."

"Safe for who?" asked Josie.

"Yeah, for vampires!" declared Lina.

Sammy laughed, stomping up the wooden steps.

"Aw, c'mon you guys! Looks cosy!"

Muttering darkly, they filed up the stairs. Atop the porch, Lina's foot went through the rotten planking.

"Fuck! Safe my ass!" she squawked. "Some help here – pleeeze!"

Ignoring her, they entered. Cat switched on the light.

"Oh!" said Cheryl.

Behind the corroded and impenetrable window panes, it was bright and neat and tidy. The furnishings were modern and cheerful and all was warm and welcoming. There was even a color TV.

"Cool!" said Janey.

Sammy and Josie were already channel hopping, arguing over what to watch. The door banged open and Lina came in under a storm cloud.

"Gee, thanks guys!" she put on a show of limping, bending to rub her ankle.

Smiling, Cat clapped her hands, getting their attention.

"You each have a room upstairs," she told them. "Take your pick; you'll all find bags on the bed with everything you need."

She laughed as some turned and made a dash for it, to be first to the top of the stairs. Sammy used her brawn but Janey bumped and slithered round her.

"No fair!" Sammy yelled, off balance, as Cheryl slid past her.

Josie played it cool, sauntering up the stairs with exaggerated elegance.

"Do you mind!" complained Lina, bringing up the rear, still favoring her sore ankle.

A small side room was crammed with state of the art radio equipment. Headphones clamped to her head, Cat was tuning in, leaning close to the microphone.

"Hi, Aiko, we're bedding in for the night," she reported. "You're going to love these characters!"

There was a knock on the doorframe. Cat removed the 'phones and turned in her swivel chair.

"Huh," Janey looked around. "Secret agent alright."

She was holding up a sky-blue track suit top; turning it round to display white lettering across the shoulders: TRACK AND FIELD.

"Very fancy," she said. "But why do I need it?"
Cat stood up, walked over to her and ruffled the black crop gently.
"You all have one of those."
"She grinned and tapped the side of her nose mysteriously.
"All will be revealed...."

They were driving through the night, under the harvest moon.

"Terminate with extreme prejudice...."

Three jet black vehicles with tinted glass. Gun barrels glinted.

Cat left the communal bathroom, wrapped in a towel robe, and walked the length of the dim landing towards the door of her room. It was catching up with her now and she yawned luxuriously.
"Hey...?"
When she opened the door and switched on the light she saw Janey and Cheryl reclining stark naked on her bed, side by side.

Oh my Lord...!

They were grinning at her provocatively, up for a dare.
Cat stood and stared, her senses overloaded.
"Don't you like us?" asked Cheryl.

Ooohhhhhh...!

The ache inside was so bad Cat thought she was going to break in half. On the outside, she merely smiled.
"You're adorable – and dangerous."
Cheryl's pout ripened. Janey frowned.
"I'll take dangerous," she growled, nudging Cheryl with her elbow. "You can have adorable."
"No thanks!" Cheryl elbowed her back.
They pretended to tussle, rolling on the bed, rumpling the sheets. They put on a show, grunting and panting like the phony wrestlers they liked to watch on TV.
They darted quick sharp glances at Cat, to make sure she was watching.
"Okay, thank you ladies! That's quite enough!"
Laughing, Cat scooped up her blanket from the floor. She flung it so it spread out and floated down to cover them.
"I'm very flattered, really I am," she told them warmly. "But we're all tired and I think we've had enough fun to last us a while."

The armed men disembarked. Locked and loaded, they entered the vast grey cornfield, moving silently towards the farm house.

The wild girls sat on the bed, wrapped up together in Cat's blanket.
"Did Warden Hansen hit on you?" Janey asked.
Cat grinned.
"How do you think I got you all those privileges?"
Then a disgusting thought came to her.
"How about you?" she asked. "Did she try it on you?"
"Sure," Cheryl shrugged. "We did the old bag favors and she gave us candy."
Janey opened her fist to show Cat the colorful sample of pills clustered on her palm.

That bitch!

Cat frowned.
"There's a time and place for that and this isn't it. You're in training now."
She held out her hand, cupping it. Passively, Janey surrendered them.
"Okay Coach."
Cheryl's pale brow furrowed.
"When are you going to tell us what we're in training for?"
Cat did that tapping the side of her nose thing again.
"All in good time," she said. "You're gonna love it!"

In the depths of the cornfield, the man on point stopped in his tracks with a low grunt of surprise.
"Huh…?"
He went rigid. He folded in the middle, bent double. Then his spine snapped back, arching him upright violently, bent backwards like a bow.
"AAAARGH—!"
His terrible scream was strangled abruptly as his body split open and exploded. The men behind him recoiled in horror, splattered with gore.

"What the fuck—!"
In the house, they all heard the screaming from the cornfield.
"Holy shit!"
They burst out of their bedrooms onto the landing.
"What the hell is going on?"
The distant screams mingled with gunfire, sustained and out of control.

Whoever you are, you're shit out of luck boys!

Cat went the length of the landing, shoving them back into their rooms.
"Stay inside!" she shouted. "Just stay inside!"

The screams dwindled, the gunfire became more spasmodic. Then silence.

Poor dumb bastards!

The corn dripped with blood.

Cat went back into her bedroom. Wide-eyed, Janey and Cheryl were holding each other under the blanket.
"Can we…?" Cheryl gulped. "C-can we…?"
Sucking in a deep breath, Janey finished for her.
"Can we sleep with you tonight?"
When Cat looked doubtful, Janey shook her head emphatically.
"No, I don't mean that," she was pleading. "I mean can we sleep with you tonight?"
There was movement on the landing and Cat's doorway filled with Josie, Sammy and Lina.
"We were about to ask you the same thing," said Josie.
"Aw, pleeeeze…!" said Sammy.
Lina just nodded jerkily, speechless.

Oh my babies!

Cat's laugh embraced them all.
"Oh, don't any of you guys believe in wearing pajamas!"

Cat got them organized. They collected their mattresses and carried them downstairs to the living room.
Clearing the furniture, they put the mattresses together in a mosaic to make one giant bed big enough to accommodate them all.

Oh, what the heck…!

"Here, try this…."
They were still looking all around them nervously. Cat distributed some small red and white capsules.
"These will help you sleep."
The pills worked. Cat slept in the middle with the others tucked up tight around her. They slept soundly till morning.

The sky above the cornfield was dull and colorless.
"Good morning!"
They were gathered on the rickety porch, restored to their leathers and denim and T-shirts with their defiant slogans.
"Look at that!" Sammy pointed.
A black cloud of carrion crows swirled in the sky above the corn.
"Dead meat!" said Janey.
She started down the porch steps. Cat grabbed her leather-clad arm.
"You don't want to see that."
Janey shrugged her off.

"Yeah I do."

She was off and running with Sammy hard on her heels. The others couldn't let the side down and followed swiftly.

Okay, you asked for it!

As Cat jogged after them she heard their short sharp shrieks and exclamations, muffled by the thickly planted corn stalks.

Cheryl came running past her back towards the house, her eyes wide and horrified, her hand over her mouth.

"Oh shit! Oh shit! Oh shit…!" she was panting.

It was worse than she expected.

Fuck…!

A broad swathe had been carved out of the corn as if by a giant scythe. In this crudely hacked clearing the bodies lay sprawled about, some still clutching their useless guns.

"Oh my God…!"

On her knees, Lina was scrubbing vomit from her chin. And then she did it again.

"Ohhh….!"

Josie had her back turned, standing with her eyes squeezed tight shut, that familiar exercise, blanking it again.

How many times can you do that before it doesn't work anymore?

The corpses were reduced to raw chunks of meat; headless, limbless, burst open and turned inside-out. The crushed corn was pooled with coagulating blood and entrails.

Janey just stood and stared, she couldn't tear her eyes away.

"Holy cow!" said Sammy. "Wow!"

And then Janey was twisting this way and that, her eyes getting larger and larger, starting to panic. Cat stepped in front of her, blocking her view.

"Don't worry," she said gently. "They only come out at night."

Nobody wanted any breakfast. Except Sammy.

"Mmmm!" she grinned at Cat with her mouth full. "You make great ham and eggs!"

"Oh fuck you!" croaked Lina and ran upstairs to the bathroom.

They heard her shouting and pounding when she discovered that Cheryl had locked herself in there.

The others all sprawled around on the big communal bed looking numb.

Josie lifted her head and stared at Cat with eyes like dark lasers.

"Are you going to tell us what that was all about?"

Cat raised her eyebrows.

"I don't know, I've never seen it," she replied apologetically.

She raised a pale smile.

"It came with the house. Best protection you could wish for – as long as you don't go out at night!"

She glanced at her watch and then towards the grimy windows.

"We expecting company?" Janey asked.

"Any minute now," Cat replied.

Lina and Cheryl re-entered the living room bickering and shoving each other. Lina won that contest against the lightweight slimmer girl and Cheryl rolled onto the sea of mattresses.

"Hey!"

Janey stood up to defend her. Lina just glared at the world in general and sat down.

Josie rolled her eyes.

Grinning, Sammy gobbled another forkful.

Cat smiled inside.

Good, things are getting back to normal!

And then the gang was on its feet, alarmed, at the sound of wheels approaching and crunching to a halt outside.

"It's okay," Cat assured them. "They're here."

She went quickly to the front door and threw it wide open. The gang backed deeper into the living room and stood in a tight bunch.

"Come right in!"

They were surprised to see three very attractive young women who looked fit and capable in their functional blue overalls and combat boots.

The new arrivals smiled at the girls who responded instinctively with deep suspicion. They mellowed somewhat and relaxed visibly when they saw Cat welcoming them so warmly.

They also registered the respect and even hero worship glowing in the young women's eyes as they lined up before Cat as though for her inspection.

"The Boss sent us," their leader confirmed. "Whenever you're ready...."

Cat turned and grinned broadly at her young charges, who stood watching and wondering. Suddenly, they really did look like children.

"Go pack your bags," she told them. "These people will take them to where we're going."

As they exited the farm house, the young women were slamming the back doors of a pale grey van. They climbed into the cab and drove off, down the long dirt road that skirted the cornfields.

The gang stood at the foot of the porch steps watching the van diminish into the distance. Cheryl glanced over her shoulder at Cat, locking the door behind them.

"I'll be glad to see the back of this place!" the blonde girl shuddered.

Chuckling, Cat thudded down the steps and surged past them, making for a leaning old barn where the red Olds was sheltered.

"C'mon you guys!" it was a battle cry. "Let's get this show on the road!"

As they drove out along the fringes of the cornfield, her passengers eyed the strangely grey expanses warily.

"Don't worry!" Cat laughed.

She could sense the mood lighten as they left the fields and the dirt roads and had the blacktop under their wheels again.

"Let's have some sounds!" they chorused.

Cat activated the 8-track and marveled at the rejuvenating effect of Iggy and The Stooges.

The secret air field hummed with activity.

"Come on! Hustle!"

The aircraft parked in front of the hangar was the distinctive twin-prop, twin-boom Cessna O-2A that had gained fame in 'Nam in its role as Forward Air Control.

"Let's go!"

Its Service insignia and stencils had been erased, rendering it anonymous. Men in drab overalls clamped grey steel cylinders onto rails mounted beneath the thin wings.

"Oh wow!"

"This is so cool!"

The red Olds rolled down the Old World main street of Free Town, past the quaint houses and smiling young people.

"I'm glad you like it," said Cat. "It's going to be your home for a little while."

The reaction they were getting was not what they were used to. Just friendly, welcoming smiles; no ugly comments, crude suggestions or wolf whistles.

Lina stood up in the back seat.

"Hey, that pretty boy looks just like Jesus!"

Josie grabbed the waistband of Lina's cut-off denim shorts and pulled her down.

"You're long past saving, Jugs."

Lina waved and flashed the long-haired young hippie an evil grin. He turned bright pink.

"Oh, I don't want him to save me!"

She chortled lewdly.

"Well, not like that!"

Janey twisted in the front seat to glare at her. Their eyes locked, sparking.

"What's your beef?" Lina demanded. "You don't like men anyway!"

Cat felt Janey go rigid beside her, sensed her coiling inside.

"Just shut the fuck up, why don't you, Lina!" Cheryl snapped, surprising herself.

Lina's temper was coming to the boil.

"Yeah right! And she's not the only one!" she shouted. "Just because I happen to like boys!"

Janey was the thunder and Lina the lightning. Up front, Cheryl's strained paleness was disturbing. In the back, Josie was making herself small, aware that Sammy, grim-faced and menacing, was clenching her fists.

That's enough!

Cat slammed on the brakes hard. Her passengers were jolted forward and back and were suddenly all grabbing each other for support.

"Hey!"

"What the f—!"

Cat slapped her palm on the dash, the crack of a whip. Her voice was cold steel.

"Let's have no more of that, shall we!"

Their wide eyes were fixed on her anxiously.

Oh, don't worry, I still love you!

"It's a dangerous world out there and all you guys have is each other!"

Cat warmed, pointing at the Peace Flag fluttering above the old Civil War cannon.

"So why don't you just try and love one another, huh?"

For a moment there was absolute stillness. Janey contorted her body backwards, cupped Lina's hot face in her hands.

"I love you!" she stated fiercely.

She planted a hearty smacker on Lina's flushed cheek.

"Oh!" Cheryl exclaimed.

Josie's jaw dropped, as she slid down in her seat, fearing she'd be next. Beside her, Sammy laughed out loud.

"Yay…!"

Lina just sat back passively. Her face was blank but Cat could see that tears were pricking her eyes.

Yes, you could all do with a bit of love!

She let the red 442 roll on across the town square, where small groups gathered around the strumming guitars and a sweet scent was in the air.

"Hey, smell that?"

"Oh yeah!"

And then they were distracted by an unexpected sight.

"Hey…?"

"We're going to church?"

Cat laughed.

"You'll see!"

John Warburton was waiting for them on the church steps, in the embroidered caftan that he saved for special occasions.

"Welcome! Welcome!"

Intrigued, the gang saw Cat, suddenly girlish, run to him and throw herself into his arms. They watched as they hugged until it looked like their bodies would merge together.

"This is my Uncle John!" Cat said breathlessly, urging them forward.

They shuffled towards the church tentatively, suddenly shy. He radiated sunbeams, warming them all.

"So these are your young runaways," he said heartily. "Come in! Come in…!"

Restored to his familiar combat fatigues, the Colonel spread the map out on the table.

"This is it…!"

His finger traced the flight path for the pilot and co-pilot, zipped into their flight suits.

"Let's make it a good one!"

They were all naked in the bubbling hot tub – Uncle John with his brawny arm around Cat's glistening shoulders and all five spaced out in a semi-circle facing them.

John Warburton was drawing on an enormous joint, as fat as a Havana cigar. He passed it to Cat, who drank deep and tilted her head back, eyes closed. Plucking it from her fingers, he offered it across the steaming water.

"Do you ladies partake…?"

Like shy schoolgirls, they all looked to Cat. She only sat there, her beautiful breasts floating on the surface, her long lashes lowered, head lolling gently from side to side.

"Uh…yeah…thanks…!"

Seizing the moment, Janey splashed across and grabbed it.

"Careful!" laughed Uncle John. "Don't drop it!"

They passed the joint along the line, from end to end and back again. Then watched, entranced, as the two Chinese girls attended to them, in tight green silk slit to the hip, pouring perfumed oils into the bubbling water.

"Ooohh…"

The scented oils made swirling rainbows on the surface. Under the exotic lamplight, they were gleaming, golden. In all their confused lives, living life in the raw, they'd never felt like this before.

"…wow…!"

They looked around, seeing each other as if for the first time. They felt – perfect.

John Warburton beamed at them in an avuncular fashion.

"There's always a home for you here if you want it."

He could almost hear the cogs turning, as their battered young minds grappled with the concept.

"Home!" said Cheryl. "What's that?"

Cat opened her eyes; they were dark and sad.

"Don't ask me!" she replied.

Their eyes zeroed in on her, questioning. Cat sighed and squeezed her Uncle closer to her.

"I was an embarrassment to my parents," she explained. "I interfered with their social and political ambitions."

She kissed John Warburton on the lips, smiling when his flourishing moustaches tickled her. Then her face was set in stone again.

"Uncle John had to kill my father to stop him killing me."

It took a lot to shock them; this succeeded. Cat shrugged.

"It's a long story...."

The atmosphere chilled momentarily. Until Sammy started giggling; it often had that effect on her.

"Dare ya, Janey!"

Grinning, she held her nose and submerged herself until the top of her head disappeared.

"Huh!"

Janey could never resist a challenge. Closing her eyes, she sank below the oily surface, as they competed to see who could stay under longer.

Go Sammy...!"

"Come on, Janey...!"

The rest shouted encouragement, taking sides.

"Aw...fuck...!"

Janey exploded out of the water, making it splash over the rim of the tub. Sammy stayed down while the others cheered and then rose more gracefully, looking smug.

"I'll beat you one day, surfer girl!" Janey panted.

"In your dreams!" laughed Sammy, scarcely out of breath.

Lina suddenly squealed and squirmed, making waves that rippled across the water.

"Oooh! The bubbles are turning me on!"

Cheryl snorted.

"You're always turned on!"

Josie arched her eyebrows.

"I think some of us need to get laid."

Cat laughed, her eyes gleaming saucily.

"Well, I always said that you should have called this place Free Love, Uncle John!"

Footfalls rang on the coiled wrought iron staircase that led up to the landing and the hot tub.

"Careful Cat!" laughed Selena. "You're corrupting them!"

Selena came into view, followed closely by Aiko. With a cry of joy, Cat stood up to welcome them, the fragrant oil and water cascading from her glorious contours.

"Oh no, more like they're corrupting me!"

Aiko shook her head reproachfully.

"And you've already been corrupted quite enough as it is, Cat."

Selena and Aiko were both completely naked.

"Come on, make room…."

The girls were awestruck.

"Budge up, Miss Warburton…."

They didn't know where to look, their senses overwhelmed; by their golden goddess and these new arrivals: the ebony Warrior Queen and her dangerously exotic companion.

"So, what do you think of my niece's new protégés, Selena?" beamed Uncle John.

Aiko was looking at them with x-ray eyes. Selena's imperious gaze raked over them slowly.

They felt like they were being turned inside-out; and they all watched Cat, seeking some hopeful sign.

Selena nodded solemnly.

"They're everything you said they are, Cat…."

The gang let out its pent-up breath in a collective gasp, their taut bodies released the coiled tension.

And now Aiko was grinning as if to say: "only teasing!"; and Selena was smiling broadly.

"Okay, bruthah an' sistahs, let's rap!"

It had been a long day; Cat got ready for bed.

There was a soft tapping on her door. She slipped on her white towel robe.

"Come in!"

Uh oh…!

Sammy stood hesitantly in the door frame. She was in her sleep wear, a loose singlet and briefs.

I knew this was coming….

"Come in," Cat smiled. "And shut the door."

Sammy stood looking down at the floor, the walls and everywhere but at her. Cat stepped forward and bent to look up into her face, still smiling encouragingly.

"You were a great gym teacher!" Sammy blurted.

She had the look of someone thinking that's not what I wanted to say at all.

"Thank you, I enjoyed it. You were great pupils."

Silence. Cat waited, her face open, expectant.

"Do you go undercover a lot?"

"Oh yeah, I've been a news reporter, a bikini wrestler, titty dancer…."

"Cool!"

"And a groupie."

"Oh wow! Who'd you fuck? Anybody real famous?"

The memories made Cat wince.

"I was part of the stage show for a band called 666."

"Fuckin' A!" Sammy was impressed. "They were heav-eeee, Man!"

"And, for the record," Cat insisted. "Me and Aiko put on a show of batting for the other side just so we didn't have to screw any of those assholes!"

"Put on a show?" Sammy looked disappointed.

"Well, let's say we didn't have to try too hard."

Sammy looked away again. When she spoke, Cat sensed even more that there was something else she wanted to talk about.

"What happened to them? They found the tour bus all burned out but no bodies?"

How do I explain that they were all consumed by a black Boss Mustang that was driven by the Devil!

"Uh, dunno," Cat lied. "I wasn't there at the time."

"Yeah, sure…," Sammy smiled knowingly.

A taut silence. Sammy's face looked strained. She was looking up and down and sideways again.

Cat stepped closer and put her hand on Sammy's arm.

"Come on," she asked softly. "What do you really want to talk about?"

Sammy took a step back and then jerked up her head and looked Cat straight in the eye.

"Do you like me?"

Coming from her, it was more like a challenge than a question.

"Of course I like you!"

Sammy shook her feathered mop vigorously.

"No, I mean do you like me!"

Oh Sammy!

Sammy saw Cat hesitate and her eyes sparked angrily.

"C'mon, you swing both ways – you just said so!"

Cat shrugged.

"It's all part of life's rich tapestry."

Sammy blinked; that was too complicated for her. Her anger was nearing detonation.

"It's just a game to you," her voice was raw. "But it's my life, it's who I am!"

Cat held out her hands, her face contorting with pain.

"I'm sorry, I didn't mean—!"

Sammy shook her head again, backing away.

"I get it, you don't fancy me."

"What!"

"Everyone wants to fuck Cheryl, girls and boys; same with Janey, she's so hot, she can have whoever she wants; Lina's the Hollywood Sex Machine; and Josie's the Prom Queen!"

Poor baby!

"It's just like being back at school again, I'm the plain one!"
Cat gestured dismissively.
"No way! You're beautiful!"
Sammy snorted.
"Yeah right, don't tell me, I'm beautiful inside and that's what really matters!"

Ohhhhh…!

Cat slipped off the robe.
"Let me convince you."

The Cessna accelerated down the runway and lifted off.
Gaining height, it leveled and began to bank, heading for the sunrise.

The morning was bright and invigorating.
Cat and Sammy strolled together into the town square. Sammy slid her arm around Cat's waist and squeezed.
"Thank you…."
Cat smiled at her tenderly.
"Just tell me you're beautiful."
Sammy revived that hearty laugh of hers.
"I'm beautiful!"
Lounging on the sunlit grass, Lina and Josie were preening and smiling for a group of young male admirers.
Cat grinned, shaking her head.
"I see those two already have a fan club!"
Janey was shooting hoops, going one on two with a pair of burly long-haired youths. One made the mistake of trying to block her and ended up on his backside. With a smug grin, Janey held out her hand and hauled him to his feet.
Cheryl sat a little way apart on a park bench, looking both ways sullenly, at Janey and then at the boys drawn like moths to the flame to Josie and Lina.
"That's Cheryl," muttered Sammy. "Stuck in the middle as usual."
And then her face lit up, full of life.
"Way to go, Janey…!"
Waving, Sammy left Cat and galloped towards the basketball court. Janey laughed and flipped her the ball.
"Wooo!"
Sammy took it in stride, sidestepped both boys effortlessly, sprang high in the air and planted the ball in the basket.

Cat was applauding as she crossed the grass. As she passed them and their courtiers, she tipped a big wink to Lina and Josie.

Be gentle with them, ladies….

Janey left the court and was trotting towards her, bright-eyed, her face shining.
"Have fun last night…?"
She cocked a knowing eye at Cat.
"Sorry, please don't think I was playing favorites."
Janey smiled with unaccustomed softness.
"No," she whispered. "You did good."

The Cessna O-2A dipped its wing and descended, swooping low, hugging the rugged contours of the desert landscape.
The co-pilot began his calibrations.
"ETA eight minutes…!"

"Hey, Princess!"
"Good morning Cat!"
Cat saw three familiar figures emerge onto a narrow balcony framing the base of the wooden church steeple. John Warburton, Selena and Aiko, arm in arm, all wearing matching caftans.

Oh Uncle John! A three-way, huh?

As Cat waved back, a shrill klaxon sounded, shattering the mood.
"Take cover!"
The square was emptying. Astonished, the young newcomers saw grassy doors open on the lawn nearby them, revealing concrete steps plunging downwards.
The girls stood and stared at Cat in confusion. She gestured urgently.
"Go down!" she shouted. "Go down!"
And then they all heard the engine noise and saw it coming.
The suitors grabbed Josie and Lina by the hand and tugged them towards the sunken stairs.
"No! Go down!"
Janey and Sammy dashed to Cat's side and stood there, fists raised, as though to punch the onrushing aircraft out of the sky.
Seeing this, Lina and Josie tore themselves free and were running across to flank them, Cheryl scampering hot on their heels.
There was a bang above and behind them; a "whoosh" that made them duck. A rapid jet trail of white smoke raced by over their heads, arcing upwards, with a black arrowhead.
"Oh f—!"
The Cessna vanished in an oily orange and black fireball.

"Shit!"

They threw themselves in a heap, hugging the grass, as smoking fragments came sizzling down all around them.

"YOW!!!"

Cheryl was rolling on the ground, the billowing flares of her tight denims on fire. Sammy pinned her while Janey tore off her precious leather and used it to smother the flames.

"Fuck! Fuck! Fuck…!"

The fiery rain pattered out. Cheryl rolled Sammy off and sat up carefully. She eyed her ruined pants ruefully and then heaved a huge sigh of relief.

"Thanks, you guys.…"

As they hoisted her to her feet Cheryl hugged them both warmly, rare color in her cheeks. Sammy looked pleased.

They gathered around Cat, dusting themselves down. She beamed at them proudly.

"You're amazing!"

They shone back at her, for once totally united.

"Everyone okay?"

John Warburton was striding towards them. He had a compact rocket launcher balanced on his broad shoulder.

"Where did that come from?" Cat gasped.

He grinned, his moustaches bristling.

"Oh, I always like to keep one handy!"

Selena and Aiko were coming up behind him. Aiko handed a walkie-talkie to her chief, the size of a house brick.

"This is Able-Baker One," Selena was saying briskly. "Launch the strike now!"

"Attack formation…!"

The blue-grey made the gunships virtually invisible against the bright sky.

"Select your targets…!"

They came in two waves, insect-like predators.

"LAUNCH!!!"

The air strip vanished beneath a tide of bubbling fire.

"LAUNCH!!!"

The flames paled and evaporated; the black smoke thinned and wafted away. All that was left was a vast scorched stain.

"Target destroyed!"

"Just as we thought.…"

Behind its folksy façade, Free Town hid a high-tech laboratory.

"Worse than we thought.…"

They'd scoured the wreckage of the downed Cessna O-2A and salvaged one of the steel grey cylinders. It was opened and analyzed by young men and women in masks and chemical suits.

They watched them through thick sealed safety glass.

"In early World War Two," John Warburton explained. "Nazi scientists were experimenting with invisible poisonous gases that could be spread by air over conquered territories or those they were planning to invade...."

Cat shuddered. Her Uncle looked grim; he'd seen the ghastly effects of toxic agents employed in Viet Nam.

"Those gases were designed to be selective," he continued. "Formulated to target a specific race or age group, to eliminate all undesirables in one fell swoop and leave only those useful to them, as slave labor."

"Oh Jesus!" Cat was beginning to see where this was going.

"That's right," said Selena. "And someone's reviving those experiments."

"Only this time as an instrument of social control," Aiko elaborated. "It looks like the targets are the campuses and the ghettos."

There was a shocked silence, crushed by the enormity of it.

"Get your people back on the firing range, Princess," said John Warburton. "You'll be flying out soon."

Cat was struck dumb, her eyes deep wells of horror. Selena took her hands and squeezed them gently.

"It's down to you, my superstar," she said with warm intensity. "We need you to take your new team and cut it off at the source!"

Something in the wreckage stirred.

The black crust burst open, charred beams were flung aside.

The Colonel rose into view. His olive drab was smudged and tattered, his regulation flat-top singed.

"Bitches...!"

His eyes blazed in his blackened face.

"You're going to die!" he screamed. "You're going to die slow!"

CHAPTER 11

INFILTRATION

"Anunciando la llegada del vuelo 787 desde los Ángeles…!"

The airport was named after the National Hero; his stern bronze bust overlooked the entrance. He was eclipsed by technicolor blow-ups of El Presidente in a variety of Presidential poses and gaudy uniforms; all displaying what he fondly regarded as his best side.

El Presidente's voice could be heard grating on an endless tape loop from a tinny tannoy system, exhorting the masses to greater effort.

"Jeeez!" Janey grunted, unimpressed.

The Arrivals Terminal rang with empty echoes.

"Switch on your happy faces, ladies," said Cat, as they lined up at Passport Control.

They took eagerly to pistol and rifle shooting, grenade throwing, knife fighting and unarmed combat. Then came the art of the disarming smile.

"Oh, come on, make an effort!"

It had proved to be the most difficult part of their training. It suited Sammy's affable nature and Janey had surprised her with a very pretty smile.

"Huh!"

The best Cheryl could manage was a sarcastic rictus, with dead eyes. Lina was all shark's teeth, the gleam in her eyes intimidating. Josie's interpretation was lofty, mocking.

Oh, heck…!

Still, it was better than the sullen suspicion with which they usually confronted strangers.

"So, you are from America, eh?"

The passport official was mock-military glinting with tired brass. Behind him lurked the not-so-secret policeman in a wrinkled linen suit. They made for a comedy duo, the former very fat the latter very thin.

"You are athletes, yes?"

They were in their blue and white track suits and gleaming white Hi-Tops with a gold star on them. Their bulging kit bags were slung over their shoulders.

"No kidding, numb nuts…." Lina muttered.

Josie rapped her on the ankle with her toe. Lina turned and glared at her.

Uh-oh!

Cat stepped up to the counter, igniting her widest and most ingratiating smile.

"That's right," she gushed. "We're due to compete in the Inter-Continental Youth Games two months from now...."

The secret policeman was assessing her mechanically; her obvious assets made no impression on him. Shuffling the pages of her fake passport absently, the fat man was distracted, undressing the girls with his eyes.

Like 'em young, huh?

The forced smiles were becoming more and more brittle by the second. Cat could sense them coming to the boil behind her.

"We've come here for altitude training," she spoke quickly. "And to keep away from press attention and spies from rival camps."

The secret policeman lent forward and muttered something in the fat man's ear. The official couldn't tear his eyes from Cheryl and on his first attempt stamped the counter top instead of Cat's passport.

"You've got an admirer there," Sammy whispered.

"Gee, thanks!"

He took his time with their passports, one by one, his eyes lingering over them when he checked their photographs.

Oh shit!

When Janey clenched her fists, Cat took her by the wrist and jerked her away.

"Come along, ladies...!"

Smiling at the officials till she thought her face would split, Cat hustled them towards the tall glass doors and the glare outside.

"Holy fuck!"

On the broiling concrete fore court, they were assailed by a withering blast of light and heat. The humidity was crushing; in an instant their faces were shining, their hair was damp and they were tugging down the zippers of their track suit tops.

Spreading her arms, Cat got them moving.

"Let's get to our hotel."

"Huh!" said Janey. "I bet they've never heard of air conditioning!"

"Ooooh!" said Lina. "Things are looking up!"

A young man was strolling towards them with a welcoming smile. He was easy on the eye.

"Taxi, lovely American ladies...?"

Showing her teeth, Lina strode forward boldly and slung her bag over his shoulder.

"Aw shit!" grumbled Cheryl. "A bitch on heat twenty-four hours a day!"

With Lina's killer curves commanding attention, the rest were left to carry their own bags and heave them into the trunk.

As they struggled to wedge them in they threw dark glances at their buxom companion. All except Sammy, laughing, making the heavy weight seem as light as a feather.

Cat watched them, smiling.

So far so good!

The grubby taxi drove them through the cramped and dusty streets.

"Jeez!" Janey exclaimed. "What a —!"

Cat tapped her discreetly on the knee.

"We're visitors here," she murmured. "Let's try and be polite."

What they saw was mostly crumbling Old Colonial, its baroque ornateness blurred and corroded, punctuated by ugly concrete modernity.

The locals all seemed to get around on creaky bicycles and sputtering lightweight motor scooters. What cars that weren't slate grey and emblazoned with "Policia" were ancient and held together with rust.

Josie forced a window down as far as it would go to try and get some air. The tepid ventilation was canceled out by the stench of garbage flowing freely in the gutters.

"That's going to be difficult," she stated.

They saw soldiers carrying guns and people stepping meekly off the sidewalk to make way for them.

"I don't think I'm gonna like it here," Janey said out of the side of her mouth.

The thin secret policeman frowned, glancing at his watch. He rapped his fingers on his desk top impatiently.

Finally, his phone rang and the switchboard told him that his international call had been put through.

"Please speak up, Colonel, I can hardly hear you…!"

….

"Yes, it may be just a coincidence, Colonel, but they fit the list of suspect persons you advised us to look out for…."

….

"Certainly, Colonel, it shall be done…!"

"Just lie still you little bitch!" her mother was shouting. "And let him do what he wants!"

Cheryl woke in a cold sweat, choking on her scream.

She was biting the pillow, its mustiness clogging her nostrils. For a moment, panic paralyzed her. She twisted her body, rolling onto her back.

She thought she was hallucinating; and then she realized that it was real. "Oh fuck…!"

In the semi-darkness, the ceiling above the bed was moving, enormous cockroaches, scuttling to and fro.

Cheryl freaked. A white flash exploded behind her eyes.

She leapt from the bed and was out the door. Wearing only a thin T-shirt that barely preserved her modesty, she hurtled down a winding staircase and past the dozing night porter.

Out into the moonlit empty street. She kept on running.

Mere cockroaches didn't faze Janey, she was used to sleeping rough.

"C'mon, wake up…!"

Sammy had to shake her hard to jolt her into consciousness.

"Hmmm…uhhh…what the fuck…?"

Sammy grabbed a fistful of Janey's cotton singlet and heaved her upright.

"Cheryl's gone!"

"Wha…? How do you know?"

Sammy looked awkward.

"I…I went to see if she wanted…company…."

"Huh!" said Janey, offended. "Well, we'd better tell Cat!"

Cheryl's straining breath echoed down the lamp-less empty side streets. Her bare feet splashed in the raw sewage that overflowed in the gutters.

She ran blindly, the white heat frying her brain. She wanted to run forever, to run off the edge of the world.

"Hola, bonita…!"

Steel shod footfalls on the cobbles.

"A dónde vas?"

She ran slap bang into a Police patrol, squat stone-faced men in shabby uniforms.

"Vamos a divirtámonos un poco!"

Two pinned her to the wall by her widespread arms. Leering, their Sergeant flicked at the short hem of her T-shirt. The others loomed behind him, licking their lips.

Cheryl hardly struggled, staring past them with glazed eyes.

"Sostenla!"

Motherfuckers!

Cat attacked swiftly and silently. The dulled blade of the combat knife flickered like black lightning.

The Sergeant opened his mouth; only a harsh gargle and blood came out, his throat slit neatly.

The men holding Cheryl let her go. She slid down the wall and sat on the dirty sidewalk.

They clawed clumsily at the flaps of their holsters. The black blade gutted one, sinking in and slashing across. He clutched at his entrails as they spilled out.

The other received the point in his eye socket, penetrating to the brain. Blood spurting, his body jerked spasmodically until the knife was withdrawn; and then sagged limply to the ground.

That left two, drawing their guns. They weren't quick enough.

"Mine!"

Janey punched him out, laid him flat on his back, the pistol skittering away across the cobbles. Cat, all in black, descended on him like a bird of prey. Quickly, surgically, she cut his throat.

"Leave one for me!"

Sammy sank her fist into the last man's midriff, folding him like a piece of paper. She smashed her brawny forearm down on the back of his neck.

As he rolled on the ground, Cat finished the job with her knife. Dark blood mingled with the flowing garbage in the gutters.

"Holy shit!" Sammy exclaimed.

"You're something else!" gasped Janey, stepping back to avoid an expanding pool of blood.

"So are you!" said Cat. "Thanks!"

Her eyes steeled, flipping the knife from hand to hand.

"Look away!" she said.

They didn't of course. Cat bent low over the Sergeant's body. Deftly, she tugged back his head to enlarge the slice in his throat and then pulled his tongue out through it.

"Aw, shit!" Sammy exclaimed.

"Oh, that's gross!" gasped Janey.

Cat wiped her hands clean on the corpse's shirt.

"It'll make it look like a gang vendetta," she explained. "The local law is up to its elbows in all kinds of corruption."

Cheryl moaned, rubbing her eyes, staring at the scene of carnage.

"Wha…w-what happened…?"

Janey and Sammy went to her and helped her gently to her feet. Janey smoothed the blonde fringe back from her pale forehead.

"It's okay, babe," she whispered tenderly. "It's okay…."

"What the fuck!" Lina launched herself at Cheryl. "What's the fucking problem with you?"

Josie frowned.

"This isn't the first time, Cheryl," she backed Lina up. "Get a grip on yourself!"

Cheryl swayed, her face agonized, clamping her hands to her ears.

"Hey!" Janey shouted. "Leave her alone!"

Sammy stepped in to confront Lina and they glared, in each other's faces.

Cat's dingy hotel room rang with the sound of them shouting. Fists were raised.

That's enough!

"THAT'S ENOUGH!"

Cat's voice was a thunderclap, drowning them out. Silence.

"Thank you!"

She pointed to the bed.

"Now sit down, all of you!"

They squeezed along the length of the creaking mattress, shoulder to shoulder, looking embarrassed and uncomfortable.

Cat stared down on them sternly from a very great height. They'd never seen her so angry and it frightened them.

She sucked in a deep breath and let herself cool down.

"Alright," she began evenly. "We'll have no more of that."

She paced up and down along the line.

"You're five very strong and very individual personalities and I want it to stay that way…."

She mellowed.

"I'm not trying to change you or to tame you. I just want you to direct your considerable energies outwards not inwards."

Her flashing eyes galvanized them.

"I want you to destroy not self-destruct!"

Janey and Lina were side by side, trying not to let their bodies touch. Gently, Cat cupped their heads in her hands and tapped them together.

"Do I make myself clear?"

They looked crestfallen, contrite.

"Oh, come on!" Cat laughed. "You know I love you!"

Both were grinning, relief washing over them.

"Yes Coach!" they chorused.

Her fierce eyes burning, Lina suddenly bent forward to look past Janey; at Cheryl, sat slumped and moist-eyed.

"Aw fuck it Cheryl!" Lina confessed. "I was so scared for you!"

"Me too!" said Josie, her voice breaking.

Cheryl's face crumpled and the tears flowed. Janey embraced her. Sammy pounced on Lina and kissed her on the lips.

"Ugh! Agh! Get off me…!"

Lina made a face, scrubbing her mouth with the back of her hand. But behind her hand she was laughing.

And now the room chimed with laughter. Cat clapped her hands.

"Good! That's better!" she declared. "Now get packing and let's get the heck outta Dodge!"

In the ballads they called him "El águila de las montañas" – "The eagle of the mountains".

He was tall and strikingly handsome; dashing, in his olive-green battledress, with the M1 carbine slung over his broad shoulders. Framed by long wavy hair, complemented by a short beard and moustache, his piercing eyes gave him a Christ-like intensity.

He tugged off the black beret with its red star and ran his fingers through his hair.

"Ahora camaradas…."

In various shades of olive drab, his commanders gathered round the makeshift table, in the tent that made for their temporary headquarters, deep in the dripping jungle. Some were stocky simple peasants; a few were paler intellectuals; two were women. All carried guns and all looked at their leader reverently.

"…este sera nuestro objetivo…."

He spread the crumpled map out with the flat of his hands, the paper creased by the crushing humidity. Beads of sweat fell from their foreheads as they craned closer and spotted it darkly.

The map was a hand-drawn architectural plan: a main building, smaller subsidiary structures and a perimeter wall punctuated by small squares denoting watch towers.

"Esto llevará una planificación cuidadosa …."

They seemed to know the entire Deep Purple songbook. And they could sing it louder than a stack of Marshalls.

Oh, this is cruel and unusual punishment!

The battered old station wagon rattled and banged over the ruts and potholes of the crude rural roads.

"Ow!" complained Josie. "I think I've lost a filling!"

Up front, Janey turned to scowl at their driver.

"You did that on purpose!"

Cat looked innocent.

They passed tumbledown farm shacks roofed with rusty corrugated iron. Fields were worked by bent men and women and tired mules, bare footed children following them.

"Jeez!" Sammy remarked. "What a life!"

Yeah, while fat El Presidente lives in a palace!

In the distance, their destination, a range of sawtooth mountains carpeted with mottled green jungle, looming against a blank and glaring sky.

The road began to rise and narrow, twisting and turning as the jungle enveloped them. The daylight speared and flashed through the onrushing green canopy high above.

It was psychedelic, an assault on their senses, all this light and space, accustomed as they were to the dark alleys of the urban jungle.

"Aw man!" Janey yelled. "I'm freakin' out!"

The silhouette, circling high in the sky, was a familiar one, in these parts. The awesome span of the Giant Condor.

Only this bird was mechanical, its impulses guided by computer programing. Its glinting eyes were cameras, its call was a radio signal.

Guided to its target, the drone circled downwards in a slow characteristic spiral and then released its payload. A small dull metal canister trailing hooks designed to snag and conceal it in the dense tree tops.

Its descent concluded, it dangled in the branches; a tiny green pin light winked on.

A world away, Aiko looked up and grinned.

"Target is marked," she declared. "And the transmitter is activated."

Selena nodded solemnly.

"Okay, Cat, now do yo' stuff!"

"We're here!"

"Uh, where…?" asked Janey.

Dusk was falling. At the top of the winding trail, a cluster of rough cabins clung tightly to a ragged gash hacked out of the steep thickly wooded slopes.

"Our base of operations!"

Cat bounced out of the driver's seat, glad to stretch her long legs. The others exited slowly and stiffly. They bent and flexed and then stood looking dubious. All except Sammy, whose glass was always half full.

"Cool!" she pronounced brightly.

"Yeah right!" groaned Josie.

Janey, the street kid, knew all about sleeping rough, with nothing but old newspapers for a blanket.

"Aw heck!" she shrugged. "They've got a roof, what more do you want!"

Lina made a strained sound and was shuffling up the slope towards the cabins with short careful steps, bent over and clutching herself.

"A bathroom would be nice!"

"Right on!"

Cheryl dashed after her.

The outdoor latrine didn't faze them.

Yeah, you're used to it….

The stinking, overflowing facilities in the clubs they frequented, where you only got in if you were under 18; bait for much older predators – where they got their stuff in little bags; and paid "in kind" in the cubicles, or the alley outside.

Only now you're the hunters not the prey…!

It was an echo from a lost world. Primitive drums were throbbing, a dark pulse that seemed to come from the bowels of the earth.

The village stood in a clearing by a sluggish brown river. A jumble of conical huts, fashioned out of mud and straw. Campfires cast a wavering glow.

A dismembered human torso was turning slowly on a spit. It crackled, dripping. Above it dangled a display of severed limbs. Skulls grinned from atop long pikes.

152

The encampment was a hive of activity. Clad in brief aprons of grass, young women with black eyes and flat faces crouched in chattering bunches, whetting stone daggers. Naked children helped stoke fires, fanning the stinking yellow smoke. Wrinkled old women with dried out teats sucked their gums gleefully, tending a bubbling cauldron.

They were preparing a feast – but something else had to be fed first....

A low rhythmic chanting swelled and merged with the drums. Stark naked save for the whorls and symbols painted on their bodies, masked by carved skulls, the warriors were dancing.

Their chanting ebbed and flowed. This ritual was focused on a gaping cave mouth, festooned with strange talismen representing exotic animals and the human form.

Two tall wooden posts stood close together a little way back from the mouth of the cave, wrapped in vines of multi-colored flowers. In a stained and shredded safari suit, a man stood bound spread eagled between them.

His name, not that it mattered, was Ernesto Diaz and he was a surveyor for a major logging company.

"Esto es una locura…!" he was screaming.

His cries were drowned out by the drums and ancient chorus as he strained against the thick fibers that bound him.

"…No puedes hacer esto!"

There was a sound from the fathomless depths of the cave, of something gigantic stirring. It made the ground tremble.

Instantly, the warriors fell silent, the drums ceased pounding.

A glowing green vapor was exuding from the mouth of the cave, creeping slowly, steadily, carpeting the earth, advancing towards the man tied between the posts.

The warriors watched, trembling; behind them, the women drew their children close.

"Aaaaiiieeeee…!!!"

The surveyor screamed once, writhing, his eyes bulging with terror. He went rigid and then slumped, his body sagging limply.

The luminous mist had accumulated around his feet. It rose to envelop and conceal him. The nauseating stench of corruption descended on the camp site. The villagers inhaled it ecstatically, as though it was perfume.

The green fog thinned and began to roll back into the cave. All that was left hanging between the posts was a stripped and gleaming skeleton.

The dawn was greeted with little enthusiasm.

"Aw, c'mon Cheryl…!"

There was a sort of outside shower, a roughly made wooden booth with a rope and pulley and a large perforated bucket. Water was supplied by a stream tumbling down the steep slope, diverted into a zinc-lined reservoir.

They lined up with their towels, jostling impatiently.

Cat, ever the early bird, had beaten them all to it. Now she was enjoying breakfast and smiling at the muffled sounds of frustration.

"All happy now…?"

Mysteriously, the larder had been well stocked for them and she was heaping their tin plates with eggs and bacon. They tucked in lustily; all except Josie who was pushing the food around her plate with her fork.

"You know," she announced. "I'm thinking of going vegetarian."

Silence; Josie carried on undaunted.

"It's terrible what we do to animals…."

She was on a roll.

"If you want to save Nature," she declared. "You've got to eliminate the human race."

"Oh yeah?" said Janey wearily. She'd heard this before.

"Sure! Man is the only species that has no place in the natural order of things. We cut down the forests; we plow the fields or pave them over; we pollute the air…."

Their eyes were glazing over.

"We enslave animals as beasts of burden, hunt them for sport and breed mutations as pets; we breed them just so they can be slaughtered for food. Man is an aberration, a freak of nature!"

"Yeah," growled Janey. "Men are a fucking aberration all right!"

"And I've known some real freaks!" Cheryl added.

Lina's eyes lit with a voluptuous gleam.

"Ooooh! I can't imagine a world without men!"

Sammy reached across the table.

"Well, Mother Teresa," she told Josie. "If you don't want it I'll have it!"

Josie's stomach rumbled. They all laughed as she grabbed onto her plate.

Sammy beamed as Cat offered her a second helping.

"I thought I heard drums last night," she mumbled, her mouth full.

"Me too," said Janey. "Far away."

Yes, I heard them too….

There was a small metal cube with a strange dial on the table next to Cat's plate. They hadn't noticed it before. Now their heads all turned as it suddenly started bleeping and the dial glowed.

"Hey! What's that?"

Cat's face lit up, the dial's radiance reflected in her eyes. Her smile embraced them all.

"We're in business!"

The day was spent working off those ham and eggs – running and exercising, becoming acclimatized to the higher altitude.

"Aw…!"

"…Shit!"

It left them wringing the sweat out of their T-shirts.

"H-holy…f-f-f—!"

Cat stood and surveyed them, the coach's whistle clamped between her grinning teeth. Sweat on her always seemed to glow, golden.

"Awwww…tell the truth, Cat!" Cheryl complained. "You're not from this planet!"

Chuckling, Cat blew a short sharp blast on the whistle.

"Hit the showers ladies!"

"You mean shower!"

Battle was resumed as they scrambled to be first in line.

That night, Cat's invisible demons returned, pursuing her relentlessly down the dark alleys of her nightmares.

Her demons assumed a physical presence, a glowing green mist that flowed hard on her heels, sizzling ominously, as stark terror froze her to the marrow.

She woke with a wild cry, gasping, her heart pounding till she thought her ribs would crack. Her body was a block of ice.

"Ohhhhhh…!"

There was a tapping on her door.

"W-who…who is it…?"

Janey and Cheryl, in the singlets they adopted as sleep wear.

"We heard you…."

"Are you okay?"

Cat just sat in bed and looked at them, speechless, her throat constricted, the fear lingering in her eyes.

They advanced into the room and climbed onto the bed, one on either side of her.

"It'll be alright…."

"We're here now."

CHAPTER 12

ATTACK!

The week passed by in a blur of sweat and physical exertion.

"Come on…!"

Cat set a challenging pace and they surprised themselves by keeping up with her.

"That's it – you're doing it!"

She had plenty to work with. The inherent stamina of youth and instinctive belief in their own indestructibility.

In Sammy she had a physical phenomenon and Janey was a natural athlete. All of them had spent their young lives surviving on their quick wits, fleetness of foot and propensity for decisive action.

They had killed to survive; and had come through that experience remarkably undamaged, even empowered.

"Hup! Hup! Hup…!"

Day by day, Cat watched them becoming faster and more skillful.

"I'm proud of you…!"

"Lookin' good, Lina!" laughed Sammy. "I think your ass has got smaller!"

They flinched, waiting for the explosion. But Lina only flashed her teeth at her.

"Yeah," she retorted. "And your biceps are even bigger!"

That's better….

There would be friction, flare-ups and sparks flying, with five distinctive and powerful personalities. However, the spirit of competition was becoming a healthy one, a positive force.

The ties that bound them now went deeper than mere circumstance, necessity and survival.

You're a sisterhood!

Aiko entered the office, brisk and purposeful.

"We have the pictures from the drone."

Selena sat at her desk, her chair swiveled to study the panoramic map of the World spanning the wall above and behind her.

Aiko glanced at her watch, estimating the time zones.

"Do you want me to transmit them?"

She was talking to the back of the chair. Selena was fixated by one winking light amongst many, sprinkled like stars across the map.

"Chief…?"

Selena sucked in a deep breath, heavy with emotion. When she jerked the chair around her face was grim, determined.

"Yes, send it!"

Cat slapped the table top.
"Gather round…!"
Sensing something important, they sat with bright expectant faces. Suddenly, they looked even younger and a chill twisted deep inside her.

Oh, what am I getting you all into!

Puzzled, they watched her cross to a tall set of shelves laden with crockery and kitchen utensils.
"Uh, what—?" asked Janey.
Cat smiled.
"Magic!" she replied. "Watch!"
She pressed something and the collective jaw dropped. The entire assembly and all its contents descended, sliding smoothly and soundlessly down into the floor.
"Holy…!" exclaimed Lina.
A hidden alcove was revealed, packed with gleaming electronics.
"Fuck!" Sammy finished for her.
Laughing, Cat caught a tin cup that had rolled off its perch and tossed it to her.
"Catch!"
Sammy deflected it and Cheryl had to duck.
"Hey!"
The cup clattered into a corner. Impatient, Josie got up and walked over for a closer look.
Smiling, Cat was tapping a code into a numbered keyboard.
"Hey presto!"
There was a faint humming sound and a narrow sheet of paper began to scroll out. Cat tore it off and held it up for Josie to see. Josie raised her eyebrows, a hundred questions in her eyes.
Cat led her back to the crowded table.
"We've established places equipped like this one all over the world just in case we need them."
She rolled the scroll out onto the table top; the girls secured its corners with their hands.
"Okay…."
The monochrome image was rendered grained and streaky by its electronic transmission but was still quite legible.
"This is our target!"

The canvas-topped truck had been de-commissioned by the U.S. Army nearly a decade ago. You could still see traces of the white star, now supplanted by the national crest.
"Detengase aquí!"
The officer rode in the cab. The tail gate crashed down and the soldiers came spilling out of the back.

"Mira tus armas!"

They locked and loaded. Their worn Garand rifles had long ceased to be part of the G.I. armory. The olive drab uniforms they wore were faded, the helmets ill-fitting.

Their Sergeant, a burly grizzled veteran, came to attention.

"Los hombres estan listos, Capitan!"

The Captain cut a sharper figure, a pistol with ivory grips holstered at his hip. His moustaches were waxed and his eyes were keen, eager for glory and advancement.

One man bore a bulky radio on his back, the long antenna wafting. It crackled into life. Immediately, the Captain extended his hand and glared impatiently.

"Muevete, hombre!" the Sergeant bellowed. "Más rápido!"

The Captain snatched the handset.

"Are you in position, Captain…?"

The voice was heavily distorted by the airwaves; the officer saluted automatically.

"Si Señor! Estamos listos!"

The voice's obvious authority cut through the interference and atmospherics.

"Then get on with it!"

As did the threat looming behind it.

"And remember! I want them alive!"

They set out before dawn and marched all morning.

"Keep it up.…"

Now there was no complaining, just quiet determination. They knew this was for real.

"Not far.…"

Used to it by now, they bore the crushing humidity which became even more suffocating as the day moved past noon. They made light of the bulky back packs slung on their shoulders.

The bright blue track suits had been exchanged for tiger-striped camouflage, the white sneakers for combat boots. They obviously liked it; it put a swagger in their stride.

Cat kept shifting her position, taking point, then rear guard, on the flank. She hefted a 9 mm Uzi with a folding shoulder stock, her finger poised above the trigger.

She smiled.

Patience my dears.…

The dense jungle screened them from view. They were marching parallel to the fast flow of a broad river, close enough to hear the water churn and gurgle.

You're going to get all the action you could ever wish for!

Suddenly, Cat stopped. She raised a bent arm, her fist clenched. Folding her legs, she hunkered down till the dripping undergrowth came above her head.

In perfect synch, the others copied her, vanishing in an instant.

Creeping soundlessly, Cat led them towards the crumbling river bank. Sweat beading on their faces, they peered through the fringes of the undergrowth.

Uh huh!

Ahead of them, the river curved in a broad sweep. The shallow crook of the bend formed a crescent-shaped bay with a crusty discolored beach. Cleared to a stubble of stumps and scrub, the ground angled up from the beach to a low plateau.

On that shelf of bare earth and patches of scrappy grass, stood a sprawling mansion, a faded Colonial relic, a mere shadow of its former glory.

Scattered around it was an assortment of huts and out-buildings. Beyond, the land sloped upwards, containing the old house and its compound in a lushly overgrown green amphitheater.

Cat was observing through a pair of binoculars. She saw figures on the balconies, patrolling the grounds; watch towers armed by heavy machine guns.

Janey was lying close by. Cat handed the field glasses to her; Janey had a look and passed them down the line.

"This is it…!"

They called themselves "Simba", "The Lions".

"Dig it, mah bruthas…!"

Their midnight rendezvous was a drab apartment in a run-down block, one of a dwindling number still occupied in this neglected part of the City.

"It's goin' down!"

They wore the uniform: black leather over black turtle-necks, black pants, black shoes. Some wore black shades indoors. Their Afros were flags of defiance. The only permitted adornment was a tribal amulet or a pendant in the shape of a clenched fist.

There were guns on the table, guns perched on the threadbare sofa, stacked in the corner, on the sagging mattress in the bedroom. Under the kitchen counter, there was a cardboard box full to the brim with dynamite.

Their leader had exchanged his "slave name" for that of an African warrior. Standing at the head of the table, he unfurled long rolls of paper. Blueprints and floor plans that betrayed the secrets of a Federal Bank.

"We're gonna stick it to th' Man!"

"Everyone okay…?"

She didn't need to ask.

An intense electricity radiated from them. A thirst for revenge, revenge on a world that had mistreated them.

Yes, you channel that!

"Get ready!"

Delving into their back packs, her team armed itself variously. There were Ingram MAC-10 9 mm machine pistols and color-coded grenades. Sammy was fitting the sights to the extendable tube of a portable rocket launcher.

"Done!"

Sammy looked up and grinned. The others were focused, their eyes clear and bright, cradling the guns in their laps.

"Synchronize watches...."

The Uzi slung at her hip, Cat finished assembling the Remington M40A1 sniper's rifle and its long scope.

"Let's go!"

Across the roof of the shabby apartment block dashed men in another kind of black, M16s slung across their backs. They looked like beings from another planet, in night vision goggles and chemical masks.

The roof was festooned with bent TV aerials and the stalks of ventilators. The armed men knew exactly what they were looking for, singling out one ventilator and detaching its onion dome.

Two masked men hoisted a long grey cylinder. They directed the nozzle into the shaft of the ventilator and opened a valve.

Cat glanced at her watch.

Her team would be fanning out along the concave slope that girdled the rooftops. There they would watch and wait, at set intervals, concealed by the thick undergrowth.

Cat scanned the target area through the sniper scope, making subtle adjustments. She checked her watch again.

Two minutes....

"Okeh, this is how it's gonna—!"

The leader was stabbing with his finger, making indentations in the paper. Suddenly, he stepped back, his eyes bulging, clutching at his throat.

"AAA-AGHH...!"

His body spasmed and then jack-knifed as he toppled forward, crashing down on the table.

The others threw back their chairs and jumped to their feet. One pulled a pistol from a shoulder holster.

"UUUUGG-GG-GHHH...!"

The room was full of dead men.

Go...!

Janey lobbed the first grenade into the grounds of the compound. Lina's and Josie's were in the air as it exploded.

"Wooo...!"

They each had a sack full and dispensed them according to their color coding.

"…eeeeee…!"

The shrapnel bombs detonated with a searing flash and a smoking fountain of dirt, spraying scalding razors that sliced anyone within fifty feet to ribbons.

The ground ran with rivers of blood. In her sniper's roost, Cat was targeting the men in the watch towers, manning the 50 cal. machine guns. She did it quickly and clinically, all clean head shots.

Job done, she slung the long rifle, exchanging it for the Uzi. She began moving down the tangled slope.

Janey maintained the steady bombardment with the deadly fragmentation grenades. Josie and Lina had changed color and were tossing smoke bombs. The seething compound became choked by a purple-grey fog.

"Hey!" Lina showed her fangs. "Purple Haze!"

Now it was Sammy's turn. Crouched behind her, Cheryl slid the rocket with its bulbous head into the rear port of the launch tube and slapped her on the shoulder.

"Good to go!"

Cheryl ducked, covering her ears. Her lips warped in a mirthless grin, Sammy squeezed the trigger.

"Oh yeah!"

The recoil hardly budged her. There was a boom, a whoosh. With pinpoint accuracy, the missile took out a barracks block, as men were still spilling out of it, jamming on their helmets and fumbling with their rifles.

The structure erupted in a ball of flame, blown into matchwood. Men on fire staggered and fell, their arms pinwheeling. Others crawled screaming across the bloody ground, trailing mangled limbs.

"Go! Go! Go!"

Ecstatic, Cheryl slotted another rocket home. Sammy whooped and fired again.

Spread out right and left, Janey, Lina and Josie were all lobbing fragmentation grenades again, pulling pins and throwing them down into the smoke.

Caught up in the moment, Janey was pulling the pins with her teeth, just like in the movies.

Down below, blinded by the purple fog, a few survivors were blundering about, firing aimlessly. In their blind panic, they thought the smoke heralded a mass attack, that the grenades were mortar fire and the rockets heavy artillery.

And then the bombardment ceased.

Cat had reached the foot of the slope, the Uzi held ready at the hip. Flanking her, the team had left its positions and were coming down, converging to join her, cocking the bolts of the 9 mm Ingrams.

"Muévase más rápido!"

The Captain cursed vividly, wiping the sweat from his face with his sleeve.

"Más rápido!!"

As they filed past him, making heavy weather of the dense jungle, he gave the last man in line a swift kick up the backside.

"Te resultará difícil si no los encontramos!"

What he was really thinking was "It will go badly for me if we don't find them!"

They had the layout of the wrecked compound memorized and moved through the purple swiftly, thinning from thick fog to a fine mist.

"Watch it…!"

They advanced in loose formation, like trained infantry.

"On the right…!"

Anyone who got in their way was chopped down with a short burst of 9 mm. They stepped over the bodies as they lay twitching.

"Two on the left!"

Cat took them to the foot of the wide wooden steps that led up to the front doors of the mansion. They stood in the shadow of its faded grandeur.

Shrieking obscenities, a man burst out onto a long balcony above them, a pistol in his hand, firing wildly. A sharp retort from Cat's Uzi and he toppled over the rail, landing at her feet.

Cat made a sign and Janey, Lina and Josie stepped up, juggling the explosive metal eggs on their palms. Eyes blazing with fierce determination, they wound up like Major League pitchers.

"Strike one!"

"Strike two!"

"Strike three!"

They hit the dirt. Glass shattered as they hurled the grenades through the tall windows on either side of the doors. Laced with licks of flame, smoke billowed out over the top of them as they lay hugging the ground.

With debris still falling around them, they sprang to their feet. Cat led them in a rush up the steps. Her kick bent the doors inwards and then Sammy's shoulder charge blew them off their hinges.

The dim entrance hall was veiled by acrid smoke and tangled with wreckage and corpses, its tarnished chandeliers hanging askew. Shadowy figures staggered about.

"Watch out!"

Sammy's momentum had carried her some distance into the room; she lost her footing and slid face down on the floor. Blackened and in tatters, a man with blood dripping from his charred face was lurching towards her, brandishing a gun.

Cheryl fired from the hip. The back of his head exploded. She stood over the body with pure hate glowing in her blue eyes.

"Go…!"

They made their way swiftly and methodically down the twisting corridors and through the many rooms of the old house, pausing to roll grenades around corners and then fire bursts into the smoke. Anyone they didn't kill simply turned and ran away from them.

They arrived at a long passage barred by steel doors.

"Do your stuff, Biceps!" said Janey.

Sammy had the rocket launcher slung across her strong back.

"Give me room…!"

Retreating, they huddled around the corner. They heard the dull boom and then Sammy was diving on top of them as the missile impacted.

"Yikes!"

They peered around the corner, waiting for the smoke to thin. The entire corridor seemed to be warped and buckled outwards. The steel doors had fallen in.

"Go! Go…!"

Cat led them in a wild charge.

Smoke had infiltrated the laboratory; elaborate constructions of glass jars and rubber tubing had been toppled by the concussion and lay smashed, strewn all over the floor.

"Nein! Nein!" he was screaming, his hands to his face, staring in horror at the ruins of his dreams.

Cat recognized him at once.

"You look just like your photograph, Herr Doktor."

The team stood shoulder to shoulder staring at him, wondering how this insignificant little man could be the perpetrator of such enormous evil.

Walking towards him, Cat slapped a fresh magazine into the Uzi and cocked the bolt. The Doctor stumbled backwards, flapping his hands.

"Nein! Du kannst das nicht tun!" he babbled. "You cannot do this! I am valuable! I have knowledge! I have worked for your government…!"

Cat sneered contemptuously, her eyes chips of green ice.

"Oh yes, Doctor," she replied coldly. "I'm sure they were glad to have you…."

For a moment, hope flared in his wide eyes.

"But I can't let that happen again!"

She flicked the Uzi to semi-automatic and put a single shot in the middle of his forehead.

Josie stood over the body and spat in his dead face. In solidarity, the others took turns to follow her example. They looked at Cat.

She hawked and spat.

"If we had time, I'd piss on him!"

She looked around the wrecked laboratory.

"Okay, plant the charges. Let's burn this place to the ground!"

"Mira Capitán!" the sergeant exclaimed. "Es ese humo?"

The Captain tugged his field glasses from the case slung around his neck.

"Ahí, Capitán! Hacia el oeste!"

Yes, it was, a distant smudge in the bright sky, rising above the vast expanse of rolling tree tops.

He could hear it ringing in his ears: opportunity, salvation, the call to glory.

"Con rapidez!"

The shockwaves generated by the delayed explosions rippled the green canopy of the jungle. Far behind them, the old mansion was reduced to a charred heap of rubble.

"Wooo!"

Cat's squad was retracing its steps back along the path that ran parallel to the river bank.

Mission accomplished!

They were buzzing. They felt invulnerable, all-conquering. And that's when it all went wrong.

Their path ascended steeply and alongside them the ground fell away, vertically, to the fast-flowing water far below. They were triumphant, over-confident, careless.

Suddenly, the cliff edge crumbled and, with a yell, Josie vanished. They dashed across and craned to look over.

"Aw, shit…!"

She was clinging one-handed to the twisted cable of a gnarled tree root growing out of the cliff face.

"Hold on…!"

Lying on her stomach, Sammy had Janey by the ankles and was lowering her down. Lina spread herself with all her weight across Sammy's back to stop her sliding over the edge.

Suspended upside-down, Janey waved her arms.

"Reach up!" she shouted. "Give me your hand!"

Hanging by one hand, Josie glanced fearfully at the murky water rushing by below her dangling feet. Her legs thrashed as she was seized by a spasm of panic.

"Don't look down!" Cat yelled.

"Come on, Josie!" exhorted Cheryl. "You can do it!"

Janey reached down, extending her arms.

"Give me your hand, Princess," she said calmly.

Gulping, Josie summoned up all her strength and willpower and stretched up desperately with her free hand. Janey clamped onto her wrist.

"And the other one!"

Groaning with effort, sweat dripping from her contorted face, Sammy flexed her strong arms and was hoisting them slowly. Across her back, Lina pressed down hard.

As the human chain rose inch by inch, Cat and Cheryl lay down at the cliff's edge and reached over to help.

"C'mon…C'mon…!"

Locked to Josie's wrists, Janey was dragged slowly up onto the path on the lip of the vertical cliff. Straining, Cheryl had a double handful of her waistband; Cat was reaching out for Josie.

"UGH…!!!"

Josie's strained features rose into view, streaked with sweat and grime.

"Oh my God oh my God oh my God…!!!"

They were sprawled on the path, panting, exhausted, weak with relief.

"…oh my God, oh my God…!!!"

That's when the Captain's patrol blundered upon them.

"No te muevas!"

Their guns were on the ground, tossed aside as they dashed to Josie's rescue.

"Manos arriba!"

Only Cat reacted, diving and rolling for the Uzi. Coming up in a crouch, she let loose a burst that took down two of the soldiers.

Fumbling with the bolt, one of the soldiers lifted his rifle awkwardly and fired. He got lucky.

"AH!"

Cat twisted violently and went over the edge.

"No!"

Horrified, they watched her body fall limply, saw her splash into the swift current that carried her away.

"Oh no…!"

Frozen, they stood in stark disbelief, still searching the river as it flowed around a distant bend.

The soldiers were advancing. The Captain leered.

"Manos arriba!"

CHAPTER 13

GIRLS BEHIND BARS

"Más rápido!"

They were roped together loosely in single file, their wrists bound in front of them.

"Muévase más rápido!"

A soldier prodded Janey in the spine with the muzzle of his rifle.

"Don't do that again, motherfucker…!"

She gave him a look that froze him to the marrow.

They marched for hours in the stifling heat, winding their way through the humid jungle. Holding their heads high, they were careful not to stumble, determined not to show any sign of weakness.

The Captain walked up and down the line, gloating over each in turn. They steadfastly ignored him. They'd stood up to some of the toughest cops in the U.S. of A.; they weren't going to let these assholes get to them!

"Aaiii…Bonita…!"

A slab-faced soldier couldn't resist Lina's curves any longer. He lunged suddenly, grabbing for her.

"Fuck off, you dickless…!"

Lina clenched her bound fists and propelled them into his chest.

"UGH!!!"

His breath was jolted out of him, the ill-fitting helmet flying from his head.

Using the slack in the rope, Sammy jumped forward and head butted him in the face. With a yelp, he staggered and fell, his nose mashed to a bloody pulp.

As he rolled in the dirt, clutching his face, Cheryl calmly kicked him in the groin. He whined and curled into a fetal position.

Josie was over him, poised to stamp on his head. His comrades intercepted her, raising their rifle butts.

"Eso es suficiente!"

A pistol shot froze them. The Captain was aiming his pistol at the sky. He fired again for emphasis.

"No los queremos dañados!"

His thin lips curving in a vicious leer, the Captain approached Lina. Stroking his moustaches, he was undressing her with his eyes.

Lina was quivering from top to toe, her angry eyes sparking.

"Cool it…," Janey muttered.

The Captain flicked Lina's long hair with the barrel of his gun. He let it roam over her shoulder and down her arm. She stood rigid, staring past him.

"Mas tarde, pequena puta," the Captain hissed. "We have much time…!"

"Uuuuhh…hhhh…hhh…!"

The fast current swirled her, sucked her down and then spat her to the surface, gasping. It scraped her over jagged rocks, choking her with foam; it snagged her painfully on driftwood and then ripped her free again.

"AAAHH…HHHH…!"

The water hissed and churned, battering her. She was dazzled by blinding flashes of sky slashing through the rush of overhanging treetops; and was then sucked down into the dark depths again until her lungs were bursting.

"Uhh…uuhhh…uuuuhh…hhhhh…!"

After toying with her and tormenting her for an eternity, the river lost interest and deposited her on a narrow beach walled in by the jungle.

Her head throbbed with a dull pain and her vision was blurred. That lucky shot had creased her temple.

"Akkk…aaagghhh…gghhh…!"

Blinking, she vomited water. She pressed her hand to the side of her head, looked at her palm and saw blood.

Her ears were full of water. She shook her head and instantly regretted it.

"AH!"

The pain made her nauseous; she threw up again.

Oh…f-f-fuck…!

She heard something. Feebly, she scraped her wet hair back from her face and tried to push herself up. Her arms crumpled like paper.

"Oh…f-f-fuck…!"

Her vision flickered in and out of focus. She saw bare feet and strained to lift her head; it seemed to weigh a ton.

She reached as far as a pair of naked brown knees. And then the clouds closed around her and everything went black.

"Jeez!" Lina panted. "This is one way to lose weight!"

They were confined in a steel box sunken in the earth, roofed at ground level by heavy iron bars.

At the center of the baked dry prison yard, it caught the full blast of the sun at high noon. The sun seemed to hang there forever, right above them, unwilling to move.

"Awww, fuck…!"

The heat inside the box was suffocating. Their combat gear had been replaced by faded blue prison shirts and baggy pants, soaked with sweat. Sweat dripped from their faces, from the tips of their matted hair.

They leant on each other, breathing in salty sweat and rank body odor.

"Hey!" gasped Sammy. "I've hung out in some dives in L.A. that are worse than this!"

That raised a few weak grins. But not from Cheryl.

"I can't believe it!" she muttered sorrowfully. "Cat's dead!"

Janey squeezed her sagging shoulder.

"No, she isn't."

"How do you know?" asked Lina.

"We all saw it!" said Josie.

Janey frowned, her dark eyes determined.

"I know she's alive! I just know it!"

Shadows fell across them, silhouettes blotted out the sun.

The Captain was looking down on them through the bars, wafting his hand in front of his face as he wrinkled his nose, assailed by the smell.

"Well!" he snapped. "Do you feel like talking?"

As one, they flipped him the finger.

Drums.

A primeval heartbeat that seemed to come from the bowels of the earth. It enveloped her, deep and slow burning.

Cat groaned. Raw, inhuman sounds were ripped from the depths of her soul. Suddenly, there was a weird, high piping treble. The dizzy squall of the reeds cut shrilly through the demented pounding of the drums.

Naked, Cat screamed and writhed insanely. She was floating, wrapped in a roaring fire. It tossed her this way and that, bending and distending her body. A hideous pain blew up within her and burst from her gaping mouth in a howl of agony.

The drums battered her. The shriek of the pipes was a physical thing, flaying her skin. Figures loomed out of the red flames. Horrid gargoyles were capering, feathered demons. Her flesh on fire, Cat clutched and clawed at herself, screaming.

With a hop and a skip, the dancing devils departed. All at once, Cat was hovering in a ring of broad, brown faces, smiling women, her scalded flesh soothed by soft hands that stroked and fluttered, anointing her with scented oils.

The pipes were cooing like doves, the drums murmuring. Searing pain mellowed slowly to a delicious, exquisite aching. Wide-eyed, Cat twisted and arched her shining body. The skilled hands caressed and petted her, roamed over her, bold and uninhibited, exploring and invading her.

Agony and ecstasy. Cat moaned and undulated. Her whole body tingled warmly, rocked in a cradle of intoxicating perfumes.

Faster and faster. The hands and the flutes and the drums in concert, shimmering, then shuddering, an electricity that gripped and galvanized her, her body leaping, out of control.

The lip of a wooden cup dipped to let a thick syrup drip down upon her eager tongue. Cat sighed, as a warm numbness crept along her trembling limbs.

The boom of the drums rang hollow, the piping splintered into a brittle clash of echoes. Suddenly, Cat was falling, plummeting through red clouds, sucked into a whirling blackness.

By dusk, they were totally drained.

The steel retained its heat and they were still propped against each other, their heads drooping on each other's shoulders. They had barely enough energy left to whisper encouragement.

They started as a gate grated open in the barred roof above them.

"Ahora, putas…!"

The Captain had returned, flanked by a squad of burly prison guards.

"Have you changed your minds?"

They just stared at him. The Captain's thin lips curved into a cold smile.

"Sacalos de alli!"

A long ladder was lowered into the sweat box.

"Up…!"

They hesitated, doubting if their weak legs were up to the climb.

"Quickly!"

Frowning, Janey led the way up the ladder, the others followed slowly and stiffly. Sweat soaked the cheap stuff of their prison garb. The guards' eyes were glittering, licking their lips.

"Ass wipes…!" Lina muttered.

They stood swaying, gulping in great draughts of the milder evening air. Cheryl and Josie sagged, slumping to their knees.

Sneering, one of the guards seized them by the hair and hauled them upright. Cheryl shrieked and slapped him weakly; he laughed and twisted till she screamed again.

"Fucker…!"

Shouting hoarsely, Josie raked her fingernails down the guard's fat face. He bellowed and released his grip, drawing back his fist as Josie reeled, her vision blurring.

Janey summoned up all that she had left and punched the guard in the mouth. Spitting blood, he fell on his back.

Where she got it from she'd never know; suddenly Sammy was on him, straddling him, her thumbs hooked into his windpipe.

"AAAKKHH…HHH…!"

The other guards were booting Sammy in the ribs.

"UUGGHHH…!"

They had to do it several times before she finally let go and rolled off. She scrambled to her hands and knees, hair falling across her blazing eyes; felt the cold muzzle of the Captain's pistol pressed into the back of her neck.

"That's enough!"

Now all the guards had guns drawn. The gang formed into a line facing them, fists clenched, radiating fury and defiance.

The Captain was smiling again.

"You will find that you are not so tough," he gloated. "We have other, more extreme methods!"

Their expression didn't change. The Captain snapped his fingers at the guards.

"We will give you the night to think about it…!"

Her naked body sagged limply, splayed out between the posts.

"Uuuuuhhh…!"

Cat's skin glistened with oil, bronzed by the torchlight. Her golden hair was garlanded with exotic flowers.

They tightened the twisted fibers that bound her, spread eagled, until her limbs were strained.

"AAAAAHHH…HHH…!!!"

They heard screams.

"Aw shit!"

That night, they were confined in a dank and gloomy dungeon, chilled by contrast with the oven-like sweat box. Sustained by stale water and a thin gruel served in tin bowls, they sprawled side by side on dirty straw mats.

"Ugh!" grunted Lina, holding her nose.

The cell was fetid with the persistent odors of urine, excrement and vomit. A large metal bucket was their toilet. Dark stains on the stone floor looked a lot like blood.

Josie stirred the lumps in her watery stew.

"What the fuck is this junk?"

"Don't ask!" said Janey.

They were assailed by the screams again, rising in pitch and then trailing away.

"Oh fuck!" yelped Cheryl, covering her ears.

The screams went on and on – shrill, inhuman, nerve-drilling – curdled with pain.

Their wide eyes glowed in the semi-darkness.

"We've gotta get out of this place!" said Sammy.

The drums were throbbing behind her eyes. They were boiling her blood.

Stretched taut between the posts, her gleaming body was quivering. Torches sent out long tendrils of glowing red smoke that coiled around her. She jerked and screamed as though lashed by barbed wire.

Arching her body, Cat strained against the binding fibers till the posts creaked.

The drums beat her into submission. Dully, she watched a surreal apparition materialize from the luminous red veils, insubstantial, her vision fractured.

He was wizened and bent, his wrinkled skin coppery in the torchlight. His cadaverous features were part concealed by a mask fashioned from a human skull.

He was crowned by a tall crest made from the long tail feathers of a sacred bird. His loins were girdled by a belt of shriveled shrunken heads. Bangles and beads and strange amulets clanked on his wrists and ankles, draped his scrawny chest.

Capering and shuffling in short dancing steps, he approached her. The drums fell silent. He was chanting, a shrill repetitive mantra. Surrounding them, the villagers were on their knees, their chorus a deeper counterpoint.

Their Shaman was brandishing a flint dagger. He flourished it before Cat's glazed eyes. She moaned softly.

His incantation became staccato, his broken yellow teeth clashing. The tribespeople were groaning, ecstatic, rocking backwards and forwards on their knees.

With a flick of the razor-edged flint, the Shaman cut off two trailing inches of Cat's fair hair as it fell across her face. Crying out, she spasmed and shook her head wildly, her golden mane flailing as the garlands of flowers fell between her widespread feet.

Holding the bright tuft between thumb and forefinger as though it was something very precious, the Shaman brought it to a shallow bowl of smoldering incense, mounted on a crude wooden tripod. He let it flutter down into the wavering glow which flared up and vented a tall shower of sparks.

A great moan erupted all around. The drums thundered again.

Deep within the cave something mighty stirred. In the dark fathomless depths, a green glow expanded and the spectral mist was creeping out across the trembling ground.

It was past midnight when they all succumbed to the effects of the day's ordeal and slipped into a troubled sleep. The cell vibrated with the muffled moans and mutterings of their nightmares.

A rattle of keys and squeal of hinges stirred some of them but they only mumbled and rolled over.

"Mmmm…mmphh…hhhh…!"

A shadow draped Lina as she lay curled up on her side.

"Uh…wha…?"

Strong hands gripped her arms and lifted her; another was clamped over her mouth.

"Mmmm…hhhh…."

Groggy, convinced that she was still dreaming, she hardly resisted as they frog-marched her out of the cell.

The drums were demented. Long ripples surged through the tightly pressed gathering as it rocked on its knees with arms raised high.

The crawling green mist sent out feelers, probing, slithering like glowing snakes across the ground.

Cat's eyes were wide and terrified. Her shining body wanted to writhe and twist and tear itself free. Spread taut between the posts, all it could do was strain and quiver.

The Shaman was prancing, whirling. He wielded a long staff decorated with feathers and tinkling charms. With it he made elaborate passes in the air, creating whorls and swirls in the red smoke.

Cat shrieked in agony. Her body convulsed as though galvanized by an electric charge. Her limbs jerked against the ropes with such violence that her joints were almost dislocated.

The radiant green mist was tickling her toes.

The clouds in her brain were clearing, pierced by lightning flashes of alarm.

"Hey!" Lina shouted. "Where are you creeps taking me?"

She squirmed and planted her feet, the guards twisted her arms up behind her and half dragged, half carried her between them.

"Motherfuckers…!"

They forced her down a lengthy whitewashed corridor. She expected the door at the end of it to open onto a gruesome torture chamber.

"Ah, welcome, my dear…."

Instead, Lina was confronted by the Captain's well-appointed living quarters; carpets and polished furniture, bathed in a mellow lamplight.

"Come in and make yourself comfortable…."

He ordered the two guards to remain stationed outside the door.

"Por favor…."

He was out of uniform, resplendent in a monogrammed dressing gown.

Warily, Lina settled on a plush sofa. The Captain approached and sat beside her, a full wine glass in each hand.

"Uh, thanks…."

She drained it in a single gulp. The Captain smiled knowingly.

"I see that you are a young woman with healthy appetites."

Lina shrugged sullenly. His sharp eyes were devouring her, his mind forming vivid images of what lay beneath her threadbare prison garb.

"Ah, but of course, with a body like that!"

She stared at him stonily. The Captain stood and was pacing the room.

"I would hate to see such a body destroyed…."

He stopped, standing over her.

"You will talk, you know," he stated bluntly. "They all talk in the end."

Lina said nothing, staring straight ahead.

"And your friends," the Captain continued. "It can go very hard on them."

Lina gestured dismissively.

"Aw shit, I don't owe those bitches anything!"

The Captain looked interested.

"Oh yes?"

"I look after Number One!"

"Indeed…?"

"They got me into this mess. Fuck 'em!"

He sat down again beside her and put his hand on her knee.

"So, you will tell me everything," he said. "Who you are working for and how much they know?"

Lina shrugged again.

"Sure! Why not?"

She stood, facing him.

"But first…."

She was teasing the buttons of her drab top.

"You gotta do something for me!"

The Captain's eyes stood out on stalks. His jaw dropped. Drooling, he scrubbed his chin with the back of his sleeve.

"Hey!" said Sammy. "Where the fuck is Lina?"

Bewildered, their eyes scanned the cell anxiously.

"Oh shit!" groaned Josie. "I thought it was just a dream!"

She told them about the shadowy phantoms that had come and taken Lina away.

"What are we going to do?"

Janey frowned at her.

"Lina can look after herself," she growled. "Don't worry about her!"

She turned to Cheryl.

"Okay, babe, do your stuff!"

Cheryl nodded. Striding across the cell, she gripped the bars and rattled them. She was screaming.

"Let me outta here! I can't take anymore…!"

The others increased the volume by cat-calling and hurling abuse at her, calling her a coward and a traitor.

"I'll talk! I'll talk…!"

Lina spread herself across the bed.

"Well…?"

The Captain stared, disbelieving.

"Come on, I want it!"

Muttering foul obscenities, he ripped off the long dressing gown. Clad only in a pair of striped boxers, he threw himself upon her.

Groaning, he was mauling her feverishly. Lina laughed, her eyes wild.

"Fucker…!"

Fangs bared, she clamped her thighs around his rib cage.

"AAAAGGHH-GGHHH…!!!"

Clenching her teeth, Lina was crushing and grinding.

"UUUUGGHHH…!!!"

His mouth gaped, showing his tongue; his eyes bulged, the red veins in them bursting.

"AAAGGHH-GGHHH…!!!"

Outside the door, the guards looked at each other and shared a dirty grin.

"Esa pequeña puta le está dando un buen tiempo al Capitán!"

His face was turning purple.

"I…I c-c-c-can't b-breathe…!"

Lina squeezed harder, arching her back, putting her whole body into it.

"AAAIIIHHH…HHH!!!"

The Captain's ribs crackled and then crunched. Blood bubbled on his contorted lips.

"Ggghhh…hhh…"

His eyes rolled up in their sockets as his head drooped forwards.

Sweating, Lina maintained the pressure. Then she spread her thighs and kicked his sagging corpse off the bed.

"Motherfucker!"

In the small kitchen, she went through the cupboards and drawers.

"Hah!"

Lina crossed to the door and knocked. When the two guards opened it, she was standing there grinning saucily at them, one hand cocked on her hip.

"Hi, guys! Wanna join the party?"

She was wearing only the baggy shirt; most of the buttons were missing. Entranced, they stumbled into the room.

"Aw c'mon, don't be shy…!"

The bolder of the two lurched towards her.

"UH!"

Lina's right hand whipped out from behind her back. The long blade of a carving knife flashed, an arc of light.

Eyes popping, the guard clutched at his throat, blood spilling through his fingers. He staggered away across the room, his knees dissolved and toppled him onto the sofa.

Lina stepped nimbly around him and was bearing down on her next victim.

"C'mon, limp dick…!"

He fumbled with the flap of his holster; Lina drove the blade into his belly, twisting it and ripping across.

Scrabbling vainly to hold in his guts, the guard fell on his knees and swayed forwards onto his face.

Lina danced her bare feet away from the tide of blood. Quickly, she retrieved her prison pants and dressed herself. She paused to survey her handiwork.

"Yeah, Cat," she muttered grimly. "You trained us well."

There was a large ring of keys hooked on the disemboweled man's belt. Hah!"

She grabbed them and was out of the door.

They called themselves "The Dark Lords".

"We gonna fuck them Spick muthas up good!"

Afros weren't mean enough for them. They distinguished themselves by their shaven skulls. All wore mirror-lensed shades and black varsity jackets with blood red sleeves. Dipped in blood, that was them.

They waited on neutral ground, a disused asphalt basketball court surrounded by abandoned tenements gutted by vandalism and arson.

"An' here they come…!"

Their rivals had dubbed themselves, with grim irony, "The Saints" and their colors were studded black leather and denim. The emblem on their backs was an upside-down cross.

Bitter foes, they shared a rage at the world. And they were about to take it out on each other.

"Yo ready?"

"Holy fuck!"

Lina burst out laughing.

She returned bearing the keys in triumph; then just laughed again and tossed them away.

"Cocksucker…!"

Sammy sat on the guard's chest. Gripping him by the ears, she was smashing the back of his head on the stone floor, again and again, splatting in a sticky puddle.

Cheryl jerked her knee up into her man's groin. When he groaned and doubled up, she brought the edge of her hand down crisply on the back of his neck. She heard the crack and saw him crumple lifeless to the floor.

She stood over the body, looking at her hand, impressed.

"Wow…!"

Josie snapped a long leg up in a high balletic kick. Impacting on the guard's chin, it shattered his jaw. Spitting blood and teeth, he sprawled on his back. She came down with her knee on his throat, crushing his windpipe.

"NNNNNGGHHH…HHH…!!!"

Janey had her victim's head in a vice. Her lips drew back, baring her clenched teeth in a vicious snarl. Eyes blazing with hate, she flexed her shoulders and twisted. His head was wrenched sideways, his neck snapped.

"Woooo!"

They were she-wolves, standing over their prey, bloody, breathless and victorious.

Cheryl was flexing her fingers, rehearsing the death blow.

"Thanks Cat!"

Janey flung an arm around her shoulders.

"Yeah!" she panted. "Now let's go find her!"

"We ready!"

Spread across the open space, they were tooled up for the occasion with switchblades, cycle chains and bats spiked with nails. No guns, that was the agreement; otherwise, anything goes.

Poised to launch themselves at each other, a noise in the sky made them all look upwards.

"What the—!"

A helicopter was bearing down on them, skimming the rooftops of the empty tenements.

"It's the fuckin' Pigs!"

"No, man, it ain't got no Po-lice markin's!"

The chopper hovered low enough for them to detect white faces within the bubble canopy. Long grey cylinders were mounted on the landing skids.

"Wha' the mutha-fuck…!"

"Back off yo' muthas, get the fuck outta—!"

They began falling, one by one and then in twos and threes, until no one was left standing.

The helicopter hovered a moment longer and then rotated, rose and flew away, vanishing in the haze.

The glowing green mist enveloped her ankles….

"Aaaaahhh…."

….crept up her splayed calves….

"….uuuuhhh…hhh…."

….up to her knees….

In her fevered nightmare, Cat was writhing madly, consumed by green fire. The tight bonds confined her struggles to a convulsive shudder.

AAAAAAAHHHH…!!!

Moaning, the villagers shrank back from the expanding green cloud, concentric ripples radiating outwards through the densely packed mass.

While Cat screamed and the villagers groaned fearfully, the desiccated Shaman seemed immune to the green vapors, submerged to his waist, chanting, brandishing his mystical staff.

"Fuego!…Fuego…!"

The relentless pounding of the drums was penetrated by a sharper percussive sound, the staccato clatter of machine-gun fire.

The encampment was encircled by a glittering chain of muzzle flashes, bright stars sparking in the surrounding darkness, beyond the ruddy glow of the torches. The tribes people were falling like wheat cut down by the scythe.

"Ataque! Ataque…!"

In their mottled olive drab, the guerillas came in from all sides, spraying lead from the hip.

Screaming in terror, those that could made a dash for the dense jungle, scrambling over the fallen. The rest lay in twitching heaps, twisted and mangled.

"Cese el fuego…!"

The drums were silenced; the gunfire died away.

The creeping green mist drew back from the naked form spread eagled between the posts, receding quickly back towards the cave.

The wizened Shaman was crawling towards the posts on his hands and knees as the luminous mist retreated behind him.

Groaning, he strained to raise the weird staff and point it at his denied sacrifice. Shaking it feebly, he made the charms rattle. Blood spilling from his mouth, he was whispering hoarsely, an ancient spell.

With a moan, Cat's head rocked back and, for an instant, the guerilla leader thought he saw her wide eyes glow green. He dismissed it as a trick of the light and squeezed the trigger.

His narrow chest pulverized, the Shaman was slammed backwards, spasmed once or twice and lay dead. The guerilla leader looked down at the corpse contemptuously.

"Supersticiones tontas…!"

Then he remembered Cat.

"Libérala!"

They cut the binding fibers. As Cat slumped, moaning, they supported her gently, dazzled by her.

The guerilla leader was sporting a battered brown leather battledress jacket. He took it off and draped it around her. He cupped her chin in his hand and looked deep into her eyes.

"Foolish superstitions," he told her. "We will cure the people of that!"

Cat's vision was fuzzy. She was seeing in soft focus and with his long dark hair and beard his intensely handsome features looked even more Christ-like.

Oh my God…I've died and gone to heaven!

Loud detonations made her flinch. They had set charges and were demolishing the entrance to the cave. The guerilla leader put his arm around Cat's waist and let her lean on him.
"Vamonos!"

The sign said "ARSENAL" in faded letters that glimmered faintly in the darkness dappling the empty quadrangle.
"This must be it," whispered Janey.
They had exploited the random pools of shadow, avoiding detection by the sleepy sentries in the watch towers.
"Jeez!" muttered Lina. "This shithole is run worse than fucking Fairburn!"
The door had only one simple old padlock.
"Okay Muscles…," Janey stepped back to give Sammy room.
It was child's play; a quick twist and a jerk and the lock popped. They opened the door carefully, wary of rusty hinges. Sealing it behind them, they switched on the light.
"Oh yeah!"
The Armory was a long shed made of concrete blocks with a domed corrugated roof. In the dusty yellow light, they were rewarded by racks of rifles and sub machine-guns and stacks of metal ammunition boxes.
Cat had given them a trained eye. They ignored the obsolete bolt-action long arms and went straight for the automatic weapons, checking the specs on the boxes.
"Nine-millimeter Parabellum!"
Josie struck a cover model pose, the folding butt-stock on her cocked hip.
"Suits you," said Cheryl, with just a hint of envy.
Josie grinned.
"The ultimate fashion accessory," she stated boldly. "Every girl should have one!"
"Right on!" said Lina, slapping in a loaded magazine.
Janey shook her head; her bold grin lit up the room.
"Okay, let's go!"

It was always darkest just before the dawn.
"The girls…!"
They marveled at Cat's powers of recovery, as they paused to dress her, just like them, in battledress.
"My girls…!"
She was energized, driven, on a mission.
"I have to find them!"

The rebel leader was smiling as he put an M1 carbine in her hands.

"I know where they are," he assured her. "And that is where we are going."

A rosy dawn was creeping over the prison walls. The shadows were shrinking, threatening to expose them.

From within a dimmed barracks block, they could hear sounds of waking, saw a light flicker on, then another.

"Let's go!" hissed Janey.

They gripped their weapons tighter. In a bunch, they made their move.

Their target was a dilapidated concrete store-shed set against the main wall in a corner of the yard.

"Go, go…!"

The plan was to hoist and haul each other from its flat roof to the top of the wall and then swing down to freedom from there.

The odds were stacked against them.

"Fuck!"

It was the incompetence of the guards operating the searchlights in the watch towers.

"Aw...!"

Had the lights been efficient and consistent, they might have been able to time their movements and avoid them.

"….shit!"

Employed lazily and randomly, the searing beams had the unintended advantage of surprise.

"Look out!"

The would-be escapers were pinned against the long low frontage of the concrete store-shed, snared in a broad circle of sizzling white light.

A fast-firing machine-gun cut loose above them with a sound like tearing canvas. A strand of dusty plumes erupted at their feet.

"Inside!" Janey screamed.

Fickle fortune now switched sides and favored them; the gun had promptly jammed. They could hear the gunners cursing and hammering.

Sammy was already kicking in the wooden door, splitting it. Lina synchronized with her and it swung inwards.

Slamming it behind them, they hurled themselves into the dim interior, cluttered with stacks of discarded furniture, scraps, paint cans and tools. A pale glimmer filtered in through small grime-streaked windows.

They flinched and ducked as the machine-gun revived and glass shattered, spraying them with glittering shrapnel.

"Yike!"

"Holy shit!"

Janey lifted her machine-pistol above her head, thrust the muzzle through a gap in the smashed glass and squeezed off a burst.

They could hear shouting as men came piling out of the barracks, shirt-tails flapping, some in their underwear, cocking the bolts of their rifles.

Demolishing the surviving window panes with the telescopic butt stocks, Lina and Sammy let rip simultaneously, spitting fire.

As they drew fresh magazines from bags slung across their shoulders, Cheryl and Josie deputized for them. A spatter of rifle fire was drowned by the heavy machine-gun and they ducked down again.

Then silence as those inside and out wondered what to do next. The mixed bunch of soldiers and guards was distracted by the arrival of a faceless minor functionary, a civilian, panting, pale with shock.

"El Capitán está muerto!"

Left rudderless, the men hesitated. Inside, they all looked at Janey.

"What now?" asked Josie.

"We hold out!" Janey snapped.

"Till when?" said Cheryl.

"Till Cat comes!"

Sammy nodded. Lina looked skeptical. Janey's eyes burned into her.

"I know she's coming!

CHAPTER 14

VIVA LA REVOLUCIÓN!

The long column snaked along the jungle trail.

Oh Christ no!

Cat's blood froze.
She seized the rebel leader's arm.
"Listen…!"
He raised a clenched fist.
"Detener…!"
He nodded grimly.
"Yes, I hear it."
A distant popping of rifles was interrupted by crackles of automatic fire.
Cat had a tight grip on his sleeve.
"We have to get there – fast!"
Her eyes were desperate, pleading.
"Before it's too late!"
He gazed at her intensely.
"We will be there in less than an hour…."
His eyes flashed. He raised his fist again.
"Vámonos!"

"YOW!"
Janey yelled, blinded by a blast of concrete dust, her face peppered by a hot spray. She reeled backwards and fell. Cursing, she rocked on her back, covering her face with her hands.
"Cocksuckers…!"
Snarling, Lina emptied a full magazine through a smashed window.
"Die you mother —
" —fuckers!"
Spent brass tinkling at their feet, Josie and Cheryl took her place as she crouched down to reload.
"Shit!" Lina declared. "I've only got four mags left!"
Outside, their enemies had scattered for cover. They laid siege to the concrete shed, targeting the small windows, framing them with puffs of dust. The machine-gun in the tower had jammed again.
"Me too," Cheryl said breathlessly. "Four!"
Frowning, Josie shook her satchel.
"Three here!"
Kneeling over her, Sammy pulled Janey's hands apart. Her face was masked by blood.
"Oh fuck!" Janey wailed. I'm blind!"

Her eyes narrowing, Sammy tore off the sleeve of her flimsy prison shirt. "Hold still…!"

She used it to wipe Janey's face clean. Then sat back, grinning.

"Aw, it's nothing," Sammy laughed. "Just a few little bitty splinters!"

Blinking, embarrassed, Janey sat up. Scowling, she shrugged Sammy off as she tried to haul her to her feet.

"Okay, okay," she growled. "I can do it!"

Grinning broadly, Sammy slapped her on the back.

"Jeez!" Janey yelped, sitting down again.

Rifle bullets were impacting around the windows, propelling dust and chips of concrete into the room. A lucky shot came straight through and scarred the wall above and behind them. They ducked instinctively.

"Heck," scoffed Sammy. "These assholes can't shoot for shit!"

Taking a deep breath, Janey regained her dignity.

"Hey wait!"

Lina, mouthing obscenities, was poised to open fire again. The others were flanking her, slapping in fresh magazines.

"Short bursts!" Janey told them. "We gotta save ammo!"

The battery of telephones on El Presidente's desk were all ringing at once. Sweat dripping from his swarthy jowls, he struggled to juggle the receivers.

"Debes detenerlos antes de que lleguen a la capital!"

Panic glazed his bulging eyes.

"Lucharás hasta el último hombre!"

Slamming the receiver down, he clawed at his throat, popping the buttons of his high gold braided collar. Shoving back his gilded throne, he freed his paunch from the elevated desk and heaved himself to his feet.

His face was very dark, his eyes bulging. Sweat flowed down his face and stained the armpits of his sky-blue uniform. His chest felt constricted, his breathing labored. He felt twinges in his left arm.

"Idiotas!" he croaked. "Estoy rodeado de idiotas!"

In the watch tower, the faulty machine-gun stuttered into life again and then let rip.

"Aw shit…!"

The long burst stitched the window line, subjecting those inside to a blizzard of dust and splinters.

"Yow!"

Sat on the floor, they brushed themselves off, shaking debris from their hair. The machine-gunning ceased abruptly, replaced by the ongoing patter of rifle fire.

Josie peered glumly into her empty satchel. She gripped the gun cradled in her lap.

"This is my last magazine."

Their enemies were improving. Ragged volleys were coming through the windows, splatting on the back wall inside and dislodging chunks of discolored plaster.

Picking grit from her long hair, Lina stared grimly at Janey.

"Got any ideas?"

Janey opened her mouth but before she could speak a massive detonation made the floor beneath them shudder. The walls vibrated as strands of dust trickled down from the ceiling.

"What the fuck was that?" yelled Cheryl, jumping to her feet.

They could hear shouts, smaller explosions and the inconsistent rifle fire swamped by bursts of fully automatic.

Janey stood up. She was beaming.

"It's Cat!"

In a rumpled linen suit, the Colonel stormed down the plush carpeted corridors, lined with dignified oils and hunting trophies.

"Where is he?"

A uniformed flunkey tried to bar his way.

"El Presidente is seeing no one, Señor, he—!"

The Colonel grabbed him by the throat and slammed him into the wall.

"Get outta my way!"

He kicked open the gilded double doors of the Presidential Suite.

"Colonel! I—!"

In the bed chamber, El Presidente's frock-coated valet was packing his master's monogrammed luggage. The Colonel took him by the scruff of the neck and threw him out the door.

"What the hell do you think you're doing?" the Colonel bellowed.

Backing up hastily, El Presidente flapped his hands.

"It is over!" he babbled. "The rebels, they are marching on the capital!"

He sat on the four-poster bed and began sobbing, his face in his hands.

"All is lost!"

Enraged, the Colonel seized him by his tasseled epaulettes and jerked him to his feet.

"You stinking piece of trash!" he spat. "You'll damn well stay and fight!"

Eyes bugging, El Presidente shook his head violently.

"No! No! It is useless! I—!"

He gasped and clutched his left arm. His body spasmed, his face turning purple.

"Aaagghh…gghhh…!"

Foam flecked his writhing lips.

"….ggg-gg-ggghhhh…!"

His eyes rolled back, his legs sagged.

The Colonel released him and let his twitching body slump to the floor. He stared down at the dead dictator, sneering.

"Fuck it," he muttered. "We don't need you anymore…."

The charges reduced the prison gates to splinters that blew inwards like a hurricane.

"Ataque! Ataque…!"

The rebels surged into the yard.

At their leader's side, Cat jerked the M1 carbine to her shoulder and took out the machine-gun crew in the tower as they fed a fresh belt into the breach. One fell back out of sight, the other screamed all the way to the ground.

"No dispares! Nos rendimos!"

The fighting was over in minutes. Any desultory resistance was swiftly mown down. The survivors emerged from cover, throwing away their rifles and raising their hands.

Flushed with victory, the rebel leader slung his carbine and stood surveying the scene. He barked orders, gesturing towards the cell block. A squad separated, ran to it and shot the locks off the doors.

"Now," he pronounced. "We will free our people!"

Nearby, Cat was casting around anxiously – and then she heard a familiar voice.

"Hey Cat!" said Sammy. "We've been waiting for you!"

Tired and bedraggled but grinning through the grime, her team trooped out of their battered fortress.

Oh, you're wonderful!

They stood in a line, their arms draped across each other's shoulders, guns in hand. Cat slung her carbine and ran to them, her arms flung out wide. She enfolded them, trying to embrace them all at once.

"We thought we'd lost you!" gasped Cheryl, the breath squeezed out of her.

"We all did," admitted Josie. "All except Janey…."

"She said you'd come back for us!" exclaimed Lina, awestruck.

Cat clasped Janey's shoulders and drew her close. Janey's eyes were very deep and dark and wide.

"We held out all morning," she mumbled shyly.

Beaming, Cat stroked Janey's smudged cheek and plucked a speck of concrete from her hair, powdered with dust.

"You're so special," she whispered.

Cat laughed and clapped her hands.

"You guys are something else! I love you!"

They were distracted by sounds of activity in the prison yard. The cell block was disgorging pale emaciated figures in shabby prison garb, men and women of all ages. Some were too weak to walk, supported tenderly by the young guerilla fighters.

"Muévase más rápido!"

A very different group was being herded into the open. Uniformed prison guards, junior officers and non-coms, officials in civilian clothes, united by the fear in their eyes.

"Mas rapido, escoria!"

They were being prodded at gunpoint, made to stand in a line facing the prison wall.

Oh hell…!

The rebel leader was martialing a firing squad. As the full horror of their situation struck them, the men facing the wall began to quake, some sobbed, others prayed.

"Listo…!"

There was the sound of weapons cocking. Several fell to their knees, moaning.

Cat's team showed mixed emotions. Sammy and Lina stood and watched, stone-faced, unflinching. Josie was blanking it again, in that secret place inside her head. Cheryl looked down, her eyes fixed on the ground.

"Apunta…!"

Cat stood rigid with her fists clenched at her sides, helpless.

I can't stop this!

"Hey!" Janey shouted. "Wait a minute!"

She strode up to the rebel leader, standing with his arm raised.

"I've got a better idea!"

They heaved open the hatch in the bars roofing the iron sweat box. There was barely enough room for all their captives, wedged together tightly, scarcely able to breathe.

The rebels stood back and let Sammy and Lina slam the barred hatch shut. They all wanted to participate, so Josie ceremoniously handed Cheryl the padlock and watched as she snapped it shut.

Janey stood looking down through the bars, at all the frightened eyes glaring up at her. Their stark terror was reflected as a vicious gleam in her eyes.

"If you shitheads are real lucky," she snarled. "Somebody might come by in a month or two!"

He sighed contentedly, a low rumble deep in his broad chest.

A finger, encrusted with gold and diamonds, ran down the columns of figures that filled the fat leather bound ledger; one that the Tax Man didn't know about.

"Lookin' good…!"

Mr Big leant back in his padded black leather throne. He closed his eyes, day-dreaming of empires.

His reveries were interrupted by a knock on the door. He grunted, irritated.

"Yo!" he snapped. "What is it!"

Instinctively, his hand crept beneath the jacket of his lime green silk suit, tickling the pearl grips of a gold-plated .45 automatic. His left hand folded round the ruby-eyed silver skull crowning the scepter that doubled as a sword stick.

One of his minions stuck his head around the door, topped by a purple crushed velvet fedora.

"Three weird-lookin' honkeys sayin' they here t'seeya...."

Glowering, Mr Big gestured with the ghoulish cane.

"Muthafuck!" he growled. "Show 'em in!"

His visitors scoped the gleaming stripped pine and all mod cons of Mr Big's H.Q., secluded behind the Disco dance floor of the JOOK JOINT, unlit and empty in the middle of the day.

"You've done well for yourself...."

The speaker was stocky, in vigorous middle age, his iron-grey hair cropped close to his skull. His two subordinates were younger, taller and broader, with fair hair trimmed to a flat-top. All wore impenetrable shades, even indoors, and black suits and ties.

"Yeah," Mr Big made conversation reluctantly. "Bizniss is good...."

He rose from his ebonized desk, his awesome bulk seeming to fill the room. With deliberate slowness, he moved across the office and approached an embroidered African panorama that spanned the far wall; a pride of lions commanding a water hole.

His broad palm stroked the richly textured surface; it was obvious who the mighty maned male was meant to be.

The grey-haired man cleared his throat impatiently. Mr Big turned and frowned at him.

"I ain't happy," he rumbled. "Havin' this stuff here in mah place!"

The grey-haired man pursed his thin lips, adjusting the knot of his black tie.

"You're being well rewarded for it," he replied icily. "We supply you with your stock in trade, we suppress the competition and turn a blind eye to your activities. We...."

"Okeh! Okeh!" Mr Big raised his huge hands. "I get the picture!"

He delved behind the hanging tapestry. There was a click, a soft whirring and the heavy cloth rose, rolling up smoothly.

The men in black were stepping forward as a broad polished steel door was exposed.

"Thank you...."

Frowning, Mr Big stood aside. There was a small key pad mounted on the riveted door frame. The grey-haired man hesitated.

"Sure! Sure!"

Muttering, Mr Big turned his back. The grey-haired man tapped in a secret code. The sliding door whispered open. A flight of wide concrete steps was revealed, descending into darkness.

The grey-haired man eyed Mr Big sternly.

"Wait here!"

He began to go down, his colleagues following. Below them, light expanded automatically. The door closed behind them.

Dusk was slowly purpling.

"Comienza a correr...!"

With their superiors entombed in the sweat box, the humble foot soldiers were rudely evicted through the demolished gates, to take their chances in the jungle.

They ran for it, scattering, fearful of a bullet in the back. Manning the walls, the rebels jeered them.

"Corre, perros! Corran por sus vidas!"

The prison was being looted thoroughly. The Armory was emptied of ammunition and automatic weapons; the obsolete rifles were ignored.

"What do you think?" asked Josie, twirling like a catwalk model.

Cat smiled.

"Very glamorous."

The team had discarded their hated prison uniforms and were decked out as guerilla fighters in mottled olive drab, machine-pistols slung on their shoulders.

Lina was unbuttoning, airing her cleavage.

"Aw, c'mon!" Cheryl rolled her eyes.

"If ya got it," Lina smirked. "Flaunt it!"

She was already attracting lingering looks from male admirers.

"Ooooh!" she radiated encouragement. "Some of these guys are hot!"

Josie flicked out at her.

"Hey Jugs!" she protested. "Leave some for me!"

Uh oh!

Janey and Sammy had gone back to stand by the caged roof of the sweat box.

That's not good...."

Cat left Lina and Josie to take their pick of would-be suitors. Flashing a dark look at her flirtatious companions, Cheryl went with her.

"Hey...?"

Janey and Sammy stood a little way back from the bars. They could hear the groaning and gasping within. Their faces were inscrutable, giving nothing away.

Cat put her arms around them.

"Come on," she murmured. "Come away...."

It all caught up with Janey. Her eyes welled up as her face began to crumple. Cheryl jumped forward and hugged her fiercely. Sammy ruffled her black hair.

As they walked away, they became aware that they were being closely watched by several young women in battledress.

"It looks like you have a fan club," Cat chuckled.

The young women smiled shyly, hopefully, their eyes questioning. When Janey and Sammy hesitated, Cat placed her palms between their shoulder blades and gave them a gentle push.

"Go on," she insisted. "If Lina and Josie can have some fun then so can you."

Cheryl was hanging back. Cat inclined her head, smiling at her quizzically.

"Well…?"

The young women were communicating with Janey and Sammy by expression and body language.

"Aw, hell…!"

Cheryl laughed and trotted away to join them. Grinning, Sammy drew her into the fold.

As the cheerful group set off to find some privacy, Cheryl turned and looked back.

"What about you?"

Cat gleamed saucily.

"Oh, I think somebody might have plans for me!"

That night, Cat and the rebel leader made love in the Captain's bed.

He treated her as though she was a marvelous toy. He would be gentle and then surprise her, sometimes abruptly, sometimes slow and with exquisite cruelty.

He would take her to the brink and then pause and leave her seething and imploring, demanding, moaning obscenely. He would watch her for a little while and then start again.

After an eternity of agony and ecstasy, he brought matters to a shattering conclusion, her cries of release drowning his animal grunts.

They lay side by side, bathed in sweat, chests heaving.

He fell asleep immediately. Cat lay staring at the ceiling. She looked across at his hawk-like profile.

Oh man, there's a mean streak in you!

The terminal building was seething, clamoring, bursting at the seams.

Desperation in their strained faces, men, women and entire families were barging and shoving, scrambling over each other, abandoning their luggage in heaps, competing to bribe their way onto a plane going anywhere.

"Get outta the way…!"

The Colonel's physical presence and the ready violence in his eyes cleared a path for him through the heaving mass. Altercations and fist fights were breaking out all around but no one dared challenge him.

To make his point, the Colonel punched an unfortunate who blundered into him, pole-axing him and laying him flat.

"Asshole!"

Out on the tarmac, a gargantuan four-engine transport was loading, a horde of uniformed officers and civilian officials jostling to get up the ramp, their wailing wives and squalling children in tow.

The Colonel shouldered his way through and mounted the ramp. A burly National Air Force crewman barred his path.

"No, Señor …!"

He put one hand on the Colonel's chest; he had a pistol in the other.

"This flight is for government personnel only!"

Snarling, the Colonel drew a .45 from under his jacket. He rammed the muzzle into the crewman's mouth.

"Oh yeah? Says who!"

The crewman spat blood and broken teeth. The Colonel tossed him off the ramp.

Inside the crowded cavernous hold, the Colonel's gun cleared a route for him all the way to the cockpit. He kicked in the metal door and put the muzzle to the back of the pilot's neck.

"Get this crate off the ground – now!"

At the first push, the regime had collapsed like a house of cards. Any token resistance soon melted away.

"Viva la Revolución …!"

When the rebels entered the capital Cat rode at the head of the procession, standing in a captured Jeep at the side of their proud leader.

This is incredible!

The streets were lined with cheering crowds. Women threw flowers, laughing children ran alongside the slow-moving column of vehicles.

"Oh wow!" Josie gasped.

"This is so cool!" Lina exclaimed, plucking a red rose out of the air.

The team rode in an open truck with their fellow fighters. The guerillas were waving and competing to catch the flowers, giving the clenched fist salute, the V-for-Victory.

Cheryl was amazed. Janey looked stunned. Laughing, Sammy wrapped them in her strong arms.

"Lap it up, you guys, we're heroes!"

As night fell, the mood changed. Under cover of darkness, the revenge killings began, inflicted on those who had lacked sufficient status to escape, the petty officials and informers.

While his troops trashed the Presidential Palace, the rebel leader made his headquarters in what passed for the old capital's best hotel.

"The people speak…!"

Beside him at the window of his suite, Cat saw bodies dangling from lamp-posts in the avenue below. He saw the look on her face and put a firm hand on her shoulder.

"We must harden our hearts," he told her. "In the interests of justice."

I don't like this brand of justice!

She said nothing and just turned and left.

Crushed by disillusionment, Cat wandered into Janey's room. Janey turned away from the window, her face grim.

"Meet the new Boss," she said. "Same as the old Boss!"

Cat nodded sadly.

"Today's heroic freedom fighter," she replied. "Is tomorrow's ruthless dictator."

She smiled wearily.

"Get a good night's sleep. We're out of here in the morning."

Cat had a strange dream.

She dreamt that she was a powerful animal, a beast of prey, stalking through the jungle beneath a blazing green Moon.

All was green and glowing. Her eyes glowed. She could see in the dark, as she weaved her way soundlessly through the undergrowth and tall trees.

She couldn't see her prey although she knew that it was human. She could smell fear. She could smell blood. It excited her.

The radiant green foliage parted and there was a vague form running ahead of her, a silhouette, a shadow.

It stopped and turned towards her. It had no face.

A jewel in the cultural crown of the glittering City by the Bay, the Museum of Anthropology rejoiced in its resemblance to a Mayan temple. Encrusted with fantastical carvings, it was a towering, stepped pyramid of honey colored stone.

Lord of the long Gallery of the Ancient Americas was a gleaming black obsidian idol, a terrifying demon, veined with glistening crystal.

Ten feet tall, it had the head of a grotesquely stylized jaguar, the body and talons of a giant condor with feathered wings outspread, the scaly tail of a giant lizard. In its fearsome claws, it impaled the limp body of a man and was gnawing off the head with its hooked beak.

"All quiet…?"

"All quiet."

At midnight, the Museum was dimmed and silent, bathed in a subdued blue night light. The only sound was that of the regular foot patrols, men in brown uniforms and peaked caps, wearing security company badges.

They made leisurely circuits in pairs, spread out at set intervals. Bored and complacent, they talked baseball, beer and women, putting the world to rights.

Their route took them to the long shadow of the grim black idol. It always made them feel uneasy.

"Jeez! That thing gives me the creeps!"

"Yeah, ugly mother ain't he?"

As they turned to move on, one of the security guards started, cursing.

"What the hell…?"

His colleague looked around nervously. He saw nothing out of place.

"What? What're you talking about?"

The other man's face was shiny with sweat, pale in the ghostly half-light.

"The eyes!" he gasped. "Did you see its eyes?"

Cat and her team were sped away from a private airstrip. They were enclosed in an unmarked grey personnel carrier driven by fit young women armed with M16s.

After a long flight, interrupted by several brief stop-overs that saw them hustled from plane to plane, Cat's charges were all dozing, some snoring softly.

Cat smiled to herself.

Poor babies! I really put you through it!

Suddenly, in a split second, she was somewhere else.

She was invisible; she could see and not be seen. She was running down a maze of shadowy subterranean corridors, crowded with grey faceless figures that seemed to melt and pass right through her.

"Mmmm…wha—?"

Wedged between Sammy and Janey, their sleepy heads resting on her shoulders, Cheryl was awake.

Cat was back.

"What is it?" she asked.

Cheryl's pale brow furrowed.

"Uh…oh, nothing, I just thought I saw…."

Sitting opposite her, Cat leant forward, her body language questioning. Cheryl hesitated.

"Uh…I thought I saw your eyes glow bright green!"

I thought I saw something too!

Cheryl yawned and shrugged, making Janey and Sammy stir and mumble.

"I was imagining things," she decided. "Must be jet lag."

Further down, Josie grumbled.

"Hey, pipe down!" Lina muttered. "Some of us are trying to get some sleep!"

By the time the Colonel was back in the U.S.A. he was in a foul mood.

Fuck 'em! They could damn well come to him!

He waited impatiently at the secret air base, the hub of "Black Ops". It gave him time to get back into dress uniform, dressed to impress, with the rows of hard-won ribbons on his chest.

"Goddamn it…!"

He practically kicked the door down, bursting in on them. Sat around a long table, they jumped in their seats. Grey-faced men in suits that denoted their seniority, stern men in high-ranking uniform.

His face dark with fury, the Colonel slammed his fist on the head of the table. He wanted to slam their heads together.

"This whole project has been one long fuck-up!" he raged. "Your goddamn shit pile of nigger pimps and pushers, tin-pot comic opera banana republic dictators and mad scientists!"

He pounded the table again, making their coffee cups jump in the air.

"All brought down," he bellowed. "By some crazy female and a gang of juvenile delinquents!"

A two-star general stood up abruptly.

"That's enough, Colonel!" he snapped. "Remember who you're speaking to! You work for us, you know!"

The Colonel had boiled over. He took a deep breath, his broad shoulders rising and falling.

"Yeah," he growled. "And sometimes I wonder why I bother!"

One of the men in suits cleared his throat nervously.

"It's not all bad news, Colonel," he ventured. "We've made a great deal of progress...."

The pin-striped man next to him piped up.

"Yes indeed," he stated. "We have been able to achieve far greater selectivity in our test runs...."

A third chimed in.

"And the Doctor's formula has enabled us to increase the stockpiles we have stored over here."

Breathing hard, the Colonel sat down heavily.

"Okay, okay," he conceded. "But now we have to escalate the program!"

He paused, his eyes narrowing to slits of fire.

"And I'm going to exterminate those little bitches and their goddamn den mother...!"

CHAPTER 15

THE CURSE

"Are you okay…?"
Cat seemed distracted.

No, I'm not okay!

"Oh…yeah…sure…just not been getting enough sleep lately…."
They had been provided with grey one-piece jump suits. Selena scanned their faces; pale and tired, their eyes full of chaotic images and memories.
"Alright then…."
She had the contents of an open box file spread across her desk. Aiko stood nearby, neat and efficient in her regulation pale blue blouse and darker blue mini-skirt.
"It all fits," Selena began. "They're getting more ambitious…."
She glanced at Aiko, who continued for her.
"Yes, and whoever's behind this has clearly adopted the Nazi plan to target potential threats and those they regard as undesirables…."
Selena retook the baton.
"And it's carried on even after you destroyed the source and wasted the Doctor. They must have other means of production somewhere and stockpiles here in the U.S.A."
Her young guests looked discouraged. Selena rose and came out from behind the desk. Smiling, she walked along the line.
"You guys did an awesome job!"
Color warmed their cheeks, their eyes mellowed.
"You were right about them, Cat," said Aiko.
Cat seemed far away again. She jerked herself back and smiled faintly.
"Yes…yes…they're amazing….!"
Selena clapped her hands, bringing the meeting to a close.
"Okay, our intelligence resources are working on it," she stated. "When we have more to go on you'll be back in action!"
Aiko ushered them cheerily to the door. Cat hung back.
"I'll be with you in a minute…."
Approaching Selena, she lowered her voice.
"Can I have a word….?"

They waited in a bright ante-chamber. As the minutes ticked by, they began to look worried.
Cheryl cleared her throat nervously.
"Cat's not right…."
Janey sat hunched beside her, looking down at her feet. She nodded.

"I know…."

Time passed. They sat in silence, staring at the floor. The door opened.
"Hey, guys…."
Cat came in to join them. They didn't like what they saw. She looked grey and weary; the golden glow had gone out of her.
"Listen," she told them. "I'm going to leave you for a little while…."
They looked dismayed.
"Don't worry," Cat smiled softly. "I'm not going far."
Deep concern clouded Sammy's face. Cat bent and squeezed her hand.
"I'm going to stay at my beach house," she explained. "I just need some time by myself near the ocean."
They weren't reassured.
"For how long?" Cheryl asked sulkily.
Cat cupped her smooth cheek in her hand.
"Not long…."
She surveyed them, raising a smile.
"Anyway, you guys will be busy," she declared. "When you've had some rest, Aiko is going to be refining your skills."
They looked unhappy but resigned. As they trooped out to board a waiting personnel carrier, Janey dawdled, plucking Cat's sleeve.
"You want some company tonight?" she asked. "Might help you sleep."
Sighing, Cat hugged her.
"That's so sweet of you," she murmured. "But I'll be heading off now."
Janey was disappointed.
"We don't like being without you."
Cat took her hands.
"You'll do fine without me," she insisted. "And I'll be back soon."
The transport was parked in the well of a deep elevator shaft. The others were boarding.
"First, you'll have a thorough check-up," Cat was saying. "You've all been through hell."
"We don't need a check-up," Janey blurted. "We need you!"
Tears were trickling down Cat's cheeks.
"Please understand," she whispered. "I need to be alone for just a little while!"
Janey hung her head; when she looked up her dark eyes were smoldering.
"We'll miss you."
Gently, Janey reached out and plucked a tear drop from Cat's cheek, balancing it on her finger tip.
"A keepsake," she said. "Till you come back."

"Did you see it?" asked Selena.
Aiko looked puzzled.
"See what?"
Selena pursed her lips thoughtfully.

"I'm not sure...something...."
"Like what?"
"In Cat's eyes!"

The modest beach house stood on stilts, back from where the tide rolled onto the sandy shore, up against a rust-colored cliff fringed by tall grasses.
"We're home, baby...."
Cat eased off and let the red Olds roll smoothly.
The way to the garage was under the house, between its lofty pillars. Steel doors were set into the wall of the cliff. Activated by an invisible beam, they gaped open soundlessly.
"Hi, children...."
A yellow T-top Corvette ZL-1, its swift shark-like contours emphasized by tapering black racing stripes. In their chrome sheathing, gleaming side exhausts proclaimed extravagant power.
"I've missed you!"
The Chevy Chevelle SS 454 was midnight blue with white stripes streaking along the hood; basic black inside with few frills and trimmings. A brute; a battering ram.

Home sweet home...!

Inside, the beach house was kept simple, woven mats on a bare wooden floor, a few large cushions thrown down casually.
Beaded curtains screened a small, functional galley and a separate bedroom bare except for a tall wardrobe and a Japanese-style mattress on the floor.
Posters on the walls advertised bygone jazz festivals. A portable TV stood on a stool in the corner. The telephone was on the floor.
Going straight to the bedroom, Cat crossed to the tall wardrobe. She opened the doors and stepped inside.
The room behind the wardrobe was a polished steel strongbox. Neon strip lights lit automatically as she entered, her movements made jangling reflections.
Racked securely on the wall, a customized carbine, fitted with a sniper scope; a Skorpion machine-pistol; a Remington pump shotgun with folding skeleton butt; and a government-issue M16.
Cat checked the steel shelves stacked with cartons of ammunition, the wooden boxes stenciled with specs that denoted smoke and gas and fragmentation grenades. She admired a portable rocket launcher and its finned projectiles.
She arrived at a steel cabinet mounted on the far wall and opened it, twiddling the combination lock briskly.
Smith & Wesson .357 Magnum; .45 Colt automatic; 9 mm Beretta; a chromed Walther PPK, with pearl grips.

Hello, old friends!

The subterranean gymnasium doubled as a basketball court. It was bright and gleaming, state-of-the-art.

"Oh hell…," muttered Cheryl.

"Never thought Hell was going to look like this!" said Josie out of the side of her mouth.

They sat on the mats in their singlets, gym shorts and sneakers. Their faces and bare limbs were shining, their shoulders heaving as they caught their breath.

Looking lean and athletic in a pale blue track suit, Aiko had hardly broken sweat.

"What was that?"

Josie gulped.

"Nothing…nothing Miss…er…."

"Rarin' t'go!" Cheryl panted, rolling her eyes.

Aiko flashed an evil grin.

"Glad to hear it," she informed them. "Thanks to Cat, you've mastered the basics, but you still have a lot to learn!"

A narrow balcony ran all along the front of the beach house. As the sun set, Cat was standing there, gazing out at the sea.

She wore a suede halter top with beaded fringes and faded denim cut-offs secured low and snug on her hips; her feet were bare.

Expertly, she manufactured a joint, just a small one, a mild one. The sun was sinking slowly into the sea and the sand was like molten gold, the red cliffs glowing.

The last searing sliver of the sun vanished below the horizon. The dark tide rolled in. Sighing, Cat turned and went inside.

A tangle of cables powered her sole luxury, an expensive hi-fi and its tall twin speakers, spread wide apart in opposite corners of the main room. Mellow funk oozed from them, Marvin's voice like spooned honey.

Oh yeah man, heal me…!

With the joint in her hand, Cat came dancing in from the balcony, making her hips swing slowly from side to side. She hip-swayed around the room, smiling dreamily as she surfed on the mats, sliding on the polished floor.

"That was the basics!?!!" Lina groaned.

Making a loud complaining sound, Janey slumped, lying prostrate, arms splayed out, the picture of martyrdom.

Sammy jumped to her feet, grinning wolfishly.

"Bring it on!"

Screams shredded the night.

He dragged her by the hair into the alley.

"Bitch!" he snarled viciously. Yo' bin holdin' out on me!"

Her shrill protestations were choked off cruelly as he clamped his hand on her throat.

"Lessee what we got here…!"

His other hand was rooting roughly in her ample cleavage, making her squeal and squirm, pinned against the slime-streaked wall.

"Ah-huh!"

He yanked out a crackling wad of bank notes.

"Yo' lyin' ho'!"

Stuffing the cash into his hip pocket, he back-handed her savagely across the mouth. She reeled, blood spilling from her lips.

"I'll give yo somethin' so yo remember not t' cheat me agin!"

The blade of a cut-throat razor flashed in the gloom. The hooker cringed, her knees giving way.

"No, baby, no!" she wailed. "I won't do it again, I swear…!"

He drew back the razor.

"Too late, bitch, yo' gonna—!"

A guttural sound rumbled behind them, swelling to fill the dim alleyway. A deep growl escalated to a deafening roar, crashing down upon them.

"Wha' the—!"

Slanting eyes, huge and yellow and glowing. Red in tooth and claw, snarling and slavering.

Shrieking, the hooker slid down the wall.

The pimp pulled a gun. He got off one wild shot and then was babbling, screaming as he was ripped apart, disemboweled and dismembered, his head torn from his shoulders.

Splattered in blood and shreds of flesh, the hooker moaned and fainted.

Blood streamed down the walls of the narrow alley. The roaring diminished to a dark rumble; claws retracted as furred feet padded away silently.

Just before dawn, a strange vehicle drew up quietly and parked in the shadows at the rear of the JOOK JOINT.

Long and tall, the tanker was greyly anonymous, its rear end encrusted with dials and tubing.

The four-man crew was shrouded in chemical suits and goggled masks with long snouts that hissed with every breath. They moved with speed and precision, clamping thick hoses to sockets revealed by a metal hatch in the ground.

Red needles traversed the gauges. The hoses were detached and retracted automatically. Cab doors slammed shut.

Deserted roads took the tanker to the eroded borders of the city, a wasteland of rubble and demolition.

"It's here – let's go!"

A trio of insect-like helicopters was lined up on a smoothed rectangle.

"Go!"

Hoses were unrolled from the rear of the tall tanker and stretched to connect with canisters mounted on the long tail booms of the choppers.

Zipped into a flight suit, through tinted lenses, the Colonel was observing every detail.

"This time," he told the pilots. "I want to see it for myself!"

"Nice try!" said Aiko.

Janey got up gingerly, rubbing her backside.

"Owww…!"

She shot a resentful glare at Aiko, who just grinned at her. The others looked apprehensive; no one wanted to be next, not even Sammy.

Aiko was looking at Lina.

"Could you take Cat?" Lina asked bluntly.

Aiko's brow furrowed.

"I might be more skillful," she suggested. "But Cat would go on fighting till she was dead."

She beckoned Lina towards her.

"That's the trick," Aiko smiled. "You have to be ready to die!"

"For the last time," Detective Wilson was exasperated. "What did you see?"

The hooker was in the hot seat, flanked by two massive, menacing patrolmen. Although Detective Wilson was paunchy and half their size, he exuded power. Menace glittered in his piggy eyes.

The hooker just mumbled through her bruised lips and shook her head, her wide eyes swollen with fear and disbelief. Dried blood spotted her heaving cleavage.

"Aw, c'mon, Mona," said Detective Keegan.

Tall and lean and greying, he suited the role of "good cop". He leant over her, smiling, encouraging.

"We know you couldn't have torn the bastard apart like that.…"

"Bad cop" to the core, Wilson growled and shoved his partner out of the way. He gripped the frightened hooker by the wrists, pinning them to the arms of the chair.

"What did you see?" he barked. "You must have seen something!"

Her teeth chattered.

"Eyes…!"

"What?"

"Eyes!"

"Whaddaya mean eyes?"

"Eyes!" she screamed. "That's all I saw, Mistah – eyes!"

She was strung out, desperate. Her breath steamed the glass panes of the lonely phone box.

"Ohhh…!"

No one answered her frantic calls.

"Ohhh…please…!"

It was Friday night and everyone was out celebrating.

"Pleeeeze…!"

She was barely fifteen, pert and budding in a silver glitter tube top and skin tight red satin leggings.

"Awwww…shit…!"

Sobbing, she banged the receiver down again and again.

"Shit! Shit! Shit…!"

She didn't look pretty tonight. Her pale face was haggard, her scarlet lipstick smeared. Panda eyes streaking down her cheeks, her long blonde hair was matted and rat-tailed.

She stumbled away from the phone box, leaving the receiver dangling. The deserted street was menaced by forbidding dark expanses of wasteland on one side and a fenced-off garbage dump and incinerator on the other.

She stopped and searched hopefully in both directions.

"Hey…!"

Miraculously, she saw headlights. Waving her arms, she staggered into the middle of the road.

"Hey…!"

The car was big and expensive. It slowed, rolled a little way and then stopped. The girl stumbled to catch up with it and bent to peer through the side window, scraping her hair back from her face.

"Hi there!" said a friendly voice.

She saw a good-looking wealthy couple in their mid-thirties, flashily dressed for a night on the town.

"Need a ride sweetheart?"

They smiled broadly at her. The woman was sitting in the back.

"Uh…," the girl struggled to focus. "C-can you t-take me to the b-bus stop on—?"

"We can take you all the way home, little lady," the man declared. "Climb on in…!"

The sandy plateau overlooked the star-spangled vista of the city at night.

"Oooohhh, Johnny…!"

On the back seat of his prized Camaro, his proven "pussy wagon", he was way past second base and heading for third. The girl was throbbing.

Suddenly, she started and went stiff.

"What was that?"

Annoyed, he tried to continue; she sat up, pushing him back.

"Didn't you hear that?"

He made a grab for her. The girl shrieked and was staring wide-eyed over his shoulder.

"Look—!"

"Huh? Wha—?"

"Eyes!"

A deep vibration made the car rock slightly. And then the eyes moved on.

"Uh…this isn't the way," the girl mumbled nervously.

The road was unlit and flanked by fathomless darkness. The flashy couple was laughing as if sharing some secret joke, passing a vodka bottle to each other.

"Hey, chill out, sweet cheeks!" the man told her.

"Yeah!" smirked his wife, her face suddenly distorted and ugly. "Join the party!"

Leering, the man clamped his fingers on the girl's thigh. She screamed and made a grab for the door handle but it was locked.

"Let's have none of that…!"

The woman leant over the back of the passenger seat and wrapped her arm tight around the girl's throat, choking off her terrified cries.

The man's hand was yanking down the tight tube top.

"Now let's see what you've got…!"

The woman was laughing shrilly, her eyes crazy.

"Come on sweetie, play the—!"

A roar, a screech of rending metal as mighty claws raked the roof of the car and peeled it back like a tin lid.

"OH MY G—!"

"Wha—?"

An immense force lifted the man out of the driver's seat and into the blackness above.

"AAAAAGGGHH-GGHHH…!!!"

A deluge of blood rained down into the topless car, drenching the girl and the woman cringing into the back seat.

"NOOO-OOOOO…!!!"

In an instant the woman was plucked into the night and was gone.

"AAAAAAIIIIIEEEEEEE…!!!"

Snarling – shredding – ripping – bone crunching – a fountain of blood.

Somehow, the girl found herself outside the car, soaked in blood, sprawled in the gloom by the roadside. The roar was now a deep rumble, making the earth vibrate beneath her.

She saw eyes, huge and slanted and glowing yellow. She sat up, stunned, her brain scrambled; the eyes seemed to look deep into her soul.

It was almost purring. And then it was gone. The girl got up and ran.

Seen from the air, P.S. 99 was besieged by a blighted urban sprawl scarred by burnt-out shells and open wounds of waste ground.

Once a bright beacon lighting the way to a better future, the high school was decayed and neglected, infected by hopelessness.

It was contained by high fences topped with razor wire. The doors with plywood panels replacing smashed glass were guarded by men in uniform, tasked with frisking the pupils for drugs and blades and the occasional gun.

"Looks like shit…!"

In the sky above, the Colonel adjusted the headphones clamped to his domed flying helmet, jerked the small boom mike down to his chin.

"A dung heap crawling with vermin!"

The choppers made two passes, circling slowly. The kids milling and jostling, tossing basketballs in the shabby playground didn't even look up. They were used to Police eyeballing them from above.

The flight made a third pass just for good measure. There were strange gauges on the control panel. They looked out of place, like something from the future. They sank from full to empty.

The Colonel looked out through the Perspex bubble of the canopy. The mass in the playground below was still scuffling and swirling.

"I don't see anything happening!"

Sat nearby, a flabby middle-aged man shook his helmeted head. His voice crackled in the Colonel's headphones.

"That's not how this new variant works, Colonel...."

"Yeah? Then how?"

The Colonel gripped the scientist's arm till he felt the bones creak.

"And in plain English!"

The scientist grimaced with pain.

"Th-the formulation will t-target only young black males," he explained. "The symptoms will begin to manifest themselves as they reach adulthood and be diagnosed as an incurable genetic disorder found only in the colored races."

He flexed his arm carefully.

It works like a time release capsule, Colonel."

The Colonel was nodding. His eyes gleamed.

Yeah, like a time bomb!"

Grunting and groaning, Lina hauled her chin above the bar.

"Come on!" called Aiko. "Three more...!"

Job done, Lina dropped down onto the mat, blinking sweat out of her eyes.

"Aw, Cat!" she panted. "Come back soon!"

Aiko laughed.

"Cheryl, your turn – gimme fifty!"

"F-fifty!" Cheryl gasped. "What is this, goddamn Boot Camp?"

But she did it. She looked pleased; and surprised with herself.

"Well done!" Aiko clapped her hands.

"No fair!" Lina complained, glancing down ruefully at her chest. "I'm carrying all this extra weight!"

Sammy didn't stop at fifty and went on to one hundred, with scarcely a bead of sweat to show for it. She grinned and flexed her biceps.

It was a challenge that Janey couldn't resist.

"One hundred!" she croaked, releasing the bar.

They all looked at Josie.

"Oh God...!"

"Let's have some sport!"

The scientist was a nervous flyer. Alarmed, he saw the Colonel reach down the side of his seat and produce a lightweight mini-rifle with a telescopic sight.

The Colonel tapped the pilot's shoulder and was pointing downwards. The scientist's stomach rose into his mouth as the pilot gave a quick thumbs-up and made the chopper dip and descend steeply.

As it leveled out, the Colonel was sighting through the long scope. Then he grabbed the pilot's arm and was pointing again.

The helicopter was banking and then hovered.

"Perfect...!"

A collection of crusty, filthy derelicts was clustered on a shallow dome of rubble, squabbling over a bottle. Like the schoolkids, they barely glanced up at the sound of the whirring rotors.

The sound obliterated the pop-pop-pop of the automatic rifle.

The tramps jerked and fell, one by one, piling on top of each other. One got up and tried to stagger away. Pop! – down he went again.

Up above, the Colonel detached the short magazine and slapped in another, already scanning for more targets.

In his mind's eye, he was back in 'Nam, winging low over the paddy fields, strafing gooks with the .30 cal., racking up his body count.

"The good old days...!"

"Aw, c'mon guys...!"

Bad deeds under cover of night.

"Gimme a break, can't you...?"

Three off-duty cops, moonlighting as enforcers. They could have been clones – hulking, flat-tops and grim expressions.

"T-tell Jimmy to give me just a little more time!"

A squat butterball, round and pink-faced, in a loud check suit and trilby.

"I g-got a sure-fire thing goin' in the three-thirty," he stammered. "I'll have the dough, no problem...!"

He was consumed by their shadow as the three giants closed in on him, shoulder to shoulder. They filled the narrow span of the garbage-strewn alleyway, blotting out any residue of light that filtered from the deserted street.

"No time, dirt bag," one of the cops growled. "You had yer chance!"

He was slipping a set of knuckle-dusters onto his huge fist. The others slid sawn-off bats from under their jackets.

The little man backed off till he bumped up against the wall.

"No...please...guys...don't—!"

A piercing snarl descended into deep growling that made the narrow walls quiver and shake off brick dust.

"Fuck—!"

And then a roar that signaled attack.

"Jesus Christ!"

The cop with the brass knuckles was suddenly headless. He stood like a statue, a fountain, as blood cascaded from the raw stump of his neck, ten feet in the air.

As his knees began to crumble, his partners pulled their .38's and emptied them, blazing away.

"Over there...!"

One thought he detected movement in the shadows; he thought he saw....

"Eyes!"

His arm with the hand holding the gun was ripped from his shoulder. As the arm fell on the ground the hand spasmed, firing one last shot.

He screamed, turned and lurched away down the alley, into the gloom. He made it halfway, blood pumping from him, then stopped, swayed and sagged downwards.

The third cop, his eyes bulging with terror, was now dry-firing, oblivious, snapping the hammer of his empty gun. As he stumbled backwards, his legs were cut off at the knees. He fell straight down on his stumps, in a great splash of blood. His belly was raked, lacerated, his guts spilling out.

"Oooohhhh…hhhhh…!"

Huge glowing eyes were blinding him. The little man fainted and lay flat, his face in his hat.

Growling, the eyes receded. They left behind a spotted trail of blood that looked like black tar, leading to the mouth of the alley.

Janey triggered her small cassette recorder and greeted the pale glimmer of morning with the raw blast of the MC5 and "Kick Out The Jams".

The slumbering bunks around her were jolted into life.

"Yay!" cheered Sammy, instantly alert, sitting up and throwing out her arms.

Josie groaned, rolled over and put the pillow over her head.

Cheryl slept on blissfully. Propped up on her elbows, Lina glared at her. Screaming, she snatched up a plastic beaker and hurled it at Janey's head.

"You bi—!"

Most of the water went over Lina. With an evil grin, Janey fielded the plastic cup deftly, her hand like a catcher's mitt.

"Rise and shine…!"

The strip neon lighting ignited, making them squint and blink.

"Aw…!"

Aiko was in the doorway, in her track suit, smiling at them.

"Up and at 'em, ladies…!"

"Uh!"

Cat woke suddenly. Although it had been a warm red night, her body was like a block of ice.

Her head was muzzy, a grey fog behind her eyes.

"Ooooohhh…!"

She pushed herself up off the oriental mattress rolled out on the floor.

"OH!...OWWW…!!!"

Sudden pain, sharp and scalding, a black flash as she zoned out momentarily.

"Owwwww….!"

Her stomach churned. Feeling weak, she got her breath back. All over her naked body goose bumps were now beads of sweat.

She had clutched her upper arm. When she took her hand away blood was sticky on her fingers. There was blood on the sheets.

Cat stood shakily and shuffled into the tiny bathroom. She peered into the mirror.

"Shit!"

There was a deep furrow seared into the flesh. It was still oozing. Numbly, Cat wadded some tissues, soaked them and dabbed the wound gently. Opening a small wall cabinet, she splashed on some disinfectant. It stung like hell.

"Ow, fuck…!"

Just a flesh wound, she reassured herself.

"Fuck! Fuck! Fuck!"

Wincing, Cat tested her arm; a bit stiff but functional. She unwrapped and taped on an Army field dressing.

And then it hit her.

Oh my God! I wasn't dreaming!

She was shivering again. Donning a towel robe and wrapping it tight around her, she picked up the phone. Her voice was quavering.

"Hello? Uncle John…?"

At the heart of the Museum of the Ancient Americas, the Professor's oak-paneled study was a museum within a museum, housing an extraordinary collection of exotic artifacts, trophies of a lifetime spent questing for knowledge.

Sat in a leather armchair, Cat looked around her in wonder.

"You've had an amazing life, Professor…."

The old man smiled, his high forehead gleaming in a mellow, antique light. It was reflected in the gold-rimmed pince-nez perched on the bridge of his long thin nose.

"From what you've told me, my dear Miss Warburton," he observed. "Your life has been no less extraordinary lately."

Cat smiled bleakly.

"My Uncle John said that you might be able to help me?"

The Professor let his head tilt back, his eyes warmed by fond memories.

"Ah, John Warburton," he sighed. "A great adventurer; and such a generous benefactor!"

Cat's smile now had some light in it.

"Yes," she said. "He's been very generous to me too."

The Professor came back to the present.

"Well," he suggested briskly. "It's obvious that you are the victim of some ancient curse…."

He expected skepticism, but Cat craned forward in the deep padded armchair.

"Can the curse be lifted?"

The Professor's lofty brow creased in thought.

"That remains to be seen."

Cat looked disappointed. The Professor leant across stiffly and patted her hand.

"On the plus side," he commented. "It appears that the beast's retribution is confined to the guilty while sparing the innocent – or at least the less guilty."

Cat sighed.

"So it would seem."

The Professor was nodding. He took off his eye glasses and polished them with a large handkerchief.

"Which means that you have some measure of control over it."

"Perhaps...."

"Yes indeed," he assured her. "The force of your personality has to some extent transformed a curse into a power, albeit a very strange one."

Cat was dubious.

"I'm sure I don't want it!"

He patted her hand again. He wasn't too old to be smitten by her.

"It may well go in time. Or it might be possible to exorcise it...."

"Oh God, I hope so!"

His knees creaked as he rose and turned towards his desk, piled high with ancient parchments and leather-bound volumes.

"I will have to do some further research...."

Lowering himself slowly into the seat behind the desk, he began shuffling his papers.

"Meanwhile," he resumed after a short pause. "You must continue to assert yourself and learn to control these manifestations, so they occur only when you want them to."

Cat raised her eyebrows.

"That's a tall order, Professor."

"He was beaming at her.

"Oh, you can do it, Catherine," he clapped his hands together. "You are John Warburton's niece after all, so I'm certain you can!"

Cat went to the door with fresh hope in her heart. As she opened it, he spoke again.

"I almost forgot," he exclaimed. "We've had some odd goings-on right here in our museum!"

"Oh?"

"Yes, one of our most popular exhibits has vanished! The truly grotesque idol of a so-far un-named demonic deity."

"Stolen?"

"How could one steal a ten-foot tall stone statue? It weighs a ton!"

"So...?"

"It has simply disappeared – very strange...!"

The gleaming walls of the underground gymnasium resounded to the sounds of hard work.

"That's much better!" Aiko shouted.

They were scrambling like agile monkeys, to the very top of long ropes that dangled from the high ceiling. Descending in a swift spiral, they would touch down, take a deep breath and do it again.

"Good!" Aiko encouraged them. "Very good…!"

They glimpsed Selena watching them from the doorway, her face expressionless. They redoubled their efforts and were rewarded with a smile.

Selena caught Aiko's eye and signaled to her. Aiko blew a shrill blast on her whistle.

"That's enough…!"

They slid down and stood by their ropes, breathing deep and evenly.

"Well done!"

Sheathed in a skin-tight bronze catsuit that accentuated every curve and muscle of her Amazon's body, Selena stalked across the gym. She caught sight of the pull-up bar.

As the team stood and gaped, Selena did a quick twenty-five with one arm and twenty-five with the other. Strolling nonchalantly over to join them, she was smiling warmly.

"Woo!" she exclaimed. "You guys must be tough!"

They seemed to grow visibly. But now she was looking deadly serious.

"We've had a positive lead," she told them. "Time to go into action!"

Their eyes lit up. Selena turned to her second-in-command.

"Aiko, get Cat back here!"

They cheered, clapping, pumping their fists in the air. Grinning, Aiko rolled her eyes. Selena laughed out loud.

CHAPTER 16

TOTAL WAR

Cat commanded the dance floor. She'd returned to the JOOK JOINT as a spy but she couldn't resist the beat.

The pulsating multi-colored dance floor was jam packed. Status and dance chops were measured by the extent of one's aura, the amount of elbow room one could secure for oneself.

Cat shone in a fine pearly mesh micro-dress that was almost transparent and silver sandals that laced up her calves. Her aura was a force field keeping all admirers, jealous rivals and would-be suitors at a distance.

It was a shame, because some of them took her fancy.

Sorry, man, that's not what I'm here for tonight....

Her vision blurred suddenly. The whirling lights and glitter balls swirled, a whirlpool sucking her down.

What—?

The clean metronomic beat began to disintegrate and become something dark and primitive, crushing her skull.

No! Not now!

Straining every fiber, she held herself together and the moment passed. The lights re-focused, the music chiming like a bell.

Cat left the dance floor and strode swiftly to the bar.

"Jack Daniels – double!"

The bartender marveled as she slammed it back. The warming jolt restored her.

"And again!"

This time she sipped slowly, settling on a bar stool. She kept one eye cocked on a dimly lit door tucked away to the side – a door that said: NO ENTRY.

"Move it! We got t'git this shipment out t'nite!"

In the secret warehouse, they worked late into the night.

"C'mon, hustle!"

A production line of long tables was staffed by near naked women of all ages, constructing house brick sized packages and wrapping them in tape and black plastic.

They were stripped because it made it hard for them to steal and conceal. Each one of those bricks was worth a four-figure sum.

Tough-looking men patrolled the aisles between the tables, mean eyes glittering. They wore the uniform, exaggerated suits in vibrant colors and exclusive Italian leather.

A hard slap echoed like a pistol shot. A squat woman reeled, clutching her mouth, blood seeping through her fingers.

"An' don' yo go spillin' any or—!"

Steel barn doors blew inwards at either end of the huge structure, crashing to the concrete floor. Pale grey armored vehicles rolled in over them and screeched to a halt.

"Hey—!"

"Fuck—!"

The carriers disgorged lithe figures in black jump suits and ski masks. They wielded M16's and used them with surgical precision, cutting the men down before they got off a single shot.

Screaming, the women threw themselves to the ground, rolling under the tables.

"Out! Out!"

Prodding with their gun muzzles, the invaders winkled out the terrified women and herded them into a far corner. They were told to dress quickly and leave.

Heavy jerry cans were lifted out of the back of the armored carriers. They were carried to the tables and the liquid contents poured out. Soaked, the stacks of wrapped packages melted, becoming a greyish sludge that drained onto the floor.

A slim figure tugged off the ski mask. Glossy blue-black hair tumbled to supple shoulders. All around, the others copied her.

"Mission accomplished, Chief," Aiko spoke into a walkie-talkie. "Now it's up to Cat!"

The hard core of her squad was revealing itself, young and keen-eyed.

Sammy's grin was blinding.

"Wooo!"

Janey and Cheryl backed away from the gooey tables, their hands over their mouths and noses.

"Yuk…!"

They heard a groan; crawling painfully on the ground, a man was stretching bloody fingers for his gun.

"Watch out!"

Her face blank, Josie stepped forward and put a single shot into the back of his skull. Swiveling on her heel, she reached into a breast pocket and was combing out her long dark hair.

As Josie passed by, preening herself, Lina rolled her eyes skywards and clapped a hand to her forehead.

"Aw, for—!"

"Yeh, what…?"

Mr Big cursed and grabbed a gold-plated telephone.

"What yo want this time o' night!"

He was secluded in the back office with his closest cohorts, tuned in to the live relay of a basketball game. The sound was turned up to subdue the muffled throbbing from the dance floor.

"Say agin, I can' hear yo!"

He had big money on this game and didn't like being interrupted.

The tinny voice in the earpiece was babbling. Mr Big sat up straight, his eyes widening.

"Yo say what!"

He drew a bejeweled finger across his throat and a henchman cut off the commentary.

"Say that agin!"

His bull neck seemed to swell above his jazzy collar and necktie. Veins throbbed in his temples.

"Muthafuck!" he bellowed. "Fuck! Fuck...!"

He wrenched open a desk drawer, withdrew a fancy pistol and jammed it inside his jacket. Rising from his throne, he seized the skull-topped scepter.

"Git yo guns and bring the cars roun'," he snarled. "We got trouble!"

At the bar, Cat saw the NO ENTRY sign swing outwards.

Here we go...!

Mr Big came out fast and angry, his phalanx of bodyguards barging a path for him through the packed dancers, awash on a sea of swirling rainbows.

A young woman was pushed over. One glance from a sharp-suited hulk was enough to stifle any hint of protest from her dwarfed boyfriend.

Cat retrieved a beaded shoulder bag from the barman.

"Thanks...."

She slid off the bar stool. Conveniently, the toilets were located just beyond the door sign-posted NO ENTRY. The tuxedo-clad bouncers didn't waste a second glance on her migrating casually in that direction.

Side-stepping quickly, Cat opened the swing door a crack and slipped through. A softly-lit corridor led straight to the office door.

"Huh!" she grunted dismissively.

It had a keypad-coded lock. Delving into her bag she extracted a small silver cube and clamped it to the doorframe.

She keyed in numbers. A tiny green pin light winked on. Then another, then a third. In short time, five green lights were blinking simultaneously.

Cat heard the lock click. She turned the handle and inched the door open. Reaching into the bag, she came up with a pair of futuristic goggles. She put them on and rotated the coin-edged rims of the thick lenses.

Leaning forward, she peered around the door.

"Beautiful...!"

The goggles exposed a web of light. Invisible to the naked eye, the beams crisscrossed the office at varying heights.

Let's go…!

Advancing into the room, Cat was high-stepping and ducking. She knew what she was looking for.
"Yep!"
Behind the hanging tapestry, she found the secret door.

That's all I need to know!

Every second counted. Cat re-negotiated the beams and left the office, letting the door lock itself behind her.

Halfway down the corridor, it happened again.
"Uuuuhh…!"
That strange seizure gripped her. Everything blurred; the lamps became fuzzy; the long passageway began to warp.

No…!"

Her eyes flashed yellow, the pupils elongating into slits. She felt her fingertips tingle and saw her nails start to grow.

No! No! No—!

Her body clenching till she feared it would break, Cat willed the corridor to twist back into shape.
In a cold sweat, she stumbled to the swing door at the end of the passageway. Breathing deeply, she calmed herself, peered through a crack and then slid out.
The pumping sound and light assaulted her. Cat dashed into the women's toilet and shut herself in a cubicle. Chilled and queasy, she threw up in the toilet bowl.
Stumbling out of the cubicle, Cat stared at herself for what seemed like an eternity in the long mirror above the wash basins, searching deep behind her eyes.
Two flashy women came in, high and giggling. They looked at her curiously. Swallowing hard, Cat left quickly.

In the shadowy car park, she subsided into the black leather cockpit of the yellow Corvette ZL-1 and plucked the CB handset from the dash.
"Hi Selena," she reported, forcing strength into her voice. "Your intel was correct, it's here alright.…"

Alarmed, his dark-suited soldiers backed up hurriedly, getting out of his way.
"No good cocksuckah…!"

Mr Big kicked one of the bleeding corpses, making it roll across the splattered concrete floor.

"Bunch 'o pussies!"

He was incandescent, raving, throwing the tables around, smashing them into matchwood.

One mangled casualty had the misfortune to survive long enough to have the story squeezed out of him.

"Yo dumb fuck!"

And then just long enough for Mr Big to hoist him above his head, snap his spine and toss him away like a ragdoll.

"Fuckin' pansy asswipe!"

Mr Big ran out of tables to smash. The toxic goo had splashed his purple crushed velvet suit and his jacket was smoking in patches.

He was still ranting, oblivious to it even when it flickered into flame. A bodyguard plucked up the courage to rush in and rip it off his giant frame.

"Bitches…!"

His reward was a mighty buffet that laid him low, semi-conscious.

"I'm gonna skin them little ho's alive!" Mr Big roared, his eyes bulging, foam bubbling on his lips. "I'm gonna hang 'em by the—!"

Cat's eyes blazed.

"I want this mission, Selena!" she demanded. "I have unfinished business with that piece of garbage!"

Selena leant across her desk and studied Cat solemnly. Aiko was watching closely. Cat felt herself being turned inside out.

"Please…!"

After a short pause that for Cat seemed to last forever, Selena sat back in her chair and nodded decisively.

"Okay," she said. "You've got it!"

Cat let out her breath in an explosive sigh.

"Thank you!" she gasped.

Selena's stern expression softened. She smiled, her eyes warming.

"Take your young hit squad with you," she commanded. "They all know what bad dope can do so they'll be highly motivated."

"Yes," Cat replied enthusiastically. "They'll be up for it!"

Selena smiled again.

"I'm sure they will."

Cat got up and left to brief her team, a spring in her step.

Aiko stayed behind.

"What is it, Chief?" she asked. "Is something wrong?"

Selena's eyes were clouded.

"Maybe I should send you with her…."

Aiko looked surprised.

"She'll be fine," she said. "Why, don't you trust her?"

Selena stood up quickly.

"I'd trust Cat with my life," she stated forcefully. "But she's not right, she's still damaged."

Aiko nodded sadly.

"Yes, but...."

"But what?"

"This time," Aiko suggested. "This time it's something different...."

The Colonel was losing control. He could feel it slipping through his fingers. He'd never felt that way before and he didn't like it.

He seized a quailing scientist by a double handhold of his white lab coat and shook him till his teeth rattled and the thick horn-rimmed spectacles flew off his nose.

"It s-s-should w-work, C-C-C-C-Colonel," shaken violently, the frightened egghead stammered. "Th-the f-formula c-c-can b-be ad-ad-adapted t-t- s-s-select young f-f-f-females...!"

The Colonel let him go and he fell back onto a stool at his lab bench.

"You'd better be right!" the Colonel snarled.

He stormed out, knocking over a humble lab technician who was stooping to retrieve the scientist's glasses.

"You damn well make it work!"

The coke-bottle lenses crunched under the Colonel's boot.

After the briefing, Janey came alone to Cat's underground rooms.

"Cat...?"

Janey hesitated in the doorway, looking down at her feet. Smiling, Cat smoothed the black fringe away from her downcast eyes.

"Yes?" she replied gently.

Janey looked up at last, her eyes wide, searching.

"Cat, do you ever get scared?"

Terrified...!

Cat smiled again, ushering Janey inside.

"Sure I do," she said matter-of-factly. "There's nothing wrong with being scared, it keeps you sharp."

That sounds like such bullshit to me now!

Janey looked doubtful.

"I'm not allowed to show it," she frowned. "Not when I've been elected leader of the gang."

Cat squeezed Janey's shoulder.

"You're a born leader."

Janey's shoulders sagged.

"Yeah right, except that I'm scared all the time!"

Oh, me too!

"That's what real courage is," Cat told her.

"What do you mean?"

Cat went and sat on her bed, an arm around Janey's shoulders, drawing her down to sit beside her.

"Courage isn't about being fearless," she explained. "It's about overcoming one's fear and getting the job done."

Gently, she pulled Janey closer to her, till their faces were almost touching.

"You're very brave, Janey…."

With a broken sound, Janey wrapped her arms around Cat and clung on desperately.

"Just hold me – please!"

The Colonel dominated the head of the table. His subordinates scarcely dared to breathe.

"Alright," he barked. "One last time…!"

His hand made sweeping passes over a mosaic of aerial photographs.

"We go in first with the blockbuster bombs and when we've opened it up the choppers follow up with the gas".

He slammed his fist into his palm.

"We're going to exterminate that black she-wolf and her cubs!"

The C.I.A. man was a classic of his kind. Faceless and grey, you'd never look at him twice. You'd never guess how much dirt and blood he had on his hands.

He had one eccentricity, one guilty pleasure. The pink frosted doughnuts sold at the small corner coffee shop on his way to work, the bland office block that hid its identity behind a contrived corporate mask.

He would have one at his desk with his takeaway coffee while planning his day.

"May I have the situation report on Operation Veneno Lento?"

"You'll find it in your in-tray…."

A day that might include undermining a foreign currency by infecting it with counterfeit, to topple a government with a different world outlook.

"Bring me the Kornikov file…."

Or discrediting an important figure on the other side by sewing misinformation, false rumors, so his masters would wrongly suspect him of treachery and have him liquidated.

"Right away…."

All in a day's work.

"Hello again, you really do like our doughnuts don't you!"

There was a new girl at the coffee shop. She had only been there a few weeks and had already made a big impression on the C.I.A. man.

She was pert, curly blonde and baby blue-eyed and a pretty picture in her pink uniform; she had a friendly way about her that was starting to give him illogical thoughts.

"Can't start the day without them!" he replied; it was the only time he raised a smile in his entire working day.

Her laugh sent a quiver through him. He thought of his wife, sour-faced and dumpy, and sighed as he turned reluctantly and made for the door.

Behind him, the blonde girl's smile evaporated. Her handbag was tucked under the counter. Reaching into it surreptitiously, she found a small device and pressed a button twice.

Boy, this is my lucky day…!

In the coffee shop car park, there was a dusty blue delivery truck. Parked close by, a jaunty bright yellow foreign compact.

"Oh, I don't know…!"

The hood was propped open and projecting from it was a short skirt riding up dangerously, long shapely thighs and shiny stiletto-heeled boots.

"Hi there! Please can you help us…?"

The entreaty came from a doll-faced, generously proportioned blonde, standing anxiously beside the stricken car. She had hair down to her waist, her curves barely contained by a skimpy halter top and denim cut-offs low on her hips.

Her companion emerged from beneath the hood and revealed herself to be a striking redhead with green eyes and tempestuous tresses. She strained her spangled tube top.

They'll never believe this in the office!

The grey man set down the box of doughnuts.

"Well, let's see now…."

The young women fluttered around him.

"Oh thank you, that's so kind…!"

"We're just hopeless with mechanical things!"

His imagination was going into overdrive; it was rare and exciting.

"It's my pleasure," he said, poking around under the hood. "Now, I think…."

He felt a sharp prick in his thigh.

"Wha—? OW…!"

Standing up sharply, he banged the top of his skull on the underside of the hood. Baffled, he turned to stare at them, rubbing his leg and his head simultaneously.

Still smiling, the baby-faced blonde was holding a syringe spiked with a long needle. The syringe was empty, a bead of clear liquid dangling from the point.

"Wha…w-what have you…d-d-done…?"

Everything swam around, then went dark. The redhead caught him under the arms before he fell to the ground.

The blonde slapped her hand on the side of the dirty delivery van. The back doors swung open. Young women in overalls helped lift the unconscious man inside.

The redhead slammed down the hood of the yellow compact and slid into the driver's seat. The blonde swung in beside her. The engine gunned. The van doors crashed shut.

"Let's go!"

Cat read it in their body language, a fierceness bordering on lust, lusting for the kill.

You're starting to enjoy it!

They didn't have to say anything. It radiated from them. It glinted viciously in their eyes, framed by the black ski masks.

And isn't that what I do best – kill!

Silently, they unhooked the grapnels from the lip of the low wall framing the flat roof. They pulled up the ropes and coiled them around their shoulders.

Traversing the roof space swiftly, they weaved through the aerials, ventilators and generators, moving soundlessly on rubber soles. They melted into the patterned shadows, dodging the moon.

As they crouched closely around her, Cat was checking the magazine of her machine-pistol, making sure that the egg-shaped stun grenades were attached securely to her webbing.

Her assault team mimicked her, synchronized.

"Ready…?" Cat whispered.

"Ready!" they hissed in chorus.

Jogging briskly to the roof's edge, overhanging the front of the building, they craned over, locating the glow of a curtained panoramic window.

Cat secured the grappling hook and wrapped the rope around herself. Standing on top of the low wall, she turned and flexed her long legs, preparing to abseil downwards.

Roping up, the team sprang onto the wall on either side of her.

"Go…!"

Squirming, the C.I.A. man screamed, his bare buttocks drumming on the table in a paroxysm of pain.

"C'mon, asshole!" Selena snarled. "Spill!"

Aiko knew all the pressure points. The grey man screamed again, writhing.

"Okay, okay!" he croaked. "I'll talk…!"

Selena was pacing her office grimly.

"Someone high up has sold us out!" she fumed. "Those mad fuckers know where to find us!"

As Aiko watched anxiously, Selena went to her desk, snatched up a chromed handset and punched in a code.

"This is A-1 – deploy all early warning systems and alert Air Command!"

She was heading for the door.

"Okay Cat, we'll take care of business!"

It slammed behind her.

"You do your stuff!"

"Aw sheeeeet…busted flush agin!"

In a well-appointed ante-chamber, Mr Big's soldiers were sharing a late-night order of ribs, hunched over a keenly contested game of cards.

"Of all the dumb luck…!"

"Read 'em an' weep, bruthah!"

Dim silhouettes descended silently on the other side of the curtains. Glass shattered and cascaded, crashing downwards, the heavy drapes billowed.

"Fuck—!"

The metal eggs were rolling and bouncing across the carpet, converging on the card table.

"Jeez—!"

An obliterating flash, a crushing concussion. The table was flipped into the air, the chairs flew back.

Cat seemed to float into the room on the end of the rope, releasing it and touching down lightly.

The bodyguards were scattered around the floor, shrouded by a blanket of white smoke. Two were unconscious, others crawled groaning; one sat up, his hands pressed to his shattered eardrums.

"Go! Go…!"

As Cat advanced into the fogged ante-room, her team surged past her, to the polished slab of a heavy door.

A twin battering ram, Lina and Sammy body-slammed the door off its hinges. The others were right behind them.

"Wha…?"

Mr Big stood behind his monumental desk, in the company of two of his closest aides. The shockwaves had rippled into the office and they were dazed, their ears ringing.

Mr Big's henchmen came together in front of the desk, shielding their Boss. Swaying, their vision blurred, they jerked pistols from shoulder holsters.

"F-f-fuck you…!"

"Bitches!"

Cheryl and Josie were walking towards them, the machine-pistols ready at the hip. They chopped the two men down with a short burst.

The guns were part of them; they were machines – killing machines.

In the ante-chamber, the last thing the dazed bodyguards saw was eyes, glowing yellow in the smoke.

"AAAAA-AAGG-GGGHHHHH!!!"

It tore them limb from limb, ripping the flesh from their bones. Blood sprayed the walls, dripping from the ceiling.

As her team-mates fanned out to cover her, Janey closed in on Mr Big, the muzzle of her machine-pistol zeroed on him.

His shiny gun slipped from his fingers. The braggadocio was seeping out of him; he appeared to be shrinking to half his size. He saw death in Janey's eyes.

"Naw, wait!" he babbled. "We kin do 'o deal…!"

Janey stopped, her feet firmly planted.

"No deal, motherfucker!" her voice was jagged. "No more street kids wasted by your shit!"

She triggered a burst into his groin. His brutal features contorted with pain as his immense bulk folded and began to topple.

He rolled on the floor, groaning and clutching himself. The others stood over him, emptied their magazines, chopping him up.

"That's ruined his suit!" said Sammy.

They turned as Cat came into the office. She surveyed their handiwork, radiating satisfaction.

"I'm done!" she told them.

They thought they glimpsed a strange light receding in her eyes, the pupils re-forming, rounding. Not possible; they dismissed it.

The black ski masks were tugged off. They shook out their hair, their faces shining. Lina and Sammy made a move to go and look inside the ante-room, as smoke drifted into the office.

"No!" Cat snapped. "Don't go in —!"

They were already gone. They came back quickly, wide-eyed and very pale.

"What the fuck?" gasped Lina.

Turning away, Cat went swiftly towards the large hanging tapestry.

"Come on!"

They followed and she showed them the hidden door.

"Holy —!"

At the foot of the secret staircase, they were confronted by a neon-lit concrete chamber furnished with racks of sinister grey steel cannisters.

"Yikes…!" whispered Cheryl.

In a trance, she reached out to touch one of the cylinders. Sammy took her arm and pulled her away.

Cat unclipped a walkie-talkie from her belt. It crackled into life.

"All clear!" she declared. "Come and get it…!"

Her team had edged away nervously. All except Janey, who stood at Cat's shoulder. They linked arms.

"They won't be using this stuff again!"

Cat was frowning.

"I'm afraid there's more out there – somewhere!"

Dark specks swarmed across the pale disk of the rising sun. They streaked across the glowing desert, towards a horizon spiked by the sprawling vista of the city skyline.

"Close up, Red Flight!"

A distant drone, like the buzz-saw war cry of angry wasps.

"Roger, Leader...!"

Predatory gunships, bristling with firepower, flying top cover for the smaller insect-like choppers, laden with the evil grey cannisters.

The tip of an arrowhead was a trio of brutish heavyweight Skyraiders in three-tone camouflage, hauled through the air by their massive four-bladed props.

"ETA...!"

Their square-tipped wings were laden with racks of blunt-nosed bombs, designed to penetrate and burrow deep before exploding with devastating force.

Target coordinates were vectoring them to the zone of derelict warehouses and factories on the decaying outskirts of the city, the disguise worn by Selena's underground headquarters.

"Attack formation...!"

By dawn, a fleet of unmarked trucks had filled the JOOK JOINT's car park.

Some were armored and specially sealed, equipped for dangerous cargoes. Others were canvas-topped transports, disgorging lithe figures in overalls and chemical suits.

Cat led her team out to greet them.

"Load it up," Cat said. "And then burn this fucking place to the ground!"

Janey flashed an evil grin.

"Right on!" she exclaimed. "Disco sucks!"

As the new arrivals flooded past her Josie appeared at Cat's shoulder.

"Here," she said. "A present...."

She was offering Mr Big's scepter. In the silver skull, the ruby eyes were twinkling.

Cat took it from her, baring her teeth.

"Thanks! I'll give it to Selena...."

The attackers were snared like flies on the glowing web of the radar screens.

"Bandits entering Sector Four...!"

Selena's pale grey interceptors were F-5A Freedom Fighters, small and nimble and punching far above their weight.

"I see them!"

Helmeted and G-suited, Selena directed three flights, each formated in the tried and tested "Finger-Four". They packed twin cannon and a clutch of air-to-air Sidewinders under their wings.

Selena flicked a switch on the snout of her oxygen mask.

"Tango Leader to Tango Flight", her strong voice crackled in every cockpit. "Tear them apart...!"

She banked; in smoothly timed succession, her squadron mirrored her.

"Break them up and make it count – we have to get them all!"

Her pre-dawn briefing echoed in their cockpits – "We have to get them all while they're still over the desert. We can't risk any of them going down over a built-up area with that poison gas on board!"

One by one, they rolled over and plummeted down in a slashing attack.

"Geronimo…!"

The gas-bearing choppers were the priority targets. Led by Selena, the first flight of four F-5A's flamed them with their cannon on the first pass.

The second wave matched them, the sky full of bubbling flame, stained with oily black smoke.

"It's like shooting rats in a barrel…!"

The stricken choppers spiraled down, disintegrating, made scorched splashes on the desert floor.

Few of the grey gas cannisters survived intact. Most were crushed, splitting open. Their toxic contents were vaporized harmlessly, turning the flames a translucent purple.

"A turkey shoot!"

The mission thwarted, the bulky Skyraiders ditched their bombs in the empty desert and turned to engage. The third flight of F-5A's used their superior speed and power to make a diving attack, the muzzles of their cannon flashing.

One Skyraider blew up and fell as a rain of smoking fragments. Another had its fuselage chopped in half. The two segments spun down like falling leaves as the pilot ejected.

The remaining Skyraider made a run for it, jinking and weaving. An F-5A sent a missile streaking after it, an unerring arrow trailing a long plume of white smoke. It mirrored the Skyraider's desperate maneuvers, closing in on its tail. Both vanished in a ball of fire.

"Watch out!"

One of the helicopter gunships got a missile away.

"On your six, Tango Leader!"

Instinctively, Selena flicked her F-5A into a corkscrewing climb and turn that threw the projectile off balance, sending it off course. In her peripheral vision, she glimpsed it veer away aimlessly.

"With you, Leader!"

The F-5A's swarmed and released a volley of missiles. In a bouquet of fireballs, the gunships were swatted out of the sky.

A sole survivor promptly landed, the crew running in all directions with the rotors still turning, scattering into the desert.

Well done, ladies!" Selena broadcast to her pilots. "Form up and head for home…!"

"They have an air force?"

The Colonel was incredulous.

"A fucking air force!!!?!"

He hoisted the terrified young Captain by a hand clamped on his throat.

"You're supposed to be my goddamn Intelligence Officer!" he bellowed. "And you didn't know anything about it?"

He shook his red-faced junior violently, making his arms and legs flop like a doll's.

"G-G-Gharrk-kkk-kkkkhh…!"

The Captain's eyes bulged, his tongue sticking out.

"You useless fuck!"

His eyes slits of fire, the Colonel tightened his grip.

"G-G-G-Ggggnnn-nnnghhh-hhhh…!"

Cartlidge crunched and popped. Pink froth bubbled on the Captain's tongue and writhing lips. His eyes rolled up in their sockets.

"Bah!"

The Colonel tossed him aside. The Captain's limp corpse rolled to the feet of a group of quailing lab-coated scientists, their thick spectacles fogged by perspiration.

Cringing and fawning, their leader, his sagging features paling, crept forward fearfully.

"We still have the V-Weapon, herr Oberst," he croaked. "We still have the rockets!"

He wanted to shrink into his shoes as the Colonel loomed over him like a giant thunder cloud.

"Yeah," he grated. "The fucking rockets…!"

He seized the scientist's arm.

"Will they ever be ready?"

The former Nazi missile man felt his bones bend and his fingers go numb.

"We are still having t-trouble b-b-balancing the gyros," he stuttered. "A week…t-t-ten d-days…t-two weeks at the m-m-most…!"

CHAPTER 17

BATTLE OF HOLLOW MOUNTAIN

Some might have heard of Area 51. They would never have heard of this place. To those in the know, the code word was "Hollow Mountain".

"You're fired!"
The Colonel drew his .45 automatic and shot the "de-Nazified" scientist through the head. His brains splattered the white lab coats of his stunned subordinates.
As they stood, pale and shocked, the Colonel strode along the line, brandishing the big pistol under their noses.
Who wants the job…?"

And that's exactly what it was – a craggy hollowed out peak that dominated a spectacular snow-capped mountain range.
To the east, the snowy summit surveyed a vast grassy plain and beyond that a patchwork quilt of farmland, speckled with small towns.
Out west, rolling foothills descended and smoothed out into a band of pale desert. This surrendered to the relentless advance of suburbia, a green belt girdling the glittering towers of the City on the Bay, the shimmering horizon of the sea.

A paralyzed silence. The Colonel made his choice.
"Von Hirsch!" he snapped. "You're in charge now!"

The rocky shell of Hollow Mountain was supported by a spiraling, multi-layered cone of steel and concrete.
A complex architecture housed weapons stores, barracks, laboratories, food and fuel dumps, camouflaged machine-gun and artillery emplacements, missile silos.

Von Hirsch was gaunt and stooped, his thinning grey hair scraped across his skull, wire-rimmed spectacles slipping down the narrow bridge of his nose. He went as white as chalk.
"I…I-I-I…!"

"Project Hollow Mountain" was conceived as a refuge for the political and military élite. An oasis in a nuclear desert. For a desperate last stand; a base for any counter-strike against an enemy invader or civil insurrection.

"I'll give you one week to have those goddamn rockets ready to go!"
The Colonel loomed over the frail scientist, his giant shadow crushing him.

"You got me?"

The German stiffened, found that he couldn't click his heels in soft shoes. "Jawohl, herr Oberst!"

Unknown even to those in the know, "Hollow Mountain" now stood for a secret concealed within a secret, the dark core of a conspiracy.

Secure in the knowledge that Hollow Mountain was impregnable, unconquerable!

Back in The Day, they called it "Search and Destroy".

The countryside was scoured for traces of an elusive enemy. One by one, the humble hamlets were raked over, turned inside out, looking for the tell-tale signs of Viet Cong sympathizers, aiders and abettors.

"You know what we're here for, Lieutenant…!"

The Colonel was just a young shave-tail then, razor sharp, keen as mustard.

"Yessir!"

Already a legend, "Big John" Warburton sported a sandy-colored crew cut and was solid muscle, not an ounce of fat on his brawny frame.

He wore regulation olive drab but his unquestioned authority was shadowy. As were his credentials; it was rumored that he'd been there since '62, as an "Advisor", in the vanguard of J.F.K.'s Military Assistance Command Vietnam.

"Equipment, food supplies and hidden weapons," Big John reminded the impatient young officer.

"Yessir!"

The villagers were herded together, chattering nervously, some flapping their hands in feeble protest. When the village elders tried to intercede, they were shoved aside. Children clung to their mothers' skirts.

"In here, Lieutenant!"

In a long low barn, the rough floorboards were torn up to expose bulging sacks that bled rice when bayonetted.

John Warburton let the grains sift through his fingers.

"I guess Charlie won't be eating tonight."

The Lieutenant sneered triumphantly.

"Burn it!" he barked. "Burn the whole thing down!"

The villagers wailed as the barn went up in flames. As they watched anxiously, the patrol fanned out through the village, kicking in walls, stabbing the ground with bamboo stakes, probing for hiding holes and escape tunnels.

"Watch out!"

A dry wind fanned the flames and a straw-roofed hut next to the blazing storehouse ignited in a shower of sparks.

The burning structure stood on short stilts. As the fire intensified, a group of young men in the familiar black pajama-suits came scrambling out.

"Heads up!"

They made a frantic dash for the surrounding brush and the dense jungle beyond.

"Cut 'em down!" the Lieutenant screamed.

There was a clatter of automatic fire as his men opened up with their M16's. On the fringe of the screening brush, the slight figures tumbled, their momentum rolling them over.

"Steee-rike!" someone exulted.

John Warburton accompanied the Lieutenant as he sauntered over to tally up the score.

"Five...."

Grimly, "Big John" produced a wad of paper and a pencil stub and made a note of it. Not much of a body count.

Grinning, the Lieutenant turned one of the corpses over with the toe of his boot. He let something flutter down onto its chest, torn open by exit holes.

"Numero uno...."

A home-made playing card, the ace of spades emblazoned with the notorious skull and crossbones.

Counting them off, the Lieutenant decorated the other bodies similarly.

"Jesus!" said John Warburton. "This one's barely fifteen years old!"

The Lieutenant shrugged.

"Little gooks grow up to be big gooks."

John Warburton stared at him.

"Whatever happened to winning hearts and minds?"

The Lieutenant laughed harshly, walking away.

"Blow the little fuckers' brains out...."

More huts were burning. The Lieutenant's tall figure merged into the pall of smoke.

"And they've got no minds left to worry about!"

As John Warburton turned to follow him, something moved behind his back.

He swiveled. The dead boy was sitting up slowly. Tears of blood were flowing from his accusing eyes. He raised his thin arm, pointing at him.

"AAAAHH—!"

He was awake. Cold sweat chilled him, shone on his face.

"Uuuuhh...hhh...?"

Beside him, Selena stirred, threw back the covers and sat up.

"What is it, lover?" she said softly. "The bad dreams again?"

He got out of bed, padded naked across the dimmed room and poured himself a stiff whisky.

She heard him gulp it down, breathing heavily, his broad shoulders heaving.

He poured himself another and walked back towards the bed, the glass in his hand.

"The same dream, every time...."

Selena propped up the pillows and settled back, watching him, her head tilted slightly, her eyes gentle.

"Lady," he stated. "I want in on this one – I've got a score to settle with that S.O.B.!"

Twin engines droned through the night, hauling heavily-laden, anonymous DC-3's in two tight formations of four.

Vibrations tingled through the metal skin of the fuselage, amplifying the tension, their faces colorless in the hard light of icy bulbs.

Sat across from them, Cat looked at her girls, dressed for war, and suddenly felt very sad.

They were de-humanized, by the dulled helmets and the shapeless mottled-drab jumper's smocks, the heavy laced-up boots. More like machines, in their complex harness, the bulky parachute packs humped on their backs, the weapons strapped across their chests.

"Hey, Princess…."

Uncle John sat beside her, in the battle gear that brought back so many mixed memories. He read Cat's expression and reached out to squeeze her knee. She turned her head and smiled, stroking his hand.

Selena was checking her watch.

"This will take careful timing…!"

Ahead of the old reliable DC-3's, circled a single Boeing 707. Its external grey blandness concealed a wealth of top secrets.

"All systems green…!"

Young women wearing headsets sat studiously at an array of busy consoles, bathed in pulsating rainbows. Focused intently, their world consisted of the shifting and rotating grids on the screens in front of them.

"Scramblers engaged!"

Cat warmed as her team all looked to her for affirmation. She smiled deep into their questing eyes.

Sammy grinned broadly, with a big double thumbs-up. Lina's eyes flashed fiercely. Janey nodded, dark and determined. Cheryl's eyes narrowed, her lip curling to show her teeth.

Josie squirmed uncomfortably on the steel bucket seat, fiddling with the chin strap of her helmet.

"Live with it, Your Highness," said Lina. "You'll just have to muss up your hair!"

Giving Lina the evil eye, Josie unbuttoned a compartment in her baggy cargo pants and brandished her comb.

Lina groaned. Ripples of laughter rolled the length of the crowded fuselage, swelled by the seated ranks of Selena's female commandos.

That's my girls!

"What the—!"

"Sir…?"

In the deep concrete Control Center, at the heart of Hollow Mountain, the screens fluttered. Everything went blank.

Green light!

"Let's go!"

From nose to tail, they stood and hooked on their jump lines.

"Give 'em hell…!"

Aircrew heaved the sliding door back and stood aside as Selena went first. John Warburton grinned at Cat and patted his belly.

"I was carrying a lot less ballast the last time I did this!" he shouted over the roar of the slipstream.

He gripped the metal door frame and was gone. Tapping each in turn on the shoulder, Cat ushered her team forward.

Janey's expression was eloquent as their eyes met. And then she looked straight ahead and vanished into the rushing blackness.

"Geronimo!!!!"

Sammy hurled herself into space. Her laughter trailed behind her.

With exaggerated poise, Josie swaggered to the open door, smiling wryly. Flipping Cat a stylish salute, she stepped into the void.

"Oh no you don't!" Cheryl protested, as Lina shaped to push her out. She gave Cat an extravagant wink, took a short run up and sprang into thin air. Her rebel yell echoed after her.

Not to be out-done, Lina whooped, wild-eyed, pumped her fist and surged out into the starless night.

Cat suddenly felt very alone.

You're not my babies anymore….

Selena's amazons were lined up behind her, ready and able.

Swallowing hard, Cat jumped into the icy blast. The usual momentary terror was overcome by exhilaration as the wrench of her harness confirmed that the chute had opened.

All around her, she saw blossoming parachutes, like long strands of pale pearls in the vast darkness. She heard the receding hum of the DC-3's, glimpsed their winking tail lights, as they turned for home, mission accomplished.

"Brace…!"

On silent wings, great birds descended in expansive spirals out of the night sky.

"Brace…!"

Piloted with soft hands, they sank smoothly, as though they rode on invisible rails.

"Brace…!"

Arms wrapped around knees drawn up to their chins, their helmeted heads tucked in. They knew that it always sounded much louder inside than out, the familiar scraping, creaking and crunching.

On approach, the long straight wings rocked precisely as final adjustments were made. Spread out across the broad plain, the gliders slid to earth, in rapid, perfectly timed succession.

"Go! Go! Go…!"

The first boot on the ground was Aiko's.

"Let's go!"

The slab-sided fuselages disgorged a fast flow of helmeted figures, bristling with weaponry.

A swooping wind fanned Aiko's shoulders.

"Here come the heavies!"

She was sprinting into their swirling slipstream as they came grinding down.

"Move it…!"

They were as big as a barn. Rear hatches were lowered into ramps. Pushed and pulled, a cargo of scaled-down artillery pieces and crated ammunition.

Aiko was consulting an elaborate contour map. She craned up at the pale ghost of Hollow Mountain, looming over them, then scanned across the dark plain, dappled deep blue and black.

Her section chiefs clustered around her. In the gloom, their eyes glittered keenly, their lithe frames charged with savage electricity.

"Okay! You know what to do…!"

Klaxons blared, a call to arms.

"Action stations!"

Roaring into life, venting an acrid pall.

"Mount up!"

Hatches clanged shut. Gears and bearings whined as turrets rotated and long gun barrels came erect.

Crushing tracks squeaked and clattered as the big beasts lurched into motion.

"We'll be there by dawn, Colonel…!"

Leading from the front, he flew the Commander's pennant.

"Outstanding!"

Adjusting his headset, he thumped the gun breach with his fist.

"We'll have those bitches…!" he exulted. "Right where we want them!"

Cat saw it all through a distorting yellow filter that bathed the teetering crags in an eerie spectral glow.

She saw familiar shapes shifting, distending, extending. Arms expanded into leathery wings, tipped with vicious claws; legs contorted, bent and scaly, spiked with disemboweling talons.

Razor-edged beaks slavered ravenously, golden orbs gleamed in grotesque skull sockets.

"G-GG-GGGGAAAAAGG-GGHHH!"

Flesh-rending, shrieking harpies, they descended, smothering the hapless patrol and wrapping it in their hooked wingspan.

"AAAAAAAAAAAAGGG-GGGHH-HHHH!"

Her vision cleared. The murky sulfur thinned into icy blue.

Oh…!

The demons were gone.
"Cat…?"
In their place her team stood waiting on her expectantly.
"Hey…?"
They straddled the sprawled bodies, blood dripping from the blackened blades of their heavy combat knives.
"Cat…?"
She blinked, scrubbing her eyes.

Wha…?

Snagged between some rocks, a blood-stained walkie-talkie crackled urgently.
"Control to Baker Two! What's happening out there?"
John Warburton stepped past his niece and scooped it up quickly.
"Uh…Baker Two to Control," he responded. "All clear, false alarm…."
All around them, across the dark and snow-dusted slopes, shadowy squads were ditching the grey shrouds of their chutes and were forming up and moving swiftly to their rehearsed positions.
Selena had found an elevated vantage point. Her radio operator perched beside her. Heralded by puffs of static, came crisp confirmations that all was going according to plan.

"Our security systems are still down, Colonel, we're running diagnostics…!"
Standing tall in the turret, the Colonel squeezed the headphones tighter to his ears and shouted into his chin mike.
"Have you sent out patrols?"
"Yes Sir, nothing to report!"
The Colonel nodded grimly, his eyes sparking.
"Go on full alert!" he barked. "And ready the missile silos!"

"Why was Cat looking at us like that?" Cheryl whispered.
"Dunno," Janey shrugged.
She shivered suddenly, a cold spasm. She frowned, puzzled, her brow furrowing.
Her shiver was infectious.
"Yike…!" breathed Sammy.
Startling images flashed behind her eyes – claws and golden eyes.
There was blood on her hands.
"What did we just do…?"
Josie halted abruptly, head cocked, listening.
"What!" snapped Lina, bumping into her.
Josie shook her head.
"I thought I heard something…."

They all listened. Just the gusting wind, moaning on the dark mountainside.

"Like what?"

"I'm not sure…like wings…."

She hesitated.

"Inside my head…."

They moved on, negotiating the dangerous escarpments. Cheryl nudged Sammy's shoulder.

"Did you see it too?"

"A fucking nightmare," Sammy whispered hoarsely. "With my face!"

Within the summit of Hollow Mountain, the polished walls of sunken silos cast crazy reflections, a giant funhouse mirror, reverberated by sirens and pulsating red lights.

The shifting reflections were bloated and distended. Strange figures in silver suits and helmets with thick plate visors went through the well-rehearsed motions – only this was no drill.

Loops of heavy hoses were uncoiled and connected, twisted and clamped tight. Cables snaked and slithered across the tiled floor.

Dials fluttered, gauges climbed, glowing green columns of data filled busy screens.

The silver forms departed and curved exits slid shut behind them. Hissing, dense white vapors of liquid oxygen rose to fill the gleaming shafts.

An escalating vibration made the smooth grey columns of the rockets quiver with keen anticipation.

"GO!"

They were sucked into a blinding, ringing vortex, corkscrewing down and down and down….

"GO!"

An avalanche of grenades rolled ahead of them, tumbling down steel spiral steps, clanging like a cracked bell.

Below them, the detonations tolled, booming echoes rising, as they pushed through the waves of concussion washing over them, through the swirling wind of smoke and shrapnel.

"GO…!!!"

Battered by light and sound. Thunderbolts and lightning. Riding an earthquake, surfing on the shockwaves.

The rip and rattle of rapid fire; rasping bursts, shouts and screams and the unmistakable sound of hot lead impacting on flesh.

Wading waist deep in smoke and bodies, kicking aside the bloody hands that grabbed at their legs.

Fountains of crimson, spraying the pock-marked smoke-stained walls. A maze of metal corridors transmitted the terrible cacophony of a slaughterhouse.

Below, the dark plain, its sweeping horizons rimmed by the tentative glimmer of the dawn, peeping over the edge as though afraid to show itself.

Aiko was watching with grim satisfaction, as her efficient squads spread out and dug themselves in, assembling their portable artillery.

Then she felt it, vibrating through the thick soles of her combat boots. They all felt it, pausing and glancing up for a moment.

It's begun…!

Craning her head back, she probed the looming phantom of the mountain. Faintly, carried on the gusting wind, she thought she heard the muffled sounds of battle.

She swore that she saw the shadowy crags tremble. And then, as she watched, straining her eyes to pierce the gloom, great slabs of snow detached and slid down slowly before crumbling into a tumbling rumbling tide.

Every fiber of her being wanted to be there, all guns blazing. But she had a job to do. She stepped down nimbly from her vantage point, clapping her hands.

"C'mon! Pick up the pace there…!"

The thunder that Cat heard was deep inside her. It shook her bones. It was boiling her blood.

She could see through sealed steel doors and walls transformed into glass. She could see transparent skeletal forms, commando squads fanning out down long corridors that radiated in a descending spiral.

Her senses were amplified; she was supernatural. She could detect a heartbeat. She could see heat. The muzzle flashes that raked the corridors were scalding, the gore that spurted and pooled was glowing. Thunder flashes were over-loaded momentary white-outs.

The reverberating iron-bound passageways were suffocated in smoke. Cat could detect radiant humanoid shapes moving within it, advancing towards her. She squeezed the trigger and saw them fall like targets in a fairground shooting gallery.

She felt god-like – invulnerable. It was terrifying, exhilarating.

"Prepare to commence count-down…!"

Clanging like warped cathedral bells, the cables disconnected automatically and fell away, withdrawing, re-coiling.

The gleaming shafts throbbed with mounting tension, a dull pulse in counterpoint to the shrill hissing of the glistening vapors.

In the neon-lit control room, the air tingled with the electricity of keen anticipation. Shirt-sleeved technicians mopped their brows, ties at half-mast, hunched tensely over their twitching dials and busy screens.

Lab-coated scientists circled in a tight huddle. Their pale faces were taut and anxious.

"Are you certain, Gerber, that the projections are accurate?"

"Jawohl, if the warheads detonate at the precise altitude, the cloud will spread sufficiently…."

On a long table, they had unrolled the intricate grid of the city plan. A specific geometry was outlined in red.

"To cover the *entire* Black ghetto sectors?"

"Almost certainly, allowing for slight variables in the wind."

They flinched, as they felt the vibrations of distant explosions and gunfire. They seemed to be coming nearer.

"Well, let us hope that we all live to analyze the results of this experiment…!"

Preoccupied, the sweating technicians were oblivious, manipulating the knobs and switches robotically.

"Zero minus…!"

Fully automatic, Cat's team hosed the descending, spiraling steel maze.

Choreographed, they operated in pairs – Cat and Janey; Cheryl and Josie; Lina and Sammy – shoulder to shoulder, as one pair changed magazines, the next took over.

They were relentless, washing any resistance away, stepping over the bodies as they fell, kicking them aside, unfeeling – fully automatic.

A pale dawn was advancing over the horizon, gaining courage and color, coming up fast behind the tanks as they rolled forward across the plain, trailing long glowing plumes of dust.

The Colonel was standing proud in the lead turret, his polished helm gleaming. He was Alexander, Julius Caesar….

Suddenly, the spiral maze played its tricks and the enemy was behind them.

Shit…!

They didn't lift their weapons. They didn't shout. They didn't fire. With blank eyes, they just kept shuffling on warily.

What the…?

Wreathed in the smoke of battle, her team was translucent, becoming transparent. Their presence was scarcely detectable, a mere shimmer, a trick of the light. She saw her own hands fade away; and the weapon they were holding.

Am I doing this?

"Look out!"

She heard Janey's shout, resounding out of thin air.

The enemy stumbled to a halt. They looked all around, bewildered.

"Get 'em!"

Sammy's disembodied yell prompted a ripping invisible volley that mowed the opposition down as they stood there gaping. They died with a look of utter confusion on their faces.

Oh I—!

And then, suddenly, they were solid, substantial, smoke curling from the muzzles of their machine-pistols.

"Huh...?"

Sammy was patting herself.

An odd expression on her face, Janey reached out and poked Lina with her finger. In a trance, Lina extended her arm and reciprocated.

Cheryl was holding her hand up to her eyes, studying it intently, front and back. For a second, she was sure that she could see the bones through the flesh.

"What was all that about?" asked Josie.

Wide-eyed, Cat just shook her head dumbly. She thought she heard distant drums and the trilling of primitive flutes.

"Uh-oh!"

They all heard the wail of an urgent siren, slicing shrilly through the metal walls.

Cat slotted in a fresh magazine.

"C'mon!" she shouted. "Let's go!"

"Two minutes and counting...!"

Hull down, they opened fire.

"Incoming...!"

Hunkered down in their slit trenches and foxholes, Aiko's rearguard weathered the storm, a hurricane of shockwaves and shrapnel.

"Keep your heads down!"

Her radio operator huddled tight to her, Aiko focused the twin-lensed periscope that projected above the lip of the trench. There was a brief lull in the rain of vicious metal and the veils of smoke thinned.

Behind a ring of regular muzzle flashes, stark in the half-light of dawn, she saw armored half-tracks disgorging swarms of infantry.

The tanks were rearing up out of the shallow folds in the plain that concealed them, the machine-guns in their hulls winking, flame spurting from their cannons as they rolled forward.

"Get ready!" Aiko shouted into the handset. "Here they come...!"

Steel doors crumpled like tin foil.

"Freeze, motherfuckers...!"

Rolling back the years, John Warburton was "Big John" again, the old familiar Stoner with its drum magazine like a toy in his hands.

Muscular security types made the last mistake of their lives. Squeezing off single-fire from the hip, John Warburton drilled them, one-two, double-tap, one in the chest, one in the head.

"Leave some for me, Daddy!"

Selena was a split-second behind him. And just as fast, she matched his score.

"Get 'em…!"

Fanning out to flank them, a squad of Selena's élite commandos, lithe and purposeful.

They riddled the crowded control desks, puncturing the metal panels, splintering Perspex and plastic. Screaming, the technicians died in their chairs, the impact swiveling them, swiping them sideways, tearing them into bloody rags.

Their pristine lab coats defiled by the carnage, the scientists cowered in a corner, all trying to hide behind each other. Some fell on their knees, as Selena and John Warburton advanced on them vengefully.

Their chief, the cadaverous von Hirsch, was red-faced and shrieking, spittle spraying from his thin lips.

"Du Schwein!" he screamed. "Du kannst es nicht stoppen!"

His boney trembling finger was gesturing at a surviving TV monitor, mounted high on the bloodstained wall.

"Die Raketen! Die Raketen sind geflogen! Sie können sie jetzt nicht aufhalten!"

There were four such monitors, in a row, suspended on steel brackets. Each displayed the grainy image of a long sinister cylinder, propelled by its tail of flame.

Selena cried out in dismay. John Warburton cursed with rage and frustration.

The German was incandescent, triumphant. His mouth was foaming.

"Heil…!" he ranted. "Sieg Heil! Sieg —!"

Point blank, Selena blew his head off his narrow shoulders. His brains sprayed his subordinates, who howled and flung themselves to the floor.

Ignoring them, John Warburton was pacing the wrecked control room.

"Fuck it!" he growled. "The bastard isn't here!"

Selena stared at him, wide-eyed. She pointed at the screens.

"Forget about him!" she exclaimed. "What about that?"

Inflating his broad chest, John Warburton pulled himself together.

"You saw the dossier," he said quietly. "That stuff works by delayed action.…"

He raised a weak smile.

"The effects take years to show," he told her. "We'll just have to hope we can find an antidote."

Selena rolled her eyes skeptically.

"Yeah…some hope!"

She gripped his arm, her fingers crushing to the bone.

"How many are going to die?" she gasped. "Have we failed…?"

Silence.

A final strand of spent brass tinkled on the polished floor. Pooled blood lapped at their toecaps.

They had run out of people to kill.

"Now what?" said Lina.

Cat closed her eyes. But she could still see.

"Huh!"

Sammy snapped in a full magazine and looked around hopefully. She turned to Janey, who shrugged, eyebrows rising. Cheryl and Josie glanced at each other sideways.

Cat's inner vision was telescoping. Like a zoom lens, it transported her….

What's happening to me?

Down the shining corridors, up the spiraling stairways, cutting through the craggy, rocky crust of the mountain, racing across the vast plain….

NO…!!!

A tide of steel was driven on by a roaring wind of fire.

"Steady! Steady…!"

Relentless waves of infantry came crashing over the folds and furrows of the plain, a boiling surf the vivid muzzle flashes of their guns.

Rocking and bobbing on the flood, the tank formations, giant sea monsters, venting flame as they roared, spewing destruction.

"Hold! Hold on…!"

Seething breakers of fire and steel smashed against the hasty ramparts of sand-bagged earth.

"OPEN FIRE!!!"

The first waves were repelled, dashed into a towering spray of sparks and smoking fragments. Sucking themselves backwards, they paused to regroup, before swelling and surging forward again.

Portable artillery, sunken in protected pits; shoulder-borne rocket launchers and a cross-fire of light machine-guns and grenade-throwing M79 "bloop guns". The plain became a grid of killing zones, bodies heaped in piles.

"Pour it on…!"

Tracks snapped, disassembled, disengaged from sprocket wheels and flopped out uselessly on the ground. Gun barrels drooped limply. The receding tide left strewn debris behind it, smoking hulks and corpses.

"LET 'EM HAVE IT!!!"

Even as Aiko broadcast her warlike exhortations, she knew that each respite was only temporary, that her embattled force was a mere pebble on the beach, trying to hold back the ocean.

It was only a matter of time.

"Let's go!" Cat shouted.

They surfaced and were traversing the jagged precariously tilted flanks of the mountain – Cat and her team in the vanguard of Selena's commandos.

As they progressed, they swept the mountainside clean. They pin-pointed the heavy machine-gun and artillery emplacements that were harassing Aiko's besieged rearguard on the plain far below, as it strained to resist the advance of the Colonel's tank force.

"Clean 'em out!"

With ruthless efficiency, they lanced the enemy positions. They punctured them with rocket launchers, cracked them open with grenades and washed them out with the searing jets of flame throwers.

The scrambling, screaming survivors, human torches, were mown down by the deadly spray of machine-pistols.

Go team!

Oily coils of black smoke belched from the viewing slits of the camouflaged bunkers.

"Ugh!"

"Jeee-zus…!"

Assailed by the stench of scorched flesh, Josie and Cheryl took a step backwards, covering their mouths.

"Yike!"

Sammy gulped a slug from her canteen, sloshed it in her mouth, gargled and spat.

"Gimme…!"

Lina reached out and grabbed the flask from her.

Hunched down in a rocky outcrop, Cat was scanning the plain below through a pair of field glasses. She cursed violently.

"What is it?" Janey asked.

A cascade of small stones heralded the arrival of Selena and John Warburton, negotiating the perilously steep angles warily.

"What's going on down there?"

Cat stood slowly, heedless of ongoing exchanges of fire all around them. Her eyes flashed green fire.

"Trouble!"

"Don't let them outflank us!"

The hail of fire pouring down on them from the mountainside was diminishing and becoming more erratic, but it was still coming, taking its toll.

We must hold…!

Aiko ducked as a shell burst buffeted her, deluging her in smoking clods of earth and small stones. Shrapnel hissed and whizzed dangerously close.

They mustn't get past us and reach the mountain!

Its tracks grinding, a tank was rolling straight at her, intending to crush and bury her within her sand-bagged command post.

"Look out!"

A wrinkle in the ground made the tank rear upwards, exposing its soft underbelly. Two lithe commandos sprang out of their slit trench and darted towards it. Rolling underneath, between the churning tracks, they clamped circular charges to the thinner skin.

Oh God!

The charges detonated with a scalding flash. One young woman had scrambled far enough to be tossed by the blast back into the trench. The other died, killed instantly by the concussion.

"Bastards…!"

Aiko's eyes burned with tears of rage. A file of infantry had been tailing the tank, using it for shelter. As it rocked and tilted sideways, they were exposed.

Rising from cover, her face distorted with rage, Aiko emptied the magazine of her M16, slaughtering them.

Her example inspired battle cries all along the hard-pressed line. Their resistance intensified – No retreat! No surrender…!

CHAPTER 18

CAT'S CLAWS

Cheryl screamed.

"What the f-f-f—!"

Cat was transforming.

"Holy—!"

Cat was rising, spreading her arms wide, to embrace the world. She was floating, weightless. She was golden, light radiating from her.

Those around her retreated, afraid to be touched by it. Her aurora expanded and enveloped them. In the pale chill of dawn, they were illuminated, warmed and protected.

Bathed in glowing gold, John Warburton was transfixed, murmuring an ancient Eastern mantra. He fumbled in the deep pockets of his battledress for the amber prayer beads, his lucky charm.

In the strange glow, Selena was made of noble bronze. She was galvanized by a supernatural electricity.

"Aaaaaaaaahhhh…!!!"

Janey screamed, jolted by it.

"Ooooohhh…hhhh…!"

Josie moaned, her eyelashes fluttering. Her head rocked slowly from side to side, long brown hair swaying across her face.

Cheryl's paleness was tinted rose gold. Her slim body was vibrating.

Janey was a dark flame, eyes like glowing coals. Lina seethed, her shoulders heaving.

Solid gold, Sammy wrapped her strong arms around herself, so tight she could scarcely breathe.

"Uuuhhh.hhhh…!"

Slowly, Cat stretched out her arms. Bright beams of light fanned out from her fingertips, spanning the war-torn, smoking plain.

They were spread thin, stretched to breaking point.

They mustn't turn our flank!

They were going to, and Aiko knew it. It was only a matter of time – and time was running out.

She saw a tank roll over one of her forward positions, burying its occupants alive in their foxhole.

Oh Jeee-zus…!!!

"Hold on! Hold—!"

High above her, a supernatural sound filled the sky, defying the noise of battle.

Cat's lips were moving. Flowing from her, a timeless incantation resounded off the looming slopes and rang out across the plain.

Far below, Aiko lowered the binoculars and wiped her eyes. She couldn't believe what she was seeing.

The single chanting voice became a mighty chorus, a swelling hymn that rolled across the sky.

Ohhh…hhh….

The sound was a wind that grew in strength until it was a hurricane that swept away the advancing waves of infantry.

OH…!!!

Battered but unbowed, Aiko's troops were rising recklessly, out of their slit trenches and foxholes. Standing on the hastily piled sand bags, they lifted their weapons above their heads, cheering.

OH MY GOD!!!!

Cat was a blinding light. She was white heat and those around her reeled back, slipping and sliding on the steep slope.

The chanting sky echoed with the rolling thunder of drums. The shrieking wind whistled over the heads of Aiko's celebrating warriors and descended upon their enemies, wiping the plain clean of them.

"Look —!"

The stone idol was there, ghastly and gargantuan. Its eyes glowed redly; fire gusted from its fanged jaws.

Rampaging, a raging destroyer, it bowled the tanks over. Their shells burst impotently around it or rebounded off its stony armor, as it crushed them like tin toys.

The sound coming from Cat was a sustained and shattering shriek. The sky was boiling.

Swarms of hideous demons swooped on leathery wings. Cawing and croaking hoarsely, they pursued the fleeing survivors across the plain.

As they ran frantically in all directions they were hoisted in their talons, ripped to shreds by their slavering saw teeth.

Standing on the ramparts of her command post, Aiko squeezed her eyes tight shut.

No…no…no…!!!

She opened them. It was real; it was happening.

"Cat!"
The sky was calmer now, simmering. The drums were murmuring; the music was lilting.
"Cat…?"
Her light became a soft glow. Below, the grotesque idol tossed aside the crumpled shell of the last remaining tank. It turned ponderously and across the soaring distance their eyes met.
Cat seemed to smile secretly and then exhaled a whisper that carried all the way across the plain. Something ancient and mystical.
The idol bowed its monstrous head. It folded its arms across its chest and began to dissolve, becoming transparent, fading until it had vanished completely.

They were breathing again.
"H-holy fuck!" Sammy exclaimed. "You really do have super powers!"
Cat was shaking her head, dazed and confused.

I don't want them!

Janey reached out tentatively to touch her.
"We'll have to think of a super hero name for you!"
"Super Cat…!"
"Wonder Cat…!"
Cheryl laughed.
"How about Cool Cat?"
"Or Crazy Cat," suggested Lina.
Cat laughed at that, nodding, and they all joined in.
"I'll take that!"
All except Selena. She was looking up anxiously at the sky.
"The rockets!" she cried. "What about the rockets?"

Miles above, the flight of four rockets was on the ethereal fringe of the Earth's atmosphere and was arcing on the edge of Space, stars and galaxies twinkling above them.
They commenced a shallow curve, poised to plunge towards their target.

Miles below, the Ghetto was waking to another day of ducking and diving, the daily struggle for survival.
Children made their beds on the fire escape in summer because there was no room for them inside. They stirred and climbed back in again. Their mothers toiled to control them as they ran wild, despairing but still praying for deliverance.

Above them, the rockets were tilting, poised to eject their toxic contents before proceeding to a secret splashdown in remote waters.

The streamlined nose cones were opening, like the petals of a flower. And like a gust of pollen carried on the wind, a cloud of tiny silver globes expanded, floated and then began to descend.

Twinkling in the blue sky, it would seed the Ghetto and infuse the blood of its restless malcontented Youth.

There death would lie dormant, timed to emerge in adulthood as a previously unknown and incurable disease; programmed genetically to target the males of a specified minority.

A minority deemed undesirable – for the good of the country.

Cat smiled at Selena; her eyes sparking strangely.

"Rockets?" she said. "What rockets…?"

Gazing upwards, she made a dismissive movement with her hand, as though she was wafting something away.

The cloud of silver globes evaporated, became a glittering dust that dissipated harmlessly.

At the mouth of the Bay, as the gleaming Cityscape receded behind it, the fishing fleet was readying its nets.

"What the hell…?"

The dull thud of a sonic boom made crew on the deck and skippers in the wheel house duck suddenly.

Four great splashes, four tall columns of white water in a row, half a mile off the bow. The shockwaves reached them, making the boats rock slowly.

"What the fuck was that?"

"Beats me…."

"YOU FUCKING BITCH…!!!!"

He was clawing his way up the rocky slope, his hands raw and bleeding.

"YOU'RE DEAD!" he screamed. "I'M GOING TO—!!!!"

The Colonel was bruised and battered, tattered and torn.

Beneath the stains of battle, he was costumed like his hero, General George S. Patton: polished helmet; riding breeches and boots; tailored tunic festooned with ribbons; Sam Browne belt supporting twin ivory-handled Colt Peacemakers.

"I'M G-G-G—!!!!"

He was deranged, his face scorched and scabbed with blood. As he clambered up frenziedly towards them, he was firing wildly with a pistol in each hand; and kept on and on although the hammers were clicking on empty.

Eagerly, Cat stepped forward to meet him.

"Come and get it, motherfucker!"

John Warburton reached out and grabbed her arm.

"He's mine!"

Cursing, the Colonel tossed away the spent revolvers. On a confined plateau of flat ground, the two big men circled each other

Take him, Uncle John!

They engaged in a whirlwind, a deadly martial ballet of chops and kicks and blocks.

Cat and Selena were bobbing and swaying, shadow boxing. Janey had her fist to her mouth, gnawing on her knuckles. Josie gripped Lina's sleeve, twisting the cloth tightly. Lina was oblivious, her eyes wide, thrilled.

"Kill that fucker!" Cheryl shrilled.

"Hurt him!" Sammy shouted vengefully. "Hurt him bad!"

Snarling through a mask of dust and crusted blood, the Colonel made a move that John Warburton seemed to fall for.

The others gasped, but Cat was grinning viciously.

You're fucked!

Deceived, the Colonel pressed home his attack.

"YAAAAHHH...!!!!"

John Warburton was a blur, moving with sight-defying speed. The Colonel's rush was halted abruptly. His bulk was flipped effortlessly as his weight was turned against him.

"AAAAAAAAAAAAIIIIIIIEEEEEEEEE....!!!!"

He vanished over the edge; he screamed all the way down.

He left the polished helmet behind him. Cat picked it up and gave it to her Uncle. He could see his reflection in it. He could see the dead boy, reaching his thin arms out to him.

"That was for you, son...."

The telephone jangled.

"You'd better come and see this, Professor!"

There was something in the tone of voice that made him hurry to the Main Gallery.

The Chief Curator and two uniformed guards were waiting for him.

"What do you make of this, Professor...?"

They were scratching their heads and shrugging at each other, incredulous.

"I can't believe it!" exclaimed the Chief Curator.

I can...!

Reverently, the Professor gazed up into the cold eyes of the towering stone idol, back where it belonged, commanding the long gallery.

"It just appeared," one of the guards gasped. "Right in front of my eyes!"

Exhilarated, the Professor clapped his hands, hugged himself.

"How marvelous!" he cried. "It's wonderful...!"

They stared at him blankly, shot each other worried glances.

The Professor turned and was shuffling away down the length of the gallery, as fast as his old legs could carry him, waving his arms ecstatically.

"She has mastered it!" he was proclaiming. "She has become a goddess!"

"Stop looking at me like that," Cat told Aiko's battle-weary survivors. "Like I was some kind of god!"

Her Uncle put his arm around her shoulders.

"Well, you gotta admit," he chuckled. "You put on one hell of a show!"

Cat frowned as he released her. Disturbing sounds and images were scrambling her thoughts.

Suddenly, she felt very tired, her strength draining down through her long legs. They folded beneath her as she sat on the ground.

Janey came and stood over her.

"Aw, you'll always be just Crazy Cat to us!"

Cat smiled at her gratefully and took her hand. She let Janey haul her back to her feet again.

"Thanks!"

Selena enfolded Aiko in her arms.

"Great job!" she declared. "We'd have been screwed if they'd got past you!"

Aiko was looking at Cat, surrounded by her youthful team.

"They almost did!" she sighed.

She gazed out across the smoldering wreckage of her defenses.

"We lost some," she said sorrowfully. "Too many!"

Selena nodded grimly.

"We'll remember them," she said fiercely. "Every one of them!"

John Warburton threw away the Colonel's helmet. Still gripping Aiko's hand, Selena reached out and pulled him close to her. They kissed ferociously.

"What now?" asked John Warburton, as their lips parted.

Selena's eyes flashed with fierce determination.

"The end game," she replied. "We track this evil to its source!"

"Whooooooooooooooooo…."

Top down, Cat was burnin' rubber.

"….ooooooo-eeeeeeeeeeeeeeee….!!!!"

She was rockin' and rollin'.

The yellow Corvette ZL-1 was a streak of light. She was traveling faster than light, faster than sound, out-racing the Funky declarations fan-faring from her speakers.

The giant disk of the dawning sun rolled along the vast sweep of the watery horizon, keeping pace with her. The sea gleamed and sparkled like pale gold, the surf was frothing champagne.

"Oh yeeeeeeeeeeaaaaaaaaaaaaaaaaaaaahhhhhhh….!!!!"

100…110……………140………..

The wind in the golden banner of her hair was cleansing her. She was clad only in a skimpy bikini and the thrill of the cooling blast on her skin was exhilarating.

....150....160.....................

The tour group expelled a collective sigh. Their guide bathed in it.

"Yes, ladies and gentlemen...the Oval Office!"

Crisp in her official blazer and pleated skirt, she gave them long enough to register that they were really there.

"No photographs, please," she admonished them firmly. "But we do have postcards available in the Gift Shop...."

Some were plainly disappointed not to have found the President sat at his desk waiting to greet them. The guide was ushering them out, glancing at her watch.

"And now, we'll be moving on to...!"

Her lust for speed satisfied, Cat swerved the 'Vette off the black-top of the coast highway. Onto the broad beach that separated her beach house from the sparkling ocean.

She showed off, carving along the border of sea and sand, flying on tall glittering wings of spray. She spun her shark-like ride in a dizzy "bootlegger's turn".

"Yay...!"

Her team was there to greet her.

"Way t'go, Crazy Cat...!"

They were decked out for a day by the sea. Janey and Cheryl wore skin-tight wet suits, surf boards tucked under their arms. Bikini-clad, Sammy was already on the water, astride her board, riding the curling crests of the speeding breakers.

"Hey, y'all...!"

Josie's bikini was a bold fashion statement; Lina's was downright scandalous.

Oh my...!

They were fussing over a rainbow beach blanket.

"Well," snapped Lina. "If you've got a better spot, go to it!"

Cat smiled; the sound of them arguing somehow made her feel restored, reassured.

"Hiya...!"

Cheryl let her board drop onto the sand. Janey speared hers so it stood upright. They strolled over to the parked Stingray and leant into its black leather cockpit.

Janey depressed a chromed button and popped out the 8-track. The Funky grooves were cut off in their prime.

"Hey!" Cat protested.

They over-balanced and were head down in the well of the car, rooting around.

"You got any Led Zep...?"

Behind the stately façade maintained for public consumption lay the murky corridors of power.

A color-coded phone buzzed, muffled because it was concealed in a locked drawer.

"Yes…?"

The deadpan voice was disguised, mechanical.…

Cat was glowing as she emerged from the shower, reaching for a towel.

Drying herself slowly, luxuriously, she was smiling at the sounds of her team whooping it up on the beach below her elevated dwelling.

Diverted to a window, she laughed. Lina and Josie, stretched out lazily on their enormous blanket, sat up and shook their fists, at three surfer girls galloping by and kicking up sand.

Chuckling, Cat untangled the flex of a hand-held dryer and plugged it in. Shaking out her wet hair, she leant towards the bathroom mirror.

OH—!!!

The face that looked back at her belonged to someone else.

"Oh God…!!!"

Red-eyed, leering, exposing decaying yellowed teeth filed to a point. The wrinkled, desiccated painted death mask of the village Shaman.

Black.…

Black night. A convoy of black bullet-proof vehicles with windows of jet-black glass.

They had coded license plates that warned lesser powers to back off.…

The old man was yawning and rubbing the sleep from his eyes.

"I'm sorry to disturb you, Professor.…"

The sight of her was enough to tell him that it was both urgent and desperately important.

She was ghostly pale, her features strained, hollow eyes sunk in dark circles. She'd come in a rush, in T-shirt and jeans, on bare feet.

"That's quite alright, my dear, please do come in and tell me all about it.…"

Front and rear, the secretive formation was protected by armored personnel carriers, equipped with heavy caliber machine-guns and rocket launchers.

Anyone who got in their way was forced off the highway, blasted by a barrage of flashing red lights and shrill sirens.

The Professor cut a figure from the previous century: long dressing gown that draped down to the toes of his slippers, a tasseled sleeping cap.

Cat might have smiled at the sight of him had she not been so consumed by anxiety. Instead, she doubted whether such a manifestation of quaint eccentricity could possibly help her.

"Now, my dear Miss Warburton, how may I be of assistance?"

In a rush, breathlessly, the words tumbling hoarsely over each other, Cat told him her story.

Sat behind his antique desk, the Professor listened intently. He observed her keenly, over the top of his pince-nez, his chin resting on his steepled fingers.

It felt like forever, since Janey had last seen herself in her street clothes.

She caressed the battered black leather biker jacket, encrusted with badges and symbols that proclaimed her defiant individuality and flipped the finger to the world.

Since forever, she had literally slept in it; now it seemed oddly unfamiliar.

Sighing, she pulled it tight, hugging it to her.

"Yeah, I know…."

Cheryl came and stood beside her. They filled the full-length mirror in their beach-side motel room.

"Feels strange, doesn't it?"

Cheryl had retrieved a favorite T-shirt, canary yellow with a brash challenging slogan slashed across the chest in scarlet. She held it up to the mirror, as though she was about to try it on for the very first time.

Janey was shuffling her feet. After so long in combat boots, her comfortably grimy Hi-Tops made her feel like she was walking on air.

"Jeez…!"

They studied each other in the mirror.

"Yeah…." sighed Cheryl.

Janey shivered suddenly. She reached out and gripped Cheryl's hand.

"Hey?" she asked. "We're okay, ain't we?"

Cheryl's sober reflection was looking back at her.

"I mean," Janey persisted. "We're still us, ain't we…?"

The mechanical voice cracked like a whip.

"The Colonel has sacrificed his life for his country…!"

Cat had run out of words. Out of breath, she slumped back weakly into the padded depths of a worn old leather armchair.

Time seemed to stand still. And then the Professor was smiling.

"I think I have it, my child…."

Sammy was wondering whether she had found her true self.

Sat cross-legged in front of the TV that stood in the corner of her motel room, she drifted in and out of the ball game.

Snap-click-snap…!

She could field strip and re-assemble the 9 mm Browning Hi-Power with her eyes shut.

"Oooooo…yeah!"

She twirled the gun on her forefinger.

Snap-click…click…!

Josie was right beside her, working the oiled slide. She flashed an evil grin.

"And my mom wanted me to play with dolls!"

A second voice took up where its predecessor left off, speaking with equal authority.

"We go to Plan B!"

"You must try and relax, my dear," the Professor spoke soothingly. If this is to work…."

Cat subsided into the depths of the armchair. Like a child, she wanted to curl up and hide inside it.

"Here, drink this…."

Served in a polished stone goblet, its surface was swirled and oily. As her lips approached it, Cat hesitated, flinching from its pungent odor.

"Go on, don't be afraid."

Cat took a tentative sip and recoiled, grimacing. It tasted as bad as it smelled. Even worse.

"Ugh!"

Holding the stone chalice in one hand, the Professor supported her head gently with the other.

"Go on," he murmured. "You must drink it all…."

Gulping, Cat screwed her eyes tight shut and consumed the bitter brew. Its sourness had a tang of decay and for a moment her bowels rebelled, threatening to reject it.

"Agh…uuuggghhh…gghhh…!"

The cup drained, Cat sagged backwards. Setting it down on a small side table, the old man left her. Crossing the room, he moved amongst the exotic antiquities that cluttered his dusty study.

The domed lid of an iron-bound chest creaked open and he stooped to rummage inside it.

"Aha!"

The Professor withdrew a scrolled parchment. Cradling it in both arms, his back bent, he carried it across to his desk, leaving a trail of ancient dust and dry fragments on the worn carpet.

With a grunt, he let the heavy scroll thud onto the desk-top, jolting brass ink-wells and an assortment of odd ornaments. He gazed across the room at the figure sprawled loosely in the armchair.

"We must give it time to work…."

Reclining on the bed, Lina drained a beer can, crushed it and dunked it with pinpoint accuracy in a waste basket across the room.

"Three points!"

Burping, she wiped her mouth with the back of her hand.

They watched the game for a while.

"Hey?" asked Sammy. "How many people do you think we've killed?"

Lina shrugged, diving into a jumbo-bag of potato chips.

"Dunno," she replied, her mouth full. "A hundred?"

They looked at Josie.

"C'mon, Brainbox," Sammy laughed. "Do the Maths!"

Josie was looking down at the pistol in her lap. There was an uneasy silence.

"How do you feel about it?" Lina asked.

Josie shrugged, turning her head towards the TV screen.

"Third quarter's starting…."

Cat's limbs felt as though they were made of lead.

"Mmmmmmmm…mmmm….!"

Her head tilted forward till her chin rested on her chest.

"I think we're ready now!"

Leaning over his desk, the Professor unfurled the large scroll. The yellowed parchment was wrinkled and crumbling at the edges, blotched by faded stains.

"Ah, yes…"

His eyes gleaming, the old man studied a jumble of cryptic symbols, wrapped around lively depictions of strange deities and exotic animals. Humans in ceremonial robes and feathers danced attendance.

"Now, let us see…!"

Only to the scholarly eye did it form a language. One that consisted of ancient dark arts, known to the very few.

Passing his thin hands over the parchment, the Professor began to chant, his frail body bowing rhythmically. An evocation that was all guttural grunts and tongue-clicking consonants was forced up from the pit of his stomach.

"Aaaaaaa…aaaahhh…hhhhh…!"

Cat's limp body spasmed and then arched rigidly up out of the deep armchair. Her fingers clamped on the padded arm rests.

"AAAAAIIIIEEEEE…!!!!"

Her eyes opened wide. She shrieked, mouth gaping.

"AAAAAAAAAIIIIIEEEEEE…GGGHHH…!!!!"

As her body convulsed and thrust upwards, tentacles of pale green light issued from her open mouth. They twisted and wrapped around her, as though reluctant to leave her.

Her face contorted, Cat writhed, screaming.

Behind his desk, the Professor stood erect, suddenly powerful, his arms flung out wide. His chanting grew louder and louder, making everything in the cluttered study vibrate, resonate and rattle.

"UUUUUUUHHH…HHHH…HHH…HH…!!!!"

Cat's undulations were slowing and reducing, her shrill ululations mellowing. The coils of green light were detaching from her body. As they slithered away from her across the floor they began to merge and take on a discernable form.

The Professor's strident tone was commanding and the solidifying shape seemed to cower before him.

"Be gone, evil spirit!" the Professor demanded. "Leave her and depart…!"

It was recognizable now – the gaunt Shaman, clutching his staff and draped in his evil charms.

"Go from this earthly plane to the realms of darkness where you belong!"

The glowing green ghoul made one last feeble gesture of defiance, shaking the staff just once before fading and then vanishing in a twist of twinkling vapor.

Lina's eyes clouded.

"We're all going to go to Hell," she stated. "That's for sure."

Sammy snatched the bag of potato chips from her.

"Huh!" she scoffed dismissively, stuffing her mouth, crumbs spilling from her chin.

Josie picked up the gun and worked the slide again.

"Hell?" she said darkly. "I've already been there!"

"Ooooohhh…what happened…?"

Cat sat forward gingerly and pressed her palms to her throbbing temples.

"Oh, my head…!"

The Professor was beside himself, a-quiver with glee.

"It worked!" he cried. "It actually worked!"

Cat tried to stand up. Her legs turned to water and she fell back down again, enfolded by the deep chair.

"W-w-what worked?" she mumbled in confusion.

The Professor was leaning over her solicitously, stroking her drooping shoulders and offering her a tumbler of brandy.

"Here, this will do you good…."

Cat gulped it down; some went down the wrong way and she coughed and spluttered, red-faced.

"Well…?"

Recovered, she looked at him for an explanation.

"He's gone!"

Cat frowned, bewildered, still shaken.

"Who's gone?"

The Professor was jiggling on his toes, hugging himself.

"The wicked priest," he proclaimed. "I have exorcised him; he tried to live on within you but now his evil spirit has left your body and been extinguished!"

Cat was rubbing her eyes.

"Does that mean," she asked hopefully. "That I won't have those crazy bad trips anymore?"

The Professor pursed his thin lips.

"Ah, yes, well...."

Cat's eyebrows shot upwards.

"Well what!"

The Professor was embarrassed.

"Well, you might yet retain those ancient powers...."

Cat groaned, hunched forward, her head in her hands.

The Professor hastened to pour her another brandy, pressing it upon her.

"From now on, my dear Miss Warburton, they should remain entirely at your command!"

Cat groaned again.

Brisk footfalls echoed crisply, rebounding off the polished walls.

"Come on!"

The secret tunnel, lined with pale granite, had seen service under a long line of Presidents, going back to the turn of the 19th Century. It had smuggled dangerous liaisons in and out, from giggling showgirls to cultured courtesans. It had facilitated confidential diplomacy.

"Let's go...!"

This time, it was grim-faced middle-aged grey men in suits. Red-faced and puffing, they were urged on by lean younger men in black suits, shades and ties, bulky satchels slung across their broad shoulders, a heavy suitcase in each hand.

Panting, the grey men were glancing anxiously at their watches. The men in black were cursing.

"Faster...!"

The telephone on the Professor's desk was an historical relic. Its melodic tinkle was a sound from another age.

"Yes...?"

His high forehead furrowed.

"It's for you."

Cat heaved herself heavily out of the armchair. He handed the old contraption to her.

"Oh, hi Aiko...."

In the bell-shaped brass ear-piece, Aiko's voice crackled thinly; the urgency in her voice was unmistakable.

"Cat, assemble your team – we have a job for you!"

The clandestine airfield was a charred ruin; a festering wound, black scabs and dark bruises staining the desert.

"Make it fast...!"

Starkly, the smooth runway had been repaired and made ready for use again.

"We've got no time to lose!"

The dawn was spreading from the luminous horizons. Its rosy tint glinted on the swept wings of the twin-engine Lear Jet, poised at the end of the runway, ready to leap like a dancer into the air.

The pilot was checking his flight plan, tracing the route for his deputy. The engines were turning over slowly as the black convoy sped towards them, raising a glowing tower of pale pink dust.

"They're making a run for it," said Aiko.

"No chance!" declared Selena.

"But after that...?" John Warburton pondered.

"What the — ?"

Some sixth sense made the co-pilot look up.

"Jesus!"

Claws like sharpened steel were ripping through the armor plating of the personnel carriers, shredding it like tissue paper.

"AAAAAAAIIIIIIGGG-GGHH-GHHHHH...!!!"

"YAAAAAAA-GGGHHH...HHH...!!!"

Snarling savagely, it raked out the men inside, flaying them alive, ripping them to pieces.

"AAAAARRRRRGGGGHHH-GGGGHH-HHHH...!!!"

The sealed cargo came spilling out onto the ground, metal crates bursting open and disgorging gleaming gold bars and a sparkling shower of diamonds.

Wedged between their destroyed escorts, the black limousines were paralyzed. Then they were shunting back and sideways into each other as their drivers tried to turn, reverse, go forward, in any direction that offered escape.

"Now...!"

Janey's yell had the team rising from the ground, out of thin air, cloaked in camouflage that blended them into the desert floor.

"Get 'em!" Sammy shouted.

They advanced swiftly and ringed the cars as they rocked and slid and banged together, firing their machine-pistols from the hip.

"Get 'em all!"

The ammo in their magazines was armor-piercing. Neat nine-millimeter holes punctured the gleaming bodywork as they sprayed the trapped vehicles. The jet-black windshields and side windows fractured, starred and then collapsed in fragments.

The dimly glimpsed figures inside juddered and jerked in their seats, heads rocked by the impact, arms flopping. The force of the barrage held them upright and when it ceased they folded and sagged down limply.

"Motherfuckers!" spat Lina.

Its hinges ruptured, a door detached. Blood flowed out like a red waterfall. A mutilated body slumped at Josie's feet. It groaned; she cursed, gesturing with her gun impotently.

"I'm empty."

Cheryl shrugged.

"Me too."

They watched him die.

The dead man had dragged a suitcase out with him. The clasps popped open and revealed thick wads of dollar bills. They stood and gaped.

The bundles of banknotes were wedged in tight. Cheryl tugged one out; she read the numbers on the band securing it, her eyes widening.

"Holy fuck! There must be—!"

"Look out!"

A searing whine was the pilot gunning the engines; the Lear Jet began to roll forward.

The roar that drowned the engines was supernatural. A wing was torn off at the root. The crippled plane toppled sideways, grinding to a halt.

"OH GOD NO!"

Claws carved jagged furrows down the length of the fuselage. The pilot's scream was smothered by a thudding detonation as the aircraft vanished in a ball of flame.

"Yipes!"

The hot blast bowled them over and they lay there, pressing their bodies into the ground.

Selena smiled, a vicious gleam in her eyes.

"Poor dumb bastards!"

They stared, speechless.

"Good job, you guys!"

Radiant and triumphant, Cat was standing there smiling at them.

"You're the best!"

Their minds were blank. It was beyond their powers to comprehend. They had no means of expressing what they wanted to say.

It was left to Sammy, who took all things in her stride.

She strolled over to survey the mangled remains of the armored personnel carriers, fingering the shredded claw marks in the thick plating.

She looked across at Cat and grinned.

"Cool!"

CHAPTER 19

COUP DE GRACE

"Ten…nine…eight….!"

November 1952 – charts of the Pacific showed a small dot at the tail of an uninhabited atoll.

"…seven…six….!"

It was "a small naked island" and was thus dispensable. It was eminently suitable.

"…five…four…three…!"

As was the norm, the Bomb had a quaint code name.

"…two…one!"

It all went as planned; the experiment was pronounced perfect.

The rest was dry sanitizing statistics – the fireball was "three and one quarter" miles wide; the island "became dust and ash, pulled upward to form a mushroom cloud that rose about twenty-seven miles into the sky".

They were very precise about it. The Bomb had a "yield" of 10.4 megatons, seven hundred times the explosive energy inflicted upon Hiroshima. They'd come a long way, they told each other proudly, in a few short years.

They rode back together, secluded in the sky.

The bulkheads and padding muffled the noise as twin rotors churned the hot air rising from the desert, riding the dense turbulence.

"Hey…?" asked Janey.

"Hey what?" Cat grinned at her.

She felt ten tons lighter; all was crystal clear.

Janey frowned; hesitating, she looked away.

Cat tweaked her sleeve, smiling.

"What is it?"

Janey was struggling to find the words. Cat read her thoughts.

"Is it what you saw out there?"

Janey nodded, a nervous jerk of her head.

"Uh, yeah…."

Swallowing hard, she got it together.

"That thing you do," she hesitated again. "You know…."

"Yes, I know."

"Well…?"

"Yes?"

"Uh…er…well…well, you can't, I mean…?"

"You mean can it ever attack you?"

Janey lowered her eyes, embarrassed, nodding dumbly.

Cat tucked her hand under Janey's chin and lifted her downcast face gently.

"No," she smiled warmly. "That won't happen!"

Dawn filtered through the cracks in the velvet curtains.

"Mmmmm…good morning lover…."

The "Dream Girl" escort agency combined the two oldest professions in the world. One was obvious; the other a closely guarded secret.

Pillow talk; careless talk….

"You must be very proud, General."

She was statuesque, long-legged, glossy auburn waves framing hazel eyes that radiated hero worship.

Smiling, she lit his cigar. Patting the hairy mound of his belly, the General luxuriated on the satin sheets, his body tingling with voluptuous memories.

He blew smoke at the overhanging canopy of the gilded four-poster bed, dominating his palatial hotel suite.

"One does what one must, my dear," he declared grandly. "One must be prepared to be ruthless, if one is a true patriot!"

He sucked and blew smugly.

"All undesirables must be eliminated, for the good of the country!"

Leaning sideways, he cupped a bountiful breast.

"Are you a true patriot, my dear…?"

The young woman chuckled, her eyes gleaming saucily.

"Oh General!" she cooed. "You know I am!"

She swung her long legs off the bed and sauntered across the dim bed chamber, hips swinging.

The General's eyes feasted on her curves, tinted by the rosy dawn.

"Oh God…!" he groaned ecstatically.

She undulated back to him, a ruby red wine glass in each hand.

"Let's toast the flag, General!"

He was sat up, propped against the pillows. She handed a glass to him.

"The Stars and Stripes…!"

"Forever!"

He drained it in a thirsty gulp. Setting it down on a bedside table, he reached out for her.

"Now, young lady, why don't you show me again—!"

Suddenly, he grunted, looking puzzled. He coughed.

"Uh…."

He coughed again, and again, grabbing his flabby chest.

"Wha…uuuhhh…hhh…?"

His face darkened, turning purple; he struggled to breathe. His eyes bulged.

"Aaakk…kkk…kk…!"

His body spasmed, his spine arching violently.

"Ggggg…hhhh…hhh…!

He slid down off the stacked pillows. Convulsive shudders shook him, his mouth foaming.

Standing at the foot of the bed, the young woman was calmly dressing, slipping into her seductive, low-cut costume.

She glanced at her watch.

"Thirty seconds...."

One last shiver and the General lay still. His strained features relaxed, his death mask frozen in what might pass for a warped grin.

"Hmph!"

His assassin was holding a small two-way radio.

"Mission accomplished," she confirmed. "It'll look like a heart attack; it'll look like he died happy!"

Post-1952, the map of the Pacific was less one tiny dot. To the world, the island no longer existed.

But it did; unseen, far below the surface.

The death scene was played out again, in discreet motel rooms and exclusive penthouses.

"G-G-Ghaaarrgghh...ggghh...!"

Execution at dawn.

"Aaaaarrgghh...g-g-gaaarghh-hhh...!"

It was easy to believe that the ageing bureaucrat had paid for his amorous exertions with a predictable coronary.

"Ooooogghhh...g-g-gaaaa-k-kk...kkkkk...!"

"Aaaaagghhh-gghh...ggg...hhhh....!"

"G-Gaaaarrkkk-kkk-kk-hhhh...hhh...!"

The tally included the Army, Navy, Air Force and Marines. It extended to the corridors of power, the legislature and the executive, high on the food chain. The secret world of the C.I.A. and N.S.A.

Some died in sin, playing away from home. Others died in their own beds, waking their wives with their death throes.

"OH MY G-GOD...!!!"

All it took was a puff of vapor administered in their sleep by a slender black-masked intruder, gone in the time it took for it to take effect.

One by one, they were crossed off Selena's death list.

Rubber stamped: "No suspicious circumstances".

The autopsies would find nothing sinister. There would be no trace of the "Dream Girl" escort agency. It never existed.

"Do I look fat in this?"

Josie was laughing as she struck a pose. They were all laughing, waddling like ducks, in rubber suits, their feet shod in flippers.

Cheryl had steamed up her face mask. Sammy tapped on the glass.

"Anyone home?"

Janey was experimenting with the raised tube of her snorkel, sucking loudly on the mouthpiece. Chortling, Sammy clamped her hand over the blow-hole, cutting off her air supply.

"Hey!" Janey spluttered, spitting it out.

Chuckling, Cat watched them, shaking her head.

"Okay, that will do, children," she declared. "You've had your fun…!"

Lina was scowling.

"Aw, heck!" she exclaimed, exasperated.

The wet suit looked sleek and sexy on Cat's athletic frame. They frowned at her enviously.

"You've been soldiers," she told them. "Now you're going to be sailors!"

Down there the sea seemed lifeless, abandoned. The green luminosity that filtered from the rippled surface faded into near darkness.

Even the sharks avoided it, veering away and giving it a wide berth, as though they sensed some sinister threat.

Clustered on the submerged stump of the obliterated island, the domes had been thoroughly camouflaged. Their smooth, un-natural symmetry was disguised by a ragged blanket that blended into the sea bed.

The few bold fish that did venture near enough could detect steady vibrations that pulsed from deep within, something mechanical and man-made.

The cave was a gaping maw, swallowing the green sea as it came rolling in.

"Oh, wow…!"

They stood on the dock deep within, craning to look around them, their heads tilted all the way back.

The cavern was a mighty, steel-buttressed cathedral, vastly enlarged and reinforced with smooth concrete. In a blaze of light, it rang with clanging, banging echoes, seething with purposeful activity.

Tethered to the pier on which they stood were the grey steel bullet-shapes of streamlined midget submarines.

"How do you like our new toys…?"

In basic battledress, Selena was striding along the dock towards them, smiling broadly.

She radiated strength and determination, reflected in the bright faces of Aiko and John Warburton.

"Fuckin' A, man…!"

Led by Janey and Sammy, Cat's team were hopping down and clambering all over them, testing the watertight releases of the hatches, peering through the thick lenses of the portholes in the stubby conning towers.

They looked up hopefully, at John Warburton leaning over and grinning above them.

"All bought and paid for!" he chuckled. "You'll get to play with them alright!"

Amidst all the bright-eyed enthusiasm, Cat looked strangely somber.

"Hey Selena?" she muttered out of the side of her mouth. "With all the resources at your disposal, have you ever thought of just taking over the country?"

Surprised, her Uncle straightened up and took a step backwards. Aiko blinked. They weren't sure if she was joking.

"No, Cat," Selena laughed. "Not with you there to stop me!"

Shaped like blunt arrowheads, thrusting powerfully, an undersea convoy hauled a long train of cylindrical containers, emblazoned with symbols that warned of high volatility and toxicity.

"Standby…standby…!"

Approaching the disguised domes, the convoy was escorted by a fast-moving swarm of two-man "human torpedoes". Nimble submersibles radiated probing beams into the murk.

"Make ready to secure…!"

The containers were draped around the circumference of the domes. They nestled to them tightly, like suckling young.

The process was displayed on panoramic viewing screens.

"Ach, zo…!"

He was galvanized by a religious fervor, his sparse frame quivering within the white lab coat that was a size too large for him.

"Bald! Sehr bald!"

His fever infected the military men gathered around him. For their benefit, he translated.

"Soon, meine herren!" he exclaimed. "Soon we will have die formel – the formula – refined to a new level…!"

He was beaming, his pale eyes blazing fanatically.

"Es wird perfekt!"

Don't panic!

A hissing that was a physical force, threatening to crush her skull.

Whatever you do, don't panic…!

The water level was bubbling at her knees, rising swiftly to drown her thighs. In seconds, it had enveloped her hips, wrapped around her waist.

Stay cool…!

The savage chill penetrated the rubberized second skin of the tight wet-suit.

"Nnnn…ngghh…!!!"

She gritted her teeth as it churned and frothed around her heaving rib-cage, stifling her breath, making her bones ache.

"UH…HHH…!!!"

It buoyed up beneath her armpits, surged over her shivering shoulders.

Reaching up with numbed fingers, she cupped the blunt snout of the breathing mask, testing the security of the elastic straps.

Her feet detached weightlessly from the floor of the deep tubular chamber. She began to rise.

As the water closed over the top of her head she flipped a switch. It activated her emergency air supply, flowing through a flexed tube from a square canister strapped to her chest.

Entwined in strands of glittering bubbles, her body rose rapidly, accelerating towards a bright circle high above. She kicked with her legs to propel her faster and faster.

"Here she comes!"

Janey's head and shoulders broke the churning surface and bobbed there, making waves that sloshed over the side walls of the tank and made them all jump backwards.

"Way t'go, Janey!"

Gasping, Janey tugged off the mask and trod water, tossing her wet hair back from her eyes.

"Woo!" she exclaimed. "Man, what a rush!"

Sheathed lithely in their wet-suits, Cat and Aiko flashed a grin at each other. Aiko opened her mouth but Sammy beat her to it.

"Me next...!"

He could scarcely contain himself.

"If I may say so myself," he proclaimed. "It is a work of genius!"

He was the very image of the evil genius. Desiccated, cadaverous, a glinting monocle wedged above a jutting cheekbone over which his skin stretched like sallow parchment.

In the privacy of his steel-walled quarters he could be his true self, in the all-black uniform that now hung loosely on him.

He swiveled stiffly to face a gilt-framed portrait, an icon salvaged from the ruins of a monstrous dream.

Spittle flecked his lips. He clicked his heels and raised his hand in the old stiff-armed salute.

"It is worthy of you, mein Fuhrer!"

His bent back straightened as his stooped shoulders appeared to expand and fill the baggy folds of his old uniform.

"We will provide these American swine with the means to corrupt and ultimately destroy themselves – the drugs, the tools of mass destruction...!"

His rising voice had a supernatural echo.

"The fools imagine that we serve them, but it is they who will bow to our will and our higher purpose...!"

An echo from a dark past, one that had once enthralled the adoring masses.

"And when we have done, a Fourth Reich shall rise like the immortal phoenix from their ashes!"

He wasn't accustomed to making his calls from a public phone box in the dead of night.

"Hello...?"

His hat brim was tugged low, trench coat collar turned up, like something from a bad B-movie.

"Hello...!"

The Rolex that flashed on his wrist was solid gold, like his cuff links. His college ring was Ivy League. He wore the enameled Stars 'n Stripes pinned to his expensively tailored lapel.

"Yes, that's right," his tone was low and conspiratorial. "They're getting too close...!"

Jerking the turned-up collar higher, he glanced over his shoulder.

"You've had your orders," he snapped, before slamming the receiver down. "With extreme prejudice!"

"Yeah, I know, Cat," Selena chuckled.

It was a beautiful morning with an invigorating breeze wafting in from the sea.

"I should drive American...."

On an isolated stretch of the coastal highway, they were cruising in Selena's pride and joy, an aristocratic "Silver Birch" Aston Martin DB5.

Cat made a face. Its smooth sophistication was alien to senses turned on by the rampant raw power of American Muscle.

"Hmph!"

Selena laughed.

"So, what about your Uncle's pet A.C. Cobra?" she teased. "Made in England and you're always begging him to let you drive it!"

Cat snorted.

"Yup, made in England – fine-tuned in the good ol' U.S.A.!"

A swift shadow flitted across the sloping windshield and then back again before seeming to hover above them.

"Uh-oh!"

The olive drab Huey veered low to skim the roadside parallel to them, matching their speed.

The cabin door was wide open and they glimpsed figures crouched inside, manning a heavy machine-gun on a swivel mount.

"Mutha...!"

Selena twisted the wheel and slid the Aston sideways and below the streaking landing skids.

The burst of pale tracer fanned out harmlessly above them.

"Cat...!"

She knew what to do. Eyes blazing, Cat flipped up a lid on the padded rest between the front seats. Her fingertip selected from a panel of small silver switches.

The Aston's trunk opened on slick hydraulics, revealing three short polished tubes projecting upwards.

"Go!"

Selena nudged the accelerator. Taking the chopper pilot by surprise, the silver DB5 surged ahead of him.

"Now!"

The pilot saw the muzzles of the rocket launchers but had no time to react.

"Boom…!"

The fireball illuminated the refined interior of the Aston Martin and boiled hotly in the rear-view mirror.

"Yike…!"

They ducked, hunching their shoulders as they felt the flash on the back of their necks.

"Wooo-eeeee…!"

At a safe distance, Selena pulled over. The mangled wreck had rolled down off the edge of the highway. Black smoke was casting a long shadow across the beach.

They flinched again as ammo blew and created a brief firework display, strands of smoking tracer arcing into the blue sky.

"Let's get out of here!"

Grinning, they high-fived and were on their way, leaving the scene of destruction far behind them.

"We must be very close," Selena stated.

She unhooked a CB handset from the dash.

"Aiko, it's a go…!"

Jumping out of a plane was second nature to them now.

"Woooo…!!!"

Aiko counted them off.

Steady…steady….

This was a bigger and better thrill.

They were walking off the ramp of a giant C-130, spilling from its cavernous belly. Skinned in rubber, wearing masks connected to tanks on their backs, flippers strapped to their feet.

They were jumping into the vast shining ocean.

"Geronimo…!!!"

There was no reassuring jump line to do the work for them.

"Woooo…oooooo…oooooooo….!!!"

They went spread-eagled, in controlled free-fall, stacked in an ascending column.

"Yeeeeee-hah…hhhhh….!!!"

Poised on the lip of the ramp, Aiko counted most of them off before stepping into the void. She tilted down and nose-dived, her arms tight to her sides, legs clamped together, her body a swift arrow.

As she flashed by, overtaking them, they whooped, their shrill cry whipped away by the jet stream.

Not yet…!

Aiko flattened out, spread herself and slowed dramatically.

Not yet...!

Star-shaped, they felt like they were floating eternally. There was no sense of falling, only the air tugging at their outspread limbs.

Almost...!

They watched the large color-coded gauges strapped to their wrists.

Almost...!

The sparkling surface of the sea was accelerating to meet them.

Now!

The rising column disengaged, the links in the loose chain fanning out, making room for themselves.
"NOW!!!"
In perfect synch, they pulled the ripcords.

Yes...!!!

Rectangular, ribbed canopies opened and acted as sudden air brakes, as the sea surged close enough to mist their curved visors with spray.

And now!!!

As the wave tops strained up towards their dangling webbed feet, they slapped the release catch on their chests.
The harnesses parted and the detached chutes floated away. They plunged into the deep green gloom.

Cat vaulted into the open T-top of the shark-like yellow Corvette. The black cockpit embraced her.
Overlooking Cat's beach house and the sand and the sea, Selena stood leaning on the flank of the silver DB5.
She looked out across the vast expanse of shining water, where it melted into the horizon. She could almost hear the sounds of battle, so many miles away.
"I'll be at base H.Q. with your Uncle...."
Selena swung down into the exclusive grey leather.
"Make it fast, Cat, I think they're going to need you."
She twisted the key.
"You know what to do...!"
Cat shivered, charged by a strange electricity. She nodded.

Yes, I know what to do!

Beneath the surface, in the luminous zone where the sunlight penetrated, the column re-formed, in order of battle.

Suspended in the green glow, all eyes were on Aiko, waiting for her signal.

Go!

It came as a decisive slash of her hand, chopping downwards towards their target, the disguised assembly of domes, glimpsed dimly down below.

Their bodies rotated, dipped and dived, arms tight to their sides, streamlined.

The yellow Corvette was a streak of summer lightning on the twists and turns of the highway, tracing the outline of the rugged coast.

The wind in her hair, she drove on a razor's edge; she took it to the limit. She was ice cold, focused like a laser.

As they descended into the murky depths, their keen eyes penetrated the encrusted disguise. They identified a large central dome, linked by watertight arteries to lesser satellites stationed at all four points of the compass.

Aiko's hand signals were eloquent.

The seabed was undulating and fissured, strewn with giant boulders, testament to centuries of seismic activity. Tall dense patches waved their mottled fronds in the currents.

Perfect…!

It was the ideal hiding place. They waited.

Cat let the 'Vette roll out to the very tip of a dagger-shaped promontory.

"Okay, baby…."

She got out and stood beside the car. The wind whipped at her hair. Far below, the waves smashed against the rugged cliffs, raising a mist of salt spray that swirled around her face.

"Show me what you've got!"

Eyes glowing, Cat stroked the smooth angles of the low-slung bodywork.

"Show me!"

They didn't have to wait long.

Here they come…!

A routine patrol, six men armed with spear guns, escorted by a small two-man submersible shaped like a broad spearhead.

Right on time!

As the intruders watched from their place of concealment, the submersible docked, nestled to the crusty slope of the main dome. Shouldering their weapons, the patrol hovered around it.

Okay...!

A section of encrusted skin was detaching from the surface of the dome. It revealed itself to be the tall rectangular entrance to an airlock.

GO!!!

Flexing her legs, Aiko rose from cover. Left and right, the ambushers responded to her.

Aiko's spear transfixed the patrol leader through the neck. He spasmed, arms and legs jerking, in a cloud of dark blood.

Another was spread-eagled against the curved wall of the dome as a spearpoint smashed through the glass of his face mask. The man beside him jack-knifed, his body folding over the shaft projecting from his belly.

The rest were floating away limply, leaving trails of blood in the water. The door to the airlock gaped open.

"Show me!"

Cat's voice rang above the frothing of the waves. As she caressed it, the yellow car began to change.

A broad back rippled with powerful muscles, upholstered by shimmering feathers, each a gilded spear point.

Extended muscle-play powered an enormous wingspan, wings that beat slowly. With a flash of gold, a fan of long tail-feathers rose and expanded. A long neck supported a noble gilded head, with mellow eyes belied by the fierce sickle curve of its beak.

The great golden bird opened its jaws to emit a low throbbing call. Flexing its long neck, it looked back at Cat as she climbed on board. The feathers on its wide shoulders plumped up to accommodate her, sitting her up and making her comfortable.

Cat saw herself reflected in the golden eyes. And she was golden too.

Go! Go!

Aiko's command was unspoken, but they all heard it, a forceful double-pump of her fist.

A chance encounter with a humble rating in a tan jumpsuit ended with a hand over his mouth and a swift sharp blade across his throat. That was Sammy.

The spear guns had been exchanged for silenced machine-pistols unzipped from waterproof sheaths. Anyone they met in the bright coiling corridors went down before they had a chance to raise the alarm. Janey and Lina saw to that.

The grenades that Cheryl and Josie tossed into the Radio Room hardly made a sound, just a dull bump. There was no fire and smoke; they killed by concussion.

Oh Cat, you've done a great job!

They were seeking the laboratory at the heart of the dome. Steel security shutters were coming down.
"Uuuuugghhh…ggghhhh…!!!"
Slinging her weapon, Sammy took hold with both hands. Gritting her teeth, putting her whole body into it, she halted its descent.
"Come on!" Janey yelled.
Shoulder to shoulder, the others lined up alongside Sammy as she took the strain.
"Heave…!!!"
The gears were grinding; something metallic twanged and the steel curtain rose abruptly, making them stumble backwards.
"Watch it!" Aiko shouted. "It could be toxic!"
Surged in, they flicked their weapons to single-fire.
"Get them!"
The silencers popped as they cleared the premises with surgical precision, knocking down the lab-coated figures as they scrambled frantically, looking for a place to hide.
"See?" Sammy grinned. "Nothing broken!"

The head man was cornered in his private lair, wearing his black uniform adorned by the polished death's heads.
His boney fingers were scrabbling in the drawers of his desk, raking his shelves clean, scooping out cardboard files and stacks of paper.
"Nein! Nein…!"
He lurched towards them, yellowed documents spilling from his shaking hands, strewing them at their feet.
"I c-can help…." He babbled shrilly. "I have so much more to tell…!"
Stunned, Josie was confronted by his monstrous décor.
The infamous flag with the crooked cross; crisscrossed ceremonial daggers; a framed oil painting of his Master as man of destiny; the precious photos of himself in his exalted company; personal gifts in pride of place.
"He's mine…!"
Her eyes flamed, scalded by tears.
"Nein…!!!"
She shot him once in the belly and then straddled him as he twisted and screamed on the floor.
The others froze. The screaming went on and on. Josie stood over him, stone-faced. She saw his distorted features melt and become those of her perverted Uncle.

"Aw, fuck!"

Janey stepped forward and put him out of his misery with a bullet to the head. Her face contorting, Josie rounded on her.

Sammy seized Josie's gun hand by the wrist. She squeezed and her fingers went limp, letting the machine-pistol fall.

Cheryl put an arm around Josie's shoulders and led her from the room.

"Jeeez...!" breathed Lina.

Janey looked numb.

"I never thought," she muttered. "Anyone could hate more than me...."

Like a child in a storybook, Cat was suspended on a cushion of air, the mighty downdraft of the great golden bird's wings. She settled gently on its feathered back as it flew away with her, across the shining sea.

"Here they come...!"

Someone had triggered an alarm before he died.

"Get ready!"

Of the four satellite domes two functioned as stores, the others were evidently barracks.

Armed men were disgorged into the connecting shafts that linked them to the central dome. Viewing screens showed them hefting explosives and heavy weaponry. They meant business, advancing rapidly.

"Pile it high!"

Aiko made the dash from the sealed accessway on one side of the main dome to the other.

"Higher...!"

Her squads were constructing barricades, manhandling heavy furnishings, anything that wasn't nailed down.

Already they could hear telltale noises from outside.

They're planting charges!

Aiko flicked the switch to fully automatic, her sights set on the source of the threat, the inevitable breach and the rush that would follow.

At her side, Sammy tossed a tubular-framed chair lightly to the very top of their improvised barrier.

"Oh man!" she laughed, the light of battle in her eyes. "I bet Cat wishes she was here for this one!"

The mythical giant extended its mighty wingspan, floating majestically on a thermal.

Here goes...!

Cat rose and stood confidently on its broad back, astride the gilded feathers rippled by the wind. The swirling sheen of her golden mane was enriched, she was radiant.

The creature turned its noble head to gaze at her, its eyes warming and mellow.

Cat smiled and dipped her head in acknowledgment.

"Thank you!"

An explosion jolted them, had them reaching up to steady objects toppling from the heights of the makeshift barricade.

The steel bulkhead was buckling. They braced themselves.

A second detonation made everything creak and rattle. The door seals were bulging.

They all looked to Aiko and were surprised to see her smiling.

"Cat?" she slapped Sammy on the shoulder. "Oh, but she is here!"

And then Cat was leaping, in an extravagant swan dive, arcing down into the sea....

The next one will blow it wide open!

They heard the gong-like sound of the magnetic clamps fixing the charges to the door frames.

"Steady...!!!"

And then they heard screams.

"What the f—?"

Piercing shrieks of terror came needling through the steel.

The deep sea was churning; a storm that enveloped the connecting shafts, lifting them off the ocean floor and bending them.

Water was coming through the cracks, the men in the shafts were splashing knee-deep as they waded frantically back the way they'd come, desperate to escape.

In the central dome, they watched it all on the viewing screens.

"Holy shit!"

"No way...!!!!

A seething underwater cyclone was battering the shafts and crushing them. The air inside was vented in twisting tornadoes of bubbles.

Claws like curved scimitars did the rest, ripping the crumpled shafts to shreds. Limbs outspread, drowned bodies rose, rotating, spun by the bubbling twisters.

In the main dome, absolute silence. Everyone waited for someone to say something.

"Woooo!!!"

They could rely on Sammy to break the tension. And then they were all hooting and hollering.

"Uh...uh...?"

Janey shuffled awkwardly, looking down at her feet.

Lina and Josie just stared.

"Wow!" blurted Sammy. "Holy fuckin' cow…!"

Cat stood before them, looking slightly dazed, a little sheepish, dripping wet.

Cheryl came close and gazed deep into her eyes.

"Oh man!" she exclaimed. "I'm glad you're on our side!"

"I'm sorry, Mr President," the switchboard operator apologized. "I just can't reach him…."

Slumped at his desk in the Oval Office, he ran his fingers through his thinning reddish hair, his blue eyes sparking with annoyance.

"Well," he snapped. "Try harder!"

He slammed the receiver down.

"Goddamn…!"

His square head sunk deeper into his humped shoulders, till he had no neck at all. Exasperated, he crashed his fist onto the desk top.

"Goddamn it to hell!"

He fumbled clumsily with the constricting knot of his tie.

"What the fuck is going on?" he shouted into the mocking emptiness of the room. "No one's answering the phone today!"

The Potomac flowed darkly under a moonless sky, its timeless currents tinted, glinted here and there by occasional lights from the shore.

"Steady as you go…!"

The river forked at the broad blunt end of Theodore Roosevelt Island.

"Steer two-point-nine…!"

In line abreast, the thin stems of the periscopes carved the black glassy surface as clean as a razor, leaving barely a trace.

"Two-point-nine, aye…!"

Their course took them down the flank of the island, down past its narrow tip called Little Island, threading the spans of the Theodore Roosevelt Bridge.

"Keep her steady…!"

As the island slipped behind them into the night, they saw their landmark shining above the shore, the floodlit columns of the Lincoln Memorial; and ahead, the approaching arches of the Arlington Memorial Bridge.

"All stop!"

The lights were burning late deep in the bowels of 1600 Pennsylvania Avenue.

"Well…?"

Two very important men were the sole occupants of the long conference table.

"What do you make of it?"

The escape chamber was barely large enough to accommodate John Warburton's brawny bulk.

Cat had to turn away to hide her expression as he squeezed himself into the steel tube, the rubber of his wetsuit squeaking.

Oh heck! If he gets stuck in there the mission's over!

Wedged in tight behind her by the confines of the midget sub's hull, Cat's team were quivering with suppressed laughter. She could feel its vibrations.

They were keen, bright-eyed. This was the end game and they knew it.

The gilt-framed faces of past notables stared down at them solemnly, offering no assistance.

"I can't say, the signal was completely garbled, and then cut off entirely…."

"The Chief has been chasing after me all day, I can't keep dodging him forever."

"We'll see him in the morning…."

It must have been a trick of the light, they could have sworn that the painted faces were frowning at them.

"Right now, we need to get our story straight!"

Sizzling and bubbling brightly, the thermic lance made short work of the mossy bars.

With a twitch of their flippers, they paddled backwards as the broad circular grate toppled slowly and thudded on the riverbed.

Neat…!

There was now a gaping hole in the wall of roughly hewn stone slabs that buttressed the river bank down below the surface. Advancing warily, they shone their lamps into the void.

Selena dipped and swam inside, a splash of light preceding her. The flooded tunnel was wide enough to allow Aiko to swim alongside her.

John Warburton hovered at the tunnel mouth and ushered Cat inside, pumping his fist to signal "Go!". As she surged forward, Cat rolled to give her team a big thumbs-up; bunched close behind, they reciprocated boldly.

In an instant, they were gone, into the tunnel, leaving only a thinning trail of bubbles.

The First Lady seized the twisted blankets, re-covering herself. Pulling them up above her head, she burrowed into the pillow.

Beside her, the President tossed and turned, mumbling and snorting.

"Damn it…!"

He lashed out and knocked over the bedside lamp, fumbling for his watch. His wife groaned.

"It's three in the morning…!"

They stood and marveled, looking all around them.

"It's just as you said," Selena stated.

They had emerged onto a gravelly underground beach. Under a high domed brick ceiling, a dark tunnel mouth confronted them enigmatically.

John Warburton grinned at them, pleased with himself.

"Yep!" he declared. "This is it!"

In the pale lantern light, they were shedding the rubber skin of the scuba gear, exchanging it for khaki.

"This escape tunnel goes way back, to the Civil War," John Warburton told them. "The way we came in was just above the water level back then."

Under Aiko's supervision, waterproof kit bags were unzipped and weapons distributed. The man-made cavern echoed with the sound of locking and loading.

Cat was reading the map of the city with her mind's eye, estimating the distance to their objective. Her Uncle read her thoughts.

"At the double-quick," he told her. "We can be there in half an hour."

Selena glanced at her watch.

"Okay," she said. "We wait!"

"What!!?!"

The President's eyes bulged. Red in the face, his shirt collar was choking him. One hand supporting him as he leaned across his desk, he wrenched at the knot of his tie with the other.

"You say you did what!!!??!!"

Despite themselves, they felt guilty about leaving a trail of muddy footprints on the blue gilt-edged carpets.

"Hey," said Cat. "Just what we're looking for!"

The sign on the door said: OFFICIAL TOURS – OFFICE. They knocked politely and went inside.

"Hi there…!"

It was early and only the Supervisor was there, a pleasant-looking woman in early middle-age, wearing the regulation blue blazer and beige skirt.

"Oh my God!"

Horrified, she backed up at the sight of the guns, turning ghostly pale. John Warburton stepped forward, smiling broadly.

"There's no need for concern, Ma'am," he reassured her. "We haven't come for you…."

As the woman sagged against her desk, he took her gently by the arm.

"Would you be so kind as to show us the way to the Oval Office?"

Gulping, she struggled to speak. Instead, she reached behind her, fingers scrabbling on the desk top. Stammering, she brandished a glossy brochure, the pages rattling.

"T-t-there's a f-f-floor p-plan on p-p-p-page t-t-t-two…!"

John Warburton beamed.

"Why so there is, Ma'am, this will do nicely!"

Selena and Aiko exchanged wry glances, rolling their eyes. Cat chuckled.

Didn't think to bring one of our own!

They tied and gagged the trembling woman to her chair. A deft touch from Aiko rendered her unconscious.

John Warburton led the way, flourishing the lavish brochure.

"Hey," he told them. "I always wanted to take one of these tours."

Two big square-shouldered men in black suits came around a corner. They were joshing, boasting.

"I'm tellin' ya, that babe was built like—!"

He was demonstrating with his hands. In that pose he stopped and gaped.

"Who the hell are you?"

And then both men were reaching for their guns.

"Don't kill them!" Selena hissed.

Aiko was spinning, a deadly ballerina. Her heel connected with the point of her target's chin. He slammed back against the wall of the corridor and slid to the floor.

Cat was a guided missile. Her left hand chopped the Secret Service man's wrist and the pistol slipped from his numbed fingers. Her right was a blur and whipped his head around. Glassy-eyed, he crumpled at her feet.

It hardly made a sound. They stepped back and looked at their leader; Selena smiled at them.

"Nice job!"

The President sat slumped at his desk, his head in his hands. It muffled his anguished groan.

"What are we going to do…?"

He addressed his question to the two men standing before him. He repeated it to no one in particular, a cry of despair.

"What are we going to do!!!?!"

Suddenly, they didn't feel like the two most powerful men in the country, after the President. Their job titles rang hollow – Counsel and Assistant to the President for Domestic Affairs; Administrative Assistant to the President and Chief of Staff.

Utterly deflated, they shuffled their feet like naughty children, looking down at the carpet.

"Uh…."

"Well, we…."

The door set into the curved wall of the Oval Office crashed open.

"Good morning gentlemen!"

Cat wasn't as formal as her Uncle.

"Up against the wall, motherfuckers!"

Gotya!

White-faced, they did what they were told, raising their hands high above their heads.

Selena took in the President's dumbfounded expression.

"You really didn't know anything about this," she sneered. "Did you, Mistah President?"

Pop-eyed, sweat shining on his face, he shook his head jerkily.

"Jeez!" Cat exclaimed. "Then you really are as dumb as you look!"

He nodded vigorously.

The Chief of Staff leant forward.

"Is that you Warburton…?"

They looked surprised.

"You know this turkey?" Janey asked.

John Warburton sighed heavily, his eyes clouding.

"We were at Yale together," he explained. "A hundred years ago!"

The Chief of Staff's eyes frosted contemptuously.

"You look like a goddamn hippie!"

Some of his defiance rubbed off on his co-conspirator, who lowered his hands, scowling.

"You used to be a patriot Warburton!"

John Warburton smiled coldly at him.

"I still am!"

Breathing heavily, the President lurched forward, stepping between them.

"W-what are you g-oing to d-d-do…?"

Selena adjusted the machine-pistol in her grip, centering it on the Chief of Staff's chest. Wide-eyed, he staggered back into the wall.

"You can't kill us!" he shrieked. "That's treason!"

Selena curled her lip.

"No," she told him. "It's a public service!"

She triggered a short burst that made a bloody mess of his expensively tailored shirt front. He flung out his arms, his feet lifted off the floor.

John Warburton was poised but Cat beat him to it. Her burst took the Counsel's head clean off his shoulders, splattering the vintage wallpaper. The decapitated corpse stood stock still for a moment and then crumpled.

"Goddamn!" John Warburton protested.

"Sorry," Cat shrugged apologetically.

There were sounds in the next room and then burly men in black suits were bursting in upon them, brandishing guns.

"Don't—!" Selena shouted.

"We know!" yelled Janey.

Cat's squad were on them like a whirlwind, eager to demonstrate all they had learned.

"YAH…!"

"HAH!"

Janey still clung to the old ways – she couldn't resist it. The fancy new moves laid him wide open. Her old-fashioned kick left him feeling like his balls were in his mouth. Vomiting, he blacked out with the pain.

By contrast, Josie was a dancer, poetry in motion. She seemed to be coming at him from all sides. Bewildered, humiliated, her victim blundered onto the swiveling high kick that splintered his senses.

HAAIIEEE…!!!"

Cheryl's war cry fractured his ear drums. She displayed her vicious streak, flicking her fingertips across his eye sockets. Blinded, he retreated.

Coolly, she stalked him, waiting till the wall brought him up short. She detonated short punches, one-two, on his solar plexus, and when he folded chopped him on the back of the neck.

Sammy didn't waste any time. She walked through his attack, shrugging it aside, parrying with her strong forearms.

She did it all with her fists. Her rapid left jabs pole-axed him, driving him backwards. A short left to the lower ribs doubled him up and brought his chin down onto the right uppercut that came up to meet it.

"Hey, no fair guys!"

Lina had two to contend with. Side-stepping nimbly, she was faster than sight. Her savage backhand spun one round, drooling blood. She dipped her shoulder and body-slammed the other into him.

As they tried to regain their balance and disentangle themselves, she grabbed them by the scruff of the neck and smashed their heads together.

"Wooo!"

Laughing, Cat and Aiko were high-fiving.

"Cat!" Aiko declared. "I think we did a good job there!"

Cat reached out to wrap Janey in her arms.

"Holy fuck, guys!" she exclaimed. "You've got a beast in you too!"

Caught up in their celebrations, they had almost forgotten about the President, who was edging towards the door, stepping gingerly over the fallen.

"Hey!" said John Warburton. "Where do you think you're going?"

He stopped and jerked his hands high in the air again.

"D-d-don't k-kill m-me!" he pleaded.

He quailed as Selena advanced on him, looking grim. She seized him by the collar, marched him to his desk and sat him down hard.

"You're gonna live, Mistah Prez!" she informed him.

Her voice had the ring of steel.

"You're gonna get some good people in and you're gonna destroy every trace of this whole mess so it can never happen again!"

He was almost crying with relief, sagging in his chair.

"Yes, yes…of course…you can count on me…!"

Selena eyed him sternly.

"I sure hope so," she stated. "Because we'll be watching you!"

Grinning broadly, Aiko waited while Cat's team pocketed some souvenirs and then led them out. John Warburton flipped a mocking salute before turning on his heel to follow them.

Selena reached out and took Cat's hand. Linked together, they strolled towards the exit.

At the door, Cat turned her head and stared back across the room. For a moment, the President swore that he saw her eyes change shape and glow golden.

"Remember," her voice rang all around him. "We'll be watching!"

They slept, bathed in electric blue.

Suddenly, Janey squealed.

"Wha — ?"

A shape was moving under the rumpled blankets, creeping towards the head of the bed.

"Jesus!"

Cat was twisting, reaching for the pistol on the bedside table, her long hair veiling her naked breasts.

Now Janey was laughing, as something warm and supple slid between them.

"Hi there!"

Cheryl's blonde head popped up and nestled into the pillows.

Oh you little minx!

Cat was laughing too, Janey squeezed Cheryl in a fond headlock. Cheryl squeaked as their legs tangled.

"Hey…?"

The door swung wide open. Sammy led Lina and Josie into Cat's motel bedroom, in the scanties of their improvised sleep wear.

"Yay!" declared Sammy. "Slumber par-tay…!"

"Mmmphh…!"

Lina stirred, frowning; someone's big toe was prodding her.

She lifted her head from the pillow and surveyed a tangled scene.

"Mmmm…?"

Somewhere in the middle, Cat had taken refuge by submerging herself under the covers.

"Hey…." Josie whispered.

Janey was snoring softly, like the purring of a large cat. Her face half buried in her pillow, Cheryl was making cute little whiffling noises.

Lina raised her eyebrows. Somehow, Josie had contrived to slide herself between the salt 'n pepper pair of them.

"It was the only way I could get them to stop," Josie mouthed, rolling her eyes. "So I could get some sleep."

Janey turned over in her sleep and her bare arm draped lazily across Josie's waist.

"Oh, good night!" Josie muttered and closed her eyes.

Dreaming, Sammy curled up and cradled her head on Lina's belly.

"Aw…."

Lina opened her mouth and then shut it again. In the blue half-light, Sammy looked so peaceful.

… heck…!

Lina must have moved because Sammy woke suddenly, opening her eyes to see Lina staring at her. Alarmed, she jerked her head up.

"I didn't do anything, Lina!" she exclaimed. "I swear!"

Josie kicked out her long legs like a child having a tantrum and rolled onto her front, clamping a pillow over her head.

Wide awake, Janey and Cheryl were watching anxiously.

Lina looked at Sammy for what seemed an eternity. Then she heaved a theatrical sigh. Reaching out slowly, she pressed Sammy's tousled head back down onto her stomach.

"Shut up and go back to sleep…."

As Lina closed her eyes and drifted away, her fingers were soothing Sammy's hair.

"Sleep…!"

Janey and Cheryl stared, open-mouthed.

"Who are you?" asked Cheryl. "And what have you done with Lina?"

Dozing off, Lina growled.

"Sleep damn you – now!"

The humped covers were quivering, vibrated by Cat's muffled laughter.

"And you…!"

They said goodbye to Cat at her beach house, on her beach, as the surf frothed like champagne between their bare toes.

"I'll miss you so much," Cat said huskily, tears pricking her eyes.

"Same here," Janey whispered, her eyes burning, welling over. She couldn't say any more and walked away quickly.

"Be bad," Cat said to Cheryl, stroking her silky fair hair.

Cheryl sniffed back a tear, smiling bravely.

"I will!"

Sammy's embrace crushed Cat's breath out of her.

"Oooof!"

They laughed and hugged again. Suddenly, Sammy was serious, her eyes misting.

"Thanks," she said softly. "For making me proud of who I am."

As ever, Josie played it cool.

"Well," she declared. "It's been an experience!"

And then the mask crumpled and she sprang to hold Cat tight.

"Love you…!"

Head down, frowning, Lina was trying to find the right words. She looked up slowly as Cat laid a soft hand on her shoulder.

"Knowing you," Lina attempted. "Has made me a better person."

Cat smiled. "Me too."

Janey returned.

"You sure you're not mad?" she asked Cat.

"About what?"

"That we decided not to join the organization?"
Cat squeezed her hand.
"No, I'm not mad, of course not."

I'm glad – you deserve to have a chance to enjoy being young!

Janey hesitated.
"It's just that we have other plans."
"Oh yes?"
Sammy stepped up behind Janey and slapped her on the back, bending her double.
"Yep!" she declared. "We're gonna form a band!"
Cat was amazed.
"A band? Can you guys play instruments?"
They were all laughing, as they waded into the sparkling surf.
"No," yelled Janey. "But after what we've been through how hard can it be?"

For a complete list of
Midnight Marquee Press
books and movies,
visit our website at
www.midmar.com